Rhoda

By Ellen Gilchrist

Ellen Gilchrist

A LIFE IN STORIES

LITTLE, BROWN AND COMPANY
BOSTON   NEW YORK   TORONTO   LONDON

First Edition

The characters and events in this book are fictitious.
Any similarity to real persons, living or dead,
is coincidental and not intended by the author.

Excerpts from "Begin the Beguine," words and music by Cole Porter. Copyright © 1935
by Warner Bros. Inc. (Renewed). "The Desert Song" words by Otto Harbach and Oscar
Hammerstein II, music by Sigmund Romberg. Copyright © 1926 by Warner Bros. Inc.
(Renewed). "Embraceable You," words by Ira Gershwin, music by George Gershwin.
Copyright © 1930 WB Music Corp. (Renewed). By permission of Warner Bros.
Publications Inc.

Excerpt from "Me and Bobby McGee" by Kris Kristofferson and Fred Foster. Copyright
© 1969 Combine Music Corporation. By permission of SBK Blackwood Music Inc.

"Pictures in the Smoke" and an excerpt from "Inventory" from *The Portable Dorothy Parker*
by Dorothy Parker, introduction by Brendan Gill. Copyright 1926, renewed 1954 by
Dorothy Parker. By permission of Viking Penguin, a division of Penguin Books USA Inc.

Library of Congress Cataloging-in-Publication Data

Gilchrist, Ellen
    Rhoda: a life in stories / Ellen Gilchrist. — 1st ed.
        p.   cm.
    "Back Bay book."
    ISBN 0-316-31464-1
    1. Manning, Rhoda Katherine (Fictitious character) — Fiction.
    2. Women — United States — Social life and customs — Fiction.   3. Women
poets — Fiction.   I. Title.
PS3557.I34258R48   1995
813'.54 — dc20   95-8087

10   9   8   7   6   5   4   3   2

RRD-VA

*Published simultaneously in Canada
by Little, Brown & Company (Canada) Limited*

Printed in the United States of America

Contents

Introduction

I INVENTED RHODA MANNING on a beautiful fall day in New Orleans. That morning I set out to write a story with a description at the beginning. I was new to fiction writing at the time and if I read something I liked I would immediately try to write something similar. I think that I had just been shown a description of a tree in a book by John Steinbeck. The description ended with the words "it was everything a tree should be." That took my breath away and made me want to describe something that fully, with that finality. A vision came to me of the pasture beside my grandmother's house. In good years it would be a pasture. In bad years it would be pressed into service as a cotton field. I saw the pasture in all its beauty and my cousins and my brother in the center of it building a broad jump pit. The famous Broad Jump Pit to which I was going to be denied access. The Broad Jump Pit was famous in my family long before I wrote about it.

As I began to describe the pit I realized I was seeing it from the perspective of the roof of the chicken house, an octagonal-shaped structure that was one of my favorite hideouts on the plantation. "Think how it looked from my lonely exile atop the chicken house," I wrote. That was the first time I wrote in

Rhoda Manning's voice and as soon as I typed the line I knew the little girl as I know myself. By noon I had finished a draft of the story, which is called "Revenge," and which is the second or third completed short story I ever wrote in my life. I had the story and I had the central character but she did not yet have a name. She was almost Shelby, from "Summer, an Elegy," but not quite. I had darkened the persona in Shelby, to accommodate the death that shadows that story.

There are no shadows in Rhoda. Rhoda is passion, energy, light. If germs get inside her, her blood boils up and devours them. If she loses a pearl ring, it's proof there is no God. If it's necessary to drop an atomic bomb to save Western Civilization, she's ready. I had the character by the end of that morning's work but I did not have a name.

I went out to run in Audubon Park. The most self-assured woman in New Orleans was running her four miles. This was a woman who had declared, *at the height of the running craze*, that it was obsessive to run more than four miles a day. I began to run along beside her. "I wrote a funny story this morning," I said. "May I name a little, fictional girl for you?"

"What's she like?" the real Rhoda asked.

"She's powerful and she wins."

"All right. Go ahead. You may."

Now, fifteen years later, I have written many stories about Rhoda. Some of them are blatantly autobiographical and some are made up. Many are true to the real essence of the Rhoda I created on that fall morning. Others miss the mark. If I was in a bad mood or out of sorts with myself, I would savage Rhoda. Of course I only know all this in retrospect. Or think I know it. No writer truly understands the relationship between reality and storytelling. No real storyteller gives a damn about it except in retrospect or in those rare generous moments when they think what they know can be explained.

The one thing I do know is that something wonderful happens to me when I am writing about Rhoda, especially Rhoda as a child. Because she is a mirror of myself I am able to participate in the story as I write it. I radiate with her curiosity and intelligence, her divine cynicism. I am eight and ten and twelve years old. Those memory banks are evoked most powerfully when I am writing about the child Rhoda alone with one of her obsessions. She is pinning butterflies to cardboard for one of her scientific experiments, let us say. I smell her hands, know her horror and fascination. Science demands sacrifice. Rhoda and I will pay the price. We write the names below the specimens. The cold wind of karma blows over us. We shake it off. We go on with our work.

So is Rhoda me? I don't know. She starts off being me and she ends up being my creation. Unlike me she can have varying numbers of brothers of varying ages. She can live in different places at different ages and, of course, she could have any man she wanted if she really wanted one. She has never had a sister but she has always wanted an identical twin and perhaps I will give her one. She was identical twins in the womb, let us say, and one was resorbed by the mother's body because of a lack of calcium in the diet. Rhoda goes back in a time machine and changes her mother's diet and the twins are born in perfect health. Twin Rhoda is born first, and then twin Treena Aurora, who will stick by her older sister every day of her life and be her trusted lieutenant. When it is time to study biochemistry and become Nobel laureates in science, they will share the prize.

In the meantime, we will have to be satisfied with the Rhoda I have created, in all her cosmic loneliness and hope. Here she is then, all her guises under one cover. She would probably like to think of herself being read about on an airplane above the deserts of the west, or alone in a bedroom with a plate of cookies within reach, or to some poor old lady on a sickbed, on a fall day underneath a crimson tree, or a golden one or an orange one.

Ellen Gilchrist
February 20, 1995

Rhoda

Revenge

I
T WAS THE SUMMER of the Broad Jump Pit.

The Broad Jump Pit, how shall I describe it! It was a bright orange rectangle in the middle of a green pasture. It was three feet deep, filled with river sand and sawdust. A real cinder track led up to it, ending where tall poles for pole-vaulting rose forever in the still Delta air.

I am looking through the old binoculars. I am watching Bunky coming at a run down the cinder path, pausing expertly at the jump-off line, then rising into the air, heels stretched far out in front of him, landing in the sawdust. Before the dust has settled Saint John comes running with the tape, calling out measurements in his high, excitable voice.

Next comes my thirteen-year-old brother, Dudley, coming at a brisk jog down the track, the pole-vaulting pole held lightly in his delicate hands, then vaulting, high into the sky. His skinny tanned legs make a last, desperate surge, and he is clear and over.

Think how it looked from my lonely exile atop the chicken house. I was ten years old, the only girl in a house full of cousins. There were six of us, shipped to the Delta for the summer, dumped on my grandmother right in the middle of a world war.

They built this wonder in answer to a V-Mail letter from my father in Europe. The war was going well, my father wrote, within a year the Allies would triumph over the forces of evil, the world would be at peace, and the Olympic torch would again be brought down from its mountain and carried to Zurich or Amsterdam or London or Mexico City, wherever free men lived and worshiped sports. My father had been a participant in an Olympic event when he was young.

Therefore, the letter continued, Dudley and Bunky and Philip and Saint John and Oliver were to begin training. The United States would need athletes now, not soldiers.

They were to train for broad jumping and pole-vaulting and discus throwing, for fifty-, one-hundred-, and four-hundred-yard dashes, for high and low hurdles. The letter included instructions for building the pit, for making pole-vaulting poles out of cane, and for converting ordinary sawhorses into hurdles. It ended with a page of tips for proper eating and admonished Dudley to take good care of me as I was my father's own dear sweet little girl.

The letter came one afternoon. Early the next morning they began construction. Around noon I wandered out to the pasture to see how they were coming along. I picked up a shovel.

"Put that down, Rhoda," Dudley said. "Don't bother us now. We're working."

"I know it," I said. "I'm going to help."

"No, you're not," Bunky said. "This is the Broad Jump Pit. We're starting our training."

"I'm going to do it too," I said. "I'm going to be in training."

"Get out of here now," Dudley said. "This is only for boys, Rhoda. This isn't a game."

"I'm going to dig it if I want to," I said, picking up a shovelful of dirt and throwing it on Philip. On second thought I picked up another shovelful and threw it on Bunky.

"Get out of here, Ratface," Philip yelled at me. "You German spy." He was referring to the initials on my Girl Scout uniform.

"You goddamn niggers," I yelled. "You niggers. I'm digging this if I want to and you can't stop me, you nasty niggers, you Japs, you Jews." I was throwing dirt on everyone now. Dudley grabbed the shovel and wrestled me to the ground. He held my arms down in the coarse grass and peered into my face.

"Rhoda, you're not having anything to do with this Broad Jump Pit. And if you set foot inside this pasture or come around here and touch anything we will break your legs and drown you in the bayou with a crowbar around your neck." He was twisting my leg until it creaked at the joints. "Do you get it, Rhoda? Do you understand me?"

"Let me up," I was screaming, my rage threatening to split open my skull. "Let me up, you goddamn nigger, you Jap, you spy. I'm telling Grannie and you're going to get the worst whipping of your life. And you better quit digging this hole for the horses to fall in. Let me up, let me up. Let me go."

"You've been ruining everything we've thought up all summer," Dudley said, "and you're not setting foot inside this pasture."

In the end they dragged me back to the house, and I ran screaming into the kitchen where Grannie and Calvin, the black man who did the cooking, tried to comfort me, feeding me pound cake and offering to let me help with the mayonnaise.

"You be a sweet girl, Rhoda," my grandmother said, "and this afternoon we'll go over to Eisenglas Plantation to play with Miss Ann Wentzel."

"I don't want to play with Miss Ann Wentzel," I screamed. "I hate Miss Ann Wentzel. She's fat and she calls me a Yankee. She said my socks were ugly."

"Why, Rhoda," my grandmother said. "I'm surprised at you. Miss Ann Wentzel is your own sweet friend. Her momma was your momma's roommate at All Saint's. How can you talk like that?"

"She's a nigger," I screamed. "She's a goddamned nigger German spy."

"Now it's coming. Here comes the temper," Calvin said, rolling his eyes back in their sockets to make me madder. I threw my second fit of the morning, beating my fists into a door frame. My grandmother seized me in soft arms. She led me to a bedroom where I sobbed myself to sleep in a sea of down pillows.

The construction went on for several weeks. As soon as they finished breakfast every morning they started out for the pasture. Wood had to be burned to make cinders, sawdust brought from the sawmill, sand hauled up from the riverbank by wheelbarrow.

When the pit was finished the savage training began. From my several vantage points I watched them. Up and down, up and down they ran, dove, flew, sprinted. Drenched with sweat they wrestled each other to the ground in bitter feuds over distances and times and fractions of inches.

Dudley was their self-appointed leader. He drove them like a demon. They began each morning by running around the edge of the pasture several times, then practicing their hurdles and dashes, then on to discus throwing and calisthenics. Then on to the Broad Jump Pit with its endless challenges.

They even pressed the old mare into service. Saint John was from New Orleans and knew the British ambassador and was thinking of being a polo player. Up and down the pasture he drove the poor old creature, leaning far out of the saddle, swatting a basketball with my grandaddy's cane.

I spied on them from the swing that went out over the bayou, and from the roof of the chicken house, and sometimes from the pasture fence itself, calling out insults or attempts to make them jealous.

"Guess what," I would yell, "I'm going to town to the Chinaman's store." "Guess what, I'm getting to go to the beauty parlor." "Doctor Biggs says you're adopted."

They ignored me. At meals they sat together at one end of the table, making jokes about my temper and my red hair, opening their mouths so I could see their half-chewed food, burping loudly in my direction.

At night they pulled their cots together on the sleeping porch, plotting against me while I slept beneath my grandmother's window, listening to the soft assurance of her snoring.

I began to pray the Japs would win the war, would come marching into Issaquena County and take them prisoners, starving and torturing them, sticking bamboo splinters under their fingernails. I saw myself in the Japanese colonel's office, turning them in, writing their names down, myself being treated like an honored guest, drinking tea from tiny blue cups like the ones the Chinaman had in his store.

They would be outside, tied up with wire. There would be Dudley, begging for mercy. What good to him now his loyal gang, his photographic memory, his trick magnet dogs, his perfect pitch, his camp shorts, his Baby Brownie camera.

I prayed they would get polio, would be consigned forever to iron lungs. I put myself to sleep at night imagining their labored breathing, their five little wheelchairs lined up by the store as I drove by in my father's Packard, my arm around the jacket of his blue uniform, on my way to Hollywood for my screen test.

Meanwhile, I practiced dancing. My grandmother had a black housekeeper named Baby Doll who was a wonderful dancer. In the mornings I followed her around while she dusted, begging for dancing lessons. She was a big woman, as tall as a man, and gave off a dark rich smell, an unforgettable incense, a combination of Evening in Paris and the sweet perfume of the cabins.

Baby Doll wore bright skirts and on her blouses a pin that said REMEMBER, then a real pearl, then HARBOR. She was engaged to a sailor and was going to California to be rich as soon as the war was over.

I would put a stack of heavy, scratched records on the record player, and Baby Doll and I would dance through the parlors to the music of Glenn Miller or Guy Lombardo or Tommy Dorsey.

Sometimes I stood on a stool in front of the fireplace and made up lyrics while Baby Doll acted them out, moving lightly across the old dark rugs, turning and swooping and shaking and gliding.

Outside the summer sun beat down on the Delta, beating down a million volts a minute, feeding the soybeans and cotton and clover, sucking Steele's Bayou up into the clouds, beating down on the road and the store, on the pecans and elms and magnolias, on the men at work in the fields, on the athletes at work in the pasture.

Inside Baby Doll and I would be dancing. Or Guy Lombardo would be playing "Begin the Beguine" and I would be belting out lyrics.

> *"Oh, let them begin . . . we don't care,*
> *America all . . . ways does its share,*
> *We'll be there with plenty of ammo,*
> *Allies . . . don't ever despair . . ."*

Baby Doll thought I was a genius. If I was having an especially creative morning she would go running out to the kitchen and bring anyone she could find to hear me.

"Oh, let them begin any warrr . . ." I would be singing, tapping one foot against the fireplace tiles, waving my arms around like a conductor.

>*"Uncle Sam will fight*
>*for the underrr . . . doggg.*
>*Never fear, Allies, never fear."*

A new record would drop. Baby Doll would swoop me into her fragrant arms, and we would break into an improvisation on Tommy Dorsey's "Boogie-Woogie."

But the Broad Jump Pit would not go away. It loomed in my dreams. If I walked to the store I had to pass the pasture. If I stood on the porch or looked out my grandmother's window, there it was, shimmering in the sunlight, constantly guarded by one of the Olympians.

Things went from bad to worse between me and Dudley. If we so much as passed each other in the hall a fight began. He would hold up his fists and dance around, trying to look like a fighter. When I came flailing at him he would reach underneath my arms and punch me in the stomach.

I considered poisoning him. There was a box of white powder in the toolshed with a skull and crossbones above the label. Several times I took it down and held it in my hands, shuddering at the power it gave me. Only the thought of the electric chair kept me from using it.

Every day Dudley gathered his troops and headed out for the pasture. Every day my hatred grew and festered. Then, just about the time I could stand it no longer, a diversion occurred.

One afternoon about four o'clock an official-looking sedan clattered across the bridge and came roaring down the road to the house.

It was my cousin, Lauralee Manning, wearing her WAVE uniform and smoking Camels in an ivory holder. Lauralee had been widowed at the beginning of the war when her young husband crashed his Navy training plane into the Pacific.

Lauralee dried her tears, joined the WAVES, and went off to avenge his death. I had not seen this paragon since I was a small child, but I had memorized the photograph Miss Onnie Maud, who was Lauralee's mother, kept on her dresser. It was a photograph of Lauralee leaning against the rail of a destroyer.

Not that Lauralee ever went to sea on a destroyer. She was spending the war in Pensacola, Florida, being secretary to an admiral.

Now, out of a clear blue sky, here was Lauralee, home on leave with a two-carat diamond ring and the news that she was getting married.

"You might have called and given some warning," Miss Onnie Maud said, turning Lauralee into a mass of wrinkles with her embraces. "You could have softened the blow with a letter."

"Who's the groom," my grandmother said. "I only hope he's not a pilot."

"Is he an admiral?" I said, "or a colonel or a major or a commander?"

"My fiancé's not in uniform, honey," Lauralee said. "He's in real estate. He runs the war-bond effort for the whole state of Florida. Last year he collected half a million dollars."

"In real estate!" Miss Onnie Maud said, gasping. "What religion is he?"

"He's Unitarian," she said. "His name is Donald Marcus. He's best friends with Admiral Semmes, that's how I met him. And he's coming a week from Saturday, and that's all the time we have to get ready for the wedding."

"Unitarian!" Miss Onnie Maud said. "I don't think I've ever met a Unitarian."

"Why isn't he in uniform?" I insisted.

"He has flat feet," Lauralee said gaily. "But you'll love him when you see him."

Later that afternoon Lauralee took me off by myself for a ride in the sedan.

"Your mother is my favorite cousin," she said, touching my face with gentle fingers. "You'll look just like her when you grow up and get your figure."

I moved closer, admiring the brass buttons on her starched uniform and the brisk way she shifted and braked and put in the clutch and accelerated.

We drove down the river road and out to the bootlegger's shack where Lauralee bought a pint of Jack Daniel's and two Cokes. She poured out half of her Coke, filled it with whiskey, and we roared off down the road with the radio playing.

We drove along in the lengthening day. Lauralee was chain-smoking, lighting one Camel after another, tossing the butts out the window, taking sips from her bourbon and Coke. I sat beside her, pretending to smoke a piece of rolled-up paper, making little noises into the mouth of my Coke bottle.

We drove up to a picnic spot on the levee and sat under a tree to look out at the river.

"I miss this old river," she said. "When I'm sad I dream about it licking the tops of the levees."

I didn't know what to say to that. To tell the truth I was afraid to say much of anything to Lauralee. She seemed so splendid. It was enough to be allowed to sit by her on the levee.

"Now, Rhoda," she said, "your mother was matron of honor in my wedding to Buddy, and I want you, her own little daughter, to be maid of honor in my second wedding."

I could hardly believe my ears! While I was trying to think of something to say to this wonderful news I saw that Lauralee was crying, great tears were forming in her blue eyes.

"Under this very tree is where Buddy and I got engaged," she said. Now the tears were really starting to roll, falling all over the front of her uniform. "He gave me my ring right where we're sitting."

"The maid of honor?" I said, patting her on the shoulder, trying to be of some comfort. "You really mean the maid of honor?"

"Now he's gone from the world," she continued, "and I'm marrying a wonderful man, but that doesn't make it any easier. Oh, Rhoda, they never even found his body, never even found his body."

I was patting her on the head now, afraid she would forget her offer in the midst of her sorrow.

"You mean I get to be the real maid of honor?"

"Oh, yes, Rhoda, honey," she said. "The maid of honor, my only attendant." She blew her nose on a lace-trimmed hand-kerchief and sat up straighter, taking a drink from the Coke bottle.

"Not only that, but I have decided to let you pick out your own dress. We'll go to Greenville and you can try on every dress at Nell's and Blum's and you can have the one you like the most."

I threw my arms around her, burning with happiness, smelling her whiskey and Camels and the dark Tabu perfume that was her signature. Over her shoulder and through the low branches of the trees the afternoon sun was going down in an orgy of reds and blues and purples and violets, falling from sight, going all the way to China.

Let them keep their nasty Broad Jump Pit I thought. Wait till they hear about this. Wait till they find out I'm maid of honor in a military wedding.

*   *   *

Finding the dress was another matter. Early the next morning Miss Onnie Maud and my grandmother and Lauralee and I set out for Greenville.

As we passed the pasture I hung out the back window making faces at the athletes. This time they only pretended to ignore me. They couldn't ignore this wedding. It was going to be in the parlor instead of the church so they wouldn't even get to be altar boys. They wouldn't get to light a candle.

"I don't know why you care what's going on in that pasture," my grandmother said. "Even if they let you play with them all it would do is make you a lot of ugly muscles."

"Then you'd have big old ugly arms like Weegie Toler," Miss Onnie Maud said. "Lauralee, you remember Weegie Toler, that was a swimmer. Her arms got so big no one would take her to a dance, much less marry her."

"Well, I don't want to get married anyway," I said. "I'm never getting married. I'm going to New York City and be a lawyer."

"Where does she get those ideas?" Miss Onnie Maud said.

"When you get older you'll want to get married," Lauralee said. "Look at how much fun you're having being in my wedding."

"Well, I'm never getting married," I said. "And I'm never having any children. I'm going to New York and be a lawyer and save people from the electric chair."

"It's the movies," Miss Onnie Maud said. "They let her watch anything she likes in Indiana."

We walked into Nell's and Blum's Department Store and took up the largest dressing room. My grandmother and Miss Onnie Maud were seated on brocade chairs and every saleslady in the store came crowding around trying to get in on the wedding.

I refused to even consider the dresses they brought from the "girls'" department.

"I told her she could wear whatever she wanted," Lauralee said, "and I'm keeping my promise."

"Well, she's not wearing green satin or I'm not coming," my grandmother said, indicating the dress I had found on a rack and was clutching against me.

"At least let her try it on," Lauralee said. "Let her see for herself." She zipped me into the green satin. It came down to my ankles and fit around my midsection like a girdle, making my waist seem smaller than my stomach. I admired myself in the mirror. It was almost perfect. I looked exactly like a nightclub singer.

"This one's fine," I said. "This is the one I want."

"It looks marvelous, Rhoda," Lauralee said, "but it's the wrong color for the wedding. Remember I'm wearing blue."

"I believe the child's color-blind," Miss Onnie Maud said. "It runs in her father's family."

"I am not color-blind," I said, reaching behind me and unzipping the dress. "I have twenty-twenty vision."

"Let her try on some more," Lauralee said. "Let her try on everything in the store."

I proceeded to do just that, with the salesladies getting grumpier and grumpier. I tried on a gold garbadine dress with a rhinestone-studded cumberbund. I tried on a pink ballerina-length formal and a lavender voile tea dress and several silk suits. Somehow nothing looked right.

"Maybe we'll have to make her something," my grandmother said.

"But there's no time," Miss Onnie Maud said. "Besides first we'd have to find out what she wants. Rhoda, please tell us what you're looking for."

Their faces all turned to mine, waiting for an answer. But I didn't know the answer.

The dress I wanted was a secret. The dress I wanted was dark and tall and thin as a reed. There was a word for what I wanted, a word I had seen in magazines. But what was that word? I could not remember.

"I want something dark," I said at last. "Something dark and silky."

"Wait right there," the saleslady said. "Wait just a minute." Then, from out of a prewar storage closet she brought a black-watch plaid recital dress with spaghetti straps and a white piqué jacket. It was made of taffeta and rustled when I touched it. There was a label sewn into the collar of the jacket. *Little Miss Sophisticate,* it said. *Sophisticate,* that was the word I was seeking.

I put on the dress and stood triumphant in a sea of ladies and dresses and hangers.

"This is the dress," I said. "This is the dress I'm wearing."

"It's perfect," Lauralee said. "Start hemming it up. She'll be the prettiest maid of honor in the whole world."

All the way home I held the box on my lap thinking about how I would look in the dress. Wait till they see me like this, I was thinking. Wait till they see what I really look like.

I fell in love with the groom. The moment I laid eyes on him I forgot he was flat-footed. He arrived bearing gifts of music and perfume and candy, a warm dark-skinned man with eyes the color of walnuts.

He laughed out loud when he saw me, standing on the porch with my hands on my hips.

"This must be Rhoda," he exclaimed, "the famous red-haired maid of honor." He came running up the steps, gave me a slow, exciting hug, and presented me with a whole album of

Xavier Cugat records. I had never owned a record of my own, much less an album.

Before the evening was over I put on a red formal I found in a trunk and did a South American dance for him to Xavier Cugat's "Poinciana." He said he had never seen anything like it in his whole life.

The wedding itself was a disappointment. No one came but the immediate family and there was no aisle to march down and the only music was Onnie Maud playing "Liebestraum."

Dudley and Philip and Saint John and Oliver and Bunky were dressed in long pants and white shirts and ties. They had fresh military crew cuts and looked like a nest of new birds, huddled together on the blue velvet sofa, trying to keep their hands to themselves, trying to figure out how to act at a wedding.

The elderly Episcopal priest read out the ceremony in a gravelly smoker's voice, ruining all the good parts by coughing. He was in a bad mood because Lauralee and Mr. Marcus hadn't found time to come to him for marriage instruction.

Still, I got to hold the bride's flowers while he gave her the ring and stood so close to her during the ceremony I could hear her breathing.

The reception was better. People came from all over the Delta. There were tables with candles set up around the porches and sprays of greenery in every corner. There were gentlemen sweating in linen suits and the record player playing every minute. In the back hall Calvin had set up a real professional bar with tall, permanently frosted glasses and ice and mint and lemons and every kind of whiskey and liqueur in the world.

I stood in the receiving line getting compliments on my dress, then wandered around the rooms eating cake and letting people hug me. After a while I got bored with that and went out to the back hall and began to fix myself a drink at the bar.

I took one of the frosted glasses and began filling it from different bottles, tasting as I went along. I used plenty of crème de menthe and soon had something that tasted heavenly. I filled the glass with crushed ice, added three straws, and went out to sit on the back steps and cool off.

I was feeling wonderful. A full moon was caught like a kite in the pecan trees across the river. I sipped along on my drink. Then, without planning it, I did something I had never dreamed of doing. I left the porch alone at night. Usually I was in terror of the dark. My grandmother had told me that alligators come out of the bayou to eat children who wander alone at night.

I walked out across the yard, the huge moon giving so much light I almost cast a shadow. When I was nearly to the water's edge I turned and looked back toward the house. It shimmered in the moonlight like a jukebox alive in a meadow, seemed to pulsate with music and laughter and people, beautiful and foreign, not a part of me.

I looked out at the water, then down the road to the pasture. The Broad Jump Pit! There it was, perfect and unguarded. Why had I never thought of doing this before?

I began to run toward the road. I ran as fast as my Mary Jane pumps would allow me. I pulled my dress up around my waist and climbed the fence in one motion, dropping lightly down on the other side. I was sweating heavily, alone with the moon and my wonderful courage.

I knew exactly what to do first. I picked up the pole and hoisted it over my head. It felt solid and balanced and alive. I hoisted it up and down a few times as I had seen Dudley do, getting the feel of it.

Then I laid it ceremoniously down on the ground, reached behind me and unhooked the plaid formal. I left it lying in a heap on the ground. There I stood, in my cotton underpants, ready to take up pole-vaulting.

I lifted the pole and carried it back to the end of the cinder path. I ran slowly down the path, stuck the pole in the wooden cup, and attempted throwing my body into the air, using it as a lever.

Something was wrong. It was more difficult than it appeared from a distance. I tried again. Nothing happened. I sat down with the pole across my legs to think things over.

Then I remembered something I had watched Dudley doing through the binoculars. He measured down from the end of the pole with his fingers spread wide. That was it, I had to hold it closer to the end.

I tried it again. This time the pole lifted me several feet off the ground. My body sailed across the grass in a neat arc and I landed on my toes. I was a natural!

I do not know how long I was out there, running up and down the cinder path, thrusting my body farther and farther through space, tossing myself into the pit like a mussel shell thrown across the bayou.

At last I decided I was ready for the real test. I had to vault over a cane barrier. I examined the pegs on the wooden poles and chose one that came up to my shoulder.

I put the barrier pole in place, spit over my left shoulder, and marched back to the end of the path. Suck up your guts, I told myself. It's only a pole. It won't get stuck in your stomach and tear out your insides. It won't kill you.

I stood at the end of the path eyeballing the barrier. Then, above the incessant racket of the crickets, I heard my name being called. Rhoda . . . the voices were calling. Rhoda . . . Rhoda . . . Rhoda . . . Rhoda.

I turned toward the house and saw them coming. Mr. Marcus and Dudley and Bunky and Calvin and Lauralee and what looked like half the wedding. They were climbing the fence, calling my name, and coming to get me. Rhoda . . . they called out. Where on earth have you been? What on earth are you doing?

I hoisted the pole up to my shoulders and began to run down the path, running into the light from the moon. I picked up speed, thrust the pole into the cup, and threw myself into the sky, into the still Delta night. I sailed up and was clear and over the barrier.

I let go of the pole and began my fall, which seemed to last a long, long time. It was like falling through clear water. I dropped into the sawdust and lay very still, waiting for them to reach me.

Sometimes I think whatever has happened since has been of no real interest to me.

Nineteen Forty-one

RHODA was sitting on the front sidewalk trying to set some paper on fire with a magnifying glass. She was very worried at that time about what she would do if she was lost in the woods. It would be she and Dudley alone in the woods. Dudley would have the compass but he would not tell her what it said. He would sneak off while she was sleeping and leave her there to rot. She would not panic. She would not wander deeper into the woods. She would stay where she was until help came. She would find water. She would build a fire. But how to do it? Striking rocks on flint didn't work. How many times had she tried that? Rubbing sticks together didn't work. No, the best thing to do was carry a magnifying glass at all times.

Rhoda trained the glass on an ant crossing the sidewalk. There were clouds in the sky. That was lucky for the ant.

"Get your things on," Dudley said, coming around the corner of the house, accompanied by his friend, Fat Tunney.

Fat Tunney hung back. Dudley squatted down by Rhoda. He was wearing his jodhpurs and his English riding hat. His leather riding crop was in his hand. You would never have believed he lived in Mound City, Illinois.

"Come on," he said. "Get dressed. Pop wants us to catch the horses. Fat Tunney's here. He'll help."

"I don't want to catch the damned old horses," Rhoda said. She trained the magnifying glass on Dudley's boots, thinking how nice it would be to give him a hotfoot. "I'm busy. Leave me alone."

"Come on. He wants us to saddle Dixie so you can go riding with this girl that's coming over. She's the banker's daughter."

"I don't want to go riding. You catch the goddamned old horses if you want to, since you're his slave. I'm not going back there and get in that goddamn old mud." Fat Tunney hung his head. He had never known a girl that talked like Rhoda. He had never known any people like the Mannings. They had been there six months. He didn't know what he did before they moved to Mound City. Every morning he woke up thinking about them and pulled on his clothes and went over to see what they were doing.

"That's right, Rhoda," he said now. "Your daddy said to tell you to hurry up."

"Well, I'm not going to," she said. "And get off the sidewalk. I'm killing ants."

"You better come on," Dudley said. He stood up. He was wearing his bandolier with his extra merit badges. He was going for Eagle Scout. He was trying to be the youngest Eagle Scout in America. "Get dressed," he said. "Don't make me tell you again."

Rhoda trained the magnifying glass on his leg. "Go to hell, you spy," she said. "Go back to Germany where you belong. You aren't even a citizen. You're a yellow German spy. You're really a Jap. That's why your skin's so yellow." She was referring to Dudley's malaria. He had malaria from living in a levee camp when he was small. The Mannings had lived a dangerous life. Everything happened to them but they always recovered. They had too much character to give in to fate.

"Go back to Germany," Rhoda continued. "Go salute the Führer. Go salute the Führer's bathroom." She cracked up at that, beating her sandals against the sidewalk. "Go to the German bathroom, go to the bathroom with the Japs. Ha, ha, ha, Ha, ha . . ." She was laughing so hard it hurt. Fat Tunney was laughing too but he was trying not to let it show.

Dudley and Fat Tunney disappeared around the side of the house. Rhoda got up and followed them. At the back of the property was a corral surrounded by a barbed-wire fence. Little scalps of horsehair were stuck here and there in the barbs. Little bloody pieces of Dixie and Cardinal and Straw, the last two named for the colors of Rhoda's mother's sorority.

As Rhoda came up the horses were milling around the water tank, bumping each other's flanks, slurping water, making noises. Rhoda didn't trust them. They were different from horses in books, good faithful creatures like Black Beauty or beautiful white stallions running across the plains carrying the mail. These were quarter horses and their only purpose in life was to teach Rhoda and Dudley not to be afraid.

"Get your jodhpurs on, honey," her father said. He was sitting on the gate. "Mr. Trumbo is bringing his little girl over here to ride."

"I can't," she said. "I'm menstruating."

"Oh, my God," he said, and climbed down off the fence, hoping to get to her before she said it again and the boys heard it. "ARIANE," he screamed toward the house. "ARRIIIII-ANNNEEE, get out here and get this child. Who told you that?" he demanded, taking her by the arm. "Who told you a thing like that?" His face was as red as the sun. Rhoda's mother came running out of the house and across the yard and swooped her up. "Where does she learn those things?" he was saying. "Who told her that? Who told her such a thing?"

"Sherry Nettleship's aunt told us all about it," Rhoda said. "You can't ever go swimming and blood runs down your legs. And you can't ride horses or anything like that. I've been doing it all morning. There's blood all over the sidewalk. Go look for yourself." It was an inspiration. Actually, Rhoda had spilled red Kool-Aid while she was making fire. That was what had drawn the ants. "You can die if you aren't careful," she continued. "Anything can happen when you menstruate."

Rhoda's mother took her into the house and put her in the bathtub. She knelt beside the tub looking down at Rhoda's plump apricot-colored legs, her little precious vagina, her soft round stomach, her navel, where this maddening child had actually been joined to her own body. She dripped water from her hands over Rhoda's legs. She touched her hair. She allowed her hand to rest on Rhoda's skull. Ariane Manning loved her children so much it took her breath away to touch them. A little girl, a precious sweet baby girl, her little girl, her daughter.

"Don't ever talk about that again," she said. "We don't talk about things like that. It is a long, long time before that will happen to you. When the time comes I will tell you what to do. It's a long way off, a lot of years. I can't believe Mrs. Nettleship told you a thing like that. I just can't believe it."

"She was drunk," Rhoda said. "She was drinking bathtub gin. She told us everything about it. She told me and Sherry everything there is to know."

"Oh, my God," Ariane said. "I can't believe it. I just can't believe we're in this town. Oh, my God. I just don't know. I just don't know where to start."

She took her daughter from the tub and dried her with a blue towel and dressed her in jodhpurs and a white blouse and a little checked vest. She held the boots while Rhoda wiggled her feet into them. She brushed Rhoda's hair. She dotted her neck with perfume. Stuck a handkerchief in her pocket. She stopped crying. She got a hold on herself.

When Rhoda got back to the corral the horses were saddled. Dudley and Fat Tunney were just saddling the last one, a large black and white mare named Dixie. They were tightening up the cinches. Dixie was fighting them, puffing up her belly, kicking, carrying on.

She is the worst horse we have, Rhoda thought. I bet he's going to make me ride her.

"Get on Dixie, Sister," her father called out from his command position astride the gate. "Let the boys have the geldings."

"She doesn't have any gaits," Rhoda said. "I can't stand to ride a horse that doesn't have gaits."

"You wouldn't know what to do with gaits," Dudley said. "You can hardly even ride."

"Shut up all that arguing," her father said. "Give her a leg up, Fat Tunney. Look out! Here's our company coming in the back." Rhoda swung herself up into the saddle. A languid, droopy-looking girl on an Appaloosa was turning into the yard from the road behind the place. Rhoda looked her over. She didn't look like much. She was barely even holding the reins as the horse came plodding over. Still, she was a banker's daughter. She might have a playhouse or a chauffeur or anything. "Hello," Rhoda said, as soon as the girl was near enough to hear. "I'm Rhoda."

"Well, I'm Lelia," the girl said. "I'm supposed to show you where to go."

"This is Mr. Trumbo's daughter," her father said. "That's been so nice to me. Now you girls go on and have a ride and when you get back I'll take us out for ice cream. Use your knees, Sweet Sister. Don't forget to use your knees."

"I can't feel anything through this saddle. This saddle's too thick."

"Well, don't complain about everything. Go on, then, you girls get going before it gets too hot." He climbed down off the fence and took the bridles and led the horses down the path and turned them in the direction of the road. "Ride 'em now," he said. "Show him who's boss. Let's see you ride."

Lelia's Appaloosa began to trot along the path, a nice clean little trot. Rhoda dug her knees into the saddle. She straightened her back. She had a vision of herself riding through the town, her hair flying back from her face, the eyes of the town following her, worshipping and jealous.

She dug her heels into Dixie's side. She pulled on the reins. The horse balked. Rhoda tried again. This time she jerked Dixie's head from side to side. Slapping the reins against her neck. "Get going," she said. "Come on, you goddamn old horse."

Dixie lowered her head, then rose up on her hind feet and spun in a circle. She hit the ground, then took off for the road. Rhoda clung to the reins, then clung to the mane. The horse jumped a ditch. The saddle moved, then moved again. Rhoda's head was on a level with Dixie's thighs. Her eyes were on the road.

Dixie turned and began to run along the railroad tracks. A man ran out of a house and tried to flag them down. "Let go," he yelled. "Let go. Let go and fall."

Her head hit the tracks. Then hit again. There was grass and steel and sky. Then there were faces.

Her father was there and Mr. Samuels and they put her into a car and she was going somewhere. For a long time she was going somewhere. Her grandmother seemed to be in the car, opening a suitcase, getting out presents. Her beautiful tall grandfather was there, wearing a gray suit. He was holding her head in his hands. His great blue eyes were sad. He took her into his old wicker rocking chair. He read to her from magazines. He let her smoke his pipe. He gave her money. Many quarters and nickels and dimes. As soon as the store opened she could put them in the slot machine. The slot machine was in the car. It was a Buick with a slot machine. She and her grandmother and grandfather would ride forever sticking money in the slot machine. Nickels poured out onto the seat. They had so many nickels they didn't know what to do with all of them. They threw them out the windows so the poor people could have some and play their own slot machines. The poor people caught the nickels. They held them up to the light.

When Rhoda woke up she was in her own bed and her mother was sitting beside her and Doctor Finley was there and her name was in the newspaper.

> Rhoda Katherine Manning, only daughter of Chief Engineer Manning of the U.S. Corps of Engineers, is recovering from a fall she received when the horse she was riding ran away. She received cuts and bruises and is recovering at the Manning home on Maple Street.

"I'm going to kill that horse," she said, opening her eyes, lifting her head from the pillow.

"Your father already beat it half to death," her mother said. She sighed and looked away.

"You made me do it," she said, seeing him standing in the door. "You made me ride it. And Dudley put the saddle on. He did it wrong. He didn't put the saddle on right." Dudley was standing at the foot of the bed, looking thin and yellow. "You did it," she said. "You tried to kill me."

"Don't talk like that, Rhoda," her mother said. "It was an accident. It wasn't anybody's fault."

"It was his fault," she said, sitting up higher. "He and Fat Tunney. They did it. The saddle came off. That's why I fell. You did it," she said, looking right at him. "You did it on purpose. You tried to kill me so you can inherit everything."

"Come on, son," her father said. He put his arm around his son and led him from the room. "Let your mother take care of her."

"He did it," she yelled after them. "I almost died. It's a wonder I'm not dead."

"Let me get you some supper," her mother said. "Everyone in town's been bringing food. There's quail with a glass cover and chocolate custard and everything you love."

"I dreamed about Dan-Dan," Rhoda said. She sank back into the pillows, allowing her mother to hold her hands. "I dreamed Dan-Dan and Big Daddy and I were going to sleep in those concrete wigwams where we stayed that other time. Did you tell them yet? Do they know I almost died?"

"They're on their way," her mother said. "They ought to be here soon."

"Good," Rhoda said. "I'll get them to kill the horse."

The Tree Fort

I HAVE BEEN HAUNTED lately by memories of Seymour, Indiana. A story in a magazine set me off and set me dreaming, of my brother Dudley, and the fort, and the year he lost the eye. A fort made out of Christmas trees, piled four trees high, on the flat ground where the yard ran down to meet the alley. Dudley's pyramid, a memorial to the light in his left eye.

The first time I saw the fort was on a Saturday morning in January. I was coming home from my ballet lesson, walking up the alley from Sycamore Street, dragging my ballet shoes behind me by the laces, on the lookout for anything valuable anyone might have thrown away. I had found a hand-painted card shuffler in that alley once. It could happen again at any time.

I was almost home when I saw the activity in the yard. There were three boys, Dudley and Miles Pennington and Ronnie Breiner. They were standing beside a pile of Christmas trees. Dudley had his hands on his hips. He was wearing his jodhpurs and his hunting vest. His hair was as short as a marine recruit's. My father kept it cut that way to save him from vanity. Dudley stood in the middle of his friends, a young Douglas MacArthur, mulling over his problem. As I drew nearer I could see the Clifford twins coming down the side yard dragging another tree. It was Epiphany, the sixth of January, the day good Christians throw their trees away. What was Dudley up to and how had he once again hit upon an idea so wonderful, so startling in its power and simplicity, that it was certain to ruin my life for weeks?

"What are you doing?" I called out, as I crossed the victory garden and made for the pile of trees. "What's everyone doing?"

"We're building a fort," Dudley said. "Go in the house and get us some water and bring it out here if you want to help."

"Get your own hell damn water," I said, and went on by the trees. "Why are you building a fort?"

"To have a club. We're going to have a war with Billy Bob Robbins."

"How will we stack them up?" Ronnie Breiner asked. "I don't see what's going to keep them up."

"Just get them," Dudley answered. He was slouched over on one hip, wearing all seven of his lanyards. "We'll get them up. Get us some water, Shorty, if you want to help." He always called me Shorty. He got the idea from a gangster movie. I ignored him and went on into the house to put my ballet things away. From around the corner on the other side I could see Wayne Shorter and his friends dragging two more trees into the yard. It was eleven-thirty on a Saturday morning, right in the middle of a world war, and once again Dudley had found a way to ruin my life.

By noon they had a circle of trees piled four trees high and held together with clothesline and two-by-fours. Inside the circle was an enclosed space about as large as a bedroom. They filled that with old sleeping bags and a camouflage tarpaulin. I sat on the back steps and watched the activity. I was eating a sandwich and sucking a baby bottle filled with chocolate milk. My mother had a new baby and I could borrow his baby bottles anytime I wanted to and use them to suck chocolate milk. The milk picked up a wonderful flavor as it passed through the rubber nipple. I bit off a small piece so the milk would flow more easily. I knew they could see me drinking out of the bottle but I didn't care. It never occurred to me to stop doing something just because someone was looking at me.

They were dividing up into teams now. One team to hold the fort and the other to attack. Dudley's team would defend the fort. I see him now, standing on a ladder, sighting down across his arm with a wooden rifle, both eyes still in perfect working order, mowing down the invaders, then charging out in the forefront of his men, shooting as he ran. Coming to meet him from beside the French doors were Billy Bob and his horde of scrawny kids from the new development on the other side of Calvin Boulevard. I sucked my bottle. The January sun beat down on Seymour, Indiana. Inside my little plaid skirt and sweater my hot sweaty little body sucked down the rubber-flavored chocolate milk and watched the battle of the fort proceed.

When my father came home from the Air Corps base that afternoon he immediately took over rebuilding the fort. He made Dudley and Wayne take down all the two-by-fours and stack them up in a better configuration. "Those goddamn trees could fall on someone and hurt them," he said. "You boys are going to get me sued." Then Dudley and Wayne had to labor until dark shoring up the fort and making it safe.

He did not, however, seem to mind that every dead Christmas tree on Calvin Boulevard was piled up in our back yard killing the grass, and when mother mentioned it he told her to calm down and leave the boys alone. There's plenty of grass in the world, he told her, the grass can take care of itself. I had decided to stay out of it. I didn't even tell her that Billy Bob's regiment had trampled her roses as they pulled their tanks up from the alley for a surprise attack.

That night, tired as he was and with his hands red and raw from laboring on the fort in the January weather, Dudley made the first of the rubber guns. He fashioned it from pine, although later the guns would be made of finer woods, cypress and maple and persimmon and even walnut. He made the stock by whittling down a split two-by-four and sanding it for an hour. He was just beginning on the trigger mechanism when mother made him turn out the lights. At that time I was in the habit of sleeping in his room when I got scared. I would pay him three cents a night to sleep in his extra bed or five cents to sleep curled up on the foot of his bed. I was deathly afraid of the dark in those years. I feared the insides of closets and the space beneath my cherry four-poster bed and the goblins that get you if you don't watch out and angels coming for to carry you home and vampires and mummies and the holy ghost. I would wake from dreams and go running into my parents' room in the middle of the night when I slept alone. I was pathologically, deathly afraid of the dark, of night and shadow and the wages of sin. So I was sleeping in Dudley's extra bed when he turned the light back on and went back to work on the rubber gun. He added a carved handle and a trigger made out of a wooden clothespin and then dug around in a dresser drawer for a rubber band and used it to demonstrate for me how the trigger would release the band. "Of course, we'll have to make better things to shoot," he said. "We'll have to cut up old inner tubes."

"Will you make me one?" I asked. I felt very close to Dudley that night, watching him at his desk, risking a whipping to finish his work. He was brave, braver than I was in every way, and I loved him, with his thin face and his long thin arms and high intelligence quotient and his ability to stand up to and get along with our father. I had seen our father pull off his belt and beat Dudley in front of his friends and Dudley would never say a word. He took punishment like a man. He worked like a man. He was a man. I was safe in his room. No mummy or vampire would ever come in there. It was worth five cents to get a night's sleep without having to worry about the closets or underneath the beds.

"I might," he said. "If I have time."

"Will I get to be in the fort?"

"I doubt it, Shorty. You're a girl. Girls aren't supposed to be in everything."

"I'll make one of my own, then. Can I have part of the trees?" He shook his head and went back to work, enlarging the place on the stock where the clothespin would fit and lock in.

"I'm getting a diamond ring," I said and slipped back down beneath the covers. I liked to keep my neck covered at all times when I was asleep. Even in Dudley's room you couldn't be too careful about vampires. "When Momma dies she's leaving me her ring."

"Go to sleep," he said, and held the gun up to the light to inspect it. "You're making too much noise. You're going to wake them up."

The fort became a permanent fixture in the back yard. The fort stayed. Winter progressed into spring. The Christmas trees turned brown and brittle and lost their needles and the needles were swept up and used to mulch the rose garden, which had been rebuilt by Dudley and his gang. All our roses bloomed that spring, American Beauties and Rosa Damascena, which dates back to the Crusades, and the dark red Henry Nevard and Rosa Alba, the white rose of York, and Persian Yellow and Fruehling's Gold and Maiden's Blush, our cutting of which had come to Indiana from Glen Allen, Mississippi, hand-delivered by our cousin, Lauralee, who was a lieutenant in the navy.

The fort grew, taking up all the room between the back porch and the rose garden and the alley. The cedar and pine needles were reinforced by boards donated by boys from around the neighborhood. A tower was added and a permanent scaling ladder. Paths were worn along the sides of the house as invading forces charged down the hill. Later, the spring rains turned the paths into gullies.

The manufacture of rubber guns proceeded apace. The strips of rubber were of varying sizes, as Dudley experimented with different types of inner tubes. He would sit for hours in the evenings, sanding and polishing the stocks and handles, cutting old inner tubes into strips, sewing holsters from scraps of unbleached domestic and suiting samples.

March turned into April and April into May. The Allies were winning the war in Europe. The clock in my second-grade classroom was the cruelest clock in the world. The days until the end of the school year seemed to last forever. At last my trunk was brought up from the basement and aired out and I began to fill it with T-shirts and socks and shorts and flashlight batteries. In June I was going to camp. I loved camp. I adored camp. I would have liked to go to camp all year. At camp I was the leader. At camp I had people sleeping around me every night. Without paying a single cent I had a whole room full of people to sleep with.

This year I was going to a new camp in Columbus, Ohio. Columbus Girls' Camp. A letter came with a sticker to put on my suitcase and another one for my trunk. I forgot about the fort. Who needed the hell damn fort? I was going off to Columbus Girls' Camp to row boats and swim in races and make lanyards and build campfires and sleep in a cabin with people all around me, far from the vampires and mummies and holy ghosts who inhabit real houses where families live.

*   *   *

So I was not there when he lost the eye. "The eye is a tiny balloon that grows at the front of the brain." So it said in a book I took home from the library. "The cells at the back are tuned to be sensitive to light, enabling us to see the world around us. The eye is so delicate that it has to be protected by a bony socket and eyelids to cover the window and a flow of tears to keep the window clean."

On the day he lost the eye, Dudley and Billy Bob and Miles and Ronnie were attacking as a tank corps. Wayne and Sam were inside the fort. The other boys were pushing wagons loaded with staves down from the back porch. There was an incline of about forty degrees, plenty good for accelerating wagon-tanks. Dudley was standing up in a wagon holding a loaded rubber gun and Miles was pushing him. Billy Bob was beside him in the other wagon. It was the tenth or twelfth or twentieth time they had run the wagons down the hill toward the fort. They were getting better and better at guiding them, but somehow or other this time Billy Bob's wagon ran into the side of Dudley's wagon and in the melee Dudley's rubber gun backfired and the thin band of old inner tube managed to elude the bony socket and the eyelid and dealt a blow to Dudley's eye. There goes my eye, I guess he said. It's a good thing it's on the left side. Anyway, there was blood, lots of blood. The German housekeeper held Dudley in her arms while Momma and Sam and Wayne ran for Doctor Shorter, and later that night, when the bleeding wouldn't stop, they took him to the doctors at the Air Corps base and the next day the Air Corps flew him to Memphis to an eye surgeon.

It took all summer to heal. It was September before Dudley came home with his eye still swathed in bandages.

When the bandages came off he could see light and dark and distinguish shapes, but nothing more. There were blood clots behind the iris, and the doctors were afraid to operate for fear it would set up sympathetic problems with the good eye. That's all we talked about from then on. Dudley's good eye. How to protect his good eye. How never to take chances with his good eye. How his good eye was doing. Thank God for his good eye. Pray for his good eye.

While Dudley was in Memphis the fort had fallen into disrepair. Children from all over the neighborhood came and inspected it and told each other about the tank battle. An aura of mystery and danger hung around the circle of trees, timeless, Druidic, threatening. I never went near the place. I knew bad karma when I felt it. The sleeping bags were in there rotting away but I didn't go in and drag them out. By the time Mother got home from Memphis they were filled with ants and had to be pitched out for the garbagemen.

Dudley had a strange relationship with the fort after he returned from Memphis. I remember him standing there with his big black patch on his eye, wearing his brown and white tweed knickers, his hands on his hips, looking at the fort, not defeated or scared or really puzzled even. Just standing there looking it over.

Then one day the following spring, after D-Day, when the pressure was letting up all over the United States and men could go back to ruining the lives of their children, my father looked up over his breakfast oatmeal and said, "Son, today we are going to have to get rid of those trees. Your mother wants the grass to grow back before the owners of this house return."

"They will think we are white trash," my mother added. She was poaching eggs in a black skillet, a little blue and white apron over her blue shirtwaist dress. I was sitting in the corner of the breakfast nook pulling on my hair to make it grow.

"Let's clear them out," my father went on. "Get Wayne and Billy Bob and let them help."

"I'm not helping," I said. "It's not my damn old fort."

"I'm going to wash your mouth out with soap," my mother put in. "Dudley, please do something about her."

"No one expects you to help," my brother said.

"No one expects you to do a thing," my father added. "You are a very selfish little girl."

I slid down under the table and climbed out and stood beside my mother. I didn't care what they thought. As soon as the war was over I was going to be a movie star. When I got to Hollywood I would probably never even write to them again. Dudley looked at me out of his good eye. He looked so thin and sad. I guess he was thinking about how terrible it was going to feel to have to drag all those prickly trees back to the alley and then rake up the yard and even then get yelled at and probably get a whipping before the day was out. I'm glad Daddy doesn't like me, I was thinking. The more he likes you, the more trouble you are in.

"Clean up your room," someone called after me but it was too late. I was through the dining room and past the green chair and out the door. I could feel the morning calling from the front yard and I ran on out and headed down Calvin Boulevard to see what I could find to do.

It was a glamorous spring day. The gold star in Mrs. Allen's window gleamed in the light. The apple trees in the Hancocks' yard had burst into bloom. Elsie Carter came riding down the boulevard carrying her sack of *Saturday Evening Posts*. One of my molars was about to fall out. I could taste the wonderful thin, salty taste of blood. I was eight years old. In five years darker blood would pour out from in between my legs and all things would be changed. For now, I was pure energy, clear light, morally neutral, soft and violent and almost perfect. I had two good eyes and two good ears and two arms and two legs. If bugs got inside of me, my blood boiled and ate them up. If I cut myself, my blood rushed in and sewed me back together. If a tooth fell out, another one came in. The sunlight fell between the branches of the trees. It was Saturday. I had nothing to do and nowhere to go and I didn't have to do a thing I didn't want to do and it would be a long time before things darkened and turned to night.

The Time Capsule

NINETEEN HUNDRED and forty-four. In a year the Japanese would surrender but Rhoda did not know that yet. She was worried sick about the Japanese. Forty years later she would smell a fig tree beside a bakery and remember how her swing looked down on fig trees during those fateful years while she waited to see who would win the war.

It was not an ordinary swing. It was the tallest back-yard swing in Seymour, Indiana, thirty feet high, constructed of tall pine uprights sunk in concrete shoes. The rope was an inch thick. There was a seat of solid pine fitted into the rope by hundreds of hours of Rhoda's relentless swinging. She could swing holding a doll or a sandwich. She could swing standing up or sitting down. She could swing so high the ropes snapped at the top. Every morning she would come down the back stairs and across the yard and get in and take off. Off we go, she would be singing. Into the wild blue yonder. Climbing high into the sky.

One morning in August she was swinging more slowly than usual because she was thinking about fate. Anything could happen to anyone at any time. That much was clear. You could be on the losing side of a war. You could fall in love and get married. Hollywood could come and get you for a movie star. Your mother could die and leave you her rings. You could die.

Rhoda stopped the swing. She dragged her toes in the dirt. No, she would never die. She was not the type. It was probably a lie like everything else they told you. She smelled her arms. They smelled alive. She lifted her head. She tossed her hair. To hell with death, damn it all to goddamn hell. She concentrated on the fig tree above the sandpile. Let them come with death. She would smash them in the face. She would tie them to a tree and beat them with willow whips and jump in her plane and take off for the island where her mother waited. She dug her toes deeper in the soft, loose dirt beneath the swing. Red dirt, as red as blood, not dark like dirt in the Delta, like black dirt and black skin and rivers. This was the red dirt of Indiana, where they had to live because a war was going on. This was the war and everyone must do their part. She leaned far out of the swing until the ropes cut into her arms. She dug her toes into the dirt until her sandals were covered with it. Then she pushed back off into the sky. She pumped with her arms and legs. She went higher and higher, this time she would go forever, this time she would flip the swing over the uprights and come plummeting down.

It had been a bad summer. First Gena's sister told her blood was going to come out from in between her legs one week out of every four. There was nothing she could do about it. No one was excluded. Then her father took her and her mother to see *The Outlaw* with Jane Russell and made them leave at the part where Jane was warming her boyfriend's body in the haystack. "I'll keep you warm," Jane was saying. "I'll save you." Big Dudley had grabbed them up and dragged them out of the theater. He was furious with Ariane for exposing Rhoda to filth.

But the main thing was the newsreel. The news from the Pacific did not look good. Americans were dying on every island. It was possible they would lose the war. Rhoda stopped the swing. It was time to make a time capsule. She must leave a record so future generations would know she had been here. She got out of the swing and dusted off her dress and went into the kitchen. Mrs. Dustin was there, the German lady who worked for the Mannings now that they were someplace where there weren't any black people. Mrs. Dustin wasn't nice like black people. She only worked for them because she had to. She didn't even love them. "Stay out of the refrigerator," she said now. "Your mother doesn't want you eating between meals."

"I need this matchbox," Rhoda said. She took it off the stove and dumped the matches on the table.

"Don't take that," Mrs. Dustin began, but it was too late. Rhoda was out the door, the sash of her pinafore trailing behind her. She was dressed up today, wearing a green and white checked dress and an organdy pinafore. She had a green velvet ribbon tied around her wrist to ward off the story of the blood coming out down there. Down there, down there, down there. Do not put anything down there. Do not stick anything inside yourself down there. Wash your hands before you touch yourself down there. There was a wonderful quality to her mother's voice when she talked of it, scary and worried. Now, on top of everything else, there was this goddamn story about the blood. "It happens to every single girl," Gena's sister had said. "No one can escape it. You can never go swimming again. You have to have this big lump of absorbent cotton between your legs and it hurts so much you have to go to bed." The minute Rhoda got home she had fallen down on her knees beside her bed to beg God not to let it happen to her. As usual there was no answer, so she got up and went to find her mother. "Why would Gena's sister tell you such a thing? I can't believe she told you something like that," Rhoda's mother said.

"Then it's true?"

"No, it's not exactly true. It will be a long time before it happens to you and it doesn't hurt. It's God's way of making us able to have babies."

"Blood comes out from in between your legs?"

"Yes, but not for a long time. Rhoda, you are just a little girl. You don't have to worry about this yet."

"I hate God. I hate His guts. That's just like Him to think up something like that." She left the room. When she got to the door she called back across her shoulder, "I wouldn't have your old God for all the tea in China. I think He looks like hell in that old robe."

That was the day before. Today Rhoda was on the offensive where fate was concerned. She went down the back stairs, holding the matchbox in her hand, and up on a rise to a place where she had been digging a foxhole the year before. She had abandoned the project because of a book she read about a little girl who went blind from staring at the sun. She had stayed inside for weeks after she read it. The shovel was still there. She picked it up and began to dig. Her hands were so strong and so valuable. Her mother was a princess, her father was a king, she was so wonderful and valuable. She must never die or be lost in any way. She dug as fast as she could, thinking of things that must go into the capsule. A picture of herself, the picture she sent to Margaret O'Brien after seeing *Journey for Margaret*. A man had left his luggage in London so that Margaret could get on the plane and fly to safety. I would do it, Rhoda decided. I would leave all my worldly goods behind to save a little girl. She dug awhile longer, imagining it. Then she dropped the shovel and took the matchbox inside to fill it up. She walked through the French doors and into the living room of the high-ceilinged stucco house someone in Seymour, Indiana, had copied from a picture of a French château they found in a magazine.

Rhoda took down the photograph album from a shelf and

dusted it off with her skirt and found the photograph she wanted. It was a picture of herself sitting on a Persian rug in a white dress. Yes, it would do to carry her into the future. She tore it out of the book and sat down at her mother's desk to write the message.

> My name is Rhoda Katherine Manning. I weigh 82. We are in a war. They might come at any minute. I have auburn hair and brown eyes. I was born on a plantation in the Delta and as soon as the war is over I'll be going back. Mrs. Allen's son died in the war. She has a gold star in the window and I go and visit her quite frequently. The pope wouldn't let her be my brother's godmother. She isn't allowed to go inside our church. No one tells me what to do. I am just like my father.
>
> Well, I see I am running out of paper. When you find this think of me. It is summer and the sun is shining and everything is fine around here so far. I will include my fingerprints.
>
> > Yours truly,
> > Rhoda Manning

She looked up from her writing, stuck her thumbs in the inkwell, added her thumbprints, blew the ink dry, then rolled the message up into a scroll. She went into the kitchen, got some wax paper, covered the scroll with it and added a rubber band. Then she went up to her room to see what she could find to put in the capsule. She chose a picture of Alan Ladd, a string of beads, three pennies, and an empty perfume bottle. She arranged the things neatly in the matchbox and pushed the cover shut. There. That should give them a pretty good idea of what Seymour, Indiana, was like in nineteen forty-four. She marched back out to the garden and began to dig again. The smell of the earth came up to meet her, cold and fresh. A robin called. A breeze touched her face. It was perfect. Rhoda sat back upon her heels and thought about the inside of the earth, how many things are buried there. Valuable things you could find, things you could eat. She put her face in her hands, sank back deeper on her heels, thinking of her victory garden, how small and tough the carrots were, what a disappointment. Dudley had laughed at her carrots. He said a rabbit wouldn't eat the carrots that came up in her patch. Dudley. Why did they like him so much? Why was he so good? Why did he always get away with murder? Why did he have all the friends?

He was coming across the yard toward her now, wearing his jodhpurs and his riding boots. He stopped, one hip cocked out, his black patch over his injured eye.

"Get out of here," she said. "I'm doing something."

"Let me see."

"It's a time capsule." She handed over the matchbox. He opened it and looked inside.

"You ought to put your scout pin in. There ought to be something about the scouts."

"Well, I don't have anything else. That's all that's going in."

"This is going to rot. You ought to get a tin box."

"Just mind your own business."

"I'd use tin if I was you. You want me to get you a can?" He was getting his hooded look. Rhoda grew wary. There were no meaningless encounters between Rhoda and Dudley. Every word and gesture was charged with meaning and intent. There was no meager stuff here. It was the world they were fighting for.

"Just mind your own beeswax," she said. "Just leave me alone." He backed off. He actually walked away. Turned his back and walked away. Rhoda dug a few more inches in the ground, stuffed the box in the hole and covered it with dirt. Then she got up and went into the house to see what he was doing.

He was in his room with the door shut. There was the sound

of shuffling, the sound of muffled voices, muffled laughter. Rhoda pressed her ear to the door. Laughter again. It was Cody Wainwright. They were doing something. They were talking about their secret things. She would use the hidden passageway behind the stairs. They would never know she was there. She could stay there for hours without a sound, hot and close in the little alcove behind his room.

She climbed down through the small door and into the crawl space between the dormers, walking on the two-by-fours. She sat down on the crossbeams. She prepared to listen. Nothing was going on. They weren't talking. They weren't saying anything. Someone laughed. It was Dudley. Yes, it was Dudley laughing. Cody laughed back. Silence. Only silence. They turned the radio on. It was hot. Before long she would breathe up all the air. She would die back here and no one would ever find her. She got up and beat on the wall of his room. "I hear you in there. I can hear every word you're saying. I heard everything you said." Then she climbed back out the door and turned around to face them. "I heard you," she said. "If you hit me I'll tell her everything you said."

"You're a nasty bad little girl," Dudley said. "You are as bad as anyone gets to be."

"Let's take her with us to the sweetshop," Cody said. "Let's get her a lemonade."

"She's been out in the yard making a time capsule with her picture in it." Dudley laughed and turned his back on her. "That's how much she likes herself. She thinks someone's going to be interested in her after she's dead." He laughed again, a dark vicious laugh, and took his friend's arm and left her there.

A week later Rhoda's father came home one afternoon and announced that they were moving to Terre Haute, Indiana, to build another airport. They had one week to pack up and be there. The War Department was going to build the biggest airport in Indiana and get this goddamn war over with. They were going to live in a famous writer's house, a writer named Virginia Sorensen. The writer had a little girl just Rhoda's age and Rhoda would live in this child's room. They must hurry and put everything in storage. The war was heating up. There must be more airports, more pilots, more planes. Everyone must pitch in and do their share. They must tighten their belts, pack the boxes, get on the move.

Dudley began to cry. He was afraid to go to a different school so soon after he lost his eye. Rhoda's mother put her arms around him and cried too. Only Rhoda and her father did not cry. Only Rhoda and her father had enough sense to win a war. Rhoda took some boxes up to her room and began to throw things into them, singing as she worked. "Over hill, over dale, as we hit the dusty trail. And those caissons go rolling along. . . ." She threw in her movie star pictures and her music box and her false fingernail set and her Kiddie Kurlers and her hot water bottle. She threw in her books and started on her dresser drawers. All her nice white socks. The pair of ecru rayon pants her mother wouldn't let her wear because they were tacky. She held them up to the light. There were stripes of ecru silk. She threw them in and finished off the drawer. A rumbled sheet of white tissue paper was in the bottom. She folded it and left it in the drawer. Jimmy got up out of a corner and came and stood by the boxes. He was her imaginary playmate. He had come to live with her when she was four, when her mother was in the hospital. He had stayed with her all that long year. He had sat with her on the fire escape of the apartment in Louisville, Kentucky, waiting for the bread man to come and bring the bread with the picture of the Seven Dwarfs. Rhoda hadn't seen him in a long time. Now he was here, wearing his gray suit and white shirt and black tie, wearing his cynical look. "Well, I see we're moving again," he said. "I hope you don't get a bad teacher like you did last time. I'll never forget that day."

Rhoda stopped packing. She sat down on the bed. All her courage disappeared. The day she had come to Seymour to the new school, a fat, blond teacher had put her in the bad reading group. THE LOWER GROUP. Rhoda Katherine Manning, the best reader in the world, sitting in the back of the room. She had sat there all day until they found out she could read. "It could happen again," Jimmy said. "Go find her. Make sure she knows. Go find her right now. Get it settled."

Rhoda found her mother in the bathroom packing the iodine and alcohol and Mercurochrome and hydrogen peroxide. "If you put me in a school that puts me in a dumb reading class I will kill myself. You had better be sure they don't do that."

"Oh, darling." Her mother closed the bathroom cabinet and sat down on the edge of the tub. "I'm so sorry. So sorry about everything. I'm doing all I can. I'm doing everything I know how to do."

"Just be sure about the school."

"I will. I promise I will. I'll go with you the first day and take your test scores. I'll talk to the teacher before you go there. Nothing will happen. I promise you. You're going to live in a writer's house, honey. She wrote *A Little Lower Than the Angels*. We'll get all her books and read them. It will be an adventure. We must be brave, darling, we're in a war."

"I know. You already told me that. How big a room?"

"Plenty big. Your father said it had a blackboard. And Rhoda, don't worry about the school. I will never let that happen to you again."

"It better not."

"It won't. I promise you. Things can't be perfect right now, honey. We have to get this war over. Our men are dying over there. We have to save as many as we can." As soon as she said it

Ariane regretted the words. It was not good to say dead or death to Rhoda. The child backed up and moved into the corner.

"What does it mean to die? What happens to you?" Rhoda was near the sink. She could smell the alcohol and the Mercurochrome. It smelled like the hospital where she had had her tonsils out the year before. They had strapped her to a table and put a mask on her face and dripped sleeping gas on it. Her mother and father were in the hall. Nuns were all around her, holding her down. There was nothing she could do. Her life was in the hands of nuns and strangers. Death will be like that, Rhoda thought. They will hold you down and drip poison in your nose and there will be nothing you can do and your mother will be out in the hall. She refused her mother's hands. "I can't stand to die," she screamed. "I hate God. I hate it all so much. I won't do it. They can't make me do it. They won't get me. I won't hold still. I won't go in there. Go to goddamn hell, that's what I'm going to tell them. You won't make me die, you goddamn old God, to hell with you."

Her mother had her now. Her mother had her in her arms. "It isn't like that, honey. People you love are up there waiting for you. You can be with Jesus. He died to give us everlasting life. He frees us from death."

"That's a lie. None of it is true. Nothing you ever tell me is true." Her mother dropped her arms. She sighed a long deep sigh. Rhoda was too much. Too smart for her own good. Too wild, too crazy, too hard to manage or control. She was a long way from the sweet little redheaded girl Ariane had ordered from Jesus. Thinking of Jesus, Ariane remembered her duty. She fought back. "You just calm down, young lady. You just stop all that talk right this minute."

"Make sure about the school," Rhoda said and made her exit. She went into the hall and found Jimmy waiting at the top of the stairs. She took his arm and started down. "Let's go dig up

1944

WHEN I WAS EIGHT years old I had a piano made of nine martini glasses.

I could have had a real piano if I had been able to pay the terrible price, been able to put up with piano lessons, but the old German spy who taught piano in the small town of Seymour, Indiana, was jealous of my talent.

"Stop it! Stop it! Stop it!" she would scream in her guttural accent, hitting me on the knuckles with the stick she kept for that purpose. "Stopping this crazy business. Can't you ever listen? Can't you sit still a minute? Can't you settle down?"

God knows I tried to settle down. But the mere sight of the magnificent black upright, the feel of the piano stool against my plump bottom, the cold ivory touch of the keys would send me into paroxysms of musical bliss, and I would throw back my head and begin to pound out melodies in two octaves.

"Stop it," she would be screaming. "This is no music, this crazy banging business. Stop on my piano. Stop before I call your momma!"

I remember the day I quit for good. I got up from the piano stool, slammed the cover down on the keys, told her my father would have her arrested, and stalked out of the house without my hat and gloves. It was a cold November day, and I walked home with gray skies all around me, shivering and brokenhearted, certain the secret lives of musical instruments were closed to me forever.

So music might have disappeared from my life. With my formal training at this sorry end I might have had to content myself with tap and ballet and public speaking, but a muse looked down from heaven and took pity on me.

She arrived in the form of a glamorous war widow, was waiting for me at the bar when I walked into the officers' club with my parents that Saturday night.

There she sat, wearing black taffeta, smoking long white cigarettes, sipping her third very dry martini.

"Isn't that Doris Treadway at the bar?" my mother said. "I can't believe she's going out in public."

"What would you like her to do," my father said, "stay home and go crazy?"

"Well, after all," my mother whispered. "It's only been a month."

"Do you *know* that lady?" I asked, wondering if she was a movie star. She looked exactly like a movie star.

"She works for your daddy, honey," my mother said. "Her husband got killed in the Philippines."

"Go talk to her," my father said. "Go cheer her up. Go tell her who you are."

As soon as we ordered dinner I did just that. I walked across the room and took up the stool beside her at the bar. I breathed deeply of her cool perfume, listening to the rustling of her sleeves as she took a long sophisticated drag on her Camel.

"So you are Dudley's daughter," she said, smiling at me. I squirmed with delight beneath her approving gaze, enchanted by the dark timbre of her voice, the marvelous fuchsia of her lips and fingertips, the brooding glamor of her widowhood.

"I'm Rhoda," I said. "The baby-sitter quit so they brought me with them."

"Would you like a drink?" she asked. "Could I persuade you to join me?"

"Sure," I said. "Sure I'll join you."

She conferred with the bartender and waved to my parents who were watching us from across the room.

"Well, Rhoda," she said, "I've been hearing about you from your father."

"What did you hear?" I asked, getting worried.

"Well," she said, "the best thing I heard was that you locked yourself in a bathroom for six hours to keep from eating fruit cocktail."

"I hate fruit cocktail," I said. "It makes me sick. I wouldn't eat fruit cocktail for all the tea in China."

"I couldn't agree with you more," she said, picking up her stirrer and tapping it on her martini glass. "I think people who hate fruit cocktail should always stick together."

The stirrer made a lovely sound against the glass. The bartender returned, bringing a wineglass full of bright pink liquid.

"Taste it," she said, "go ahead. He made it just for you."

I picked up the glass in two fingers and brought it delicately to my lips as I had seen her do.

"It's wonderful," I said, "what's in it?"

"Something special," she said. "It's called a Shirley Temple. So little girls can pretend they're drinking." She laughed out loud and began to tap the glass stirrer against the line of empty glasses in front of her.

"Why doesn't he move the empty glasses?" I asked.

"Because I'm playing them," she said. "Listen." She tapped out a little tune. "Now, listen to this," she said, adding small amounts of water to the glasses. She tapped them again with a stirrer, calling out the notes in a very high, very clear soprano voice. "Do, Re, Mi, Fa, So . . . Bartender," she called, "bring us more glasses."

In a minute she had arranged a keyboard with nine perfect notes.

"Here," she said, moving the glasses in front of me, handing me the stirrer, "you play it."

"What should I play," I said. "I don't know any music."

"Of course you know music," she said. "Everyone knows music. Play anything you like. Play whatever comes into your head."

I began to hit the glasses with the stirrer, gingerly at first, then with more abandon. Soon I had something going that sounded marvelous.

"Is that by any chance the 'Air Corps Hymn' you're playing?" she said.

"Well . . . yes it is," I said. "How could you tell?"

She began to sing along with me, singing the words in her perfect voice as I beat upon the glasses. "Off we go," she sang, "into the wild blue yonder, climbing high into the sky, dum, dum, dum. Down we dive spouting a flame from under, off with one hell-of-a-roar, roar, roar . . ."

People crowded around our end of the bar, listening to us, applauding. We finished with the air corps and started right in on the army. "Over hill, over dale, as we hit the dusty trail, and those caissons go marching along, dum, dum, dum . . . In and out, hear them shout, counter march and right about, and those caissons go rolling along. For it's hie, hie, hee, in the field artilll-a-reeeee . . ."

A man near me began playing the bass on a brandy glass. Another man drummed on the bar with a pair of ashtrays.

Doris broke into "Begin the Beguine." "When they begin the beguine," she said, "it brings back a night of tropical splendor. It brings back the sound of music so te-en-de-rr. It brings back a memorreeeeee ever green."

A woman in a green dress began dancing, swaying to our

rhythm. My martini glasses shone in the light from the bar. As I struck them one by one the notes floated around me like bright translucent boats.

This was music! Not the stale order of the book and the metronome, not the stick and the German. Music was this wildness rising from the dark taffeta of Doris's dress. This praise, this brilliance.

The soft delicious light, the smell of perfume and gin, the perfection of our artistry almost overwhelmed me, but I played bravely on.

Every now and then I would look up and see Doris smiling at me while she sang. Doris and I were one. And that too was the secret of music.

I do not know how long we played. Perhaps we played until my dinner was served. Perhaps we played for hours. Perhaps we are playing still.

"Oh, just let them begin the beguine, let them plaaaaay . . . Let the fire that was once a flame remain an ember. Let it burn like the long lost desire I only remember. When they begin, when they begin, when they begi-i-i-i-in the be-gui-i-i-i-ine . . ."

Victory Over Japan

W HEN I WAS in the third grade I knew a boy who had to have fourteen shots in the stomach as the result of a squirrel bite. Every day at two o'clock they would come to get him. A hush would fall on the room. We would all look down at our desks while he left the room between Mr. Harmon and his mother. Mr. Harmon was the principal. That's how important Billy Monday's tragedy was.

Mr. Harmon came along in case Billy threw a fit. Every day we waited to see if he would throw a fit but he never did. He just put his books away and left the room with his head hanging down on his chest and Mr. Harmon and his mother guiding him along between them like a boat.

"Would you go with them like that?" I asked Letitia at recess. Letitia was my best friend. Usually we played girls chase the boys at recess or pushed each other on the swings or hung upside down on the monkey bars so Joe Franke and Bobby Saxacorn could see our underpants but Billy's shots had even taken the fun out of recess. Now we sat around on the fire escape and talked about rabies instead.

"Why don't they put him to sleep first?" Letitia said. "I'd make them put me to sleep."

"They can't," I said. "They can't put you to sleep unless they operate."

"My father could," she said. "He owns the hospital. He could put me to sleep." She was always saying things like that but I let her be my best friend anyway.

"They couldn't give them to me," I said. "I'd run away to Florida and be a beachcomber."

"Then you'd get rabies," Letitia said. "You'd be foaming at the mouth."

"I'd take a chance. You don't always get it." We moved closer together, caught up in the horror of it. I was thinking about the Livingstons' bulldog. I'd had some close calls with it lately.

"It was a pet," Letitia said. "His brother was keeping it for a pet."

It was noon recess. Billy Monday was sitting on a bench by the swings. Just sitting there. Not talking to anybody. Waiting for two o'clock, a small washed-out-looking boy that nobody paid any attention to until he got bit. He never talked to anybody. He could hardly even read. When Mrs. Jansma asked him to read his head would fall all the way over to the side of his neck. Then he would read a few sentences with her having to tell him half the words. No one would ever have picked him out to be the center of a rabies tragedy. He was more the type to fall in a well or get sucked down the drain at the swimming pool.

Fourteen days. Fourteen shots. It was spring when it happened and the schoolroom windows were open all day long and every afternoon after Billy left we had milk from little waxy cartons and Mrs. Jansma would read us chapters from a wonderful book about some children in England that had a bed that took them places at night. There we were, eating graham crackers and listening to stories while Billy was strapped to the table in Doctor Finley's office waiting for his shot.

"I can't stand to think about it," Letitia said. "It makes me so sick I could puke."

"I'm going over there and talk to him right now," I said. "I'm going to interview him for the paper." I had been the only one in the third grade to get anything in the Horace Mann paper. I got in with a story about how Mr. Harmon was shell-shocked in the First World War. I was on the lookout for another story that good.

I got up, smoothed down my skirt, walked over to the bench where Billy was sitting and held out a vial of cinnamon toothpicks. "You want one," I said. "Go ahead. She won't care." It was against the rules to bring cinnamon toothpicks to Horace Mann. They were afraid someone would swallow one.

"I don't think so," he said. "I don't need any."

"Go on," I said. "They're really good. They've been soaking all week."

"I don't want any," he said.

"You want me to push you on the swings?"

"I don't know," he said. "I don't think so."

"If it was my brother's squirrel, I'd kill it," I said. "I'd cut its head off."

"It got away," he said. "It's gone."

"What's it like when they give them to you?" I said. "Does it hurt very much?"

"I don't know," he said. "I don't look." His head was starting to slip down onto his chest. He was rolling up like a ball.

"I know how to hypnotize people," I said. "You want me to hypnotize you so you can't feel it?"

"I don't know," he said. He had pulled his legs up on the bench. Now his chin was so far down into his chest I could barely hear him talk. Part of me wanted to give him a shove and see if he would roll. I touched him on the shoulder instead. I could feel his little bones beneath his shirt. I could smell his washed-out rusty smell. His head went all the way down under his knees. Over his shoulder I saw Mrs. Jansma headed our way.

"Rhoda," she called out. "I need you to clean off the blackboards before we go back in. Will you be a sweet girl and do that for me?"

"I wasn't doing anything but talking to him," I said. She was beside us now and had gathered him into her wide sleeves. He was starting to cry, making little strangled noises like a goat.

"Well, my goodness, that was nice of you to try to cheer Billy up. Now go see about those blackboards for me, will you?"

I went on in and cleaned off the blackboards and beat the erasers together out the window, watching the chalk dust settle into the bricks. Down below I could see Mrs. Jansma still holding on to Billy. He was hanging on to her like a spider but it looked like he had quit crying.

That afternoon a lady from the PTA came to talk to us about the paper drive. "One more time," she was saying. "We've licked the Krauts. Now all we have left is the Japs. Who's going to help?" she shouted.

"I am," I shouted back. I was the first one on my feet.

"Who do you want for a partner?" she said.

"Billy Monday," I said, pointing at him. He looked up at me as though I had asked him to swim the English Channel, then his head slid down on the desk.

"All right," Mrs. Jansma said. "Rhoda Manning and Billy Monday. Team number one. To cover Washington and Sycamore from Calvin Boulevard to Conner Street. Who else?"

"Bobby and me," Joe Franke called out. He was wearing his coonskin cap, even though it was as hot as summer. How I loved him! "We want downtown," he shouted. "We want Dirkson Street to the river."

"Done," Mrs. Jansma said. JoEllen Scaggs was writing it all down on the blackboard. By the time Billy's mother and Mr. Harmon came to get him the paper drive was all arranged.

"See you tomorrow," I called out as Billy left the room. "Don't forget. Don't be late."

When I got home that afternoon I told my mother I had volunteered to let Billy be my partner. She was so proud of me she made me some cookies even though I was supposed to be on a diet. I took the cookies and a pillow and climbed up into my treehouse to read a book. I was getting to be more like my mother every day. My mother was a saint. She fed hoboes and played the organ at early communion even if she was sick and gave away her ration stamps to anyone that needed them. She had only had one pair of new shoes the whole war.

I was getting more like her every day. I was the only one in the third grade that would have picked Billy Monday to help with a paper drive. He probably couldn't even pick up a stack of papers. He probably couldn't even help pull the wagon.

I bet this is the happiest day of her life, I was thinking. I was lying in my treehouse watching her. She was sitting on the back steps putting liquid hose on her legs. She was waiting for the Episcopal minister to come by for a drink. He'd been coming by a lot since my daddy was overseas. That was just like my mother to be best friends with a minister.

"She picked out a boy that's been sick to help her on the paper drive," I heard her tell him later. "I think it helped a lot to get her to lose weight. It was smart of you to see that was the problem."

"There isn't anything I wouldn't do for you, Ariane," he said. "You say the word and I'll be here to do it."

I got a few more cookies and went back up into the tree-house to finish my book. I could read all kinds of books. I could read Book-of-the-Month Club books. The one I was reading now was called *Cakes and Ale*. It wasn't coming along too well.

I settled down with my back against the tree, turning the pages, looking for the good parts. Inside the house my mother was bragging on me. Above my head a golden sun beat down out of a blue sky. All around the silver maple leaves moved in the breeze. I went back to my book.

> She put her arms around my neck and pressed her lips against mine. I forgot my wrath. I only thought of her beauty and her enveloping kindness.
>
> "You must take me as I am, you know," she whispered.
>
> "All right," I said.

Saturday was not going to be a good day for a paper drive. The sky was gray and overcast. By the time we lined up on the Horace Mann playground with our wagons a light rain was falling.

"Our boys are fighting in rain and snow and whatever the heavens send," Mr. Harmon was saying. He was standing on the bleachers wearing an old baseball shirt and a cap. I had never seen him in anything but his gray suit. He looked more shell-shocked than ever in his cap.

"They're working over there. We're working over here. The Germans are defeated. Only the Japs left to go. There're canvas tarps from Gentilly's Hardware, so take one to cover your papers. All right now. One grade at a time. And remember, Mrs. Winchester's third grade is still ahead by seventy-eight pounds. So you're going to have to go some to beat that. Get to your stations now. Get ready, get set, go. Everybody working together . . ."

Billy and I started off. I was pulling the wagon, he was walking along beside me. I had meant to wait awhile before I started interviewing him but I started right in.

"Are you going to have to leave to go get it?" I said.

"Go get what?"

"You know. Your shot."

"I got it this morning. I already had it."

"Where do they put it in?"

"I don't know," he said. "I don't look."

"Well, you can feel it, can't you?" I said. "Like, do they stick it in your navel or what?"

"It's higher than that."

"How long does it take? To get it."

"I don't know," he said. "Till they get through."

"Well, at least you aren't going to get rabies. At least you won't be foaming at the mouth. I guess you're glad about that." I had stopped in front of a house and was looking up the path to the door. We had come to the end of Sycamore, where our territory began.

"Are you going to be the one to ask them?" he said.

"Sure," I said. "You want to come to the door with me?"

"I'll wait," he said. "I'll just wait."

We filled the wagon by the second block. We took that load back to the school and started out again. On the second trip we hit an attic with bundles of the *Kansas City Star* tied up with string. It took us all afternoon to haul that. Mrs. Jansma said she'd never seen anyone as lucky on a paper drive as Billy and I. Our whole class was having a good day. It looked like we might beat everybody, even the sixth grade.

"Let's go out one more time," Mrs. Jansma said. "One more trip before dark. Be sure and hit all the houses you missed."

Billy and I started back down Sycamore. It was growing dark. I untied my Brownie Scout sweater from around my waist and put it on and pulled the sleeves down over my wrists. "Let's try that brick house on the corner," I said. "They might be home by now." It was an old house set back on a high lawn. It looked like a house where old people lived. I had noticed old people were the ones who saved things. "Come on," I said. "You go to the door with me. I'm tired of doing it by myself."

He came along behind me and we walked up to the door and rang the bell. No one answered for a long time although I could hear footsteps and saw someone pass by a window. I rang the bell again.

A man came to the door. A thin man about my father's age.

"We're collecting papers for Horace Mann School," I said. "For the war effort."

"You got any papers we can have?" Billy said. It was the first time he had spoken to anyone but me all day. "For the war," he added.

"There're some things in the basement if you want to go down there and get them," the man said. He turned a light on in the hall and we followed him into a high-ceilinged foyer with a set of winding stairs going up to another floor. It smelled musty, like my grandmother's house in Clarksville. Billy was right beside me, sticking as close as a burr. We followed the man through the kitchen and down a flight of stairs to the basement.

"You can have whatever you find down here," he said. "There're papers and magazines in that corner. Take whatever you can carry."

There was a large stack of magazines. Magazines were the best thing you could find. They weighed three times as much as newspapers.

"Come on," I said to Billy. "Let's fill the wagon. This will put us over the top for sure." I picked up a bundle and started up the stairs. I went in and out several times carrying as many as I could at a time. On the third trip Billy met me at the foot of the stairs. "Rhoda," he said. "Come here. Come look at this."

He took me to an old table in a corner of the basement. It was a walnut table with grapes carved on the side and feet like lion's feet. He laid one of the magazines down on the table and opened it. It was a photograph of a naked little girl, a girl smaller than I was. He turned the page. Two naked boys were standing together with their legs twined. He kept turning the pages. It was all the same. Naked children on every page. I had never seen a naked boy. Much less a photograph of one. Billy looked up at me. He turned another page. Five naked little girls were grouped together around a fountain.

"Let's get out of here," I said. "Come on. I'm getting out of here." I headed for the stairs with him right behind me. We didn't even close the basement door. We didn't even stop to say thank you.

The magazines we had collected were in bundles. About a block from the house we stopped on a corner, breathless from running. "Let's see if there're any more," I said. We tore open a bundle. The first magazine had pictures of naked grown people on every page.

"What are we going to do?" he said.

"We're going to throw them away," I answered, and started throwing them into the nandina bushes by the Hancocks' vacant lot. We threw them into the nandina bushes and into the ditch that runs into Mills Creek. We threw the last ones into a culvert and then we took our wagon and got on out of there. At the corner of Sycamore and Wesley we went our separate ways.

"Well, at least you'll have something to think about tomorrow when you get your shot," I said.

"I guess so," he replied.

"Look here, Billy. I don't want you to tell anyone about those magazines. You understand?"

"I won't." His head was going down again.

"I mean it, Billy."

He raised his head and looked at me as if he had just remembered something he was thinking about. "I won't," he said. "Are you really going to write about me in the paper?"

"Of course I am. I said I was, didn't I? I'm going to do it tonight."

I walked on home. Past the corner where the Scout hikes met. Down the alley where I found the card shuffler and the Japanese fan. Past the yard where the violets grew. I was thinking about the boys with their legs twined. They looked like earthworms, all naked like that. They looked like something might fly down and eat them. It made me sick to think about it and I stopped by Mrs. Alford's and picked a few iris to take home to my mother.

Billy finished getting his shots. And I wrote the article and of course they put it on page one. BE ON THE LOOKOUT FOR MAD SQUIRREL, the headline read. By Rhoda Katherine Manning. Grade 3.

We didn't even know it was mean, the person it bit said. That person is in the third grade at our school. His name is William Monday. On April 23 he had his last shot. Mrs. Jansma's class had a cake and gave him a pencil set. Billy Monday is all right now and things are back to normal

I think it should be against the law to keep dangerous pets or dogs where they can get out and get people. If you see a dog or squirrel acting funny go in the house and stay there.

I never did get around to telling my mother about those magazines. I kept meaning to but there never seemed to be anywhere to start. One day in August I tried to tell her. I had been to the swimming pool and I thought I saw the man from the brick house drive by in a car. I was pretty sure it was him. As he turned the corner he looked at me. *He looked right at my face.* I stood very still, my heart pounding inside my chest, my hands as cold and wet as a frog, the smell of swimming pool chlorine rising from my skin. What if he found out where I lived? What if he followed me home and killed me to keep me from telling on him? I was terrified. At any moment the car might return. He might grab me and put me in the car and take me off and kill me. I threw my bathing suit and towel down on the sidewalk and started running. I ran down Linden Street and turned into the alley behind Calvin Boulevard, running as fast as I could. I ran down the alley and into my yard and up my steps and into my house looking for my mother to tell her about it.

She was in the living room, with Father Kenniman and Mr. and Mrs. DuVal. They lived across the street and had a gold star in their window. Warrene, our cook, was there. And Connie Barksdale, our cousin who was visiting from the Delta. Her husband had been killed on Corregidor and she would come up and stay with my mother whenever she couldn't take it anymore. They were all in the living room gathered around the radio.

"Momma," I said. "I saw this man that gave me some magazines . . ."

"Be quiet, Rhoda," she said. "We're listening to the news. Something's happened. We think maybe we've won the war." There were tears in her eyes. She gave me a little hug, then turned back to the radio. It was a wonderful radio with a magic eye that glowed in the dark. At night when we had blackouts Dudley and I would get into bed with my mother and we would listen to it together, the magic eye glowing in the dark like an emerald.

Now the radio was bringing important news to Seymour, Indiana. Strange, confused, hush-hush news that said we had a bomb bigger than any bomb ever made and we had already dropped it on Japan and half of Japan was sinking into the sea. Now the Japs had to surrender. Now they couldn't come to Indiana and stick bamboo up our fingernails. Now it would all be over and my father would come home.

The grown people kept on listening to the radio, getting up every now and then to get drinks or fix each other sandwiches. Dudley was sitting beside my mother in a white shirt acting like he was twenty years old. He always did that when company came. No one was paying any attention to me.

Finally I went upstairs and lay down on the bed to think things over. My father was coming home. I didn't know how to feel about that. He was always yelling at someone when he was home. He was always yelling at my mother to make me mind.

"What do you mean, you can't catch her," I could hear him yelling. "Hit her with a broom. Hit her with a table. Hit her with a chair. But, for God's sake, Ariane, don't let her talk to you that way."

Well, maybe it would take a while for him to get home. First they had to finish off Japan. First they had to sink the other half into the sea. I curled up in my soft old eiderdown comforter. I was feeling great. We had dropped the biggest bomb in the world on Japan and there were plenty more where that one came from.

I fell asleep in the hot sweaty silkiness of the comforter. I was dreaming I was at the wheel of an airplane carrying the bomb to Japan. Hit 'em, I was yelling. Hit 'em with a mountain. Hit 'em with a table. Hit 'em with a chair. Off we go into the wild blue yonder, climbing high into the sky. I dropped one on the brick house where the bad man lived, then took off for Japan. Down we dive, spouting a flame from under. Off with one hell of a roar. We live in flame. Buckle down in flame. For nothing can stop the Army Air Corps. Hit 'em with a table, I was yelling. Hit 'em with a broom. Hit 'em with a bomb. Hit 'em with a chair.

Perils of the Nile

RHODA GOT UP from her seat just as the house lights were going on, licked the rest of the Milky Way from her fingers, and looked around to see if any of the boys she liked were still there. Bebber Dyson was half-asleep in his usual Saturday afternoon seat, but he was too small and dark and poor to be of any real interest to Rhoda, even if he had shown her the eight-page book when they were collecting paper for the sixth-grade paper drive.

She rubbed her tongue across her teeth and gave a little shudder thinking of the picture of Dick Tracy sticking his thing into the dog.

She waved at Bebber and he started her way. Well, he was better than no one at all she thought. After all, he was the best basketball player in the whole school. He was such a good basketball player the seventh grade let him play in their games.

It was a mystery to Rhoda that Bebber was such a good basketball player. No one knew where he came from. He didn't have a proper home. He didn't have regular meals or ironed clothes or parents that went to the PTA. All he had was a father that drank and some rooms above a store.

It belied everything Rhoda knew about basketball. Rhoda's brother had special basketball shoes and special pregame basketball training meals and his own basketball goal above the garage door to practice on. Rhoda's father even had the concrete people come and pour concrete under the goal so they could mark off the free throw lines.

But no matter how many hours Rhoda's brother stood at the free throw line practicing shots he could only get the ball through the hoop half the time.

Bebber Dyson's shots always went through the hoop. He could shoot sideways and underhanded and over his head and one-handed and two-handed and every single time the basketball went through the hoop. Perhaps it was because he stayed at the pool hall all the time Rhoda thought. Perhaps it was because he was poor. Maybe you have to be poor to be a good basketball player.

"How you doing?" Bebber said, coming up beside her, smiling his wide smile. His teeth were very white and even like a movie star's. He was wearing his blue polo shirt. He wore the same shirt nearly every day, but he was always clean and he smelled nice. He didn't smell bad like most poor people.

"Where's your friend Cynthia?" he asked. "She didn't come with you today?"

"She had to go riding with her mother," Rhoda said. "They made her go. She almost died she wanted to see this picture so much. Gene Kelly's her favorite. She loves him."

Cynthia was Rhoda's best friend. Her mother was always taking her off horseback riding on the weekends. It made Rhoda's heart burn with envy and admiration to see them going off in their boots and jodhpurs. Rhoda wondered if Bebber was in love with Cynthia. Cynthia had funny taste in boys. Come to think of it Bebber did look something like Gene Kelly.

"I don't like Gene Kelly very much myself," she said. "I think he looks like a girl."

"He's a good dancer," Bebber said.

"He's okay," Rhoda said, "but he smiles too much."

"Where you going now?" Bebber asked. "You want to go to the drugstore and see if anyone's there?"

"Sure," Rhoda said. She wasn't sure if it was a good idea to be seen with Bebber, but she liked the idea of going in the drugstore with a boy. Maybe someone would think they had a date. Maybe Joe Franke would see her and think Bebber loved her.

"Hey," she said. "You want to see what I got today. Look at this." She held out her hand. Then she froze, looking down at her hand in horror. It was gone.

The ring was gone. Her brand-new antique pearl ring that had come in the mail from her grandmother that very morning was gone. She stared down at her finger, cold and disbelieving. It was not there. Her grandmother's own pearl ring that had come in the mail from Mississippi, her long-awaited birthday ring, her heirloom, her precious heirloom pearl solitaire ring that she was not under any circumstances supposed to wear was no longer on her finger.

"Bebber," she said. "Bebber, I've lost my ring." She dropped to the floor on her knees and began searching under the seats with her fingers, running her hands through the sticky jumble of popcorn sacks and candy wrappers and Coca-Cola cups.

"What does it look like?" he said, kneeling beside her, blocking the aisle where the last stragglers from the Saturday matinee were making their way out into the sunlit world of Seymour, Indiana.

"It's a pearl," she said. "It's a real pearl solitaire set in gold. It's valuable. It's worth about a hundred dollars and my grandmother sent it for my birthday and they're going to kill me for losing it."

"Well, calm down," Bebber said. "We'll find it. Just calm down and pick up everything that's down there and shake it out." He dropped to his knees beside her, smelling the sweet sweaty smell of her blouse. She was a strange girl, a funny girl who talked all the time and acted like she wasn't afraid of anything, not even the teacher. Once she faked a faint on the playground and was taken home in the principal's car without once opening her eyes or admitting she could hear.

He had walked her home one afternoon after school, and her mother made chocolate milk for them and stayed in the kitchen talking to them while they drank it. She praised him when he picked up his glass and rinsed it in the sink.

Bebber thought about Rhoda's mother a lot. She was very beautiful and had looked straight at him out of sad blue eyes while he talked about himself. Rhoda's whole family were strange people. They had come to Seymour from the south and talked a strange soft way. Whenever he passed their house he wished he could go in and talk to Rhoda's mother some more.

"If I don't find it they're going to kill me," she said. "They're going to murder me."

"Where do you think you lost it?" he asked, running his hand up and down the grooves between the folding seats.

"I don't know," she said, "but I had it when I came in the show because I showed it to Letitia. Letitia said it was the prettiest thing she'd ever seen in her life."

"Maybe it got in your popcorn sack," Bebber said. "Maybe you ate it."

"I did not eat it," Rhoda said. Rhoda was very conscious of her figure. She hated to be reminded that she ever ate anything. "And that isn't funny, Bebber. And if I don't find that ring they're going to kill me."

"I'm sorry," he said. "I'll get the usher. We can use his flashlight. You be picking up the rest of the paper." As Bebber started to rise up from the floor he felt the ring, cold and flat beneath his fingers on the worn runner of the aisle carpet. His fingers closed around it and he stood up and stuck his hands into his pockets.

"I'll be back," he said. "You keep on looking."

He returned with the usher, and the three of them searched the floor and seats for a long time, retracing Rhoda's steps from the time she came into the theater, shaking out every piece of paper and box and cup and poking down into dozens of seats and crannies.

"Maybe you didn't really have it on," Bebber said. "Maybe you just thought you wore it."

"I had it," Rhoda said. "I showed it to Letitia."

"There's no place else to look," the usher said. "And the manager wants to close up now. We're having a special show tonight for the war effort. Everyone that brings a piece of steel gets in free. It's *Journey for Margaret* with Margaret O'Brien."

"But what about my ring?" Rhoda said. "How'll I ever find it?"

"We'll make an announcement tonight," the usher said. "How about that. We'll announce that anyone that finds it should turn it in to the box office."

"All right," Rhoda said. "I guess that's all I can do."

"Come on," Bebber said. "Let's go over to the drugstore and see if anyone's there."

"I don't feel like it now," Rhoda said. "I better go on home."

"You want me to go home with you?" Bebber asked. "You want me to help you tell your mother?"

"No," she said. "I probably won't tell her until I have to. She's going to murder me when she finds out."

When Rhoda got home she went up to her room, closed the door, and threw herself down on the eiderdown comforter. Why does everything have to happen to me she thought. *Every time something happens it happens to me.* She rubbed her face deep down into the silk comforter, feeling the cool fabric against her cheeks, smelling the queer dead odor of the down feathers. She pulled out a few pieces where the little white tips were working their way out of the silk.

The eiderdown comforter was Rhoda's favorite thing in the house. It was dark red on one side and pink on the other. Rhoda liked to roll up in it on hot afternoons and pretend she was Cleopatra waiting for Mark Antony to come kiss her.

Sometimes Cynthia would play the game with her, but Cynthia made a desultory Roman general and her kisses were brief and cold and absentminded. It was better to play Cleopatra alone.

When she was alone Rhoda pretended the bed was a barge floating down the Nile and she was the queen reclining on a silken couch being fed by slaves, her hair combed and perfumed, her sleek half-naked body being pampered and touched and adored a thousand ways. She lay still, quiet and gracious, watching the shore glide by as she surveyed her kingdom.

Rhoda's bed was a cherry four-poster, and she could lie on her stomach on top of the comforter and rock the mattress back and forth by the pressure of her feet against the footboard. She would rock like that until she fell asleep, feeling strange and lost in time, a dark queen full of languorous passions.

Today, however, the quilt was of no comfort to her. She was not due to have another valuable ring until her mother died and left her a diamond and that might be a long time as women in her family lived to ripe old ages.

It occurred to her that she might pray for the ring. Usually Rhoda wasn't much on praying. When she said her prayers at night all she thought about was Jesus coming to get her in a chariot filled with angels. She didn't want Jesus to come get her. She didn't want to be lying in a box like Jerry Hollister, who was run over in his driveway by his own brother home on leave from the air corps.

The whole fifth grade had gone to see Jerry lying in his casket. His face was white as chalk and he was wearing a suit, lying on his dining room table in a casket with his eyes permanently closed.

Rhoda didn't want anything to do with that. She didn't want anything to do with Jesus or religion or little boys lying on their dining room tables with their eyes closed.

When they made Rhoda go to church on Sundays she pretended she was someplace else. She didn't want anything to do with God and Jesus and dead people and people nailed up on crosses or eaten by lions or tortured by Romans.

This matter of the ring, however, was an emergency. At any moment Rhoda's mother might call up the stairs and ask her to bring the ring to show to someone.

I could pretend it was stolen she thought. I could say Del Rio stole it. Del Rio was the black woman who lived with them. Del Rio had come on a bus from Mississippi when Rhoda's baby brother was born. Rhoda hated Del Rio. Del Rio was always lecturing Rhoda about not drinking out of the water bottle and threatening to sic a big dog on her if she didn't stop teasing the baby. It would serve Del Rio right to go to jail for stealing.

Of course it would never work. Del Rio would kill her, would come for her with a knife. Besides, the man at the picture show was going to announce that she had lost it. Everyone in town would be calling up to see if they had found it.

I might as well pray, Rhoda said, getting up off the bed and looking around the room for a nice place to do some praying. The closet, Rhoda thought. That's the best place. She went into the closet and pulled the door shut behind her. Her dresses and blouses hung primly on their pink silk hangers. Her shoe bags hung on the door beside her bowed head.

"Well, Jesus," Rhoda said, beginning her prayer. "You know I have to get that ring back. So if you will get it back to me I promise I'll start believing in you." She waited a minute to let that sink in, then continued.

"If you'll help me find it I'll be nice to everyone from now on. I won't yell at anyone and I won't stick my finger in my crack when I take a bath. I'll quit lying so much. I'll quit hating Dudley and I'll quit giving Cokes to the baby. If you'll help me find it I'll do everything you want from now on. I'll even go overseas and be a missionary if that's what you want."

Rhoda liked that idea. She could see herself standing on a distant seashore handing out bright fabrics to the childlike natives. Rhoda was beginning to feel quite holy. She was beginning to like talking to Jesus.

"Jesus," she continued, squirming around on the floor to get in a more prayerful position, picturing Jesus on a hill surrounded by his sheep. "Jesus," she said, "to tell the truth I have always believed in you. And I'll be going to Sunday school all the time now if I get my ring back."

It was very quiet in the closet. Rhoda could feel Jesus thinking. She felt him lay his hand upon her head. Jesus said he would think it over.

Rhoda got up from her knees in a reverent manner and left the closet with her hands still folded. She was feeling better. The oppression that had weighed her down all afternoon was lifting. It was up to Jesus now. She decided to go downstairs and shoot some baskets with Dudley until time for supper.

Bebber Dyson sat down on the unmade bed, took the ring from his pocket, and examined it in the light coming in on a slant through the low windows. His face was very still, and the high Indian cheekbones of his grandfather cast long shadows along the ridge of his nose.

Bebber studied his treasure. It was an old-fashioned solitaire, a small pearl set in five slender prongs of gold.

He touched the top of the pearl with his finger, then put it on and held his hand away from him, imagining Rhoda's mother's slender white hands.

The ring was like her, elegant and still and foreign. Someday, he thought, he would drive a big car down a street to a house where a woman like that waited. Everything around her would be quiet and clean and she would hand him something to drink in a glass.

He wrapped the ring in a piece of tissue paper and returned it to his pocket.

Then he got up and made the bed, folding the corners neatly and smoothing out all the wrinkles.

Next he walked around the small apartment, emptying the ashtrays and wiping off the flat surfaces with a towel. He swept the floor, picked up the sweepings in a dustpan, and deposited them in a paper sack.

He removed his clothes and laid them on the bed to inspect them for spots. He walked over to the sink and carefully washed out the blue shirt, scrubbing it good with plenty of soap, rinsing it and hanging it on a hanger by the window.

Then he began to wash himself, very carefully and thoroughly, beginning with his hair, working down to his arms and chest and legs and feet. He washed himself as if he were some foreign object, oblivious to the beauty and symmetry of his body, to the smooth shine of his olive skin, to the order and intelligence of his parts.

He dried himself, then wiped up the mess the water had made on the floor. He brushed and parted his hair and dressed carefully in his good clothes, gray pants, white shirt, and a sleeveless dark green sweater.

He walked down the stairs and out onto the street. The early autumn dusk was magical, long rays of red slanting light catching the bottom branches of the elm trees.

He walked down Pershing Avenue to where it turns onto Calvin Boulevard, imagining what Rhoda's mother would be doing this time of day, holding her baby, laughing into his tiny face, walking around her kitchen fixing dinner, her high-heeled shoes clicking on the linoleum.

Maybe she would ask him to stay for chocolate milk. Maybe she would ask him to stay for dinner.

The light was changing now, deepening. Bebber began to hum a little tune to himself as he walked along, feeling clean and lucky, fondling the little package in his pocket, picturing the way her hair moved around her shoulders when she talked.

I will be riding up on a white horse he thought. I will be wearing a uniform and she will be standing on the porch holding her baby. It is too cold for her to be outside like that. I will give her my coat. I will put her on the horse and take her wherever she needs to go. I will walk slowly because it is dangerous to ride that way carrying a baby.

Bebber walked on down the street, the rays of the setting sun making him a path all the way to her house, a little road to travel, a wide band of luminous and precarious order.

Blue Satin

Rhoda's most easily manipulated grandmother had come to stay with Rhoda and her brothers while Rhoda's parents went off to a football game in Lexington, Kentucky. Her grandmother's name was Nell and she was very nervous about this plan. She loved her grandson Dudley, who was a perfect little man, and she was fairly certain she could care for the baby, Ingersol, even though there was only one servant in the house and that was a cleaning woman who left as soon as she could every day and didn't seem to enjoy her work. This was southern Illinois and it was a long way from the Mississippi Delta. Nell much prefered visiting her daughters in New Orleans but Ariane had begged and begged and finally she had given in and agreed to stay four days alone with the children.

The problem was Rhoda. Rhoda was a bad little girl to begin with and on top of that Ariane had spoiled her rotten. Anything Rhoda thought up to do she did. She was the most difficult child Nell had ever seen. "I don't know where that child came from," she had told her daughter a hundred times. "No one in our family was ever rude." But of course she knew where Rhoda came from. From her father and her maternal grandmother, both of whom ran roughshod over life. "Hit her with a tree if she misbehaves," Dudley said, and laughed out loud. "Hit her with a broom. Hit her with a chair."

"He always says that," Ariane added. "But he never does a thing to her. All he does is give her money."

Rhoda stood in the door to the dining room listening to them discuss her. She always listened to the adults talk. She listened to every word they said if she didn't have anything better to do. She had a lot to do. She had projects going all around the house and in the garden shed and underneath the porch. She had dead wasp collections and books she was writing and catalogs she was ordering out of for the girls on Paradise Island and holes she was digging to China and doll hospitals and crossword puzzles and codes she was making up and books she was reading. She was busy morning, noon, and night but sometimes she took time to listen to her parents talk about her. They said the same things over and over again like a lullaby. "She's just like you, Dudley," her mother would always say for the coup de grace. Then her mother would lower her eyes flirtatiously as if to say, Who but me could have given you your heart's desire, a child as wild and selfish as you are.

"Hit her if she sasses you," he'd answer. "Hit her with a broom. Hit her with a chair." Then he would take Rhoda off with him to the bank or let her drive the truck or buy her a new bicycle whether they could afford it or not. "Your mother doesn't need to be getting upset," he'd tell Rhoda. "Try to be nice to her, Sister. Try to help her a little bit with the baby."

Rhoda would try to help out with the baby but the baby bored her. She wasn't interested in babies. She was interested in pilots and queens and kings and card games and Chinese checkers and Monopoly and walking around town seeing what was going on.

The afternoon before her parents left for the football game, Dudley took Rhoda off into the yard and gave her twenty-five dollars and a lecture. "You be helpful to your grandmother, sugar," he told her. "Help her with Ingersol. I'm counting on you to lend a hand with him, Rhoda. I'm counting on you to help take care of things around here."

"What's this money for?"

"In case you need anything. In case she needs you to get something for her. Dudley will be in charge. Don't let me hear any bad reports on you when I get back. I'm counting on you to act like a big girl."

"I will. You can count on me." Rhoda smiled and let her father hug her close to him. He was wearing khaki pants and a white shirt and a fine tweed jacket he had bought in Louisville. He was the strongest man in the world and the funniest. She was going to make him proud of her. He didn't need to worry about a thing. She was going to come up to his expectations.

She put the money in the pocket of her plaid skirt and walked up the stairs to her room. Ingersol was playing on the bottom of the stairs. She patted him on the head. She overcame her disgust at his diapers. After all, he was the cutest baby on the block and the fattest.

She hummed to herself as she went up the stairs to her room. Blue heaven and you and I. And stars climbing a desert sky. A desert breeze whispering a lullaby. Only stars above you to see I love you. Rhoda rode across the desert on an Arabian stallion. Only the stars could guide her. She was wearing long robes and a burnoose. Her horse loved her so much she barely had to touch the reins. She was riding to meet her boyfriend in the night. It was Joe Franke in his coonskin cap. No, it was Hopalong Cassidy, who had been her father's roommate at Auburn University. Hoppy was waiting for her. There was a murder to solve in the desert.

Rhoda went into her room and put on her jodhpurs and a white shirt and her boots. She threw the clothes she had been wearing on the floor. She lay down upon the bed and began to read a book about some girls in England going camping. Rhoda didn't actually read books. She inhabited them. She moved into the page and across the barriers of space and time. This afternoon she was somewhere in Scotland camped near a forest.

On Friday afternoon her parents left. They packed their leather suitcases into the trunk of the new Plymouth coupe and drove off like newlyweds. Rhoda and Dudley and Ingersol and their grandmother stood on the front steps and waved until the car was out of sight. "I only hope they have a good time," Nell said. "Goodness knows, Ariane needs a rest. You all just work her to death. Help me with this baby, Sonny. Let's take him inside and get him settled." Dudley took his little brother by the hand and led him into the house. Nell sighed deeply and tugged at the waist of her dress to make it cover her petticoat. No matter how many times Ariane worked on her hems, her petticoat was always showing.

Rhoda got on her bicycle and rode over to Cynthia's house to see what was going on. Cynthia and her mother and her sisters had just returned from a shopping trip to Saint Louis. The living room was filled with fabrics and patterns and new shoes and socks and underwear. It started to make Rhoda jealous. Ariane never took her on shopping trips to Saint Louis. And she didn't have any beautiful older sisters to run through the house wearing curlers in their hair.

"I'm going shopping tomorrow," Rhoda announced. "My mother went to a ballgame so I have to go by myself. Maybe Cynthia can come along and help me." She stood there by the table full of new fabrics and looked so forlorn that Mrs. Allen forgot her natural tendency to make Cynthia spend Saturday mornings practicing the piano and dusting the living room and said, "Of course she can go. We would have taken you with us to Saint Louis if I'd thought about it. Here, look at this material.

Maybe I will make you a vest to match the one I make for Cynthia." It was a printed cotton fabric that was quilted. Rhoda immediately decided it was the prettiest thing she'd ever seen in her life.

"I hate it," Cynthia said. "It's going to make me look fat as a pig."

"No, it is not," Cynthia's older sister, Martha Jane, who was Miss Perfect Every Minute of Her Life, put in. "Don't you dare talk to mother like that, after all the trouble she goes to for you."

"It's all right," Mrs. Allen said. "If Cynthia doesn't want it, I'll make it for Rhoda." She put her arm around Rhoda and gave her a hug.

"Send Rhoda in here," Judge Allen called out from the den. "She's the only twelve-year-old in town who likes to talk about books."

Rhoda went into the den and found the judge in his easy chair reading *Twilight of the Gods*. "I'll lend you this as soon as I finish it," he said. "Tell me what's going on. Where are all the boys?"

"Cynthia is still going steady with David," Rhoda began. "But Mark is in love with her too and he keeps trying to get her to break up with David and go with him. Last week I thought she was going to start going steady with Mark, but then, at the last minute, David came over to my house and talked to her. I wish she'd go out with Harlon Childs. He's the best football player in the state. I'd go out with him if I were her."

"Who are you in love with?" The judge leaned up from the chair and smiled his darling, wicked smile at her.

"Oh, you know, the same one." Rhoda's face darkened into its tragic mode. "This boy down in the Delta who can't go out with me because he has cystic fibrosis. It's a terrible affliction. We don't know if he'll be able to walk pretty soon. I may be kin to him anyway. His name's Bobby Mann. I guess I better write to him this afternoon. He's going to have to go and live in Washington next year. It's a hopeless love."

"You better go find old Harlon Childs yourself. You can't spend your young life loving someone in Washington, D.C."

"I can't help it. I'm going to be a doctor when I grow up, anyway. I won't have time to get married and have children."

Cynthia came into the den and grabbed Rhoda's arm. "Come on, let's get out of here before Martha Jane thinks of something for me to do."

Rhoda and Cynthia went out onto the porch and lay upside down in the swing to get rid of their double chins. "What are you going to get tomorrow?" Cynthia asked.

"I don't know. We're just going shopping. We'll see what we can find." It was a fine fall afternoon. The leaves were turning on the trees. From upside down the ceiling of the porch and the trees in the front yard looked wonderful and mysterious. "I think I'll go to Arabia pretty soon," Rhoda began. "I want to go over there and see about those Arabian horses. It looks like it would be hard to ride on sand but it's not. It's easy as pie. You just sail across the sands. Those horses aren't mean like the ones our mothers ride. They are just like people and can read your mind and know the way home from anywhere."

"What are you doing?" Martha Jane had come out the door and found them. "Get up from there right this minute. Anyone going down the street can see your underpants."

"They cannot," Cynthia answered. "You're just saying that because you have a double chin and you want us to have one too."

"I have to go home anyway." Rhoda swung her legs down across the swing chains and stood up and straightened up her skirt. "I have to go help my grandmother take care of Ingersol." She started down the stairs to her bicycle. She admired Martha

Jane for being so beautiful and perfect. She wanted Martha Jane to like her and think of her as a darling little girl who always did what she was told. "See you tomorrow," she called over her shoulder to Cynthia, who was still stoutly upside down on the swing. "I'll come get you as soon as the stores open."

"They open at ten," Martha Jane said.

At nine-thirty the next morning Rhoda arrived at Cynthia's to pick her up to go shopping. She had had a hard time convincing her grandmother that she was allowed to go downtown shopping with a friend but Dudley had taken up for her and convinced Nell to let her go. "What are you shopping for?" she had asked Rhoda. "Your mother didn't say anything to me about you going shopping."

"I'm going to buy a dress to wear to parties," Rhoda answered. "I want a dress for a change that isn't navy blue or plaid."

Cynthia was waiting when Rhoda arrived. She had on her white peasant blouse and a long black skirt and a wide black belt with silver loops. She had slept all night in brown Kiddie Kurlers and her hair was curled all over her head. Cynthia and Rhoda were living for the day when they could buy permanent waves at the drug store and "give them" to each other but that day was several years away. Mrs. Allen said Cynthia couldn't have one until she was in high school and Rhoda hadn't even asked her mother yet. There had been a terrible episode with a permanent wave machine in a beauty parlor when Rhoda was only six and since then it was a subject that was never broached at the Mannings' house.

"Where are you going to shop?" Cynthia asked. They had begun to walk in the direction of the downtown square. They had passed the bakery and the turn-off to the junior high and were almost to the ice-cream parlor when Rhoda made up her mind. "I think I'll start at the Fashion M'Lady," she said. "I went there once with Momma and Doris Bordelon and they had the most beautiful clothes I've ever seen. Doris got this dress with a little bustle in the back. She's got a baby now and she lets me see him nurse at her breast. It's disgusting. His name is Little Bruce and she lets him suck as long as he wants. She just sits there and lets him do it."

"It makes me sick to think of it," Cynthia agreed. They had passed the ice cream parlor with its faint curdled smell and were proceeding past the pool hall where Bebber Dyson was chalking his cue. He waved at them. He was the best basketball player in the sixth grade. He was so good the big boys let him play with them, but he didn't have a girlfriend because he was just friends with everyone. He was friends with Rhoda and had shown her a book with cartoons of people having sexual intercourse on a table in it. She tried not to think about it but she couldn't forget those pictures. Now, looking into the poolroom, she decided the place where most of that went on was probably in the poolroom at night.

She took Cynthia's arm. They were almost to the courthouse now, where the judge might be hanging out the windows of his chambers keeping tabs on them. Sure enough, he was standing in his window smoking his pipe and saw them coming and stuck his head out the window to wave. "Where are you going?" he called out. "Where are all the boys?"

"We're going shopping," Rhoda called back to him. "I'm going to get a dress to dress up in."

At the drugstore they stopped and had lemon Cokes and shared a package of Nabs. Then they proceeded on down the street to the Fashion M'Lady. It was a small shop that was three times as long as it was wide. The front was a large plate-glass window and a door. The mannequin in the window on this day was wearing a tweed suit with suede high heels and a white suit shirt with a bow. Spread at her feet were rhinestone earrings and necklaces and bracelets and silver and brass hair combs. It was very elegant and Rhoda was sure she had come to the right store.

A saleslady met them at the door. She knew Cynthia but she did not remember meeting Rhoda. "What can I do for you girls?" she asked.

"I have twenty-five dollars. My parents are out of town. I need to buy a dress up dress in case I have to go somewhere. Do you have anything that's got a peplum on it or a bustle?" Rhoda took the money out of her pocket and held it out in her hands. She was wearing a skirt exactly like the one Cynthia had on and a white camp shirt with short sleeves. She had on a wide red belt that her mother had let her buy at the dime store. She narrowed her eyes and surveyed the saleslady. You never could tell with grown people. Sometimes they could be trusted to take you seriously and sometimes they acted like everything Rhoda did was a joke. Rhoda was not in the mood to joke this morning. She was in the mood to shop.

"Well, I'll let you look," the lady said. "What size do you think you wear?"

"I don't know. Let me see what you've got first." Rhoda drew herself up to her full five foot two inches and pulled Cynthia up beside her. "Show us what to look at. We know the kind of thing we want."

It only took three minutes of going through the racks of clothes to find the dress that Rhoda knew she wanted. It was hanging in the very back of a sales rack. It had been fifteen dollars and was now reduced to nine dollars and fifty cents. It was pale blue satin. A pale blue satin sheath with a drape around the waist. It was strapless and on the back was a large blue satin flower with white silk stamens tipped in red. It was the most beautiful dress Rhoda had ever seen. It was a dress for Betty Grable to entertain the troops. It was a dress to wear to sing in a nightclub. Blue heaven and you and I. Underneath the desert robes and the burnoose Rhoda would be wearing this blue satin sheath dress. Her strong stout body slipped into it like a knife into its sheath. When she arrived at the desert king's tent, when she dropped the robe from her shoulders, she would be standing there wearing this. The king would fall in love. He would stand stock-still and almost faint. You are too beautiful for one man alone, he would say. No time for that now, Rhoda would reply. I have to get into my jodhpurs. This message has to reach the troops. Come on, let's go. I haven't got all day.

"I'll try this on," she said.

"You're going to put it on?" Cynthia asked. She was sitting on a little stool watching Rhoda go through the clothes. She was a good lieutenant. She obeyed orders. She never questioned a thing that Rhoda did.

"Then come in here," the saleslady said. There was no one else in the store. If the little girl wanted to try on the cocktail dress, what difference did it make to her. After all, the girl had twenty-five dollars. She might really mean to buy something with it.

Rhoda put the satin dress on her little short body and looked and looked into the glass. Yes, you are too beautiful for one man alone, the king repeated. But you are just right to be my queen. You can ride like a man and we will have a lot of parties and you will of course wear the blue dress with the flower on the back. First we'll have to get married.

"I don't get married," Rhoda said out loud. "I think I'll take it," she told the saleslady. "Wrap it up."

They walked back by the drugstore and had another Coke. This time they got a cherry Coke and instead of eating Nabs they played the jukebox. They played "Open the Door, Richard" and then they played "Embraceable You." They had been in a chorus line at the Lion's Club Follies the year before and had done a routine to "Embraceable You." They drank their cherry Cokes and hummed along to the music. Then they walked on back to Rhoda's house, carrying the dress box between them by its string. It was one of the prettiest fall days there had ever been in Harrisburg, Illinois. It was a perfect day for two perfect girls. Embrace me, my sweet embraceable you. Embrace me, you irreplaceable you. Don't be a naughty baby, come to Poppa, come to Poppa, do. My sweet embraceable you.

They went singing into the house and found Nell sitting exhausted in a green chair. Ingersol had just fallen asleep after a long hard morning on his grandmother's part.

"I bought a dress," Rhoda said. "You want to see it?"

Ten minutes later Rhoda came down the stairs from her room wearing the dress. Cynthia was right behind her holding a pearl necklace they had found in Ariane's jewelry box.

"What do you think?" Rhoda asked and began to turn and turn in front of her grandmother. "Isn't it gorgeous? Aren't you crazy about it?"

"What are you thinking of?" Her grandmother stood up and began to wave her hands in the air. "Take that off immediately. Where did that come from? Rhoda, Rhoda, Rhoda, you are the craziest child I've ever seen in my life."

"You don't like it?" Rhoda was stunned. There was no end

to the insanity of grown people, especially her mother's people from the Delta.

"Oh, my," Cynthia said, and laid the pearls down carefully on a chair. "Maybe I'd better go home."

At four that afternoon Nell drove Rhoda back to the Fashion M'Lady and followed her into the store and they gave back the dress and retrieved the nine dollars and fifty cents. "I tried to tell her it wasn't suitable," the saleslady lamely defended herself.

"The very idea," Nell said. "The very idea that you would let her try it on, much less pay for it and bring it home."

"She wanted it. She had the money. Her friend was with her. The judge's youngest daughter, well, I heard she wasn't all they wanted her to be."

"Just refund the money, please," Nell insisted. "And in the future try to use some judgment."

They drove back home in silence. Nell's short legs barely reached the pedals of the old Chevrolet Dudley had left for her to drive. Her stockings, which had been rolled up above her knees and held in place with garters, were now halfway down her legs. Her petticoat was down at least an inch and a half beneath her hem. Her hands gripped the wheel. She drove down Main Street to the house and up into the side yard and parked the car.

"It is Saturday afternoon," she said, when she turned off the key. "Don't let anything else happen, Rhoda. Go in the house and find yourself something to do until supper."

Rhoda got out of the car without a word and walked up to the back door. A praying mantis was hanging on the screen. She picked him up and stuck him to her skirt and carried him inside to add to her collection. She stopped in the kitchen and got a jelly glass and transferred him to that and then covered the jelly glass with a piece of wax paper and took a rubber band out of a drawer and put it around the top. Then she took an ice pick and made a little circle of holes to let the air in.

Dudley was in the living room with Ingersol. "Because of you I had to take care of the baby," he said. "Because of you I didn't get to go to Mike Reilly's and play basketball."

"Tough luck," Rhoda called out and walked on past him and up the stairs. She considered falling down the stairs and pretending to break her leg but she decided it wasn't worth it. She had better things to do. She had to finish *Below the Salt* by Thomas Costain and she needed to work on the telephone she was making out of a shoebox.

She went into her room and locked the door. She got the cardboard telephone out from underneath her bed and also a loaf of bread and a jar of mayonnaise. She spread some mayonnaise on a piece of bread and added another piece for a top. She sat the praying mantis on a bookshelf and tapped the jar to make sure it was still alive. Then she lay down on top of her dark red silk eiderdown comforter and opened the book that was on her pillow. She took a big bite of her mayonnaise sandwich. She began to read.

A sudden draft almost extinguished the candle held by the countess. Tostig moved a screen which stood against the wall and propped it up around her, so she would have no further trouble.

"What is Richard doing in Wales?"

"He is there with his lady wife."

"His wife!" exclaimed the countess, her voice rising with surprise. "Richard is married? Why did I not know of this? And who is the bride?"

"He is married" — Tostig seemed reluctant to give voice to such dangerous information — "he is married to the Princess Eleanor of Brittany."

"This is utter nonsense! You can't know what you're saying, Tostig. The princess is a state prisoner. She is held in one of the king's castles. I believe it is Corfe, although I have never been able to get any information from my husband. He may not know himself."

"She escaped from Corfe Castle several weeks ago, my lady."

The countess stamped a foot in disbelief and exasperation. "You can't mean what you are saying! This is unbelievable. You stand there and tell me with a straight face these extraordinary things. . . ."

Rhoda grabbed the mayonnaise and added a layer to the crust of the bread. An almond-shaped piece of mayonnaise fell on the page. Rhoda wiped it off with her finger and went on reading. England was better than Arabia. In England a countess could wear all the blue satin she needed, she could stamp her feet while properly attired, she could get to be a queen while she was still young enough to know how to act, she could be heard.

Rhoda finished off the sandwich and dove back in.

Downstairs, Nell had finally managed to get Ariane and Dudley on the phone. "I can't handle her," she was saying. "She went downtown this afternoon and bought a cocktail dress in a store. I want you to tell her to stop running off all over town. And she never eats anything. She hasn't eaten a bite I've fixed her since you left."

"Let her starve," Dudley said. "Lock her in her room with bread and water."

"We'll come on home tomorrow." Ariane took the phone away from him and spoke sweetly into the receiver. "We'll be there as soon as we can."

"The princess must have lost her head completely!" exclaimed the countess. "Although she was a state prisoner, she remained high on the list of succession. By running away and marrying a commoner, she has forfeited all chance of high preferment."

"She has lost her liking for heights, my lady. The cell in which she was confined was very high. It was at the top of a forty-foot shaft in the castle wall. She was kept there for seven years! She prefers now to live on a less exalted level, even though it means being the wife of a poor knight. My lady, they are very much in love with each other."

Rhoda had left the bed now and was lying on the floor underneath it. It was a high four-poster bed and the space beneath it was just the right size for a twelve-year-old girl, her eiderdown comforter, her provisions, and her book. She sang the book to herself as she read it, here in her life, in the vast confines of the only world there is.

The Expansion of the Universe

It WAS SATURDAY AFTERNOON in Harrisburg, Illinois. Rhoda was lying on the bed with catalogs all around her, pretending to be ordering things. It was fall outside the window, Rhoda's favorite time of year. "The fall is so poignant," she was fond of saying. This fall was more poignant than ever because Rhoda had started menstruating on the thirteenth of September. Thirteen, her lucky number. Rhoda had been dying to start menstruating. Everyone she knew had started. Shirley Hancock and Dixie Lee Carouthers and Naomi and everyone who was anyone in the ninth grade had started. It was beginning to look like Rhoda would be the last person in Southern Illinois to menstruate. Now, finally, right in the middle of a Friday night double feature at the picture show, she had started. She had stuffed some toilet paper into her pants and hurried back down the aisle and pulled Letitia and Naomi back to the restroom with her. They huddled together, very excited. Rhoda's arms were on her friends' shoulders. "I started," she said. "It's on my pants. Oh, God, I thought I never would."

"You've got to have a belt," Letitia said. "I'm going home and get you a belt. You stay right here."

"She doesn't need a belt," Naomi said. "All she needs is to pin one to her pants. Where's a quarter?" Someone produced a quarter and they stuck it in the machine and the Kotex came sliding out and Rhoda pinned it inside her pants and they went back into the theater to tell everyone else. *A Date with Judy*, starring Elizabeth Taylor, was playing. Rhoda snuggled down in her accustomed seat, six rows from the front on the left-hand aisle. It was too good to be true. It was wonderful.

It was almost a week later when her mother discovered what had happened. Rhoda tossed the information over her shoulder on her way out the door. "I fell off the roof last week," she said. "Did I tell you that?"

"You did what? What are you talking about?"

"I started menstruating. I got my period. You know, fell off the roof."

"Oh, my God," Ariane said. "What are you talking about, Rhoda? Where were you? What did you do about it? WHY DIDN'T YOU TELL ME?"

"I knew what to do. I was at the picture show. Naomi gave me some Kotex."

"Rhoda. Don't leave. Wait a minute, you have to talk to me about this. Where are you going?" Rhoda's mother dropped the scarf she was knitting and stood beside the chair.

"I'm going to cheerleader practice. I'm late."

"Rhoda, you have to have a belt. You have to use the right things. I want to take you to Doctor Usry. You can't just start menstruating."

"We're going to get some Tampax. Donna Marie and Letitia and I. We're going to learn to wear it." Then she was gone, as Rhoda was always going, leaving her mother standing in a doorway or the middle of a room with her jaw clenched and her nails digging into her palms and everything she had believed all her life in question.

*　　*　　*

Now it was October and Rhoda was lying on the bed among the catalogs watching the October sun outside the window and getting bored with Saturday afternoon. She decided to get dressed and go downtown to see if Philip Holloman was sitting on his stool at the drugstore. Philip Holloman was a friend of Bob Rosen's and Rhoda was madly in love with Bob Rosen, who was nineteen years old and off at school in Champaign-Urbana.

Bob Rosen was the smartest person Rhoda had ever known. He played saxophone and laughed at everything and taught her how to dress and about jazz and took her riding in his car and gave her passionate kisses whenever his girlfriend was mad at him. She was mad at him a lot. Her name was Anne and she worked in a dress shop downtown and she was always frowning. Every time Rhoda had ever seen her she was frowning. Because of this Rhoda was certain that sooner or later Bob Rosen would break up with her and get his pin back. In the meantime she would be standing by, she would be his friend or his protégée or anything he wanted her to be. She would memorize the books and records he told her to buy. She would wear the clothes he told her to wear and write for *The Purple Clarion* and be a cheer-leader and march with the band and do everything he directed her to do. *So he would love her.* Love me, love me, love me, she chanted to the dark bushes, alone in the yard at night, sending him messages through the stars. Love me, love me, love me, love me.

Rhoda walked down Rollston Street toward the town, concentrating on making Bob Rosen love her. She walked past the ivy-colored walls of the Clayton Place, past the new Oldsmobile Stephanie Hinton got to drive to school, past the hospital and the bakery and the filling station. The Sweet Shop stood on its corner with its pink-and-white gingerbread trim. I could stop off and get a lemon phosphate before I go to the drugstore, Rhoda thought. Or one of those things that Dudley likes with ice cream in the lemonade. There was something strange about the Sweet Shop. Something spooky and unhealthy. Rhoda was more comfortable with the drugstore, where the vices were mixed in with Band-Aids and hot water bottles and magazines and aspirins.

Leta Ainsley was in the Sweet Shop. Leaning up against a counter with her big foreign-looking face turned toward the door. She had been in Japan before she came to Harrisburg. She had strange ideas and hair that grew around her lips. She was the Junior editor of *The Purple Clarion* where Rhoda was making her start as a reporter. She had let Rhoda wear her coat and her horn-rimmed glasses when the photographer came to take a picture of *The Purple Clarion* staff for the yearbook.

"I'm glad you're here," Leta said, drawing Rhoda over to a table by the window. "You wouldn't believe what happened to me. I've got to talk to someone."

"What happened?" Rhoda moved in close, getting a whiff of Leta's Tabu.

"I've been, ahh, in a man's apartment." Leta paused and looked around. She bent near. The hairs above her lip stood out like bristles. Rhoda couldn't take her eyes off them. Leta was so amazing. She wasn't even *clean*. Rhoda raised her eyes from Leta's lips; Leta's black eyes peered at her through the horn-rims. "I've been dryfucking," she said very slowly. "That's what you call it."

"Doing what?" Rhoda said. A shiver went over her body. It was the most startling thing she had ever heard. People in Harrisburg, Illinois, were too polite to talk about something as terrible and powerful as sex. They said "doing it" or "making babies," but, except when men were alone without women, no one said the real words out loud.

"Dryfucking," Leta said. "You do it with your clothes on."

"Oh, my God," Rhoda said. "I can't believe it."

"It feels so wonderful," Leta said, "I might go crazy thinking about it. He's going to call me up tomorrow. He's coming to band practice on Tuesday night and see us march. I'll show him to you."

"Good," Rhoda said. "I can't wait to see him."

"What you do," Leta went on, taking a cigarette out of its package without lifting her elbows from the table. "Is get on a bed and do it. You need a bed." Rhoda leaned down on the table until her head was almost touching Leta's hands. The word was racing around her head. The word was unbelievable. The word would drive her mad.

"I have to go up to the drugstore and look for Philip Holloman," she said. "You want to come with me?"

"Not now," Leta said. "I have to think."

"I'll see you tomorrow then," Rhoda said. "I'll turn in my gossip column stuff before class. I've almost got it finished. It's really funny. I pretended Carl Davis was Gene Kelly and was dancing in Shirley Hancock's yard."

"Oh, yeah." Leta sat back. Unfurled herself into the chair. "That sounds great."

"I'll see you then."

"Sure. I'll see you in the morning."

Rhoda proceeded on down the street, past the movie theater and the cleaners and the store where Bob Rosen's unsmiling girlfriend sold clothes to people. Rhoda considered going in and trying on things, but she didn't feel like doing it now. She was too haunted by the conversation with Leta. It was the wildest word there could be in the world. Rhoda wanted to do it. Right that very minute. With anyone. Anyone on the street. Anyone in a store. Anyone at all. She went into the drugstore but no one was there that she knew, just a couple of old men at the counter having Alka-Seltzers. She bought a package of Nabs and walked toward the park eating them, thinking about Leta and band practice and men that took you to apartments and did that to you. The excitement of the word was wearing off. It was beginning to sound like something only poor people would do. It sounded worse and worse the more it pounded in her head. It sounded bad. It made her want to take a bath.

She went home and went up to her room and took off her clothes and stood in front of the full-length mirror inspecting her vagina. She lifted one foot and put it on the doorknob to get a better look. It was terrible to look at. It was too much to bear. She picked up her clothes and threw them under the bed and went into the bathroom and got into the tub. She ran the hot water all the way up to the drain. She lay back listening to the sucking noises of the drain. Dryfucking. She sank down deeper into the water. She ran her hand across her stomach, found her navel, explored its folds with her fingers, going deeper and deeper, spiraling down. It was where she had been hooked on to her mother. Imagine having a baby hooked on to you. Swimming around inside you. It was the worst thing that could happen. She would never marry. She would never have one swimming in her. Never, never, never as long as she lived. No, she would go to Paradise Island and live with Queen Hippolyta. She would walk among the Amazons in her golden girdle. She would give her glass plane away and never return to civilization.

"Rhoda, what are you doing in there?" It was her real mother, the one in Illinois. She was standing in the doorway wearing a suit she'd been making all week. Dubonnet rayon with shoulder pads and a peplum, the height of style. "You're going to shrink."

"No I'm not. What was it like to have me inside of you? How did it feel?"

"It didn't feel like anything. I've told you that."

"But it was awful when I came, wasn't it?"

"You came too fast. You tore me up coming out. Like everything else you've ever done." Ariane drew herself up on her heels. "You never could wait for anything."

"I'm not going to do it," Rhoda said. "You couldn't pay me to have a baby."

"Well, maybe no one will want you to. Now get out, Rhoda. Your father's bringing company home. I want you dressed for dinner."

"How far in does a navel go?"

"I don't know. Now get out, honey. You can't stay in the tub all day."

Rhoda got out of the tub and wrapped herself in a towel and padded back to her room.

"Hello, Shorty," Dudley said. He was standing in the doorway of his room with a sultry look on his face. His hands were hooked in the pockets of his pants. He filled the doorframe. "Where you been all day?"

"None of your business," she said. "Get out of my way."

"I'm not in your way. We're going to move again, did you know that?"

"What are you talking about?"

"He's buying some mines. If he gets them we have to move to Kentucky. I was at the office today. I saw the maps. He's going to make about a million dollars."

"You don't know what you're talking about."

"You wait and see."

"Shut up. He wouldn't make us move in the middle of high school."

"He might have to."

"You're crazy," she said, and went on into her room and shut it out. She had gone to four grade schools. She was never going to move again. She was going to live right here in this room forever and wait for Bob Rosen to take his pin back and marry her. "He's crazy," she said to herself and pulled her new pink wool dress off the hanger and began to dress for dinner. "He doesn't know what he's talking about."

Monday was a big day at Harrisburg High School. They were taking achievement tests. Rhoda liked to take tests. She would sharpen three pencils and take the papers they handed her and sit down at a desk and cover the papers with answers that were twice as complicated as the questions and then she would turn the tests in before anyone else and go outside and sit in the sun. Rhoda considered achievement test day to be a sort of school holiday. She went out of the study hall and past the administrative offices and out the main door.

She sat in the sun, feeling the October morning on her legs and arms and face, watching the sunlight move around the concrete volumes of the lions that guarded the entrance to Harrisburg Township High School. The Purple Cougars, Harrisburg called its teams. It should be the marble lions, Rhoda thought. I ought to write an editorial about that. He told me to write editorials whenever I formed an opinion. She imagined it, the lead editorial. Not signed, of course, but her mark would be all over it. Her high imagination. He still got the paper up in Champaign-Urbana, since he had been its greatest editor.

She picked up her books and hurried into the school and up the broad wooden stairs to the *Purple Clarion* office. She sat down at a table and pulled out a tablet and began to write.

I was out in the October sun getting tanned around my anklets when it occurred to me that we have been calling our teams the wrong name. Purple Cougars, what does that mean? There aren't any cougars in Harrisburg. No one even knows what one is. When we try to make a homecoming float no one knows what one looks like. Everyone is always running around with encyclopedias in the middle of the night trying to make a papier-mâché cougar.

WE SHOULD BE THE MARBLE LIONS. Look at what is out in front of the school. JUST GO AND LOOK . . .

"What you doing, Scoop? I was just looking for you." It was Philip Holloman.

"Oh, God, I've got this great idea for an editorial. Leta said I could write one whenever I got in the mood. You want to hear it?"

"I have a letter for you." He was wearing his blue windbreaker. He looked just like Bob Rosen. They had matching windbreakers, only Bob's was beige. She had been in the arms of Bob Rosen's beige windbreaker and here was Philip's blue one, not two feet away. He was holding out a letter to her. A small white envelope. She knew what it was. At her house there were three of them wrapped in blue silk in the bottom of her underwear drawer.

"Why did he write me here?"

"I don't know. Look at the address. Isn't that a kick? God, I miss him. I miss him every day." She took the letter. *To,* Miss Scoop Cheetah, R.K. Manning, Ltd., *The Purple Clarion,* Harrisburg Township High School, Harrisburg, Illinois.

In the left-hand corner it said: Rosen, Box 413, University of Illinois, Champaign-Urbana, Illinois.

Rhoda took the letter and held it in her hand, getting it wet from her palms, and left her notebook on the table with her editorial half-finished and excused herself, breathing, still breathing, barely breathing, and went out into the hall. Philip watched her from the vantage point of eighteen years old. He liked Rhoda Manning. Everyone that knew her liked her. People that understood her liked her and people that thought she was crazy did too. Rosen was going to direct her career and someday marry her. That was clear. Anybody could see what was going to happen. She was on her way. She was going to set Harrisburg Township High School on its ear. Rosen had decreed it.

"Dear Cheetah," the letter began. Rhoda had found a quiet place in the abandoned lunchroom.

> I am going to be home this coming weekend. November 1, 2, and 3. If you will be waiting for me wearing a black sweater and skirt and brown shoes and get that hair cut into a pageboy I'll be over about 6:30 to take you to the ball game in Benton. If you have to wear your cheerleading things (Is there a freshman-sophomore game that night?) you can bring the black skirt and sweater and change at my cousin Shelton's house.
>
> If you show up in that pink dress looking like Shirley Temple you will have to find someone else to violate the Mann Act with. I have been thinking about you more than seems intelligent.
>
> Things aren't going well up here now. I have had to miss a lot of classes and will have to go to Saint Louis on the 4th for some more surgery. Mother is coming from Chicago. Tell Philip. I left it out of his letter.
>
> Did you read that style book I sent you? You *must* study that or no one will ever take your pieces seriously. Leave the feature section to the idiots. We are after news.
>
> Love,
> Bob

She went home that afternoon and took the other letters out of their drawer and got up on her bed and read them very slowly, over and over again.

Dear Cheetah,

I made it to Champaign-Urbana in the midst of the worst winter storm in history. They want me. They took me over and showed me the Journalism Department. You wouldn't believe how many typewriters they have. It must be twenty.

Coleman Hawkins is going to play here next week. Stay away from those Nabs. See you soon. In a hurry.

Love,
Bob

Dear Cheetah,

My roommate brought a cake from home and a cute habit of picking his nose when he studies. The classes look like a snap except for Biology which is going to require "thought and memory." This Williard guy teaching it has decided that science will save the world and I am going to sit on the front row and keep him from finding out I'm a History major. If at all possible.

Mother cursed out the Lieutenant Governor of Illinois at a street corner. Where in the hell do you think you're going, she was muttering and I looked at the license plate and it said 2.

Remember what I told you about those tryouts. Team up with Letitia and don't think about anything but the routine. And remember what I told you about talking to Harold about writing the play. You can do it if I did.

Big kisses,
Bob

Dear Cheetah,

I was sick in bed for two days and still can't go to class. I've memorized everything in the room including the nosepicker's daily Bible study guide. Here's his program for the day.

FOR SEPTEMBER 29

DO'S AND DON'TS

Do decide that those in power are there to take care of you.

Do listen when they speak for they are there by the will of the Lord for your benefit. Honor the ones the Lord has put over you to help you on the way to your recovery from the sickness and disease of ignorance of the Lord.

Don't be one of those that question the wisdom of older people. Sit at the feet of your parents and teachers. Let love be on our face and shine unto them the light of the Lord.

Don't let vice call out to you. The devil is everywhere. Be on the lookout for his messengers. Do not be fooled by smiles and flattery.

The nosepicker suspects me of being in the legions of the devil. He has asked to be transferred to another room. If the devil *is* on my side that will happen soon. I cough as much as possible and ask him what the Bible is and try to get into as many conversations as possible tidbits about my mother's notoriously filthy mouth. I can't wait till you meet her. She is coming to Harrisburg this summer to stay with grandmother and me.

I'm tired a lot but it's better. Write me. I love your letters and get some good laughs.

What is happening about the play? What did Harold say?

Love,
Bob

Dear Cheetah,

Back in class. Your letter came Monday. That's great about the play. I think you should call it Harrisburg Folly's, not Follies. Or something better. We'll work on it when I'm home Christmas.

Why skits? How many? Too busy to make this good. Hope you can read it. Out the door.

Bob

That was it. The entire collection. Rhoda folded them neatly back into their creases and put them in their envelopes and wrapped them in the silk scarf and put them beside the bed on the table. Then she rolled the pillow under her head. He's coming home, she said to herself as she cuddled down into the comforter and fell asleep. He is coming home. He's coming over here and get me and take me to Benton to the game. I'm not eating a bite until Friday. I will eat one egg a day until he gets here. I'll be so beautiful. He will love me. He'll do it to me. He doesn't even know I started. I might tell him. Yes, I'll tell him. I can tell him anything. I love him. I love him so much I could die.

Then it was Tuesday, then it was Wednesday, then it was an interminable Thursday and Rhoda was starving by the time she dragged herself home from school and went into the kitchen and boiled her daily egg.

"You are going to eat some supper, young lady," her mother said. "This starvation routine is going to stop."

"I ate at school. Please leave me alone, Mother. I know what I'm doing."

"You look terrible, Rhoda. Your cheeks are gaunt and you aren't sleeping well. I heard you last night. And I know what it's about."

"What's it about? What do you know?"

"It's about that Jewish boy, that Rosen boy you're going to go to Benton with. I don't know about your driving over there with him all alone, Rhoda. Your father's coming home tomorrow night. I don't know what he's going to say."

"Philip Holloman and Letitia's sister, Emily, are driving over with us. I mean, he's the editor of the paper. That ought to be enough chaperones. Emily's going. You call her mother and see." If her mother did call, Rhoda would have to try something else. "Call Emily's mother and see. We're going together. The ex-editor of my newspaper I happen to write for and the editor this year and Letitia's sister. I guess that's enough for anybody. I am so lucky to get to go with them, with some people that have some sense instead of those idiots in my grade."

"Well, if Emily's going."

"She's going."

"Please eat some supper."

"I can't eat supper. I can barely fit in my cheerleader skirt. Did you finish the black one? I have to have it. Is it done yet?"

"It's on the worktable. We'll try it on after dinner. I don't know why they want you to have black. I think it's very unflattering on young girls."

"It's just what they want." Rhoda kissed her mother on the cheek and went back to scrambling her egg. She scrambled it in several pats of butter. At the last minute she added an extra egg. If she didn't eat anything else until tomorrow night it would be all right. Already she could feel her rib cage coming out. She would be so beautiful. So thin. Surely he would love her.

"That's really all you're going to eat?"

"That's all. I ate a huge lunch." She dumped the scrambled eggs onto a plate and went out of the kitchen and through the living room and sat in the alcove of the stairs, with the phone sitting about three feet away. Soon it would be tomorrow. It would ring and his voice would be on the line and he would call her Cheetah and then he would be there and she would be in his arms and life would begin.

Then death will come, she remembered. Then you will die

and be inside a coffin in a grave. Forever and ever and ever, world without end, amen. Rhoda shivered. It was true. Death was true. And she was included. She ate the eggs.

Then it was Friday, then Friday night. Then he was there, standing in her living room, with his wide brow and his wide smile and his terrible self-confidence, not the least bit bothered by her mother's lukewarm welcome or that her father didn't come out of the dining room to say hello. Then they were out the door and into his car and it was just as she had dreamed it would be. The quality of his skin when she touched his arm, the texture, was so pure, so white, even in the dark his skin was so white. He was sick and his body was fighting off the sickness and the sickness was in the texture of his skin but something else was there too. Power, will, something like his music was there, something going forward, driving, something that was not going to let him die. She wanted to ask him about the sickness, about Saint Louis, about the operations, but she did not dare. The forward thing, the music, would not allow it. Even Rhoda, as much as she always talked of everything, knew not to talk of that. So she was quiet, and kept her hand on his arm as he drove the car. She waited.

"I'm so goddamn proud of you," he said. "You're doing it. You're going to do it, just like I said you would."

"It's just because of you," she answered. "It's just to make you like me. Oh, hell, now I'm going to cry. I'm pretty sure I'm going to cry." He stopped the car on the side of the road and pulled her into his arms and began to kiss her. There was a part of her rib cage in the back that was still sort of fat but not too fat. If I was standing up I'd be skinny, she decided. It's not fair to kiss sitting down.

"You don't ever wait for anything, do you?" he said. "I had

meant to make you wait for this." He handed it to her. Put it in her hand. The metal cut into her palm, the ruby in the center embedded in her palm. "You'll have to wear it on the inside of your bra. We aren't supposed to give them to children."

"I'm not a child. You know I'm not a child."

"Yeah, well Tau chapter of ZBT doesn't know anything except you're a freshman in high school. Don't get me thinking about it."

"Are you giving me this pin or not?"

"I'm giving it to you." He turned her around to face him. "I'm giving it to you because I'm in love with you." He laughed out loud, his wonderful laugh, the laugh he had been laughing the first time she laid eyes on him, when he was leaning up against the concrete block wall of the Coca-Cola bottling plant picking her out to be his protégée. "I'm in love with a girl who is fourteen years old."

"Say it again," she said. "Say you love me."

"After the ball game."

"No, right now. In front of Janet Allen's house. Right here, so I'll always remember where it was."

"I love you. In this Plymouth in front of Janet Allen's house." Then he kissed her some more. There were a lot of long crazy kisses. Then Rhoda pinned the ZBT pin to the inside of her bra and later, every time she jumped up to cheer at the ball game she could feel it scratch against her skin and send her heart rampaging all over the Benton football field and out across the hills and pastures of Little Egypt and down the state of Illinois to the river.

On Sunday he went back to school. Drove off down the street smiling and waving and left her standing on the sidewalk, by the nandina bushes. She walked down Bosworth Street to Cynthia's house and sat on the swing all afternoon telling Cynthia every single thing they had said and done all weekend, every word and nuance and embrace, every bite they ate at the drive-in and what kind of gas he bought and how he cursed the gas tank and the story of his mother cursing out the lieutenant governor of Illinois. When Cynthia's mother called her to dinner, Rhoda walked back home, trying to hold the day inside so it would never end.

There was a meatloaf for dinner and macaroni and cheese and green peas and carrots and homemade rolls. All her favorite dishes. After dinner her father called them into the living room and told them the news. They were moving away. He had bought them a white Victorian mansion in a town called Franklin, Kentucky, and in a month they would move there so he could be nearer to the mines. "It's too far to drive," he said. "I can't make these drives with all I have to do."

"We're going to move again?" Rhoda said. "You are going to do this to me?"

"I'm not doing anything to you, Sister," he said. "You're a little silly girl who's still wet behind the ears. I know what's best for all of us and this is what we're going to do. You're going to love it there."

"I'm going to have a play," she said. "I've just written the Senior Play. I have written the Senior Play for the whole school. They're going to put it on. Are you listening to me?" No one else said a word. It was only Rhoda and her father. Her mother was on the green chair with her arms around Dudley. "I won't leave. I don't believe you'd do this to me. You can't do this to me."

He lifted his chin. He stuck his hands in his pockets. Their eyes met. "You do what I tell you to do, Miss Priss. I'm the boss of this family."

"He can't do this to me." Rhoda turned to her mother. "You can't let him do this. You can't let it happen."

"I tried, my darling," her mother said. "I have told him a hundred times."

"I won't go," Rhoda said. "I'll stay here and live with Cynthia." Then she was out the door and running down the street and was gone a long time walking the streets of Harrisburg, Illinois, trying to believe there was something she could do.

Four weeks later the yellow moving van pulled up in front of the house on Rollston Street and the boxes and furniture and appliances were loaded on the van. Rhoda stayed down the street at Mike Ready's house talking and listening to the radio. She didn't feel like seeing her friends or telling them goodbye. She didn't tell anyone goodbye, not Dixie Lee or Shirley or Naomi, not even Letitia or Cynthia Jane. She just sat at Mike Ready's shuffling a deck of cards and talking about the basketball team. Around four o'clock she went home and helped her mother close the windows and sweep the debris on the floor into neat piles. "We can't leave a mess for the next people," her mother said. "I can't stand to move into a dirty house."

"Where's Dudley?" Rhoda asked. "Where's he gone?"

"He went with your father. They've gone on. You're going to drive with me. We need to finish here, Rhoda, and get on our way. It's going to be dark before too long. I want to drive as far as possible in the light."

"How long will it take?"

"About three hours. It isn't that far away. We can come back all the time, Rhoda. You can come back to see your play."

"I don't care about the goddamn play. Don't talk about the play. Let's get going. What else do we have to do?"

*   *   *

Then they were in the car and headed out of town. They drove down the main street, then turned onto Decatur and drove past the store where Anne Layne was working still, selling clothes to people off of racks, a frown on her face, caught forever in a world she could not imagine leaving for good reasons or bad ones, past the drugstore where Philip Holloman would sit every Saturday of his life on the same stool until it closed the year he was thirty-nine and he had to find a new place to hang out in on Saturdays. Past the icehouse and the filling station and the drive-in and past the brick fence of Bob Rosen's grandmother's house, where his gray Plymouth would come to rest. Past the site of the new consolidated school and the park where Rhoda had necked with Bob Rosen when he was still going steady with Anne Layne and past the sign that said City Limits, Harrisburg, Illinois, Population 12,480. Come Back Soon. You're Welcome.

It grew dark swiftly as it was the middle of December. December the fourteenth. At least it's not my lucky number, Rhoda thought, and fell asleep, her hand touching the edge of her mother's soft green wool skirt, the smell of her mother's expensive perfume all around them in the car. The sound of the wheels on the asphalt road. When she woke they were pulling onto the wide steel bridge that separates Illinois from Kentucky. Rhoda sat up in the seat. It was the Ohio River, dark and vast below her, and the sky was dark and vast above with only a few stars and they were really leaving.

"I don't believe it," she said. "I don't believe he'd do this to me." Then she began to weep. She wept terrible uncontrollable tears all across the bridge, weeping into her hands, and her mother wept with her but she kept her hands on the wheel and her eyes on the road. "There was nothing I could do about it, darling," she said. "I told him over and over but he wouldn't listen. He doesn't care about anything in the world but himself. I don't know what else I could have done. I'm so sorry. I know how you feel. I know what you are going through."

"No, you don't," Rhoda said, turning her rage against her mother. "You don't know. You could have stopped him. You don't know. You lived in the same house every day of your life. Your house is still there. Your mother is still there in that same house. You went to one school. You had the same friends. I don't care about this goddamn Franklin, Kentucky. I hope it burns to the ground. I won't like it. I hate it. I already hate it. Oh, my God. I hate its guts." Her mother took one hand from the wheel and touched her arm.

"Good will come of it, Rhoda. Good comes of everything."

"No, it doesn't," she said. "It does not. That's a lie. Half the stuff you tell me is a lie. You don't know what you're saying. You don't know a goddamn thing. STOP THIS GODDAMN CAR. I HAVE TO GO TO THE BATHROOM. STOP IT, MOTHER. I MEAN, STOP IT RIGHT THIS MINUTE. THE MINUTE YOU GET OFF THIS BRIDGE."

Ariane stopped the car and Rhoda strode off across a field and urinated behind a tree. The warm urine poured out upon the ground and steam rose from it and that solaced her in some strange way and she pulled up her pants and walked back across the stubble and got into the car.

"It better be a big house," she said. "It had better be the biggest house in that goddamn town."

Music

RHODA was fourteen years old the summer her father dragged her off to Clay County, Kentucky, to make her stop smoking and acting like a movie star. She was fourteen years old, a holy and terrible age, and her desire for beauty and romance drove her all day long and pursued her if she slept.

"Te amo," she whispered to herself in Latin class. "Te amo, Bob Rosen," sending the heat of her passions across the classroom and out through the window and across two states to a hospital room in Saint Louis, where a college boy lay recovering from a series of operations Rhoda had decided would be fatal.

"And you as well must die, beloved dust," she quoted to herself. "Oh, sleep forever in your Latmian cave, Mortal Endymion, darling of the moon," she whispered, and sometimes it was Bob Rosen's lanky body stretched out in the cave beside his saxophone that she envisioned and sometimes it was her own lush, apricot-colored skin growing cold against the rocks in the moonlight.

Rhoda was fourteen years old that spring and her true love had been cruelly taken from her and she had started smoking because there was nothing left to do now but be a writer.

She was fourteen years old and she would sit on the porch at night looking down the hill that led through the small town of

Franklin, Kentucky, and think about the stars, wondering where heaven could be in all that vastness, feeling betrayed by her mother's pale Episcopalianism and the fate that had brought her to this small town right in the middle of her sophomore year in high school. She would sit on the porch stuffing chocolate chip cookies into her mouth, drinking endless homemade chocolate milkshakes, smoking endless Lucky Strike cigarettes, watching her mother's transplanted roses move steadily across the trellis, taking Bob Rosen's thin letters in and out of their envelopes, holding them against her face, then going up to the new bedroom, to the soft, blue sheets, stuffed with cookies and ice cream and cigarettes and rage.

"Is that you, Rhoda?" her father would call out as she passed his bedroom. "Is that you, sweetie? Come tell us goodnight." And she would go into their bedroom and lean over and kiss him.

"You just ought to smell yourself," he would say, sitting up, pushing her away. "You just ought to smell those nasty cigarettes." And as soon as she went into her room he would go downstairs and empty all the ashtrays to make sure the house wouldn't burn down while he was sleeping.

"I've got to make her stop that goddamn smoking," he would say, climbing back into the bed. "I'm goddamned if I'm going to put up with that."

"I'd like to know how you're going to stop it," Rhoda's mother said. "I'd like to see anyone make Rhoda do anything she doesn't want to do. Not to mention that you're hardly ever here."

"Goddammit, Ariane, don't start that this time of night." And he rolled over on his side of the bed and began to plot his campaign against Rhoda's cigarettes.

Dudley Manning wasn't afraid of Rhoda, even if she was as stubborn as a goat. Dudley Manning wasn't afraid of anything.

He had gotten up at dawn every day for years and believed in himself and followed his luck wherever it led him, dragging his sweet Southern wife and his children behind him, and now, in his fortieth year, he was about to become a millionaire.

He was about to become a millionaire and he was in love with a beautiful woman who was not his wife and it was the strangest spring he had ever known. When he added up the figures in his account books he was filled with awe at his own achievements, amazed at what he had made of himself, and to make up for it he talked a lot about luck and pretended to be humble but deep down inside he believed there was nothing he couldn't do, even love two women at once, even make Rhoda stop smoking.

Both Dudley and Rhoda were early risers. If he was in town he would be waiting in the kitchen when she came down to breakfast, dressed in his khakis, his pens in his pocket, his glasses on his nose, sitting at the table going over his papers, his head full of the clean new ideas of morning.

"How many more days of school do you have?" he said to her one morning, watching her light the first of her cigarettes without saying anything about it.

"Just this week," she said. "Just until Friday. I'm making A's, Daddy. This is the easiest school I've ever been to."

"Well, don't be smart-alecky about it, Rhoda," he said. "If you've got a good mind it's only because God gave it to you."

"God didn't give me anything," she said. "Because there isn't any God."

"Well, let's don't get into an argument about that this morning," Dudley said. "As soon as you finish school I want you to drive up to the mines with me for a few days."

"For how long?" she said.

"We won't be gone long," he said. "I just want to take you to the mines to look things over."

Rhoda french-inhaled, blowing the smoke out into the sunlight coming through the kitchen windows, imagining herself on a tour of her father's mines, the workers with their caps in their hands smiling at her as she walked politely among them. Rhoda liked that idea. She dropped two saccharin tablets into her coffee and sat down at the table, enjoying her fantasy.

"Is that what you're having for breakfast?" he said.

"I'm on a diet," Rhoda said. "I'm on a black coffee diet."

He looked down at his poached eggs, cutting into the yellow with his knife. I can wait, he said to himself. As God is my witness I can wait until Sunday.

Rhoda poured herself another cup of coffee and went upstairs to write Bob Rosen before she left for school.

Dear Bob [the letter began],

School is almost over. I made straight A's, of course, as per your instructions. This school is so easy it's crazy.

They read one of my newspaper columns on the radio in Nashville. Everyone in Franklin goes around saying my mother writes my columns. Can you believe that? Allison Hotchkiss, that's my editor, say she's going to write an editorial about it saying I really write them.

I turned my bedroom into an office and took out the tacky dressing table mother made me and got a desk and put my typewriter on it and made striped drapes, green and black and white. I think you would approve.

Sunday Daddy is taking me to Manchester, Kentucky, to look over the coal mines. He's going to let me drive. He lets me drive *all the time*. I live for your letters.

                              Te amo,
                              Rhoda

She put the letter in a pale blue envelope, sealed it, dripped some Toujours Moi lavishly onto it in several places and threw herself down on her bed.

She pressed her face deep down into her comforter pretending it was Bob Rosen's smooth cool skin. "Oh, Bob, Bob," she whispered to the comforter. "Oh, honey, don't die, don't die, please don't die." She could feel the tears coming. She reached out and caressed the seam of the comforter, pretending it was the scar on Bob Rosen's neck.

The last night she had been with him he had just come home from an operation for a mysterious tumor that he didn't want to talk about. It would be better soon, was all he would say about it. Before long he would be as good as new.

They had driven out of town and parked the old Pontiac underneath a tree beside a pasture. It was September and Rhoda had lain in his arms smelling the clean smell of his new sweater, touching the fresh red scars on his neck, looking out the window to memorize every detail of the scene, the black tree, the September pasture, the white horse leaning against the fence, the palms of his hands, the taste of their cigarettes, the night breeze, the exact temperature of the air, saying to herself over and over, I must remember everything. This will have to last me forever and ever and ever.

"I want you to do it to me," she said. "Whatever it is they do."

"I can't," he said. "I couldn't do that now. It's too much trouble to make love to a virgin." He was laughing. "Besides, it's hard to do it in a car."

"But I'm leaving," she said. "I might not ever see you again."

"Not tonight," he said. "I still don't feel very good, Rhoda."

"What if I come back and visit," she said. "Will you do it then? When you feel better."

"If you still want me to I will," he said. "If you come back to visit and we both want to, I will."

"Do you promise?" she said, hugging him fiercely.

"I promise," he said. "On my honor I promise to do it when you come to visit."

But Rhoda was not allowed to go to Saint Louis to visit. Either her mother guessed her intentions or else she seized the opportunity to do what she had been wanting to do all along and stop her daughter from seeing a boy with a Jewish last name.

There were weeks of pleadings and threats. It all ended one Sunday night when Mrs. Manning lost her temper and made the statement that Jews were little peddlers who went through the Delta selling needles and pins.

"You don't know what you're talking about," Rhoda screamed. "He's not a peddler, and I love him and I'm going to love him until I die." Rhoda pulled her arms away from her mother's hands.

"I'm going up there this weekend to see him," she screamed. "Daddy promised me I could and you're not going to stop me and if you try to stop me I'll kill you and I'll run away and I'll never come back."

"You are not going to Saint Louis and that's the end of this conversation and if you don't calm down I'll call a doctor and have you locked up. I think you're crazy, Rhoda. I really do."

"I'm not crazy," Rhoda screamed. "You're the one that's crazy."

"You and your father think you're so smart," her mother said. She was shaking but she held her ground, moving around behind a Queen Anne chair. "Well, I don't care how smart you are, you're not going to get on a train and go off to Saint Louis, Missouri, to see a man when you're only fourteen years old, and that, Miss Rhoda K. Manning, is that."

"I'm going to kill you," Rhoda said. "I really am. I'm going to kill you," and she thought for a moment that she would kill her, but then she noticed her grandmother's Limoges hot chocolate pot sitting on top of the piano holding a spray of yellow jasmine, and she walked over to the piano and picked it up and threw it all the way across the room and smashed it into a wall beside a framed print of *The Blue Boy*.

"I hate you," Rhoda said. "I wish you were dead." And while her mother stared in disbelief at the wreck of the sainted hot chocolate pot, Rhoda walked out of the house and got in the car and drove off down the steep driveway. I hate her guts, she said to herself. I hope she cries herself to death.

She shifted into second gear and drove off toward her father's office, quoting to herself from Edna Millay. "Now by this moon, before this moon shall wane, I shall be dead or I shall be with you."

But in the end Rhoda didn't die. Neither did she kill her mother. Neither did she go to Saint Louis to give her virginity to her reluctant lover.

The Sunday of the trip Rhoda woke at dawn feeling very excited and changed clothes four or five times trying to decide how she wanted to look for her inspection of the mines.

Rhoda had never even seen a picture of a strip mine. In her imagination she and her father would be riding an elevator down into the heart of a mountain where obsequious masked miners were lined up to shake her hand. Later that evening the captain of the football team would be coming over to the hotel to meet her and take her somewhere for a drive.

She pulled on a pair of pink pedal pushers and a long navy blue sweat shirt, threw every single thing she could possibly imagine wearing into a large suitcase, and started down the stairs to where her father was calling for her to hurry up.

Her mother followed her out of the house holding a buttered biscuit on a linen napkin. "Please eat something before you leave," she said. "There isn't a decent restaurant after you leave Bowling Green."

"I told you I don't want anything to eat," Rhoda said. "I'm on a diet." She stared at the biscuit as though it were a coral snake.

"One biscuit isn't going to hurt you," her mother said. "I made you a lunch, chicken and carrot sticks and apples."

"I don't want it," Rhoda said "Don't put any food in this car, Mother."

"Just because you never eat doesn't mean your father won't get hungry. You don't have to eat any of it unless you want to." Their eyes met. Then they sighed and looked away.

Her father appeared at the door and climbed in behind the wheel of the secondhand Cadillac.

"Let's go, Sweet Sister," he said, cruising down the driveway, turning onto the road leading to Bowling Green and due east into the hill country. Usually this was his favorite moment of the week, starting the long drive into the rich Kentucky hills where his energy and intelligence had created the long black rows of figures in the account books, figures that meant Rhoda would never know what it was to be really afraid or uncertain or powerless.

"How long will it take?" Rhoda asked.

"Don't worry about that," he said. "Just look out the window and enjoy the ride. This is beautiful country we're driving through."

"I can't right now," Rhoda said. "I want to read the new book Allison gave me. It's a book of poems."

She settled down into the seat and opened the book.

> Oh, gallant was the first love, and glittering and fine;
> The second love was water, in a clear blue cup;
> The third love was his, and the fourth was mine.
> And after that, I always get them all mixed up.

Oh, God, this is good, she thought. She sat up straighter, wanting to kiss the book. Oh, God, this is really good. She turned the book over to look at the picture of the author. It was a photograph of a small bright face in full profile staring off into the mysterious brightly lit world of a poet's life.

Dorothy Parker, she read. What a wonderful name. Maybe I'll change my name to Dorothy, Dorothy Louise Manning. Dot Manning. Dottie, Dottie Leigh, Dot.

Rhoda pulled a pack of Lucky Strikes out of her purse, tamped it on the dashboard, opened it, extracted a cigarette and lit it with a gold Ronson lighter. She inhaled deeply and went back to the book.

Her father gripped the wheel, trying to concentrate on the beauty of the morning, the green fields, the small, neat farmhouses, the red barns, the cattle and horses. He moved his eyes from all that order to his fourteen-year-old daughter slumped beside him with her nose buried in a book, her plump fingers languishing in the air, holding a cigarette. He slowed down, pulled the car onto the side of the road and killed the motor.

"What's wrong?" Rhoda said. "Why are you stopping?"

"Because you are going to put out that goddamn cigarette this very minute and you're going to give me the package and you're not going to smoke another cigarette around me as long as you live," he said.

"I will not do any such thing," Rhoda said. "It's a free country."

"Give me the cigarette, Rhoda," he said. "Hand it here."

"Give me one good reason why I should," she said. But her voice let her down. She knew there wasn't any use in arguing. This was not her soft little mother she was dealing with. This was Dudley Manning, who had been a famous baseball player until he quit when she was born. Who before that had gone to the Olympics on a relay team. There were scrapbooks full of his clippings in Rhoda's house. No matter where the Mannings went those scrapbooks sat on a table in the den. *Manning Hits One Over The Fence,* the headlines read. *Manning Saves The Day.*

Manning Does It Again. And he was not the only one. His cousin Philip Manning, down in Jackson, Mississippi, was famous too. Who was the father of the famous Crystal Manning, Rhoda's cousin who had a fur coat when she was ten. And Leland Manning, who was her cousin Lele's daddy. Leland had been the captain of the Tulane football team before he drank himself to death in the Delta.

Rhoda sighed, thinking of all that, and gave in for the moment. "Give me one good reason and I might," she repeated.

"I don't have to give you a reason for a goddamn thing," he said. "Give the cigarette here, Rhoda. Right this minute." He reached out and took it and she didn't resist. "Goddamn, these things smell awful," he said, crushing it in the ashtray. He reached in her pocketbook and got the package and threw it out the window.

"Only white trash throw things out on the road," Rhoda said. "You'd kill me if I did that."

"Well, let's just be quiet and get to where we're going." He started the motor and drove back out onto the highway. Rhoda crunched down lower in the seat, pretending to read her book. Who cares, she thought. I'll get some as soon as we stop for gas.

Getting cigarettes at filling stations was not as easy as Rhoda thought it was going to be. This was God's country they were driving into now, the hills rising up higher and higher, strange, silent little houses back off the road. Rhoda could feel the eyes looking out at her from behind the silent windows. Poor white trash, Rhoda's mother would have called them. The salt of the earth, her father would have said.

This was God's country and these people took things like children smoking cigarettes seriously. At both places where they stopped there was a sign by the cash register, *No Cigarettes Sold To Minors*.

Rhoda had moved to the back seat of the Cadillac and was stretched out on the seat reading her book. She had found another poem she liked and she was memorizing it.

> *Four be the things I'd be better without,*
> *Love, curiosity, freckles and doubt.*
> *Three be the things I shall never attain,*
> *Envy, content and sufficient champagne.*

Oh, God, I love this book, she thought. *This Dorothy Parker is just like me.* Rhoda was remembering a night when she got drunk in Clarkesville, Mississippi, with her cousin Baby Gwen Barksdale. They got drunk on tequila LaGrande Conroy brought back from Mexico, and Rhoda had slept all night in the bathtub so she would be near the toilet when she vomited.

She put her head down on her arm and giggled, thinking about waking up in the bathtub. Then a plan occurred to her.

"Stop and let me go to the bathroom," she said to her father. "I think I'm going to throw up."

"Oh, Lord," he said. "I knew you shouldn't have gotten in the back seat. Well, hold on. I'll stop the first place I see." He pushed his hat back off his forehead and began looking for a place to stop, glancing back over his shoulder every now and then to see if she was all right. Rhoda had a long history of throwing up on car trips so he was taking this seriously. Finally he saw a combination store and filling station at a bend in the road and pulled up beside the front door.

"I'll be all right." Rhoda said, jumping out of the car. "You stay here. I'll be right back."

She walked dramatically up the wooden steps and pushed open the screen door. It was so quiet and dark inside she thought for a moment the store was closed. She looked around. She was in a rough, high-ceilinged room with saddles and pieces of farm equipment hanging from the rafters and a sparse array of canned goods on wooden shelves behind a counter. On the counter were five or six large glass jars filled with different kinds of Nabisco cookies. Rhoda stared at the cookie jars, wanting to stick her hand down inside and take out great fistfuls of Lorna Doones and Oreos. She fought off her hunger and raised her eyes to the display of chewing tobacco and cigarettes.

The smells of the store rose up to meet her, fecund and rich, moist and cool, as if the store was an extension of the earth outside. Rhoda looked down at the board floors. She felt she could have dropped a sunflower seed on the floor and it would instantly sprout and take bloom, growing quick, moving down into the earth and upwards toward the rafters.

"Is anybody here?" she said softly, then louder. "Is anybody here?"

A woman in a cotton dress appeared in a door, staring at Rhoda out of very intense, very blue eyes.

"Can I buy a pack of cigarettes from you?" Rhoda said. "My dad's in the car. He sent me to get them."

"What kind of cigarettes you looking for?" the woman said, moving to the space between the cash register and the cookie jars.

"Some Luckies if you have them," Rhoda said. "He said to just get anything you had if you didn't have that."

"They're a quarter," the woman said, reaching behind herself to take the package down and lay it on the counter, not smiling, but not being unkind either.

"Thank you," Rhoda said, laying the quarter down on the counter. "Do you have any matches?"

"Sure," the woman said, holding out a box of kitchen matches. Rhoda took a few, letting her eyes leave the woman's face and come to rest on the jars of Oreos. They looked wonderful and light, as though they had been there a long time and grown soft around the edges.

The woman was smiling now. "You want one of those cookies?" she said. "You want one, you go on and have one. It's free."

"Oh, no thank you," Rhoda said. "I'm on a diet. Look, do you have a ladies' room I can use?"

"It's out back," the woman said. "You can have one of them cookies if you want it. Like I said, it won't cost you nothing."

"I guess I'd better get going," Rhoda said. "My dad's in a hurry. But thank you anyway. And thanks for the matches." Rhoda hurried down the aisle, slipped out the back door and leaned up against the back of the store, tearing the paper off the cigarettes. She pulled one out, lit it, and inhaled deeply, blowing the smoke out in front of her, watching it rise up into the air, casting a veil over the hills that rose up behind and to the left of her. She had never been in such a strange country. It looked as though no one ever did anything to their yards or roads or fences. It looked as though there might not be a clock for miles.

She inhaled again, feeling dizzy and full. She had just taken the cigarette out of her mouth when her father came bursting out of the door and grabbed both of her wrists in his hands.

"Let go of me," she said. "Let go of me this minute." She struggled to free herself, ready to kick or claw or bite, ready for a real fight, but he held her off. "Drop the cigarette, Rhoda," he said. "Drop it on the ground."

"I'll kill you," she said. "As soon as I get away I'm running away to Florida. Let go of me, Daddy. Do you hear me?"

"I hear you," he said. The veins were standing out on his forehead. His face was so close Rhoda could see his freckles and the line where his false front tooth was joined to what was left of the real one. He had lost the tooth in a baseball game the day

Rhoda was born. That was how he told the story. "I lost that tooth the day Rhoda was born," he would say. "I was playing left field against Memphis in the old Crump Stadium. I slid into second and the second baseman got me with his shoe."

"You can smoke all you want to when you get down to Florida," he was saying now. "But you're not smoking on this trip. So you might as well calm down before I drive off and leave you here."

"I don't care," she said. "Go on and leave. I'll just call up Mother and she'll come and get me." She was struggling to free her wrists but she could not move them inside his hands. "Let go of me, you big bully," she added.

"Will you calm down and give me the cigarettes?"

"All right," she said, but the minute he let go of her hands she turned and began to hit him on the shoulders, pounding her fists up and down on his back, not daring to put any real force behind the blows. He pretended to cower under the assault. She caught his eye and saw that he was laughing at her and she had to fight the desire to laugh with him.

"I'm getting in the car," she said. "I'm sick of this place." She walked grandly around to the front of the store, got into the car, tore open the lunch and began to devour it, tearing the chicken off the bones with her teeth, swallowing great hunks without even bothering to chew them. "I'm never speaking to you again as long as I live," she said, her mouth full of chicken breast. "You are not my father."

"Suits me, Miss Smart-alecky Movie Star," he said, putting his hat back on his head. "Soon as we get home you can head on out for Florida. You just let me know when you're leaving so I can give you some money for the bus."

"I hate you," Rhoda mumbled to herself, starting in on the

homemade raisin cookies. I hate your guts. I hope you go to hell forever, she thought, breaking a cookie into pieces so she could pick out the raisins.

It was late afternoon when the Cadillac picked its way up a rocky red clay driveway to a housetrailer nestled in the curve of a hill beside a stand of pine trees.

"Where are we going?" Rhoda said. "Would you just tell me that?"

"We're going to see Maud and Joe Samples," he said. "Joe's an old hand around here. He's my right-hand man in Clay County. Now you just be polite and try to learn something, Sister. These are real folks you're about to meet."

"Why are we going here first?" Rhoda said. "Aren't we going to a hotel?"

"There isn't any hotel," her father said. "Does this look like someplace they'd have hotels? Maud and Joe are going to put you up for me while I'm off working."

"I'm going to stay here?" Rhoda said. "In this trailer?"

"Just wait until you see the inside," her father said. "It's like the inside of a boat, everything all planned out and just the right amount of space for things. I wish your mother'd let me live in a trailer."

They were almost to the door now. A plump smiling woman came out onto the wooden platform and waited for them with her hands on her hips, smiling wider and wider as they got nearer.

"There's Maud," Dudley said. "She's the sweetest woman in the world and the best cook in Kentucky. Hey there, Miss Maud," he called out.

"Mr. D," she said, opening the car door for them. "Joe Samples' been waiting on you all day and here you show up bringing this beautiful girl just like you promised. I've made you some blackberry pies. Come on inside this trailer." Maud smiled deep into Rhoda's face. Her eyes were as blue as the ones on the woman in the store. Rhoda's mother had blue eyes, but not this brilliant and not this blue. These eyes were from another world, another century.

"Come on in and see Joe," Maud said. "He's been having a fit for you to get here."

They went inside and Dudley showed Rhoda all around the trailer, praising the design of trailers. Maud turned on the tiny oven and they had blackberry pie and bread and butter sandwiches and Rhoda abandoned her diet and ate two pieces of the pie, covering it with thick whipped cream.

The men went off to talk business and Maud took Rhoda to a small room at the back of the trailer decorated to match a handmade quilt of the sunrise.

There were yellow ruffled curtains at the windows and a tiny dressing table with a yellow ruffled skirt around the edges. Rhoda was enchanted by the smallness of everything and the way the windows looked out onto layers of green trees and bushes.

Lying on the dresser was a white leather Bible and a display of small white pamphlets, *Alcohol And You, When Jesus Reaches For A Drink, You Are Not Alone, Sorry Isn't Enough, Taking No For An Answer.*

It embarrassed Rhoda even to read the titles of anything as tacky as the pamphlets. but she didn't let on she thought it was tacky, not with Maud sitting on the bed telling her how pretty she was every other second and asking her questions about herself and saying how wonderful her father was.

"We love Mr. D to death," she said. "It's like he was one of our own."

He appeared in the door. "Rhoda, if you're settled in I'll be leaving now," he said. "I've got to drive to Knoxville to do some business but I'll be back here Tuesday morning to take you to the mines." He handed her three twenty-dollar bills. "Here," he said. "In case you need anything."

He left then and hurried out to the car, trying to figure out how long it would take him to get to Knoxville, to where Valerie sat alone in a hotel room waiting for this night they had planned for so long. He felt the sweet hot guilt rise up in his face and the sweet hot longing in his legs and hands.

I'm sorry, Jesus, he thought, pulling out onto the highway. I know it's wrong and I know we're doing wrong. So go on and punish me if you have to but just let me make it there and back before you start in on me.

He set the cruising speed at exactly fifty-five miles an hour and began to sing to himself as he drove.

> *"Oh, sure as the vine grows around the stump*
> *You're my darling sugar lump,"* he sang, and;
>
> *"Froggy went a-courting and he did ride,*
> *Huhhrummp, Huhhrummp,*
> *Froggy went a-courting and he did ride, Huhhrummp,*
>
> *What you gonna have for the wedding supper?*
> *Black-eyed peas and bread and butter, Huhhrummp,*
>   *huhhrummp . . ."*

Rhoda was up and dressed when her father came to get her on Tuesday morning. It was still dark outside but a rooster had begun to crow in the distance. Maud bustled all about the little kitchen making much of them, filling their plates with biscuits and fried eggs and ham and gravy.

Then they got into the Cadillac and began to drive toward the mine. Dudley was driving slowly, pointing out everything to her as they rode along.

"Up on that knoll," he said, "that's where the Traylors live. Rooster Traylor's a man about my age. Last year his mother shot one of the Galtney women for breaking up Rooster's marriage and now the Galtneys have got to shoot someone in the Traylor family."

"That's terrible," Rhoda said.

"No it isn't, Sister," he said, warming into the argument. "These people take care of their own problems."

"They actually shoot each other?" she said. "And you think that's okay? You think that's funny?"

"I think it's just as good as waiting around for some judge and jury to do it for you."

"Then you're just crazy," Rhoda said. "You're as crazy as you can be."

"Well, let's don't argue about it this morning. Come on. I've got something to show you." He pulled the car off the road and they walked into the woods, following a set of bulldozer tracks that made a crude path into the trees. It was quiet in the woods and smelled of pine and sassafras. Rhoda watched her father's strong body moving in front of her, striding along, inspecting everything, noticing everything, commenting on everything.

"Look at this," he said. "Look at all this beauty, honey. Look at how beautiful all this is. This is the real world. Not those god-damn movies and beauty parlors and magazines. This is the world that God made. This is where people are really happy."

"There isn't any God," she said. "Nobody that knows any-thing believes in God, Daddy. That's just a lot of old stuff . . ."

"I'm telling you, Rhoda," he said. "It breaks my heart to see the way you're growing up." He stopped underneath a tree, took a seat on a log and turned his face to hers. Tears were forming in his eyes. He was famous in the family for being able to cry on cue. "You've just got to learn to listen to someone. You've got to get some common sense in your head. I swear to God, I worry about you all the time." The tears were falling now. "I just can't stand to see the way you're growing up. I don't know where you get all those crazy ideas you come up with."

Rhoda looked down, caught off guard by the tears. No matter how many times he pulled that with the tears she fell for it for a moment. The summer forest was all around them, soft deep earth beneath their feet, morning light falling through the leaves, and the things that passed between them were too hard to understand. Their brown eyes met and locked and after that they were bound to start an argument for no one can bear to be that happy or that close to another human being.

"Well, I'll tell you one thing," Rhoda said. "It's a free country and I can smoke if I want to and you can't keep me from doing it by locking me up in a trailer with some poor white trash."

"What did you say?" he said, getting a look on his face that would have scared a grown man to death. "What did you just say, Rhoda?"

"I said I'm sick and tired of being locked up in that damned old trailer with those corny people and nothing to read but religious magazines. I want to get some cigarettes and I want you to take me home so I can see my friends and get my column written for next week."

"Oh, God, Sister," he said. "Haven't I taught you anything? Maud Samples is the salt of the earth. That woman raised seven children. She knows things you and I will never know as long as we live."

"Well, no she doesn't," Rhoda said. "She's just an old white trash country woman and if Momma knew where I was she'd have a fit."

"Your momma is a very stupid person," he said. "And I'm sorry I ever let her raise you." He turned his back to her then and stalked on out of the woods to a road that ran like a red scar up the side of the mountain. "Come on," he said. "I'm going to take you up there and show you where coal comes from. Maybe you can learn one thing this week."

"I learn things all the time," she said. "I already know more than half the people I know . . . I know . . ."

"Please don't talk anymore this morning," he said. "I'm burned out talking to you."

He put her into a jeep and began driving up the steep unpaved road. In a minute he was feeling better, cheered up by the sight of the big Caterpillar tractors moving dirt. If there was one thing that always cheered him up it was the sight of a big shovel moving dirt. "This is Blue Gem coal," he said. "The hardest in the area. See the layers. Topsoil, then gravel and dirt or clay, then slate, then thirteen feet of pure coal. Some people think it was made by dinosaurs. Other people think God put it there."

"This is it?" she said. "This is the mine?" It looked like one of his road construction projects. Same yellow tractors, same disorderly activity. The only difference seemed to be the huge piles of coal and a conveyor belt going down the mountain to a train.

"This is it," he said. "This is where they stored the old dinosaurs."

"Well, it is made out of dinosaurs," she said. "There were a lot of leaves and trees and dinosaurs and then they died and the coal and oil is made out of them."

"All right," he said. "Let's say I'll go along with the coal. But tell me this, who made the slate then? Who put the slate right on top of the coal everywhere it's found in the world? Who laid the slate down on top of the dinosaurs?"

"I don't know who put the slate there," she said. "We haven't got that far yet."

"You haven't got that far?" he said. "You mean the scientists haven't got as far as the slate yet? Well, Sister, that's the problem with you folks that evolved out of monkeys. You're still half-baked. You aren't finished like us old dumb ones that God made."

"I didn't say the scientists hadn't got that far," she said. "I just said I hadn't got that far."

"It's a funny thing to me how all those dinosaurs came up here to die in the mountains and none of them died in the farmland," he said. "It sure would have made it a lot easier on us miners if they'd died down there on the flat."

While she was groping around for an answer he went right on. "Tell me this, Sister," he said. "Are any of your monkey ancestors in there with the dinosaurs, or is it just plain dinosaurs? I'd like to know who all I'm digging up . . . I'd like to give credit . . ."

The jeep had come to a stop and Joe was coming toward them, hurrying out of the small tin-roofed office with a worried look on his face. "Mr. D, you better call up to Jellico. Beb's been looking everywhere for you. They had a run-in with a Teamster organizer. You got to call him right away."

"What's wrong?" Rhoda said. "What happened?"

"Nothing you need to worry about, Sister," her father said. He turned to Joe. "Go find Preacher and tell him to drive Rhoda back to your house. You go on now, honey. I've got work to do." He gave her a kiss on the cheek and disappeared into the office. A small shriveled-looking man came limping out of a building and climbed into the driver's seat. "I'm Preacher," he said. "Mr. Joe tole me to drive you up to his place."

"All right," Rhoda said. "I guess that's okay with me." Preacher put the jeep in gear and drove it slowly down the winding rutted road. By the time they got to the bottom Rhoda had thought of a better plan. "I'll drive now," she said. "I'll drive myself to Maud's. It's all right with my father. He lets me drive all the time. You can walk back, can't you?" Preacher didn't know what to say to that. He was an old drunk that Dudley and

Joe kept around to run errands. He was so used to taking orders that finally he climbed down out of the jeep and did as he was told. "Show me the way to town," Rhoda said. "Draw me a map. I have to go by town on my way to Maud's." Preacher scratched his head, then bent over and drew her a little map in the dust on the hood. Rhoda studied the map, put the jeep into the first forward gear she could find and drove off down the road to the little town of Manchester, Kentucky, studying the diagram on the gearshift as she drove.

She parked beside a boardwalk that led through the main street of town and started off looking for a store that sold cigarettes. One of the stores had dresses in the window. In the center was a red strapless sundress with a white jacket. $6.95, the price tag said. I hate the way I look, she decided. I hate these tacky pants. I've got sixty dollars. I don't have to look like this if I don't want to. I can buy anything I want.

She went inside, asked the clerk to take the dress out of the window and in a few minutes she emerged from the store wearing the dress and a pair of leather sandals with two-inch heels. The jacket was thrown carelessly over her shoulder like Gene Tierney in *Leave Her to Heaven*. I look great in red, she was thinking, catching a glimpse of herself in a store window. It isn't true that redheaded people can't wear red. She walked on down the boardwalk, admiring herself in every window.

She walked for two blocks looking for a place to try her luck getting cigarettes. She was almost to the end of the boardwalk when she came to a pool hall. She stood in the door looking in, smelling the dark smell of tobacco and beer. The room was deserted except for a man leaning on a cue stick beside a table and a boy with black hair seated behind a cash register reading a book. The boy's name was Johnny Hazard and he was sixteen years old. The book he was reading was *U.S.A.* by John Dos Passos. A woman who came to Manchester to teach poetry writing had given him the book. She had made a dust jacket for it out of brown paper so he could read it in public. On the spine of the jacket she had written, *American History.*

"I'd like a package of Lucky Strikes," Rhoda said, holding out a twenty-dollar bill in his direction.

"We don't sell cigarettes to minors," he said. "It's against the law."

"I'm not a minor," Rhoda said. "I'm eighteen. I'm Rhoda Manning. My daddy owns the mine."

"Which mine?" he said. He was watching her breasts as she talked, getting caught up in the apricot skin against the soft red dress.

"The mine," she said. "The Manning mine. I just got here the other day. I haven't been downtown before."

"So, how do you like our town?"

"Please sell me some cigarettes," she said. "I'm about to have a fit for a Lucky."

"I can't sell you cigarettes," he said. "You're not any more eighteen years old than my dog."

"Yes, I am," she said. "I drove here in a jeep, doesn't that prove anything?" She was looking at his wide shoulders and the tough flat chest beneath his plaid shirt.

"Are you a football player?" she said.

"When I have time," he said. "When I don't have to work on the nights they have games."

"I'm a cheerleader where I live," Rhoda said. "I just got elected again for next year."

"What kind of a jeep?" he said.

"An old one," she said. "It's filthy dirty. They use it at the mine." She had just noticed the package of Camels in his breast pocket.

"If you won't sell me a whole package, how about selling me one," she said. "I'll give you a dollar for a cigarette." She raised the twenty-dollar bill and laid it down on the glass counter.

He ignored the twenty-dollar bill, opened the cash register, removed a quarter and walked over to the jukebox. He walked with a precise, balanced sort of cockiness, as if he knew he could walk any way he wanted but had carefully chosen this particular walk as his own. He walked across the room through the rectangle of light coming in the door, walking as though he were the first boy ever to be in the world, the first boy ever to walk across a room and put a quarter into a jukebox. He pushed a button and music filled the room.

> *Kaw-Liga was a wooden Indian a-standing by the door,*
> *He fell in love with an Indian maid*
> *Over in the antique store.*

"My uncle wrote that song," he said, coming back to her. "But it got ripped off by some promoters in Nashville. I'll make you a deal," he said. "I'll give you a cigarette if you'll give me a ride somewhere I have to go."

"All right," Rhoda said. "Where do you want to go?"

"Out to my cousin's," he said. "It isn't far."

"Fine," Rhoda said. Johnny told the lone pool player to keep an eye on things and the two of them walked out into the sunlight, walking together very formally down the street to where the jeep was parked.

"Why don't you let me drive," he said. "It might be easier." She agreed and he drove on up the mountain to a house that looked deserted. He went in and returned carrying a guitar in a case, a blanket, and a quart bottle with a piece of wax paper tied around the top with a rubber band.

"What's in the bottle?" Rhoda said.

"Lemonade, with a little sweetening in it."

"Like whiskey?"

"Yeah. Like whiskey. Do you ever drink it?"

"Sure," she said. "I drink a lot. In Saint Louis we had this club called The Four Roses that met every Monday at Donna Duston's house to get drunk. I thought it up, the club I mean."

"Well, here's your cigarette," he said. He took the package from his pocket and offered her one, holding it near his chest so she had to get in close to take it.

"Oh, God," she said. "Oh, thank you so much. I'm about to die for a ciggie. I haven't had one in days. Because my father dragged me up here to make me stop smoking. He's always trying to make me do something I don't want to do. But it never works. I'm very hardheaded, like him." She took the light Johnny offered her and blew out the smoke in a small controlled stream. "God, I love to smoke," she said.

"I'm glad I could help you out," he said. "Anytime you want one when you're here you just come on over. Look," he said. "I'm going somewhere you might want to see, if you're not in a hurry to get back. You got time to go and see something with me?"

"What is it?" she asked.

"Something worth seeing," he said. "The best thing in Clay County there is to see."

"Sure," she said. "I'll go. I never turn down an adventure. Why not, that's what my cousins in the Delta always say. Whyyyyyyy not." They drove up the mountain and parked and began to walk into the woods along a path. The woods were deeper here than where Rhoda had been that morning, dense and green and cool. She felt silly walking in the woods in the little high-heeled sandals, but she held on to Johnny's hand and followed him deeper and deeper into the trees, feeling grown up and brave and romantic. I'll bet he thinks I'm the bravest girl he ever met, she thought. I'll bet he thinks at last he's met a girl who's not afraid of anything. Rhoda was walking along imagining tearing off a piece of her dress for a tourniquet in case Johnny was bit by a poisonous snake. She was pulling the tourniquet tighter and tighter when the trees opened onto a small brilliant blue pond. The water was so blue Rhoda thought for a moment it must be some sort of trick. He stood there watching her while she took it in.

"What do you think?" he said at last.

"My God," she said. "What is it?"

"It's Blue Pond," he said. "People come from all over the world to see it."

"Who made it?" Rhoda said. "Where did it come from?"

"Springs. Rock springs. No one knows how deep down it goes, but more than a hundred feet because divers have been that far."

"I wish I could swim in it," Rhoda said. "I'd like to jump in there and swim all day."

"Come over here, cheerleader," he said. "Come sit over here by me and we'll watch the light on it. I brought this teacher from New York here last year. She said it was the best thing she'd ever seen in her life. She's a writer. Anyway, the thing she likes about Blue Pond is watching the light change on the water. She taught me a lot when she was here. About things like that."

Rhoda moved nearer to him, trying to hold in her stomach.

"My father really likes this part of the country," she said. "He says people up here are the salt of the earth. He says all the people up here are direct descendants from England and Scotland and Wales. I think he wants us to move up here and stay, but my mother won't let us. It's all because the unions keep messing with his mine that he has to be up here all the time. If it wasn't for the unions everything would be going fine. You aren't for the unions, are you?"

"I'm for myself," Johnny said. "And for my kinfolks." He was tired of her talking then and reached for her and pulled her into his arms, paying no attention to her small resistances, until finally she was stretched out under him on the earth and he moved the dress from her breasts and held them in his hands. He could smell the wild smell of her craziness and after a while he took the dress off and the soft white cotton underpants and touched her over and over again. Then he entered her with the way he had of doing things, gently and with a good sense of the natural rhythms of the earth.

I'm doing it, Rhoda thought. I'm doing it. This is doing it. This is what it feels like to be doing it.

"This doesn't hurt a bit," she said out loud. "I think I love you, Johnny. I love, love, love you. I've been waiting all my life for you."

"Don't talk so much," he said. "It's better if you stop talking."

And Rhoda was quiet and he made love to her as the sun was leaving the earth and the afternoon breeze moved in the trees. Here was every possible tree, hickory and white oak and redwood and sumac and maple, all in thick foliage now, and he made love to her with great tenderness, forgetting he had set out to fuck the boss's daughter, and he kept on making love to her until she began to tighten around him, not knowing what she was doing, or where she was going, or even that there was anyplace to be going to.

Dudley was waiting outside the trailer when she drove up. There was a sky full of cold stars behind him, and he was pacing up and down and talking to himself like a crazy man. Maud was inside the trailer crying her heart out and only Joe had kept his head and was going back and forth from one to the other telling them everything would be all right.

Dudley was pacing up and down talking to Jesus. I know I had it coming, he was saying. I know goddamn well I had it coming. But not her. Where in the hell is she? You get her back in one piece and I'll call Valerie and break it off. I won't see Valerie ever again as long as I live. *But you've got to get me back my little girl. Goddammit, you get me back my girl.*

Then he was crying, his head thrown back and raised up to the stars as the jeep came banging up the hill in third gear. Rhoda parked it and got out and started walking toward him, all bravado and disdain.

Dudley smelled it on her before he even touched her. Smelled it all over her and began to shake her, screaming at her to tell him who it had been. Then Joe came running out from the trailer and threw his hundred and fifty pounds between them, and Maud was right behind him. She led Rhoda into the trailer and put her into bed and sat beside her, bathing her head with a damp towel until she fell asleep.

"I'll find out who it was," Dudley said, shaking his fist. "I'll find out who it was."

"You don't know it was anybody," Joe said. "You don't even know what happened, Mr. D. Now you got to calm down and in the morning we'll find out what happened. More than likely she's just been holed up somewhere trying to scare you."

"I know what happened," Dudley said. "I already know what happened."

"Well, you can find out who it was and you can kill him if you have to," Joe said. "If it's true and you still want to in the morning, you can kill him."

*   *   *

But there would be no killing. By the time the moon was high, Johnny Hazard was halfway between Lexington, Kentucky, and Cincinnati, Ohio, with a bus ticket he bought with the fifty dollars he'd taken from Rhoda's pocket. He had called the poetry teacher and told her he was coming. Johnny had decided it was time to see the world. After all, that very afternoon a rich cheerleader had cried in his arms and given him her cherry. There was no telling what might happen next.

Much later that night Rhoda woke up in the small room, hearing the wind come up in the trees. The window was open and the moon, now low in the sky and covered with mist, poured a diffused light upon the bed. Rhoda sat up in the bed and shivered. Why did I do that with him? she thought. Why in the world did I do that? But I couldn't help it, she decided. He's so sophisticated and he's so good-looking and he's a wonderful driver and he plays a guitar. She moved her hands along her thighs, trying to remember exactly what it was they had done, trying to remember the details, wondering where she could find him in the morning.

But Dudley had other plans for Rhoda in the morning. By noon she was on her way home in a chartered plane. Rhoda had never been on an airplane of any kind before, but she didn't let on.

"I'm thinking of starting a diary," she was saying to the pilot, arranging her skirt so her knees would show. "A lot of unusual things have been happening to me lately. The boy I love is dying of cancer in Saint Louis. It's very sad, but I have to put up with it. He wants me to write a lot of books and dedicate them to his memory."

The pilot didn't seem to be paying much attention, so Rhoda gave up on him and went back into her own head.

In her head Bob Rosen was alive after all. He was walking along a street in Greenwich Village and passed a bookstore with a window full of her books, many copies stacked in a pyramid with her picture on every cover. He recognized the photograph, ran into the bookstore, grabbed a book, opened it and saw the dedication. *To Bob Rosen, Te Amo Forever, Rhoda.*

Then Bob Rosen, or maybe it was Johnny Hazard, or maybe this unfriendly pilot, stood there on that city street, looking up at the sky, holding the book against his chest, crying and bro-kenhearted because Rhoda was lost to him forever, this famous author, who could have been his, lost to him forever.

Thirty years later Rhoda woke up in a hotel room in New York City. There was a letter lying on the floor where she had thrown it when she went to bed. She picked it up and read it again. *Take my name off that book,* the letter said. *Imagine a girl with your advantages writing a book like that. Your mother is so ashamed of you.*

Goddamn you, Rhoda thought. Goddamn you to hell. She climbed back into the bed and pulled the pillows over her head. She lay there for a while feeling sorry for herself. Then she got up and walked across the room and pulled a legal pad out of a briefcase and started writing.

Dear Father,

You take *my* name off those checks you send those televi-sion preachers and those goddamn right-wing politicians. That name has come to me from a hundred generations of men and women . . . also, in the future let my mother speak for herself about my work.

Love,
Rhoda

Some Blue Hills at Sundown

IT WAS THE LAST TIME Rhoda would ever see Bob Rosen in her life. Perhaps she knew that the whole time she was driving to meet him, the long drive through the November fields, down the long narrow state of Kentucky, driving due west, then across the Ohio River and up into the flat-topped hills of Southern Illinois.

If it had been any other time in her life or any other boyfriend she would have been stopping every fifty miles to look at herself in the mirror or spray her wrists with perfume or smooth the wrinkles from her skirt. As it was she drove steadily up into the hills with the lengthening shadows all around her. She didn't glance at her watch, didn't worry about the time. He would be there when she got there, waiting at the old corrugated building where he worked on his car, the radio playing, his cat sitting on a shelf by the Tune Oil, watching. Nothing would have changed. Only she was two months older and he was two months older and there had been another operation. When he got home from the hospital he had called her and said, "Come on if you can. I'll be here the rest of the semester. Come if you want to. Just let me know." So she had told her mother and father that if they didn't let her go she would kill herself and they believed her, so caught up in their terrible triangle and half-broken marriage and tears and lies and sadness that they couldn't fight with her that year. Her mother tried to stop it.

"Don't give her a car to go up there and see that college boy," her mother said. "Don't you dare do that, Dudley. I will leave you if you do."

So her father had loaned her the new Cadillac, six thousand dollars' worth of brand-new car, a fortune of a car in nineteen fifty-three, and she had driven up to Southern Illinois to see Bob Rosen and tell him that she loved him. No, just to see him and look at his face. No, to watch him work on his car. No, to smell the kind soft whiteness of his cheeks. To see him before he died. Untold madness of the dark hour. "Now by this moon, before this moon shall wane, I shall be dead or I shall be with you."

He was waiting for her. Not working on the car. Not even inside the building. Standing outside on the street, leaning against the building, smoking a cigarette and waiting. One foot on top of the other foot, his soft gray trousers loose around the ankles, his soft white skin, his tall lanky body fighting every minute for its life.

"Hello," he said. "I'm glad to see you. Let me see this god-damn car. Where did you get this car? My God, that's some car."

"He's getting rich. Just like he said he would. Who cares. I hate it there. There isn't anything to do. No one to talk to. I think about you all the time." He slid into the driver's seat and turned around and took her into his arms. It was the first time in two months that she had been happy. Now, suddenly, it seemed as if this moment would be enough to last forever, would make up for all the time that would follow.

"I ought to just turn around and go home now," she said. "I guess I just wanted to make sure you were real."

"It wouldn't be a good idea to get in the habit of loving me. I shouldn't have let you come up here."

"I asked to come."

"So you did. Well, look here. Let's go to the Sweet Shop and get a sandwich and see who's there. I'll bet you haven't eaten all day."

"I don't want to eat anything." She pulled away. "I want to do it. You said you'd do it to me. You promised me. You swore you would."

"When did I do that?"

"You know."

"Rhoda, Rhoda, Rhoda. Jesus. Exactly where did you envision this deflowering taking place?"

"In the car, I guess. Or anywhere. Where do people go?"

"I don't go anywhere with sixteen-year-old girls. I'd go to jail, that's where I'd go. Come here." He pulled her across his legs and kissed her again, then turned around toward the steering wheel and turned on the ignition. "Talk while I drive. I'll take you out to the roadside park. It's completely dark out there. You can see a thousand stars. Remember that night Doc Stanford was here from Louisville and we played music out there? You were having that goddamn slumber party and I had to take all your goddamn friends to get you out of the house. My friends still haven't let me stop hearing about that. That cousin of yours from Mississippi was there. Do you remember that night?"

"You won't do it?"

"Hell, no, I won't do it. But I want to. If it gives you any satisfaction you'd better believe I want to." They were cruising very slowly down a dark street that led upward through a field of poplars. There was one streetlight at the very top of the deserted street. "I drive by your house every now and then. It seems like the whole street died when your family left. Everyone misses you. So your father's doing well?"

"They're getting a divorce. He's having an affair and my

mother acts like she's crazy. That's why I got to come. They're too busy to care what I do. They sent Dudley off to a boys' school and next year I'm going to Virginia. I'll never get to come back here. If we don't do it tonight, we never will. That's what's going to happen, isn't it?"

"No, we are going to the Sweet Shop and get a malt and a ham sandwich and see who's there. Then I'm going to take you over to the Buchanans' house where you're supposed to be before someone calls out the state cops. Did you call and tell them you're in town?"

"No, they don't even know I'm coming. No one knows but Augusta. And Jane Anne. She had to tell Jane Anne." He shook his head and pulled her very close to him. She was so close to him she could feel him breathe. I'm like a pet dog to him, she decided. I'm just some little kid he's nice to. He doesn't even listen to what I say. What does he want me here for? He doesn't need me for a thing. It was dark all around them now, the strange quiet weekend dark of small midwestern towns in the innocent years of the nineteen fifties. Rhoda shuddered. It was so exciting. So terrible and sad and exciting, so stifled and sad and terrible and real. This is really happening, she was thinking. This feeling, this loving him more than anything in the world and in a second it will be over. It ends as it happens and it will never be again in any way, never happen again or stop happening. It is so thick, so tight around me. I think this is what those old fairy tales meant. This is how those old stories always made me feel.

"I want you to know something," he said. He had stopped the car. "I want you to know that I would have made love to you if I had been well. If you had been older and I had been well and things had been different. You are wonderful girl, Rhoda. A blessing I got handed that I can't ever figure out. DeLisle loves you. You know that? He asks me about you all the time. He says he can't figure out what I did to deserve you writing me letters all the time."

"I don't want to talk about DeLisle."

"I'm taking you to the Sweet Shop now." He put the brake on the car and kissed her for a very long time underneath the streetlight. Their shadows were all around them and the wind moved the light and made the street alive with shadows and they held each other while the wind blew the light everywhere and her fingers found the scars on his neck and behind his ear and caressed them and there was nothing else to say or nothing else to do and they expanded and took in the sadness and shared it.

After a while he started the car and they went to the Sweet Shop and ate ham sandwiches and talked to people and then drove over to the Buchanans' house and he left her there and walked the six blocks home with his hands in his pockets. He was counting the months he might live. He thought it would be twenty-four but it turned out to be a lifetime after all.

Net of Jewels

AFTER THE NIGHT with Stanley I decided to settle down. I had had all the blind dates and sorority bullshit I could bear. Sorority meetings were held in a hot cramped attic room with everyone sworn to secrecy at the door. After we swore we sat around and talked about appointing people to committees and how to raise the grade-point average. Then we voted on things and planned the initiation ceremony.

I had been going to meetings regularly ever since I moved into the house but finally one night I couldn't take it anymore.

"Look here," I said, getting up from my chair. "The best way to raise the grade-point average is to let me go downstairs and study. I'm behind in two subjects."

"You're out of order," the president said, looking around for help. No one ever asked to leave a meeting. The girls looked embarrassed.

"I'm behind in biology lab. I need to work."

"Well, go on then. We're almost through anyway. We're almost to the prayer."

"Okay. I'm leaving." I made my escape and went down to my room and found some change and bought a couple of Butterfinger candy bars out of a machine and tried to settle down to

study. I worked on biology for a while, memorizing the classifi-
cations of animals. Then I decided to work on world history. I
was writing a paper on the Great Ages of Man. "The great ages
of man all began with political organization. There has to be a
leader, whether he is a pharaoh, a king, a caesar or a pope. The
problem comes in when the leader starts thinking he is God and
can do whatever he likes. That's why democracy was invented.
If the leader has to be voted on by the people, he has to keep in
touch with them and give them what they want."

"Rhoda." It was Irise. I hadn't seen much of her in the past few
weeks as she belonged to a different sorority and didn't go out
much except to classes.

"Irise. Where've you been? I haven't seen you in so long. I
have a thousand things to tell you." I got up and went to the
door and pulled her into the room.

"Charles William said to tell you he's got it all fixed up for
Homecoming. He got you a date with a wonderful boy. You're
going to go, aren't you? Are you still going to go with me?" She
sat down on a corner of my bed. She was all dressed up in a
green corduroy jumper and a soft white blouse with puffed
sleeves. Her face smiled out from her short brown hair. I had
forgotten how much I liked her, how much it brightened up a
room to have Irise around.

"God, I'm glad to see you. Everybody's driving me crazy."

"Can you go? He wants us to call him tonight and talk to
him about it."

"When is it?"

"Weekend after next. Can you go? Will you go? He's building the Wreck again, this thing they build out of old cars. His
won last year. It was a mountain made of beer cans with a goat
on top."

"God, yes, I'll go. I'm dying to get away from here. I shouldn't have moved in the house, Irise. They're driving me crazy. I have to study in the middle of the night. So what's his name, my wonderful date?"

"His name's Malcolm. Charles William sent me a picture to show you. Isn't he cute? Charles William said he was a Greek god." She produced a photograph of a young man with a crew cut that stood straight up on end and big features and a somber smile. I took it from her and stared down into the paper eyes. Paper and silver oxide, black and white and shadows, icon, omen, prophecy? Do the genes know what they are seeking? Do our ends seek our beginnings?

"Don't you think he's cute?"

"I guess so. What's wrong with his hair?"

"He was Charles William's roommate last year. Charles William says he's a Greek god."

"Well, I want to go. You know I want to go."

"You have to buy an airline ticket. It costs twenty-six dollars."

"That's okay. How old is this guy?"

"The same as us. He's a sophomore."

"He looks like a baby."

"I think that was taken last year. We can get the airline tickets at the airport. Oh, Rhoda, you can wear your green dress we bought at Helen's."

"I hope it fits." I got up from the bed and rummaged around in my crowded messy closet for the dress. Right before we had gone back to school in September Charles William and Irise and I had gone shopping. Under Charles William's tutelage I had bought an emerald green satin dress cut down so low in the bosom my nipples almost showed. It had a bustle of green satin in the back and was so tight I could hardly zip it.

"I think you're going to like this boy," Irise giggled again. "Charles William says you're going to like him a lot."

*   *   *

Prophetic. Twelve days later on a Friday afternoon Irise and I boarded a Southern Airlines plane and flew from Tuscaloosa to Atlanta. The plane bobbed up and down in the clouds, gained and lost altitude without warning. Passengers clutched their airsickness bags, wrote mental wills, prayed to be forgiven, prayed to live. But I was too excited to be scared. I sat by Irise and thought about my luggage. I had three pieces of luggage and a hat box. In one suitcase was my green satin dress and some silver slippers and a pair of elbow-length white gloves and a Merry Widow and a girdle and some nylon hose. In another I had three sweaters, three skirts, three blouses, six pairs of underpants, three brassieres, four pairs of socks, some penny loafers and a suit. I was carrying the third piece of luggage, a cosmetic kit with my cosmetics and a fitted jewelry case and a book. *The Collected Poetry of Emily Dickinson.* I took out the book and began reading it as the plane dropped fifty feet, then recovered, then dropped again. I tore off a piece of airsickness bag to mark a poem.

> *I died for Beauty — but was scarce*
> *Adjusted in the Tomb,*
> *When One who died for Truth, was lain*
> *In an adjoining Room —*

"'Betrayed at length by no one but the wind whispering to the wing of the plane,'" I said out loud. "Edna Millay. How do you feel?"

"I feel okay. There's nothing to be afraid of. Birds fly, don't they?" She put her hand on top of mine. "We're going to have so much fun. We're going to have a wonderful time." The plane lurched again, then seemed to settle down. Outside the window were fields of clouds. Like a recurrent dream I had when I was small of being rolled in layers of clouds. I would wake from the dream dripping with sweat and run and jump into my mother's bed.

"How long does it take? I forgot what they said."

"An hour and forty minutes. I think forty have gone by, don't you? At least forty."

" 'The young are so old. They are born with their fingers crossed. We shall get no help from them.' That's another part of the poem."

"You always tell me poetry. Tell me the one about your children are not your children." She snuggled her shoulders down into the seat. I leaned toward her and began to recite *The Prophet*. " 'Then said, Almitra, speak to us of love. And he raised his head and looked upon the people, and there fell a stillness upon them. And with a great voice he said: When love beckons to you, follow him, though his ways are hard and steep. And when his wings enfold you yield to him, though the sword hidden among his pinions may wound you. And when he speaks to you believe in him, though his voice may shatter your dreams as the north wind lays waste the garden.' "

"Oh, it's so beautiful. That's how it is."

"When did you start loving Charles William?"

"I always did. We went to kindergarten together. His momma would take me in their car. He's always lived right there on the corner and I lived in my house. I haven't ever had another boyfriend. I wouldn't know what to do with anyone else." She turned her face to mine. Her freckles stood up on her nose. Her beautiful small hands lay in her lap. The motors roared outside the window. The propellers turned. "He always takes care of me."

"We're going to have a wonderful time," I said. "I bet it's going to be the best weekend there ever was."

"Do you know the part about the children? About your children are not your children?"

"Oh, yeah. 'Your children are not your children. They are the sons and daughters of Life's longing for itself. . . . You may give them your love but not your thoughts . . . for they dwell in the house of tomorrow, which you cannot visit, not even in your dreams.' Is that the part?"

"I love that. I love to hear you say it."

"What time is it?" She looked down at her dainty little platinum watch and told me the time. "I'm going to sleep," I said. "I'm going to sleep until we get there." Then I closed my eyes and went into a dream of Almitra standing before the assembled people of some ancient village. The people moved their heads and swayed back and forth to the wisdom of her language.

Fifty-seven minutes later Irise woke me and handed me a piece of chewing gum. "We're almost there," she said. "You can see the city." The plane lurched toward the ground. We stuck the gum in our mouths, chewed furiously. A baby screamed. Our ears popped, the motors roared. We slammed into the ground and rolled down the runway.

"There they are," she said. "They're waiting for us." The plane came to a stop near the end of a board-floored covered walkway. Charles William and a tall boy in a blue shirt stood at the very edge of the walkway. Charles William was waving his hands in the air.

"What do you think?" Irise asked. "How do you think he looks?"

We climbed down the stairway from the plane and the young men walked out to meet us. Then we walked back down the boardwalk four abreast. I had barely glanced at Malcolm. I was having a hard time remembering his name. "Oh, God," I said. "You should have seen this baby on the plane. It screamed all the time. I wouldn't have a baby for all the tea in China. If I had a baby, I'd give it away."

"When's the Wreck Parade?" Irise asked. "Are we going to be on time?"

"It's in the morning," Charles William answered. "All we have to do this afternoon is get you settled and go eat dinner. Oh, Dee, there's this fabulous record shop I want to take you to. Then we're going to dinner at Cotton's Gin. Then there's a party at the house."

"Oh, God. I can't wait. Where are we going to stay?"

"At Putty LaValle's apartment. She's from Dunleith. She's gone for the weekend. She's letting you have the place."

"Oh, God. I can't wait." I stepped in a crack between the boards and caught my heel. "Well, goddamnit." I threw my pocketbook down and tried to extricate my foot. Malcolm knelt down beside me and took hold of my ankle and pulled it out of my shoe. Then he pulled the shoe up from the crack and put it on my foot. He kept his hand on my calf. I stood very still. Charles William and Irise faded into the background. I looked down into his face. He stood up beside me. "I'm glad you could come," he said. "I'm really glad you're here."

We collected the luggage and piled it into Charles William's car. Two of my suitcases had to go in the backseat. Because of that I ended up riding into Atlanta on Malcolm's lap. Talk about libido. Talk about desire. I didn't understand what we were into but I guess he did since he had been raised on a cattle farm. "You sure do smell good," he said at one point. "That's nice perfume." More profound, Anna said she should have written. And much, much older.

"It's Nuit de Noël," I said. "My mother always wears it on her furs."

"Dee," Charles William was saying from the front seat. "Did you bring the green dress? I can't wait for you to see this record shop. The owner is a friend of mine. He's dying to meet you.

Malcolm, you're going to have to give her to me for a while. I have a surprise for her." Irise leaned into his arm, happy that he loved me too. What a strange and gentle girl she was and without jealousy. A girl who could believe that she was loved.

We drove down into the neighborhoods near the Georgia Tech campus. The fraternity houses were decorated and boys and girls were in the yards drinking beer and putting the finishing touches on the Wrecks.

"What are they about?" I asked. "What do they have to do?"

"They have to run." Malcolm laughed and moved me from one side of his knees to the other. I was sweating in my wool suit. My body was suffused with heat and I squirmed around and pulled off my jacket. The smell of the starch in his shirt, the smell of shaving lotion and the fine hard line of his head beneath his crewcut. His green eyes and thick lips *so near to me I could hear him breathing.* "What are you going to do with all those suitcases?" he said. "What do you have in all of them?"

"We have to have them." Irise turned around on the seat and smiled her bright freckled smile. "Wait till you see this green dress. Then you won't mind carrying them for her."

"There's the shopping center," Charles William called out. "There's the record store. There it is." He pulled into a parking place and we all piled out and went into the store and were introduced to the owner. Then Charles William took my arm and pulled me around a corner and into a soundproof room with a turntable and bins full of classical records and Caedmon recordings of poets reading their poetry. At that time customers were allowed to play records before they bought them. "I've been dying to play this for you," Charles William said. "I can't wait till you hear it." He took a recording out of its cover and put it on the turntable. "Listen, Dee, just listen to this." He dropped the needle into its groove and Siobhan McKenna's incomparable voice began to speak the Molly Bloom soliloquy from *Ulysses.*

"Yes because he never did a thing like that before as ask to get his breakfast in bed with a couple of eggs since the *City Arms* hotel when he used to be pretending to be laid up with a sick voice doing his highness to make himself interesting to that old faggot Mrs. Riordan that he thought he had a great leg of and she never left us a farthing all for masses for herself and her soul greatest miser ever was actually afraid to lay out 4d for her methylated spirit telling me all her ailments she had too much chat in her about politics and earthquakes and the end of the world let us have a bit of fun first God help the world if all the women were her sort down on bathingsuits and lownecks of course nobody wanted her to wear I suppose she was pious because no man would look at her twice . . ." I was gasping with delight. It was the book Sarah Worley's sister had studied at Wellesley. It was the book about Ireland. "Oh, God, Charles William, I've been looking for that. I can't believe it's on a record. Let me see the cover."

"It's Siobhan McKenna, Dee. Someday we'll go to London and hear all these people and see them on the stage. We'll go and spend a summer and hear all the great people of the world and talk to them. We won't always be here, in this little place where we were born. But, listen, listen to it."

". . . O, tragic and the dyinglooking one off the south circular when he sprained his foot at the choir party at the sugarloaf Mountain the day I wore that dress Miss Stack bringing him flowers the worst old ones she could find at the bottom of the basket anything at all to get into a mans bedroom with her old maids voice . . ."

"Oh, God, I can't believe you found this."

"Isn't it beautiful? Isn't her voice the greatest thing you ever heard?" He drew near to me. His sweet embattled face above his wide soft powerful body moved in to tell me once again what he needed so desperately for me to know. "Davie discovered it. He brought me here. I want you to meet him while you're here, Dee."

"Who is Davie?"

"A boy who's very special to me. A freshman from Valdosta. I'm gay, Dee. You never listen when I try to tell you that. I love Irise. I'm going to marry her. But I like Davie too. He wants to meet you. You're going to love each other. I know you will."

I spun around, pulled a record out of a bin, shook my head, tried not to hear it. I did not want to let it in. I wanted the world to be something I could understand. I was not safe enough to grow into a larger understanding. If I changed my spin I might disappear, be dissolved, sink back into sand, heat, broom, air, as Anna would later write. "Stone walls do not a prison make, nor iron bars a cage." Where had I heard that? Why could I not forget it? How did I know that it was true so long ago and so encapsulated and so lost?

"What are you all doing in here?" Irise came into the room. "What are you listening to?"

"I thought we were going out to eat," Malcolm said. He followed Irise into the room and came and stood by me. "I thought we were going to eat and then take you to where you're staying."

My eyes met Charles William's around their heads. I didn't smile or frown or react. I couldn't react because I didn't know what to think. It was very dangerous, what he had told me, and I didn't want to be involved in danger.

"Well, let's go then," I said. "Bring the record, Charles William. We'll buy it and take it home." I took hold of Malcolm's arm. His arm was as strong as my daddy's. I leaned into his arm, into his one hundred and twenty-five I.Q. and his normalcy. What passes in the world for normalcy. I decided to ignore what Charles William had been telling me. I didn't see what I could do about it. I didn't want to be involved in it. So I turned my attention to Malcolm Martin and his perfect body and decided to forget it. "Not that I care two straws who he does it with or knew before that way though I'd like to find out so long as I don't have the two of them under my nose all the time like that slut that Mary . . ." Charles William lifted the needle from the groove and picked up the record and slid it into its cover and handed it to me. Then he pulled a second recording out of a bin and laid it on top of the first one. It was Edna St. Vincent Millay. My favorite poet. A recording of her voice. No one else gives me such gifts, a poet would later write, and I would think of Charles William when I read it.

We paid for the records and left the store and went across the street to a restaurant called Cotton's Gin and went inside and were seated at long plank tables. We ordered beer and salads and platters of french fries. "Tell about the Wreck," Irise said. "Tell us what it looks like."

"It's hidden." Charles William waved his beer glass in the air. "Over by the engineering building. We finished it last night. It's a surprise. You'll see it in the morning."

"It's the best one we've ever had," Malcolm added. "One of our alumni saw it. He said it was the best one he'd ever seen. It's sure to win."

"I wanted to decorate the house to match it but they made me stop." Charles William laughed again. "Davie and I started on a sofa, making it match the Wreck decor, but they all came in and stopped us."

"You wouldn't believe what he did." Malcom finished his beer and moved closer to me. He put his hand on my arm as he talked. Later he put his hand on my leg and I let him leave it there. This was what I had been waiting for. Poetry and music and gay conversation. Yes, I said in Molly's voice. Yes and yes and yes and yes. I forgot the disturbing elements of Charles William's life. I forgot everything but Malcolm's hand on my leg and the way it made me feel. By the time we finished lunch all I wanted in the world was to let him kiss me. Later he did kiss me, on the way to the apartment in the car and on the couch in the living room while Charles William and Irise did whatever they were doing in the bedroom.

The green dress, that's part of what happened next whether anyone wants to believe it or not. Last week, when Charles William called me from the hospital to talk for seven hours, the first thing he wanted to talk about was that dress. "Do you remember that green dress, Dee?" he asked. "That you wore to Homecoming with Malcolm?"

"Of course I do. How could anyone forget that dress? I would never even have tried it on if you hadn't been with me."

"You were gorgeous in it."

"I was, wasn't I? Or anyway I thought I was and I guess that's the same thing."

A green satin dress, the green of Irish hills, so very green, so shiny and tight and short, cut down so low in the bosom that my nipples almost showed. Only Charles William could have found that dress and made me believe I was beautiful in it. Only Charles William could have talked me into wearing it. I put it on that night with my gold high-heeled sandals and wore it out to vamp poor Malcolm Martin who was already thoroughly vamped from my having sat on his lap all the way into Atlanta. Poor Malcolm Martin, a boy as vain and cold and unloving as my father, a perfect match for my animus.

Later, much much later, we locked ourselves into the bedroom of Putty LaValle's apartment and I took off the dress and we did it. Whatever I had thought doing it would be, this was

more terrible and exciting and interesting and endless than anything I could have imagined and even if I was doing it wrong I
wanted to go on doing it.

"You might get pregnant," he said at last. "I have to get some
rubbers if we're going to keep on doing this."

"Are we going to?"

"I don't see why not. I hope so."

"Do you love me?"

"I guess so. Sure, I think I do."

"Well, I love you. I can tell you that. I think I love you to
death." I had pulled the sheet up around my breasts. Doing it
was bad enough. Letting someone look at my breasts was going
too far. "Where are Charles William and Irise?"

"I don't know. Are they in the living room? I don't know if
they came in or not. I wasn't listening."

"How will we find out?"

"We better look. God, we're drunk, aren't we? What time is
it?"

"It's four-fifteen."

"I'm going to look out the door." I got up and found a bath-
robe and put it on and looked out the door. Irise was asleep on
the sofa. Charles William was nowhere to be seen. A light was
burning in the kitchen.

"Come back to bed," he said. "Let's get some sleep."

"Okay. I guess it's too late to worry about them anyway." I
lay back down beside him and covered us with the bedclothes.
Then I curled up into his arms and fell asleep. I had done it. I
was as good as married.

The next morning Charles William introduced me to Davie.
We were at the KA house waiting for the Wreck Parade to
begin. Our Wreck had already been hauled by truck to the
starting line on Shaw Street. It was a surreal room mounted on

the chassis of a yellow jeep. Walls melted down into the wheels. Windows curved down into the seats. The steering wheel was an ellipse of melted stars. A fake motor was mounted on the side. Colored smoke poured out of the motor, red, yellow, blue, green. An engineering major was driving the thing. All Charles William had to do was stand on the street and watch it go by and wait to pick up his award as the designer.

"Dee, come here a minute." He was drinking a Bloody Mary from a silver mint julep cup. "Come back here with me, I want you to meet someone." He took my hand and led me into the kitchen where a boy with golden hair was polishing glasses with a cloth.

"This is Davie," Charles William said. "Davie, this is Dee. I want you two to love each other." The young man put down the cloth and the glass and held out a hand to me. He was shorter than Charles William, not much taller than I was, but he was very beautiful, as beautiful as a girl. He smiled at me and held out his hand. Charles William bent down and kissed him on the cheek. Light poured in the kitchen windows onto the brass pots hanging above the stove. Light rang out against the brass and fell down onto the painted cabinets and spotted our arms and hands.

"I'm so glad to know you, Dee," Davie said. "He talks about you all the time. He thinks you're wonderful."

"I need to go find Malcolm," I said. "I want to walk on down and see where the parade is going to start."

"Davie's in architecture," Charles William went on. "He's my assistant this semester. We're building a cathedral all of wood, aren't we, Davie?" He still had his arm around him. He was holding him as he would a girl. Their bodies melted into each other. Surreal. "So you and Malcolm hit it off." He giggled. "I tried to talk to him this morning, but all he would say is that you're pretty."

"What did he say?"

"I said, Don't you think she's gorgeous? and he said yes."

"What else did he say?"

"Not much. He doesn't talk much, haven't you noticed that by now?"

"I think I'm in love with him. I mean it." I took Charles William's hand. I forgot Davie was there. "Do you think he likes me? Did he say he did?"

"I told you, he said you were gorgeous. And you are, isn't she, Davie?"

"She sure is. I've been dying to meet you, Dee. He talks about you all the time."

"Well, I'm going to go and find Malcolm." I stood in the circle of the two young men. The three of us were perfectly safe at that moment, safe in each other's good graces with the sunlight pouring down through the windows and the morning of the world all around us. "I think I'll get a Bloody Mary," I added. "Is that a pitcher of them over there?"

"I'll pour you one." Davie took the glass he had been polishing and filled it with ice and poured in vodka and Bloody Mary mix. He handed it to me.

"Thank you. I'm going to find Malcolm. Are you sure I look all right?"

"Wait a minute," Charles William said. "Get me a comb." I took a comb out of my pocketbook and then, as if it were the most important thing in the world, Charles William combed my bangs down across my forehead and stood back to admire his work. "Perfect," he said. "You look absolutely beautiful."

"She does," Davie added. "You're gorgeous, Dee." I took my Bloody Mary, and, believing I was beautiful, I went back into the living room and found Malcolm and made him believe it too. We walked out onto the sidewalk and started down the hill toward the engineering school. The sidewalks were lined with young men and women in bright fall clothes. The sky was a brilliant blue. The sycamore trees golden in the clear fall air. An incorruptible mirror that cannot be contaminated by experience, Anna once wrote, meaning life. So I suppose whatever price Malcolm and I were going to have to pay for that day's ecstasy would be the proper price. "I love you," I said and took his arm.

"I love you too. You want to go back to Putty's apartment after a while?"

"I have the key." His leg brushed against mine. A marching band began to play. The first Wreck hove into view, a vehicle with a bed mounted on top. On the bed were two young men dressed as women. They were wearing pantaloons and huge balloon breasts and they were locked in an embrace. Now even the trees seemed sexual, locked in the ground by their roots. The sycamore leaves made golden beds upon the grass. Light coming down between the buildings seemed a sexual thrust. I looked up into Malcolm's face. There were specks of gold in his green eyes. Gold on the freckles of his arms.

"Let's go now," he said. "We don't need to see this damn parade."

There was a party at the house that night and Malcolm drank gin martinis and danced a crazy dance he learned from his mother's gardener. "I call it the hootchy-cootchy," he would yell, and laugh uproariously and do it again. His legs and feet moved like liquid. I could barely keep up with him. "Oh, it's me and I'm in love again," he kept singing. "Oh, it's me and I'm in love again."

At intermission I went out into the backyard. One of Charles William's projects had been turning the backyard of the KA house into a garden. There were rows of holly bushes and flower beds and a goldfish pond. Charles William and Davie were standing by the pond. As I watched, Charles William took Davie in his arms and kissed him on the mouth. He knows I'm watching, I thought. He knows I see him doing that. I was in a strange conflicted sensual mood anyway. The things that Malcolm and I had been doing all afternoon were all over me. I didn't feel guilty about doing them, just surprised and interested and amazed. I turned away from the pond. I thought of the weight of Malcolm's body on mine, the smell and taste of him, how I had thought I could kiss through his shoulder to the bone and taste the birth of blood. I had melted into his body and he into mine and that was what was meant by love. And that was what Charles William was doing now to Davie.

"Rhoda, where are you?" It was Malcolm, coming across the patio looking for me. "Come dance with me," I said. "I want to dance some more."

"What's going on?" He looked toward the pond. "Oh, that. Well, he won the Wreck Parade for us, didn't he?"

"Why is he kissing Davie?" I took his arm. "Why is he kissing him?"

"Don't you know, Rhoda? You really don't know?"

"No. And I don't want to stay here anymore. I want to leave. I'm sick of this party. Sick of people getting drunk. Let's go back to Putty's. I want to leave right now."

"I can't leave right now. Come on inside. Don't worry about other people." He led me back into the crowded living room. The KA's and their dates were becoming sweaty and wrinkled and incoherent. I saw Irise in a corner dancing with her cousin from Dunleith. A harsh yellow light filled the hallway near the front door, fell down the stairs into the darkened room where everyone was dancing. "I have to get out of here," I said. "I'm very sensitive, Malcolm. Sometimes I can't stand to be in crowds."

*   *   *

We found my coat and my sequined scarf and my white gloves with rhinestones sewn around the cuffs and got into the car and drove back to Putty's. "I have to leave in the morning," I said. "How can I go home after this? How can I leave you?"

"You can come back up. You can write to me. We can write each other letters. Come sit by me. Come over here. Put your hand back on my leg."

"I can't leave you. I won't be able to leave after this." I began to cry. Terrible tears rolled down my cheeks. I held on to his sleeve. It was Saturday night. The next afternoon I would leave. "Why did we start doing that? We shouldn't have done it. What did we do it for? Now I have to leave you. How can I go away?"

"It's all right. We'll see each other again. You can come up any time you want to." He patted my leg. He drove the car. We were going back to Putty's. We would do it again and then I would go away and never see him. It was the same thing always with my life. If something was valuable to me it would disappear. No one would ever be there to hold me in their arms when I needed them. I would always be wandering through strange houses, through unknown rooms. Malcolm pulled the car over to the side of the street and turned off the motor and pulled me into his arms. He held me while I cried. "It's all right, Rhoda," he said. "We'll see each other again very soon. It isn't only you, you know. I'm in this too." He held me away from him. He began to laugh, a wonderful boyish happy laugh. "Oh, it's me and I'm in love again," he sang in a crazy voice. "I'm in love in Georgia. Hootchy-cootchy's in the air."

It was a full moon. We did it again that night and when he left I slept and dreamed of horses racing down hills toward the water. In the middle of the night Irise came in and got in bed with me and put her small sweet hands on my back and patted me awhile. In the morning I started menstruating. Rich red blood poured out of my body so I didn't even have to fear that I was pregnant.

At eleven Malcolm and Charles William came and got us and took us out to breakfast and then took us to the airport and put us on the plane.

"You fell in love with him, didn't you?" Irise asked, when we were high above the city, rocking our way south and west to Tuscaloosa.

"Why are people always leaving each other? It seems like a dumb thing to do."

"It's just when you're young. When you get older I think you stay."

So I WENT to Atlanta for the summer. I enrolled in summer school at Emory University and moved into a dorm overlooking the medical school. It had been reasonably tricky talking my parents into the plan but I persevered and they were so caught up in their new life in Dunleith with their seven hundred admiring friends coming over to get drunk on the porch every night that they weren't as wary as they had been in the small world of Franklin, Kentucky. Also, they were sick of my sarcasm and tired of my refusal to be polite to their endless stream of visitors. They were probably relieved to think I would be somewhere in summer school. They could say to their relatives, Oh, yes, Rhoda's in summer school at Emory. She's such a bookworm, yes, she's a mess but what can we do. A mess, that's the word my north Alabama relatives used to describe me. They had had other messes to contend with, my fox-hunting grandfather being one and Tallulah Bankhead another, but in my generation I was the main mess. So I got to do what I wanted that summer, while my daddy made money and my momma spent it and my brother Dudley and his wife, Annie, tried to make a marriage out of a real mess and my little brothers threw basketballs through the hoop and shot at each other with BB guns and chased goats through the woods at Finley Island and the porch filled up at night with whiskey drinkers. When I read the *Odyssey* I thought of Dunleith. How the suitors filled our porches and drank our wine and ate our meat.

I had hardly been in Atlanta a week when I started wanting to get married. It was too hard to do it if we weren't married. It was impossible to do it in the car. It just wasn't big enough. And it was hard to do it in Malcolm's room in the KA house because people kept slamming in and out the front door and scaring me to death and because half the time we had to sneak out the kitchen door when we got through. Don't get me wrong. Doing it was worth it. Doing it was divine. The more we did it, the more I wanted to do it and the more he wanted to do it. All we wanted to do was do it. It was what we had in common and it was plenty.

"Don't you want to get married?" I asked him finally. We were parked outside the Echo Hot Dog Stand, The World's Largest Drive-In. The place was a great favorite with Tech boys and their dates. On any given night we would see two or three couples we knew. Couples coupling in their cars, couples eating hot dogs and drinking Cokes, couples in varying stages of emotional excitement and disarray. I'll say one thing for Malcolm and me, we were up to the task. We didn't have enough guilt or depression between us to fill an ashtray. "Everyone's running away," I added, taking a Parliament out of a box and lighting it with the car lighter. "We wouldn't have to tell anyone. We could keep it a secret."

"I don't know."

"Why not? You love me, don't you? Then we could rent a little apartment and have a place to do it. God, it's driving me crazy not to have anywhere to do it."

"Where would we go?"

"To South Carolina, where Avery and Mary Adair ran away. Ask Avery where they went."

"They told their folks last week. They just moved into the married dorm."

"We don't have to tell anyone. I've got enough money to get us an apartment. Let's do it. Please let's do it." I moved over to his side of the seat, put my hand on his leg, moved my hand up and down his thigh. "Oh, please, Malcolm. I want to have a place to live with you. I want it so much."

"I don't know. I guess so. I guess we could. When do you want to go?" He put his hot dog down on the dashboard and turned around to me. My hand was still on his leg. Now there wasn't any hot dog or steering wheel or drive-in or car. There was only desire. I had to get some bonding energy to keep from thinking I was going to die and he had to get some pussy to keep from being in pain, so there we were, in love in Georgia, being bounced around like the electrons and protons of which we are in all probability composed.

"Next weekend. On Saturday. We could go on Friday and get married and spend the weekend. Oh, let's do it. Say we can."

"All right. If you really want to. If that's really what you want to do." He honked the horn for the waiter to come and take the tray from the window of the car. He put the half-eaten hot dog on the tray.

"I'll have to get a wedding ring," I said. "I guess we can go buy one tomorrow."

"I guess we can."

"Let's go to Stone Mountain," I added. "Let's go do it on a blanket on the ground."

Four days later, on Thursday morning, I cut all my classes and drove down to Rich's department store and went shopping. I bought a white piqué dress with pearl buttons down the front and a white satin slip and a long white negligee and a robe. I bought some white satin slippers with fuzzy white balls on the toes. I bought a book on how to have sexual intercourse. I bought a gray and white striped sundress with a jacket and some red Capezio sandals and a tube of contraceptive jelly. I went downstairs to the coffee shop and bought two doughnuts and a cup of coffee and ate the sugar off the first doughnut while I read the book. It looked as though we had been doing it right. But the stuff about getting pregnant sounded bad. I polished off the doughnut and thought it over. The redheaded black girl behind the counter came over and stood beside me looking at the cover of the book. "Is that any good?" she asked. I was the only customer in the shop so she had time to chat.

"I guess so. Except about the contraceptives. It keeps saying something works fifty percent of the time or ninety percent of the time. But it doesn't say which one is best."

"What you been doing?"

"Nothing. I'm getting married tomorrow." I looked around to make sure no one had come in. "We're running away. My boyfriend and I. We're going to Walhalla, South Carolina. So I thought maybe I should be finding out what to do."

"Better late than never, I suppose. You better get you some rubbers and start to pray. Them babies have a way of finding their way into the world."

"Have you got any?"

"I got three. Three more than I got any use for but I love them. Don't be doing any of that rhythm business. That doesn't work. Nothing works but rubbers and they don't work too good. You ought to get you a pessary or a diaphragm."

"There's a part in here about them. I guess I could go to a doctor after I get married and get one, couldn't I?"

"Honey, you don't have to be married to get one. They give them to anybody." She reached behind her and got the pot of coffee and refilled my cup. "When's the wedding going to be?"

"We're going to drive up tomorrow and get married Saturday.

You have to get the license, then you have to wait twenty-four hours before you can get married. Some friends of ours did it. So we know where to go."

"Well, I wish you luck. What you got in all them packages?"

"A wedding dress and a trousseau. I thought I ought to have a trousseau."

"Honey, I sure am glad you came in today. I'll be thinking about you tomorrow and I'll be thinking about you on Saturday. What time you think you'll be getting married?"

"About noon I guess. High noon." I giggled. "Shoot-out in Carolina." The waitress laughed with me. We kept on laughing harder and harder and she filled my cup one more time and I gobbled down the second doughnut and drank the coffee while I laughed.

A BOY AND GIRL walking into a gray stone building to get married. It is very early in the morning. He is wearing a pair of chinos. She is wearing a long white dress with tiny pearl buttons down the front. They are holding hands. Her hand is beautiful and plump and the color of apricots. His hand is large and bony and covered with fine brown hair. They look like brother and sister. Neither of them has slept in days.

"What if we can't get it?"

"We'll get it."

"Did you bring the blood tests?"

"I told you I did."

"Oh, Malcolm. I can't believe it. I can't believe we're doing it."

"I bet they aren't open."

"Yes they are. People are going in." A man wearing suspenders walked up the steps and disappeared into the heavy polished doors. Walhalla, South Carolina, June 25, 1955. Malcolm and I are going to get married.

The night before we had made love all night in a small motel room on a lumpy bed. The motel was on a rise of land surrounded by pine trees. All night the wind sang in the trees and pine needles fell on the asphalt roof above our heads. All night long we moved our hands up and down each other's bodies and told each other secrets and said a hundred times, Are you awake, are you still awake, are you asleep yet? I love, love, love you, I said a hundred times. I love you too, he answered. Get on top of me. Stay like that. Do that some more. Don't move until I tell you to.

So it went until the sun rose above the hills and we slept awhile. At eight o'clock I woke up and looked at my watch. "Get up," I said. "It's eight o'clock. Let's get up and go get married."

"Let's sleep some more. Come get back in bed."

"No. I want to do it now. I'm afraid you won't marry me. I have to do it now."

"Oh, Rhoda."

"I can't help it. It's how I am. Come on, get up, I want to be the first person married today. I want to be the first person in the world to get married on this Saturday."

"Let's sleep a little longer."

"No, I can't wait. Please get up. Please let's do it now." I picked up a pair of cotton underpants from the floor and put them on. I picked up a white satin slip and pulled it over my head. He reached out and pulled me into the bed and climbed on top of me. "Move," he said. "See if you can move."

"I want to have ten sons who look like you. Ten tall sons to carry my coffin to the grave."

"Why do you always talk about dying?" He got up and stood beside the bed. "You're only twenty years old."

"I can't help it. That's how I think."

"Don't get your feelings hurt. I'm getting dressed. Come on, see if you still have the license. You didn't lose it, did you?"

"No, it's right here. I have it here." I pulled the license out of my pocketbook and read it. He came and stood beside me. We moved into each other's arms. Electromagnetism, Aphrodite, sunspots, whatever explains such things.

"Do you want to get breakfast first?"

"No. I want to be the first person married today in South Carolina or in the world."

"Okay, get dressed. Let's go."

The sheriff of Milan County had bought a pickup truck and a motorboat with the money he had made performing marriages on weekends, he later told us. Ten dollars here, five dollars there. It added up.

"Come on in," he said. "Have a seat while I round up the bailiff. He likes to be my witness. Well, you got a pretty day for it. I'll say that. How old are you?"

"I'm twenty," I said. "He'll be twenty next month."

"Marrying an older woman. You both from Atlanta?"

"We go to school there." Malcolm shook hands solemnly with the sheriff and handed him the license.

"That will be twenty-five dollars," the sheriff said and Malcolm got out the money and handed it to him.

"We could let Denise witness it, if we can't find Bobby. There he is. Come on in, Robert. They're chomping at the bit to say the vows. Come on in. Stand by her, boy, that's the way. Take her hand. You got the ring?"

"I've got it," I said and produced it from my pocket and gave it to Malcolm. I had been wearing it off and on for days.

"Let's go then," the preacher said. "Dearly Beloved, we are gathered here in the presence of this company, to join together this man and this woman in Holy Matrimony, which is an honorable estate, instituted of God and like unto the union between the church and our maker. Therefore, let no one enter into it lightly, but reverently, soberly and in the sight of God. . . ." I looked at the book he was holding, at the light coming in the dusty window, at the suspenders, the chairs, my shoes. I did not believe I was worthy of such a moment. I could not bear such happiness.

*   *   *

An hour later we were back at the motel packing to leave. We had stopped and eaten breakfast at a small café and endured the stares of the patrons. Every Saturday at least two or three couples found their way to Walhalla to get married. We're turning into the runaway capital of the world, the citizens must have told themselves. Old Bud Halbritton's getting rich marrying kids from Atlanta. We ought to build a new motel, now that Walhalla's finally on the map.

I didn't have to wait long for the reaction to set in. We had hardly driven fifty miles back toward Atlanta before we had an argument. God knows what it was about. Maybe I touched his leg and he told me not to. Maybe he started desiring me and it embarrassed him. Maybe he was sorry he had done it and I picked that up. I am deeply intuitive about other people's reactions and there was plenty to react to that day. My mania was rising to a fever pitch. I am married, I kept saying to myself. Now I will never be alone, never be afraid, never be sad again. Isn't that true? It must be true. If getting married doesn't work, nothing will. If getting married doesn't work, I'll never be happy. Never, never, never, never, never.

"What will we do tonight?" I said finally. We were leaving the mountains and turning onto the four-lane highway. "We could go get some Italian food and celebrate. I'd really like to drink some Chianti."

"I'm going back to the house and study," he said. "I've got classes all day on Monday."

"You're going to the house? You're going to leave me?"

"We've been gone two days. . . . I'm taking ten hours, Rhoda. I have to do some work."

"We could go up to Stone Mountain and have a picnic. You can't just take me home."

"I have to take you home. I'll be up studying all night as it is."

Adoration

IT WAS CHRISTMAS in Atlanta and Rhoda was sick every day. She was so sick she could hardly go to work. She would get better, then get worse. It couldn't have happened at a more inconvenient time because she had just been promoted to the Shopping Service at J. P. Allen's Department Store. She ran up and down the stairs in a red dress buying things for people to give to other people. She ran up and down and talked on the phone to rich ladies about their shopping problems.

She was nineteen years old and she had been married six months and she was putting her husband through school. She made four hundred dollars a month and his parents gave them four hundred more and her father gave her anything she asked him for.

She had made love to a boy one night after a fraternity party. The next week they ran away and got married. A month later she was living in a garage apartment in Atlanta putting him through school. Sex had been a big surprise to Rhoda. She had felt its mighty hand.

"What are you doing this for?" Her friend Daniel, who was an artist, had stopped by the store to take her out to lunch. "Why did you quit school?"

"I had to. I have to put him through college."

"You're crazy. Throwing yourself away."

"Of course I'm crazy, darling. Aren't we all?" She laughed a wonderful sophisticated laugh. It was Rhoda's main affectation when she was nineteen to say darling as many times as possible every day. Her other obsession was learning to dress like the salesladies at J. P. Allen's, especially a slim dark woman with a bun who wore black leather heels trimmed in brass. Rhoda made four hundred dollars a month and she charged about six hundred a month to the store and her father was still coming out ahead. Then she got sick and it all stopped.

She couldn't believe this terrible sickness, this bleeding and bleeding and bleeding. She couldn't be pregnant because she almost always wore the diaphragm. She lay in bed in the garage apartment and bled and bled and bled. Her young husband sat on the edge of the bed and worried. He thought he had wounded her. He was scared to death of Rhoda's terrible blood. He wished he had never run off and married her no matter how much money her father had. It was terrible. She was a terrible cook and she followed him around all the time and now all she did was bleed.

"Let me call my aunt Lillian. You'd better go to a doctor, Rhoda. You'd better find out what's wrong."

"I can't get up. Tell the doctor to come over here."

"They don't come out in Atlanta. Let me call my aunt."

"All right. Call her then." Rhoda lay back on the pillows. The room was dark, shrouded by the bamboo blinds she had installed in all the windows. The room was a mess, clothes were scattered everywhere. She was bleeding to death in a messy room.

"You've got an appointment this afternoon. They said to bring you in."

"I can't get up."

"Yes you can. I'll help you." Then he pulled her to the side of the bed and handed her some clothes and she put them on. Then he picked her up and carried her across the room and down the stairs and out the door. At least he's strong, Rhoda told herself. At least I had enough sense to marry someone strong.

They drove downtown and parked in a parking lot and went into a building and up an elevator and the nurse met them at the door and took them inside and put her on a table. "I'm bleeding all the time," Rhoda said. "I've been bleeding for days."

"We know," the nurse said. She put her hand on Rhoda's arm and Rhoda went to sleep. Maybe she went to sleep. She never could remember what happened next or when they told her. It always seemed she heard the news from deep within a dream. When she woke up she was in the back seat of the car. Her husband was driving her to Alabama to her mother. "What are we doing?" she said. "Where are we going? What's going on?"

"We're going to Decatur. You're going to have a baby. Rhoda, please lie down."

"Oh, my God. I don't believe it. Oh, I hope it's a boy. I want a boy." She fell into a dream. She was on Finley Island by the water. Her little boy was with her. He held onto her hand. She would teach him to swim. He would swim the English Channel. He would dive from cliffs and be a hero to end all heroes. She woke up because blood was running down her legs again, over her skirt, her legs, the car. "You have to stop and buy me some Kotex," she said. "I have to have some new pajamas. I can't show up at Momma's like this." They stopped at a store in a small town on the Alabama line and she went in and bought clean clothes and a pair of blue silk pajamas and a robe. A musty-smelling lady in a bun helped her back into the car. She lay down on the seat holding her packages and when she woke again she was in the hospital and they were all around her, her mother and her father and her husband and Doctor Greer, her own doctor who was kin to her.

"Am I going to have a baby?" she asked.

"I don't know. We'll wait and see."

"Am I or not? I want to know."

"I'm not sure if you still have it. In the morning we'll know." They gave her a shot and she slept some more. She slept for eighteen hours. In the morning they bathed her and brought her food and Doctor Greer was alone with her, his snow-white head was beside her bed, his hand was on her hands. "I think we will have to go on and get rid of this one, Rhoda. There will be plenty more." Good, Rhoda thought, I didn't want to have a baby anyway. Then she began to cry. Terrible tears. Doctor Greer patted her hand and said, "This too shall pass away."

"I like it," she said. "I want it. I like it inside of me."

"All right," he said. "We'll wait another day." A nurse appeared and gave her another shot and she went back to sleep, back into the dream of the island and the water and the boy. The boy was floating away. Come back, she screamed. She tore out into the water, swimming her best Australian crawl. He drifted farther and farther away. Come back, Rhoda called, with her mouth half full of water. Come back. I want you. Come back to me. He floated on his back, so beautiful, so perfect, so new. He would not drag her down and drown her. He was her little boy. Her father appeared on the pier. "Catch him. Goddammit, Sister. Swim, show me what you're made of." A group of ladies were around her father, in their dresses and their heels and their perfume. They loved him and he loved them. He talked to them and listened when they spoke. He never pushed them away. Was never cold to them.

*   *   *

It was dark when Rhoda woke again. She thought she must have been asleep for hours. Everything was very dreamy in the room. The white curtains swayed on their stems, the silver utensils gleamed on the enamel table. A nurse with her hat awry was by her side. A needle was in her arm. Doctor Greer was so close she could smell his shaving cream. "How're we doing?" he said.

"I don't know. You tell me."

"I think it's all right, Rhoda. I think you'll keep the baby."

"Are you sure?"

"Not yet."

"Well, make up your mind. You tell me one thing and then you tell me another. Where's my husband?"

"He's here. He wants to see you." Her husband was in the doorway. He looked very handsome in his suit. He looked very sure of himself, like a grown man, tall and brave and wide. He took her hands. He kissed her very gently. "I hope it's true," he said.

"It will be a boy," Rhoda said. "I wouldn't have anything else."

They moved to the new apartment in January. Rhoda threw the last box on the bedroom floor and sank down on the bed. Her husband came into the room. The baby was asleep in his crib. He was two months old. He was perfect. He was so beautiful they looked at him all day. They looked at him so much they almost forgot to argue. They liked him so much they were almost happy.

"Don't do that," Rhoda said. "I'm out of jelly."

"We won't do anything. We'll just put it in."

"No."

"Come on."

"Okay."

"Let's make another one. They come out so nice. I want some more."

"You're crazy."

"Please."

"Okay."

"You're an angel."

"You are too."

It was an ecstatic pregnancy. Rhoda lived on diet pills and potato chips and gin. She lived on vegetable soup and cornbread and Cokes and gin. She went to the doctor every two weeks because he was the best-looking man in Atlanta. She went down one day in July and had the baby because it was coming too soon. They cut her open and took him out and sewed her back up and later that night she wrote her father a long letter. Some days later he wrote her back and sent her some money. Her mother came and stayed and took care of her and got her a new maid and bought her some books to read. It was a good month to have a baby. There was a new book by Ernest Hemingway on the shelves. *Across the River and into the Trees.* It was a wonderful book about the excitement and romance of love in Venice between a young countess and an old army colonel who was about to die. Thank God for books, Rhoda was thinking. Since nothing ever happens around here.

It was dark in the house. A dark house at the end of a curved street on a hill in Kansas City, Kansas. It was two o'clock in the morning and it was Rhoda's birthday. She had been twenty-six years old for two drunken hours and she woke up in the dark and felt for her husband and began to laugh at something they had done at a bar. Drunk, drunk, drunk. They had been drunk since six o'clock the night before and they hadn't even had a fight yet. "Make love to me," she said. "I mean it. Do it now."

"Go put on your diaphragm."

"I don't want to. Use a rubber."

"Oh, shit, that's no good."

"It will do." She reached in a drawer beside the bed and got one out that had been there for ages. They began to giggle, laughing and making love because it felt good and was fun. In a while it became apparent that the rubber was not doing a bit of good. "Go take a douche."

"Oh, shit, I'm too tired to move."

"Go on."

"All right." She climbed out of bed and went into the bathroom and turned on the light and stood against the doorframe giggling some more. She was wearing a white silk nightgown with blue embroidery on the top and she was making a baby right that very minute and she knew it and she didn't give a damn because it was her birthday and she thought it was funny. He would be a laughing baby who would love music and have a thousand freckles. I might as well go on and have him and get it over with, Rhoda decided. I might as well go on and get him here. She put her head against the doorframe and saw his face smiling up at her and she thought it was just as funny as it could be and she adored it and she sat down on the floor and laughed some more.

"What are you laughing at?" the father of Rhoda's babies said to her. "What's all that goddamn laughing?"

"It's just funny, that's all. It's hilarious."

"Are you going to take a douche?"

"No, it's too much trouble."

"Then get back in bed."

"I will in a minute."

"We have to stop drinking so much. We have to save some money."

"I know. I think we should. I'm going to start tomorrow."

She climbed back into bed and cuddled up in her husband's arms. This one will be the swimmer, she decided. This is the one who will swim the channel for me.

1957, a Romance

IT WAS JUNE in northern Alabama. Upstairs Rhoda's small sons lay sleeping. Somewhere in North Carolina her young husband sulked because she'd left him.

Rhoda had the name. She had fucked her fat, balding gynecologist all Wednesday afternoon to get the name. She had fucked him on the daybed in his office and on the examining table and on the rug in the waiting room. Now all she needed was five hundred dollars.

No one was going to cut Rhoda's stomach open again. She had come home to get help. She had come home to the one person who had never let her down.

She went into the downstairs bathroom, washed her face, and went up to his room to wake him.

"I have to talk to you, Daddy," she said, touching him on the shoulder. "Come downstairs. Don't wake up mother."

They sat down together in the parlor, close together on the little sofa. He was waking up, shaking sleep from his handsome Scotch face. The old T-shirt he wore for a pajama top seemed very dear to Rhoda. She touched it while she talked.

"I have to get some money, Daddy," she said. "I'm pregnant again. I have to have an abortion. I can't stand to have another baby. I'll die if they keep cutting me open. You can't go on having cesarean sections like that."

"Oh, my," he said, his old outfielder's body going very still inside. "Does Malcolm know all this?" Usually he pretended to have forgotten her husband's name.

"No one knows. I have to do this right away, do you understand? I have to do something about it right away."

"You don't want to tell Malcolm?"

"I can't tell Malcolm. He'd never let me do it. I know that. And no one is going to stop me. He got me pregnant on purpose, Daddy. He did it because he knew I was going to leave him sooner or later."

Rhoda was really getting angry. She always believed her own stories as soon as she told them.

"We'll have to find you a doctor, honey. It's hard to find a doctor that will do that."

"I have a doctor. I have the name of a man in Houston. A Doctor Van Zandt. A friend of mine went to him. Daddy, you have to help me with this. I'm going crazy. Imagine Malcolm doing this to me. He did it to keep me from leaving . . . I begged him not to."

"Oh, honey," he said. "Please don't tell me all that now. I can't stand to hear all that. It doesn't matter. All that doesn't matter. We have to take care of you now. Let me think a minute."

He put his head down in his hands and conferred with his maker. Well, Sir, he said, I've spoiled her rotten. There's no getting around that. But she's mine and I'm sticking by her. You know I'd like to kill that little son of a bitch with my bare hands but I'll keep myself from doing it. So you help us out of this. You get us out of this one and I'll buy you a stained-glass window with nobody's name on it, or a new roof for the vestry if you'd rather.

Rhoda was afraid he'd gone back to sleep. "It's not my fault, Daddy," she said. "He made me do it. He did it to me on purpose. He did it to keep me from leaving . . ."

"All right, honey," he said. "Don't think about any of that anymore. I'll take care of it. I'll call your Uncle James in the morning and check up on the doctor. We'll leave tomorrow as soon as I got things lined up."

"You're going with me," she said.

"Of course I'm going with you," he said. "We'll leave your mother with the babies. But, Rhoda, we can't tell your mother about this. I'll tell her I'm taking you to Tennessee to see the mines."

"If costs *five hundred dollars,* Daddy."

"I know that. Don't worry about that. You quit worrying about everything now and go on and try to get some sleep. I'm taking care of this. And, Rhoda . . ."

"Yes?"

"I really don't want your mother to know about this. She's got a lot on her mind right now. And she's not going to like this one bit."

"All right, Daddy. I don't want to tell her, anyway. Daddy, I could have a legal abortion if Malcolm would agree to it. You know that, don't you? People aren't supposed to go on having cesarean sections one right after the other. I know I could get a legal abortion. But you have to have three doctors sign the paper. And that takes too long. It might be too late by the time I do all that. And, besides, Malcolm would try to stop me. I can't take a chance on that. I think he wants to kill me."

"It's all right, honey. I'm going to take care of it. You go to bed and get some sleep."

Rhoda watched him climb the stairs, sliding his hand along the polished stair rail, looking so vulnerable in his cotton pajama bottoms and his old T-shirt, with his broad shoulders and his big head and his tall, courteous body.

He had been a professional baseball player until she was born. He had been famous in the old Southern League, playing left field for the Nashville Volunteers.

There was a scrapbook full of his old clippings. Rhoda and her brothers had worn it out over the years. DUDLEY MANNING HITS ONE OVER THE FENCE; MANNING DOES IT AGAIN; DUDLEY LEADS THE LEAGUE.

You couldn't eat headlines in the 1930s, so when Rhoda was born he had given in to her mother's pleadings, quit baseball, and gone to work to make money.

He had made money. He had made two million dollars by getting up at four o'clock every morning and working his ass off every single day for years. And he had loved it, loved getting up before the sun rose, loved eating his quiet lonely breakfasts, loved learning to control his temper, loved being smarter and better and luckier than everyone else.

Every day he reminded himself that he was the luckiest son of a bitch in the world. And that made him humble, and other men loved him for his humility and forgave him for his success. Taped to his dresser mirror was a little saying he had cut out of a newspaper, "EVERY DAY THE WORLD TURNS UPSIDE DOWN ON SOMEONE WHO THOUGHT THEY WERE SITTING ON TOP OF IT."

He was thinking of the saying as he went back to bed. As long as nothing happens to her, he told himself. As long as she is safe.

Breakfast was terrible. Rhoda picked at her food, pretending to eat, trying to get her mother in a good mood. Her mother, whose name was Ariane, was a gentle, religious woman who lived her life in service to her family and friends. But she had spells of fighting back against the terrible inroads they made into her small personal life. This was one of those spells.

This was the third time in two years that Rhoda had run away from her husband and come home to live. Ariane suspected that all Rhoda really wanted was someone to take care of her babies. Ariane spent a lot of time suspecting Rhoda of one thing or another. Rhoda was the most demanding of her four children, the only daughter, the most unpredictable, the hardest to control or understand.

"What am I supposed to tell your husband when he calls," she said, buttering toast with a shaking hand. "I feel sorry for him when he calls up. If you're leaving town I want you to call him first."

"Now, Ariane," Rhoda's father said. "We'll only be gone a few days. Don't answer the phone if you don't want to talk to Malcolm."

"I had an appointment to get a *permanent* today," she said. "I don't know when Joseph will be able to take me again."

"Leave the children with the maids," he said. "That's what the maids are for."

"I'm not going to leave those babies alone in a house with maids for a minute," her mother said. "This is just like you, Rhoda, coming home brokenhearted one day and going off leaving your children the next. I don't care what anyone says, Dudley, she has to learn to accept some responsibility for something."

"She's going with me to the mines," he said, getting up and putting his napkin neatly into his napkin holder. "I want her to see where the money comes from."

"Well, I'll call and see if Laura'll come over while I'm gone," Ariane said, backing down as she always did. Besides, she loved Rhoda's little boys, loved to hold their beautiful strong bodies in her arms, loved to bathe and dress and feed them, to read to them and make them laugh and watch them play. When she was alone with them she forgot they were not her very own. Flesh of my flesh, she would think, touching their perfect skin, which was the color of apricots and wild honey, flesh of my flesh, bone of my bone.

"Oh, go on then," she said. "But please be back by Saturday."

They cruised out of town in the big Packard he had bought secondhand from old Dr. Purcell and turned onto the Natchez Trace going north.

"Where are we going?" she said.

"We have to go to Nashville to catch a plane," he said. "It's too far to drive. Don't worry about it, honey. Just leave it to me. I've got all my ducks in a row."

"Did you call the doctor?" she said. "Did you call Uncle James?"

"Don't worry about it. I told you I've got it all taken care of. You take a nap or something."

"All right," she said, and pulled a book out of her handbag. It was Ernest Hemingway's new book, and it had come from the book club the day she left North Carolina. She had been waiting for it to come for weeks. Now she opened it to the first page, holding it up to her nose and giving it a smell.

"*Across the River and into the Trees,*" she said. "What a wonderful title. Oh, God, he's my favorite writer." She settled further down into the seat. "This is going to be a good one. I can tell."

"Honey, look out the window at where you're going," her father said. "This is beautiful country. Don't keep your nose in a book all your life."

"This is a new book by Ernest Hemingway," she said. "I've been waiting for it for weeks."

"But look at this country," he said. "Your ancestors came this way when they settled this country. This is how they came from Tennessee."

"They did not," she said. "They came on a boat down the river from Pennsylvania. Momma said so."

"Well, I knew you'd have something smart-alecky to say," he said.

"The first book I read by Ernest Hemingway was last year when I was nursing Malcolm," she said. "It was about this man and woman in Paris that loved each other but something was wrong with him, he got hurt in the war and couldn't make love to her. Anyway, she kept leaving him and going off with other men. It was so sad I cried all night after I read it. After that I read all his books as fast as I could."

"I don't know why you want to fill up your head with all that stuff," he said. "No wonder you don't have any sense, Rhoda."

"Well, never mind that," she said. "Oh, good, this is really going to be good. It's dedicated 'To Mary, With Love,' that's his wife. She's terrible looking. She doesn't wear any makeup and she's got this terrible wrinkled skin from being in the sun all the time. I saw a picture of her in a magazine last year. I don't know what he sees in her."

"Maybe she knows how to keep her mouth shut," he said. "Maybe she knows how to stay home and be a good wife."

"Oh, well," Rhoda said, "let's don't talk about that. I don't feel like talking about that."

"I'm sorry, honey," he said. "You go on and read your book." He set the speedometer on an easy sixty miles an hour and tried not to think about anything. Outside the window the hills of north Alabama were changing into the rich fields of Tennessee. He remembered coming this way as a young man, driving to

Nashville to play ball, dreaming of fame, dreaming of riches. He glanced beside him, at the concentrated face of his beautiful spoiled crazy daughter.

Well, she's mine, he told himself. And nothing will ever hurt her. As long as I live nothing will ever harm her.

He sighed, letting out his breath in a loud exhalation, but Rhoda could not hear him now. She was far away in the marshes near Tagliamento, in northern Italy, hunting ducks at dawn with Ernest Hemingway. (Rhoda was not fooled by personas. In her mind any modern novel was the true story of the writer's life.)

Rhoda was reading as they went into the Nashville airport and she kept on reading while they waited for the plane, and as soon as she was settled in her seat she found her place and went on reading.

The love story had finally started.

Then she came into the room, shining in her youth and tall striding beauty, and the carelessness the wind had made of her hair. She had pale, almost olive colored skin, a profile that could break your, or anyone else's heart, and her dark hair, of a thick texture, hung down over her shoulders.

"Hello, my great beauty," the Colonel said.

This was more like it, Rhoda thought. This was a better girlfriend for Ernest Hemingway than his old wife. She read on. Renata was nineteen! Imagine that! Ernest Hemingway's girlfriend was the same age as Rhoda! Imagine being in Venice with a wonderful old writer who was about to die of a heart attack. Imagine making love to a man like that. Rhoda imagined herself in a wonderful bed in a hotel in Venice making love all night to a dying author who could fuck like a nineteen-year-old boy.

She raised her eyes from the page. "Did you get Uncle James

on the phone?" she said. "Did you ask him to find out about the doctor?"

"He told me what to do," her father said. "He said first you should make certain you're pregnant."

"I'm certain," she said. "I even know why. A rubber broke. It was Malcolm's birthday and I was out of jelly and I told him I didn't want to . . ."

"Oh, honey, please don't talk like that. Please don't tell me all that."

"Well, it's the truth," she said. "It's the reason we're on this plane."

"Just be quiet and go on and read your book then," he said. He went back to his newspaper. In a minute he decided to try again.

"James said the doctor will have to know for certain that you're pregnant."

"All right," she said. "I'll think up something to tell him. What do you think we should say my name is?"

"Now, sweetie, don't start that," he said. "We're going to tell this man the truth. We're not doing anything we're ashamed of."

"Well, we can't tell him I'm married," she said. "Or else he'll make me get my husband's permission."

"Where'd you get an idea like that?" he said.

"Stella Mabry told me. She tried to get an abortion last year, but she didn't take enough money with her. You have to say you're divorced."

"All right," he said. "I'll tell you what, honey. You just let me talk to the man. You be quiet and I'll do the talking."

He lay back and closed his eyes, hoping he wasn't going to end up vomiting into one of Southern Airlines' paper bags.

He was deathly afraid to fly and had only been on an airplane once before in his life.

A taxi took them to the new Hilton. Rhoda had never been

in such a fancy hotel. She had run away to get married when she was seventeen years old and her only vacations since then had been to hospitals to have babies.

The bellboy took them upstairs to a suite of rooms. There were two bedrooms and a large living room with a bar in one corner. It looked like a movie set, with oversize beige sofas and a thick beige tweed carpet. Rhoda looked around approvingly and went over to the bar and fixed herself a tall glass of ice water.

Her father walked out onto the balcony and called to her. "Rhoda, look out here. That's an Olympic-size swimming pool. Isn't that something? The manager said some Olympic swimmers had been working out here in the afternoons. Maybe we'll get to watch them after a while."

She looked down several stories to the bright blue rectangle. "Can I go swimming in it?" she said.

"Let's call the doctor first and see what he wants us to do." He took a phone number from his billfold, sat down in a chair with his back to her, and talked for a while on the phone, nodding his head up and down as he talked.

"He said to come in first thing in the morning. He gets there at nine."

"Then I'll go swimming until dinner," she said.

"Fine," he said. "Did you bring a swimsuit?"

"Oh, no," she said. "I didn't think about it."

"Well, here," he said, handing her a hundred-dollar bill. "Go find a gift shop and see if they don't have one that will fit you. And buy a robe to go over it. You can't go walking around a hotel in a swimsuit. I'll take a nap while you're gone. I'll come down and find you later."

She went down to the ground floor and found the gift shop, a beautiful little glassed-in area that smelled of cool perfume and was presided over by an elegant woman with her hair up in a bun.

Rhoda tried on five or six swimming suits and finally settled on a black one-piece maillot cut low in the back. She admired herself in the mirror. Two weeks of being too worried to eat had melted the baby fat from her hips and stomach, and she was pleased with the way her body looked.

While she admired herself in the mirror the saleslady handed her a beach robe. It was a black-and-white geometric print that came down to the floor.

"This is the latest thing in the Caribbean," the saleslady said. "It's the only one I have left. I sold one last week to a lady from New York."

"It's darling," Rhoda said, wrapping it around her, imagining what Ernest Hemingway would think if he could see her in this. "But it's too long."

"How about a pair of wedgies," the saleslady said. "I've got some on sale."

Rhoda added a pair of white canvas wedgies to her new outfit, collected the clothes she had been wearing in a shopping bag, paid for her purchases, and went out to sit by the pool.

The swimming team had arrived and was doing warm-up laps. A waiter came, and she ordered a Coke and sipped it while she watched the beautiful young bodies of the athletes. There was a blond boy whose shoulders reminded her of her husband's and she grew interested in him, wondering if he was a famous Olympic swimmer. He looked like he would be a lot of fun, not in a bad mood all the time like Malcolm. She kept looking at him until she caught his eye and he smiled at her. When he dove back into the pool she reached under the table and took off her wedding ring and slipped it into her pocketbook.

When she woke up early the next morning her father was already up, dressed in a seersucker suit, talking on the phone to his mine foreman in Tennessee.

"I can't believe I'm going to be through with all this today," she said, giving him a kiss on the forehead. "I love you for doing this for me, Daddy. I won't ever forget it as long as I live."

"Well, let's just don't talk about it too much," he said. "Here, look what's in the paper. Those sapsuckers in Washington are crazy as loons. We haven't been through with Korea four years and they're fixing to drag us into this mess in Vietnam. Old Douglas MacArthur told them not to get into a land war in Asia, but nobody would listen to him."

"Let me see," Rhoda said, taking the newspaper from him. She agreed with her father that the best way to handle foreign affairs was for the United States to divide up the world with Russia. "They can boss half and we'll boss half," he had been preaching for years. "Because that's the way it's going to end up anyway."

Rhoda's father was in the habit of being early to his appointments, so at eight o'clock they descended in the elevator, got into a taxi, and were driven through the streets of Houston to a tall office building in the center of town. They went up to the fifth floor and into a waiting room that looked like any ordinary city doctor's office. There was even a Currier and Ives print on the wall. Her father went in and talked to the doctor for a while, then he came to the door and asked her to join them. The doctor was a short, nervous man with thin light-colored hair and a strange smell about him. Rhoda thought he smelled like a test tube. He sat beside an old rolltop desk and asked her questions, half-listening to the answers.

"I'm getting a divorce right away," Rhoda babbled, "my husband forced me to make love to him and I'm not supposed to have any more babies because I've already had two cesarean sections in twelve months and I could have a legal abortion if I wanted to but I'm afraid to wait as long as it would take to get permission. I mean I'm only nineteen and what would happen to my babies if I died. Anyway, I want you to know I think you're a real humanitarian for doing this for people. I can't tell you what it meant to me to even find out your name. Do you remember Stella Mabry that came here last year? Well, anyway, I hope you're going to do this for me because I think I'll just go crazy if you don't."

"Are you sure you're pregnant?" he asked.

"Oh, yes," she said. "I'm sure. I've missed a period for three and a half weeks and I've already started throwing up. That's why I'm so sure. Look, I just had two babies in thirteen months. I know when I'm pregnant. Look at the circles under my eyes. And I've been losing weight. I always lose weight at first. Then I blow up like a balloon." Oh, God, she thought. Please let him believe me. Please make him do it.

"And another thing," she said. "I don't care what people say about you. I think you are doing a great thing. There will be a time when everyone will know what a great service you're performing. I don't care what anyone says about what you're doing . . ."

"Honey," her father said. "Just answer his questions."

"When was your last period?" the doctor said. He handed her a calendar and she picked out a date and pointed to it.

Then he gave her two small white pills to swallow and a nurse came and got her and helped her undress and she climbed up on an operating table and everything became very still and dreamy and the nurse was holding her hand. "Be still," the nurse said. "It won't take long."

She saw the doctor between her parted legs with a mask tied around his face and an instrument in his hand and she thought for a moment he might be going to kill her, but the nurse squeezed her hand and she looked up at the ceiling and thought of nothing but the pattern of the tiles revolving around the light fixture.

They began to pack her vagina with gauze. "Relax," the nurse said. "It's all over."

"I think you are wonderful," she said in a drowsy voice. "I think you are a wonderful man. I don't care what anyone says about you. I think you are doing a great service to mankind. Someday everyone will know what a good thing you're doing for people."

When she woke up her father was with her and she walked in a dream out of the offices and into the elevator and down to the tiled foyer and out onto the beautiful streets of the city. The sun was brilliant and across the street from the office building was a little park with the sound of a million crickets rising and falling in the sycamore trees. And all the time a song was playing inside of her. "I don't have to have a baby, I don't have to have a baby, I don't have to have a baby."

"Oh, God, oh, thank you so much," she said, leaning against her father. "Oh, thank you, oh, thank you so much. Oh, thank you, thank you, thank you."

He took her to the hotel and put her into the cool bed and covered her with blankets and sat close beside her in a chair all afternoon and night while she slept. The room was dark and cool and peaceful, and whenever she woke up he was there beside her and nothing could harm her ever as long as he lived. No one could harm her or have power over her or make her do anything as long as he lived.

All night he was there beside her, in his strength and goodness, as still and gentle as a woman.

All night he was there, half-asleep in his chair. Once in the night she woke up hungry and room service brought a steak and some toast and milk and he fed it to her bite by bite. Then he gave her another one of the pills, put the glass of milk to her lips, and she drank deeply of the cold, lush liquid, then fell back into a dreamless sleep.

The plane brought them to Nashville by noon the next day, and they got into the Packard and started driving home.

He had made a bed for her in the back seat with pillows for her head and his raincoat for a cover and she rode along that way, sleeping and reading her book. The wad of gauze in her vagina was beginning to bother her. It felt like a thick hand inside her body. The doctor had said she could remove it in twenty-four hours, but she was afraid to do it yet.

Well, at least that's over, she thought. At least I don't have to have any more babies this year.

All I have to do is have one more and they'll give me a tubal ligation. Doctor Greer promised me that. On the third cesarean section you get to have your tubes cut. It's a law. They have to do it. It would be worth having another baby for that. Oh, well, she thought. At least I don't have to worry about it anymore for now. She opened her book.

> "You are not that kind of soldier and I am not that kind of girl," Renata was saying to Colonel Cantrell. "But sometime give me something lasting that I can wear and be happy each time I wear it."
>
> "I see," the Colonel said. "And I will."
>
> "You learn fast about things you do not know," the girl said. "And you make lovely quick decisions. I would like you to have the emeralds and you could keep them in your pocket like a lucky piece, and feel them if you were lonely."

Rhoda fell asleep, dreaming she was leaning across a table staring into Ernest Hemingway's eyes as he lit her cigarette.

When they got to the edge of town he woke her. "How are you feeling, honey," he said. "Do you feel all right?"

"Sure," she said. "I feel great, really I do."

"I want to go by the house on Manley Island if you feel like it," he said. "Everyone's out there."

It's the Fourth of July, she thought. I had forgotten all about it. Every year her father's large Scotch family gathered for the fourth on a little peninsula that jutted out into the Tennessee River a few miles from town.

"Will Jamie be there?" she asked. Jamie was everyone's favorite. He was going to be a doctor like his father.

"I think so. Do you feel like going by there?"

"Of course I do," she said. "Stop and let me get into the front seat with you."

They drove up into a yard full of automobiles. The old summer house was full of cousins and aunts and uncles, all carrying drinks and plates of fried chicken and all talking at the same time.

Rhoda got out of the car feeling strange and foreign and important, as if she were a visitor from another world, arriving among her kinfolk carrying an enormous secret that they could not imagine, not even in their dreams.

She began to feel terribly elated, moving among her cousins, hugging and kissing them.

Then her Uncle James came and found her. He was an eye surgeon. Her father had paid his tuition to medical school when there was barely enough money to feed Rhoda and her brothers.

"Let's go for a walk and see if any of Cammie's goats are still loose in the woods," he said, taking hold of her arm.

"I'm fine," she said. "I'm perfectly all right, Uncle James."

"Well, just come walk with me and tell me about it," he said. They walked down the little path that led away from the house to the wild gardens and orchards at the back of the property. He had his hand on her arm. Rhoda loved his hands, which were always unbelievably clean and smelled wonderful when they came near you.

"Tell me about it," he said.

"There isn't anything to tell," she said. "They put me up on an examining table and first they gave me some pills and they made me sleepy and they said it might hurt a little but it didn't hurt and I slept a long time afterwards. Well, first we went down in an elevator and then we went back to the hotel and I slept until this morning. I can't believe that was only yesterday."

"Have you been bleeding?"

"Not a lot. Do you think I need some penicillin? He was a real doctor, Uncle James. There were diplomas on the wall and a picture of his family. What about the penicillin? Should I take it just in case?"

"No, I think you're going to be fine. I'm going to stay around for a week just in case."

"I'm glad you came. I wanted to see Jamie. He's my favorite cousin. He's getting to be so handsome. I'll bet the girls are crazy about him."

"Tell me this," he said. "Did the doctor do any tests to see if you were pregnant?"

"I know I was pregnant," she said. "I was throwing up every morning. Besides, I've been pregnant for two years. I guess I know when I'm pregnant by now."

"You didn't have tests made?"

"How could I? I would have had to tell somebody. Then they might have stopped me."

"I doubt if you were really pregnant," he said. "I told your father I think it's highly unlikely that you were really pregnant."

"I know I was pregnant."

"Rhoda, listen to me. You don't have any way of knowing that. The only way you can be sure is to have the tests and it would be doing your father a big favor if you told him you weren't sure of it. I think you imagined you were pregnant because you dread it so much."

Rhoda looked at his sweet impassive face trying to figure out what he wanted from her, but the face kept all its secrets.

"Well, it doesn't matter to me whether I was or not," she said. "All I care about is that it's over. Are you sure I don't need any penicillin? I don't want to get blood poisoning."

(Rhoda was growing tired of the conversation. It isn't any of his business what I do, she thought, even if he is a doctor.)

She left him then and walked back to the house, glancing down every now and then at her flat stomach, running her hand across it, wondering if Jamie would like to take the boat up to Guntersville Dam to go through the locks.

Her mother had arrived from town with the maid and her babies and she went in and hugged them and played with them for a minute, then she went into the bathroom and gingerly removed the wad of bloody gauze and put in a tampon.

She washed her legs and rubbed hand lotion on them and then she put on the new black bathing suit. It fit better than ever.

"I'm beautiful," she thought, running her hands over her body. "I'm skinny and I'm beautiful and no one is ever going to cut me open. I'm skinny and I'm beautiful and no one can make me do anything."

She began to laugh. She raised her hand to her lips and great peals of clear abandoned laughter poured out between her fingers, filling the tiny room, laughing back at the wild excited face in the bright mirror.

Love of My Life

AN AFTERNOON in August. I am in my kitchen in the little frame house on Colonial Drive in Jackson, Mississippi. I am separated from the father of my children. They are six and five and two years old. I am five feet four inches tall. I am muscular and strong. I have strong bones and red hair and straight legs. I am very, very tan. I am wearing sandals, a pair of blue cotton shorts, a tight blue-and-white-striped blouse. I have been taking Dexedrine. I take it three or four days a week. I take Dexedrine and diuretics. I never eat. Food is the enemy of what I want. I don't know what I want but I know how to get it. If I am beautiful, the thing I want will show up. I've been waiting since I was fourteen years old for the thing I want. Once I thought it was the father of my children. Once I thought it was a federal judge my father's age. I never thought it was the children. They are the price I have to pay for looking for it. I don't have to pay anymore. I had a tubal ligation. I don't have to worry about getting pregnant anymore but still I worry.

I am getting closer to what I want. I can feel it in the hot August air, in the sunlight beating down upon the sidewalk and the two-car garage and the heads of the children. I can taste it in the gin I drink. Can hear it in the music on the phonograph. My daddy is a rich man. My husband worked for him. I have a new house, a new car. I'm at home. No one can hurt me now. My father will not let them. My brothers will not let them. I am safe now. I am almost where I want to be.

Outside, in the fenced-in yard, the five- and six-year-old are playing in the water. They have a plastic pool filled with water and a hose and a Slip-and-Slide. They are happy. They've been playing for a long time without having a fight. In a few minutes my mother will come and get them and take them off to spend the night. The maid left at four and Mother's coming at five to pick them up. The only one I have to take care of is Teddy and he's asleep. I walk around my kitchen cutting up vegetables and cooking things. It is safe to cook. I took a Dexedrine this morning. You couldn't push food in my mouth.

I have a new record on the record player. Johnny Cash singing about his Indian blood. I'm into Indians today. I feel their pain, know their sorrow, ride the plains with the braves, wait for them to come to me at night. I've had the record for two days. I play it over and over. It has become me. I know the words by heart.

I put a tray of biscuits in the oven. I turn the water on to boil beneath a pan of new potatoes. I have been separated from my husband for a week. It's wonderful. I am free, and I cannot have another baby no matter what I do. I can fall in love with anyone. I can have a lover, or two lovers, or maybe three. My brothers and my daddy will let me do anything I want to do.

I stop. A dark thought has entered me. I might not get into the Casual Club, the luncheon club my mother wants me to get into. I am waiting for an invitation. Well, surely they will want me. I am so pretty. My daddy is so rich.

A car drives up. It is my mother. We round up the boys and pack their bags and put them in her car. "I wish you'd come out too," my mother says. "When the baby wakes up get dressed and come to dinner." She stands at the door. She is wearing her suspicious look. She doesn't like the way I look. She wants to know what I'm up to.

"I might. I don't think I can. Avery might come over." It's a lie. Avery is the daughter of her best friend who is married to the mayor. Avery is the president of the Casual Club. Mother wants me to be friends with Avery.

"Oh, that's nice. Well, call in a while. Call and let us know what you're doing." She is smiling, almost smiling. The boys are fighting in the backseat of the car. "Well, I'd better go on and take them. Call us, Rhoda. Call and let me know where you are."

She drives off, Malcolm and Jimmy are fighting away. It is nineteen sixty-three. There are no seat belts. It has barely begun to dawn on us that we need them. Children fall against dashboards, cut their heads, we tell them not to stand up on the seats.

I think I am barefooted now. The baby is still asleep. As soon as mother leaves I go out onto the patio to clean up the mess the children made. I open the drain on the plastic pool. Water spills out on the patio. I walk around in it. I pull the ugly plastic Slip-and-Slide over behind the air-conditioning unit so I won't have to look at it. I have a photograph of myself at this time, in this place. I am very very thin. My half-wet shirt sticks to my ribs and breasts; beneath my shorts my tanned legs are straight and shapely. I am so young. I am twenty-six years old. My hair is cut in a chin-length bob with a part on the side. I wear a barrette in my hair. If I am wearing blue, the barrette is blue. On this day, the day I met my one true love, the Indian man, the man who was my equal, who was good enough for me, on this day I think the barrette was blue. It must have been blue because my shorts were blue.

*   *   *

I walked back into the kitchen from the patio, making wet footprints on the waxed floor, singing along to the music. I started the record over. I strummed the air. It was my blue guitar.

Dudley's black Pontiac pulled up into the driveway behind my new black station wagon. I saw him get out, laughing and talking to his passenger. His passenger got out and they came into the kitchen through the screen door. "Come listen to Johnny Cash," I said. "God, it's so good. I just adore it. What are you doing here?"

"We're playing in a tournament at the club. This is Raine Matasick, Rhoda. My sister, Raine. He's my partner." I shook his hand. I took him in. Too ugly. Too foreign. Too dark-skinned. Not fat, but big, so big. Too big. He kept on smiling. He waited with his smile. He stood back while Dudley and I talked.

"What are you doing later?" Dudley asked. "There's a party at the club. They're going to raffle off the players. It's a Calcutta. You want to go with us? Sally's going."

"You can buy us," Raine suggested. "Dudley and me'll come cheap."

"Don't let him fool you," Dudley said. "He won the state tournament last year."

"Oh, yeah." I was getting interested. Not in Raine, but in the Calcutta, whatever that turned out to be. A party at the club. I could wear my new mauve linen dress. "God, my hair's a mess. You want a drink?"

"Not now," Dudley said. He put his hand on Raine's arm. "You ought to go with us, Sister. Everyone in the state's there. This is a big tournament."

"I'll have a glass of water," Raine said. He followed me to the sink and stood beside me while I filled the glass. I had a sense of the immensity of the man. Not that he was that tall or big. He was six foot three or four. It wasn't that. It was something else, a sense of mass or power. A smell that didn't belong in the same world with the Casual Club. Too dark, too big, too foreign. I looked up at him while I filled the glass. His eyes were dark, like mine. Dark sweet eyes. I would take him for an admirer. I wanted plenty of admirers. "I wish you'd sit down and listen to this music," I said. "I'm just crazy about it. I don't listen to another thing."

Teddy came walking into the room. He was wearing a wet diaper and carrying his bottle. He was still half asleep. He stopped in the middle of the room and looked around. Raine went over to him and knelt beside him and began to have a conversation. Teddy smiled. He pulled the bottle out of his mouth and hit Raine with it. They laughed together. Then Teddy came over and grabbed me around the legs. "I'll have to get a baby-sitter," I said. "I don't know who I'll find this late."

"Call Sally," Dudley said. "She's got a list. Well, listen, Sister, we've got to go. We have to meet some people down at the Sun and Sand and then we've got to go change clothes."

"My clubs are still in my car," Raine said. "I need to put them in my trunk."

I picked up Teddy and held him while they left. I was still so uninterested in this man I could pick up a child in a wet diaper and hold him against my half-wet blue-and-white-striped cotton shirt and stand in the carport barefoot and wave as they drove away. I pulled Teddy's diapers off and left them in the carport and took him inside and put him in the tub. While he played in the water I called a baby-sitter. I walked back into the kitchen and turned the record over and played the other side.

It was exciting to think of going out alone. When I went out with my husband I had a horrible time. No matter how many martinis I drank it was always an awful time. Now I was separated. Now I could go out somewhere and have a good time. Even if it was only my brother and his wife and this big, dark man who was a champion golfer. Still, I had a funny feeling. I was very excited about this evening. As soon as I had a baby-sitter lined up I got Teddy out of the tub and dressed him and gave him some biscuits to eat and then I went into the bathroom and washed my hair and rolled it up. I took my new mauve dress out of the closet and laid it on the bed. I took out earrings and a gold bracelet. I gave Teddy some cold fried chicken and a bowl of cereal and some toys to play with on the kitchen floor. I started getting dressed. I put on my new perfume, Jungle Gardenia. I put on makeup. I dried my hair and combed it. As soon as the baby-sitter arrived and took Teddy off to the backyard, I put on the dress. I looked at myself in the mirror. I was beautiful. More beautiful than I had ever been in my life. They had tried to kill me with the babies. They had tried to ruin and kill me and make me ugly but it had not worked. I had outwitted them. I was separated now and I was going out to the Jackson Country Club and find out what I wanted. I didn't know what I wanted but I believed it existed. It existed and when I saw it I would know it. I took an ice-cold glass out of the freezer and filled it with vodka. I stood in the kitchen looking out toward the carport. Soon they would come to get me. They would take me to the place where my life would begin.

After a long time he came. It was dark when he came so it must have been very late. I must have had another drink and played the Indian recording many times. The baby-sitter must have taken Teddy to his room to read to him and I must have gotten tired of waiting and finally a car drove up in the carport and I went out the screen door to yell at my brother for being late. Only it wasn't my brother. It was Raine and he was alone.

*   *   *

Many years later, after it was over, after he had come into my life and changed it, wrecked it and emblazoned it, after I had married a rich Jewish lawyer and made him miserable, after ten years, after I had divorced the lawyer and gone off to live in the Ozark mountains to write my books. After the marriages and the divorces and the beginning of the books. After the week Raine drove me to Arkansas to begin my writing life. After I left the lawyer and took up with Raine again, after so many strange and eventful years. After all of that I heard the rest of the story of that day. I heard it from Dudley on his sixtieth birthday. At his birthday party, late in the evening, beside the lake, at the borrowed river mansion. "We were driving home from the first day of the tournament," Dudley said. "We'd been hitting so well we thought we were going to win. It was the state team tournament. You never did pay much attention to sports unless you were playing, did you, Shortie?"

"No. Go on. So what happened then?"

"We were going by your neighborhood and I said, 'Raine, what would you rather do? Go down to the Sun and Sand and find some working girls or meet my sister?'

"'You and Ingersol have a sister?'

"'She just moved back here. Her crazy little husband was working for us for a while. Then she ran him off. You might like her.'

"'You and Ingersol have a sister. I don't think I can take it.' Then we started laughing and I slowed the car down.

"'She lives over by the Colonial Country Club. Which will it be?'

"'If you have a sister I want to meet her.' Raine sat back in the seat and I turned off the four-lane into your neighborhood and brought him to you." Dudley was holding a glass of wine. We were sitting on a double bench on a bluff above the river. He looked at me out of his one good eye and his face got the soft, puffy look it wore when he desired me. When he used to come to the door of my room when he was fifteen and say things to me and offer to give me things and take me places. Get out of here, Dudley, I always answered. Later, when we were older, one night he offered me fifty thousand dollars to sleep with him and I still turned him down. The pleasure of denying him something that he wanted was worth an empire of gold. "Are you glad I did?" he ended.

"It's a good thing I was listening to Johnny Cash that week. I was in my Indian mood. I wanted to meet an Indian. Yeah, I'm glad you did. He was the love of my life. The only man I ever loved that I thought, really believed, was good enough for me." I stared into Dudley's good eye. I guess he is my brother. I know he is my brother. There but for the grace of God and one X chromosome and the fact that he was born first, go I.

"I love you, Dudley," I said. "I'm glad you are my brother."

So Raine got out of his Lincoln Continental and came into my kitchen apologizing for being late and not blaming it on Dudley although, since I always blamed everything on Dudley, I'm sure I did. Then I told the baby-sitter good-bye and gave her the phone number of the Jackson Country Club and we went out and got into the car. I think it had already started. Before I noticed how other men treated him. Before Dudley or one of them or maybe Raine himself told me he had been the best football player in the South. Since I knew nothing about football except the clothes I wore to games and the parties afterward and cared less. Since I never could remember what position he had played. Since only when I saw his name on the back of the program at an Ole Miss game, with his records still intact after seven years, or when men would talk about him and games he'd played and runs he'd made and touchdowns he had scored and

passes he had caught, did I begin to envision him playing football. What I envisioned suited the image of the body that lay by
mine, that will always be the yardstick against which I measure
other men, and because of which I understand when I see love
or read about it and say to myself, I had that, I was not stinted,
my own true love, my one and only own true love.

And I was his. But that was later. On this night, when I entered the ballroom of the Jackson Country Club on his arm I
may have thought that the obeisance was for me. I was so stuck
on myself, on my daddy's money and my newfound freedom
and my thin tan body in my new mauve dress, I may actually
have thought that feeling of waters parting was about me. All
evening I kept going away from him and flirting with other men
and then going to find him again. He was so solid, it was like
going to Hercules or Odysseus, so solid, so still. Going into his
presence was not like anything I had ever known. Except, perhaps, my father, when I was young.

I don't think we stayed long at the party. We stayed for the
Calcutta and there was a large blackboard and everyone was very
drunk and bought the players for ridiculous sums. Dudley
bought himself and Raine. Either Dudley did or a rich girl from
the Delta did. After that Raine and I went out a side door and
got into his car and went to a motel. It was pretty simple really.
We got into his car and he took me in his arms and began to kiss
me. Devour me. Gently, gently, tenderly, almost in tears. I will
fall in love with you, he said. He had not had a thing to drink.
He never drank. Since he was eighteen years old and got drunk
one night and tried to kill a man he had never had a drink. I was
drunk but I was also sober. The enormity of what was happening sobered me. I can remember every moment of that night. I
can remember him rising above me on the bed and telling me
he would never fuck me again when I was drunk. I can remem-

ber him taking me home. Late, very late. The baby-sitter had called my mother and her mother and the country club. I remember him saying that he loved me. I remember the way he smelled. The next day my skin smelt of him. My left and my right arm. I did not take a bath until late in the afternoon. Until after he called and said he had to see me.

"We lost the tournament," Dudley was saying. Sitting on the bench by the river looking at me with his one good eye. "I guess that was your fault, Shortie."

"You were pimping for him. You set me up."

"You said you weren't sorry."

"I'm not," I answered. "I just want to get the story straight."

I didn't see him the next day. It was the second day, while the maid was at my house, he came and got me in the Lincoln and we drove somewhere, I don't know where, perhaps along the new four-lane highway that my father had built. "I've never felt this way about a woman," he said. "I don't know what to do." He stopped the car and kissed me. Then he drove to a park and we talked like generals planning a war. Staccato, fast, intense, the terrible intensity of desire. "I'm still married. I don't have a divorce."

"So am I. My wife's crazy."

"Where do you live?"

"In an apartment."

"We can't do it openly. He might take my children."

"She'll take mine."

"Where will we go?"

"Now?"

"No, all the time."

"We'll get an apartment."

"Okay, let's go get one."

*   *   *

Perhaps we didn't say all that that day. Perhaps all we did that day was go downtown to a hotel and make love until the sun went down. I called the maid and offered to pay her three times the amount she made. I bribed and begged her. I was two hours late. We gave her all the money that we had. We gave her too much money and she looked him up and down and shook her head. Even the maid understood. The children were there when we got home. He didn't bribe them. He sat down in a chair and let them come to him.

They didn't care. They were lonesome for their father but they were too young to know that Raine was part of that. They liked him. He went out into the backyard and threw balls to them. We got a baby-sitter. We went out to dinner and went back to the hotel and made love some more. My mother called me about fifty times. The maid and the baby-sitter wrote the messages down. It was nineteen sixty-three. There weren't any answering machines.

While we were at the hotel my mother and father came and got the children and took them to the country. They paid the baby-sitter. They called Dudley and asked him what was going on.

In the hotel room I lay upon his body and told him the story of my life. He told me how he had acquired the different scars. The worst scars were on his legs. He didn't get them on the football field. He got them in an automobile accident when a drunk man was driving. He had not thought it could happen to him. After it was over he couldn't play football anymore. He had to learn to sell insurance and municipal bonds. He learned how to play golf. He put his trophies away. He wasn't a has-been. He was a great athlete who had had a bad break. It didn't matter. In a year he was the golf champion of the state of Mississippi. People bowed their heads when he came into a room. He was

the quietest, gentlest man I have ever known. He had the soft-
est skin. He had the strangest, most unforgettable smell. He was
half Italian and half Cherokee Indian. The love of my life. The
one and only love.

Even long ago, when it was nearer, I could never remember
making love to him. We would enter a room and our bodies
would meld. It was absolutely simple. It had a beginning and a
middle and an end. I smelled like Jungle Gardenia or Estée Lauder
or L'Heure Bleue. He smelled of shaving cream and the wild
terrible smell of his body, of physical power and cunning and
coordination that was unlike anything I had ever known. Except
for my father. My father was that strong, his shoulders were that
powerful, that wide, that still. Maybe this man was my father to
the tenth power. I lay upon his body and talked to him. Later, I
would lie upon his body and cry and he would pat me like a
child. He was never in a hurry. He never made a mistake or
wasted a motion or dropped anything. He never stopped saying
he loved me and I never stopped believing it. Wherever he is,
until my death or his death, that time is always there, indelible
upon my brain and his brain. My own true love. The man with
the Indian blood and the dark skin and the gentle eyes. The un-
circumcised man. Because of him I know what books and stories mean when men and women love each other without stint
or question, in defiance of order, in defiance of self-interest or
knowledge or pain. Sex was only part of it. Sex was where it
took place, as on a stage. But sex was not what it was about. It
was because I thought he was good enough for me. Because he
believed I would one day be his equal.

I can hear his voice. So deep and rich and slowed down to a
Southern cadence. Full of humor and pathos. A black man's
voice, a foreign voice. It was not the voice of men who married

the ladies of the Casual Club or escorted their daughters to the debutante balls. Although his family would come to that, because of him, because he was a hero and they were the sons and daughters of a hero and could get soft and still be safe.

Then it was fall and we had found an apartment and I lived in it with a roommate and he only came there. He didn't live there because his wife was pregnant. When I found out about it I went crazy. I beat upon his shoulders. I got drunk and yelled at him and woke the neighbors. I called him in the middle of the night and he would get into his car and come to where I was and say he loved me and cry. Lots of times he cried. He cried because he loved me. He suffered because of me. I loved to make him suffer. He brought his children to see me and I was nice to them. They sat in my apartment being very polite and drank the Cokes I gave them and told me about their schools. I thought they were ugly children. He must have known I thought that. After that evening I never had to see them again. Instead he came and got me and took me to the airport and we flew off to North Carolina in his plane. We rented a car. We drove around North Carolina and I waited outside offices while he sold municipal bonds to men.

We took long trips together while he sold these bonds. He had several offices around Jackson. And several business partners. They were massive quiet men who had played football with him. Some were men who had thrown passes to him. Others were men who had made holes for him to run through. I didn't know how to talk to them. They were too far away from what I knew. But Raine was not. He could be anything he wanted to be. He made people like him. He was likable and kind, quiet and dependable. Until me he had not been crazy.

I wondered if he only liked my daddy's money. But he knew

it was not mine. Later, after I left him and began to find other men, he took one of the men out to lunch one day and told him the money was not mine, would not ever be mine because women didn't get to have the money in my family.

It was me he loved. Because he thought I would someday be his equal, was already his equal because of something in me that did not give up, never stopped looking, never stopped wanting, never gave in or compromised. Later, when I had my books and my name in the papers, he would call and tell me he was proud of me, would show up at my autograph parties and stand against a wall and look at me.

II

I had found something worth wanting, worth suffering for. With this blood in me that came from my daddy and liked to fight, I had found something worth fighting for. But who was I to fight, his brokenhearted wife and her children and her unborn baby?

At Christmas of that year he had to go to Chicago to a reunion of his old football team. He had been Rookie of the Year. Had scored the most points of anyone in the backfield. Then he had the accident and it was over. But these men did not forget. Life did cruel things to men and men could bear it. Could go on loving each other in this strange fraternity of professional sports, where they did for a living what lesser men dreamed of doing, outran, outlasted, outwilled each other on a playing field. Anyone could have bad luck. They loved Raine for taking the bad luck away from them. They asked him about his knees.

We had gone out to dinner with these men when they passed through Jackson, Mississippi, or when they lived in one of the towns we flew to in the airplane or drove to in the Lincoln. So now, to make me feel better about Christmas, we were going up there together to join their annual celebration.

This was the first time I knew how much he lied to me. He had lied to me all along but I had not really understood it. I was vain and I had not been lied to before. The men who marry girls whose mothers go to the Casual Club don't lie to people until they are middle-aged. They have a code. They marry you and tell you the truth until the time when they really fall in love. Then they lie to spare your feelings. They take upon themselves the burden of the lie to spare you pain.

The world that belonged to this Indian-Italian man was not that world. In his world you took what you needed no matter what the cost. If the woman yelled at you and threw things across the room, you put your arms up before your face and took the blows. Then you begged and said you loved her, you cried if necessary, you bought her sofas and cars and rings with large stones your friends got for you on the black market.

So I bought a beautiful new evening suit I saw in *Vogue* magazine and packed it in a suitcase and counted off the days until I flew with him to Chicago.

Where were my children while this was going on? I had forgotten them. My brother Dudley told my father I was going to bring Raine in and marry him. Take care of the kids, he might have said. Let Rhoda capture him.

Even my father was not immune to Raine's glory, his picture in the Hall of Fame, his name on the back of programs, his gentle manner when he came into my parents' home. Yes, my mother had seen him now. My mother knew I went to rooms and took off my clothes and lay down with this huge Indian-Italian man. She wore an expression that said this was the worst thing that had ever happened to her. Still, she paid thousands of dollars every year for fifty-yard-line seats in the stadium where he had been the hero. She read the programs too. She was not immune. Then too, he courted her. Looked up at her with his dark sweet eyes and told her that he loved me, that I was the love of his life, that he would never harm me in any way.

I enrolled in a college in the town. A small, private college in the old part of town. I went to classes when Raine wasn't around. It was the excuse for the apartment. It was what my mother told her friends at the Casual Club.

I remember packing a suitcase to go to Chicago. I remember putting my beautiful black pantsuit with lapels of black satin and the little white satin blouse into the suitcase and closing the top. I remember the drive to Nashville where we caught the plane to Chicago. I remember the drive home on the eve of Christmas Eve and how we saw the dark shape on the horizon, just at dusk, halfway between Nashville and home. I thought it was a flying saucer. I told everyone I had seen a flying saucer and Raine always said he saw it too. But I would remember anything rather than remember what happened in Chicago.

We went to the Palmer House Hotel where he had been staying on the night he had the accident that ended his career. He stayed there out of some perverse desire not to shield himself from unpleasant things. I had never stayed at a hotel that fine with a man who could pay for it with his own money. But I did not notice the hotel. All I knew was that on that night after we arrived I would put on my new suit and go to the banquet with Raine. As though I were his wife, in place of his wife, he would take me to the place that meant the most to him.

We arrived late one evening. It was bitterly cold outside. I have never been that cold in my life. The wind came around the corners of the buildings and made you run back inside. We left the hotel and he shielded me with his body and we went to a bar where pictures of him were on the walls. His friends were there and we sat at a small table and had dinner with two men who had been referees at the games. They told me stories of his glory. They walked around the bar with me. They showed me pictures of him. Young and sweet and dark, in his football uniform, holding the ball cradled in his arm. I held his hand beneath the table and thought how big it was, how perfectly designed for this football that had given him his power in the world.

He brought me here to see these pictures, I decided. But I came to go with him to the banquet as his wife. First this banquet, then he will get a divorce. As soon as this unnecessary baby that she had only to keep him gets here. As soon as that is over I will take him away from his ugly children and his ugly wife and give him to my sons for their father. To my father for a son, to my brothers for a friend, this man I love, this man who is strong enough for me, who can dodge the things I throw at him, who can bear the pain I cause him because I am his one and only love, the one he cannot bear to be without.

The next day there was a football game in the stadium where he had played. We sat on the sidelines on folding chairs. Other men and their wives were there. It was so cold they had to bring me a cape like the ones the players wore on the bench. They draped it over me. A boy brought paper bags and put them on my feet. I was a geisha at a football game, being cared for by men who could withstand the cold.

A thin black man kept running down the side of the field and making touchdowns. Raine was like that, the other men said to me. Until the black man no one has done the thing he did for us. I held his arm. I watched his face as they said these things to me. I had never seen him happy. Until this day, sitting on those folding chairs in the cold I had never known him to be happy. With me he was in such sadness, such pain. He knew he could not keep me and it made him sad. My beauty vanished when we were together. There was no beauty in me now. Only this terrible Dexedrine thinness and this will to keep and overcome him.

Think how desirable it was to him. This young girl from the Casual Club who had been turned into a tiger. Later, back in our room, we fucked each other without mercy. We beat upon each other's body, taking all the pleasure that we could, giving nothing away, taking, taking, taking.

At five o'clock he dressed for the banquet. He went downstairs to meet someone. He said he would come back for me at six. I dressed in my new suit. I ordered a martini from room service. Then I did not drink it. Six o'clock came. He was not there. Seven o'clock came. He did not come. The banquet started at seven. Something terrible must have happened. I called the banquet but they said he was not there. I drank the martini and ordered another one. Eight o'clock and nine o'clock came and went and still he was not there. I called the banquet over and over again. Finally a waiter told me Mr. Matasick had been there but he wasn't there anymore. The banquet was over. They had all gone home. I sat on the bed in my suit. Beware of enterprises that require new clothes.

At ten-thirty he returned to the room and let me yell at him. I screamed at him. I beat upon him and tore him with my fingernails. He begged me not to hate him. He said he loved me until death. He said he brought me here because he loved me. I cried myself to sleep on gin.

Driving home was when we saw the flying saucer. Coming

home on the eve of Christmas Eve. The Christmas before the New Year's Eve when I took the Antabuse and drank on it and almost died, begged to die, wanted to die to punish him.

Money was part of it. That Lincoln Continental with its seats of whitest leather. My father's money, whether I would have it or not. He had never had a poor woman in his life. They were all wealthy women, the ones before me and the ones who followed. The ones who didn't count. He said they didn't count and I believed him.

There is only one love like that, one white hot moment when a man and a woman ask everything of each other, ask sacrifice and pain and dishonesty. Mostly pain. Alone with him in rooms, in my apartment in the afternoons when my roommate wasn't there, beside him or on top of him with his dick buried deep within me. My body pulling on him to empty him and make him suffer.

James Rainey Matasick, the name is enough to make men feel inferior. Now, in my old age, sometimes I drop it in the lap of a man if he tries to flirt with me. If he's the right age, if he looks like an old high school athlete, if he dreamed of glory, I let him make his move and then I ask him if he saw Raine play. He was my lover, I say. My one and only love.

It would be nine years before I needed him again. Before I called and told him to come save me. Only this time I would be richer, surer, older. I don't know why I called him then, only I had some Dexedrine for the first time in several years and I wanted him to take me to a place he knew about, a place that once he had taken me to. I wanted to go to Arkansas. The only time I had ever set foot in Arkansas was when Raine took me to

Little Rock to visit his sister who was dying in a veterans' hospital. He had cried in my arms after he saw her and on the way home we ran out of gasoline outside of Dumas and had to walk a mile to catch a ride to a service station.

Anyway, I called and told him I had to go to Fayetteville, Arkansas, to go to school to learn how to be a writer and he met me in Vicksburg and drove me there. I made him wait outside the English Department while I went in to meet my professors. As I said, I always forgot who he was. I never thought of him as anything on earth but my lover. "Raine Matasick is outside in the car?" my professor said. "My God in heaven, tell him to come in."

III

His integrity was darkened by the lies he told to make me love him. One day at noon, at lunch somewhere, one of those expensive restaurants that come and go in Jackson like the tides, over Bloody Marys and lobster salad, in a booth, I think, not a table, although it may have been a table . . . what he said removed us from the rest of the room in such a way that it seems it must have been a booth, Dudley cheats at golf, he said. He moves the ball. He improves the lie. He couldn't look at me when he said it. It was something he had to say, something he had to unveil to me, for some reason, perhaps to ward off Dudley's telling me about his wife, that he wasn't separated from her, that she was pregnant, that when he left me, he went back to her house. Perhaps Dudley had threatened him, had said he would tell me. Perhaps my father told Dudley to put a stop to it. I can't play with him anymore, Raine said. People bet money on those games. If men stop trusting you, you're dead. I bowed my head. I was ashamed. I could believe anything of Dudley, the killer, the older brother, the one who always had the best of everything, the one my father loved the best, the one who had the power and the money. And one eye. A natural athlete who lost an eye. Yes, to make up for the handicap he might cheat. Because he has to win. He can't live if he can't win, can't be second in anything. Had been kicked out of college for letting his fraternity brothers copy off of him. Had lived his life to earn my father's love, which he could have had without lifting his finger. Because he looks like my father's father. So much like him the resemblance is uncanny. If you hold their photographs up against each other it is the same soft pretty spoiled face.

If it were true? If my brother cheated other men, what did that make me? It was a long time ago, nineteen sixty-three, I did not know you could leave, bail out, refuse to be part of such a family, a family that drank and cheated, whored around. Drank and lied and cheated, biblical sins. If I had known it, I could not have acted upon it. I had hostages, three sons, no money, no education. Three times I had escaped death by bearing them and still I was alive. I was twenty-six years old, then twenty-seven. I thought there was not much time left before it would be too late, before I would die from the deep dissatisfaction of my life. I had meant to be a writer, every moment of my life, since I was four or five or six years old, had counted myself a writer, had always written everything for everyone. Had always done it well, been praised for it, received the highest grades in English class. But that was all consumed now, consumed in the men and the babies and this terrible wealth my father had acquired and let us waste in any way we chose. As long as we stayed out of his way so he could go on making money and as long as we acted like we were happy. As long as we acted like we would never be poor, never be frightened and poor as he had been for many years. That shadow on his life, that terrible fear of being poor.

*   *   *

I stayed because I had to stay and because my mother and father were still pure, did not lie or cheat or steal or drink. They were still the puritans they had had to be to make the money, to save, then multiply it into millions of dollars, enough to last us all forever, we thought. But my father did not think so, drove his old car, wore his old suits, stayed home at night, stayed sober.

I stayed to take advantage of their purity. Later, when I was pure again, had purged myself of evil, had stopped drinking, lying, cheating, then I could leave, could refuse to let anyone suck the hard-won goodness from me. But this was much, much later, after years of work, of writing and psychotherapy, after twenty years I was good again. I think I will remain that way. I do not think anything could pull me down again into that mire of pain.

You'll be alone, people warned me. Won't you be lonely?

I've never been lonely in my life, I answered. But I've been afraid.

I have tried to find a way to articulate what it was between Raine and me, the thing that passes between a man and a woman that is not words, that carves below the words and ignites them. Fire, the black people call it.

I pity lovers, caught in that consumption. From the word *consume*. When nature takes us back, which we call love. I had been practicing for Raine. Four unwanted pregnancies. He had four children and this new one on the way. This inconvenient child. This child who was my enemy because I was consumed in this unholy fire.

When we ran out of gasoline on the road between Dumas, Arkansas and McGee, I was listening to a tape of Willie Nelson singing "Stardust." Coming back from seeing Raine's dying sister. I had been talking for fifty miles about where we would spend the night. He did not answer me. He knew he was going to spend the night with his wife and children and he knew better than to tell me so. I would have stolen the car keys, torn him with my fingernails, jumped out of the car, done anything. It was of no importance to me if he had a family. He was my lover. No other Raine existed for me. Because I was consumed by fire.

Why else down all these centuries have women lain down with men and died in childbirth? Lain down smiling, taken pleasure in it. It has nothing to do with freedom, tenderness, pity, love. *Tenderness, pity, love,* these are words we invented to forgive ourselves.

That cold December afternoon when we saw the flying saucer. Driving along the picked cotton fields, long flat fields to the east of Jackson, at dusk, just after the sun went down. The man beside me is Raine, the one who loved me so much he lied to keep me. It is the eve of Christmas Eve and in a while he will drop me off and leave me alone at Christmas. I had to escape that knowledge so much I saw an apparition, made him see it by the force of my will, gave him an apparition so we could both escape the pain inside that car. He always said he saw it. He told everyone he did. It flew along beside us, on the horizon, inside a long blue cloud.

Finally, we stopped the car and got out and stood along the highway watching it. Many years later, I saw a film about flying saucers and the people in the movie did exactly as we did. Got out of their cars and stood along the side of a road, in little groups of two and three, watching the apparition in the sky.

Perhaps we were holding hands, the tacky topaz ring he had given me upon my finger, a ring so big it would have cut into his hand if he had squeezed it. Later I gave it to a maid or lost it or threw it away. It disappeared within a year. We stood there watching the apparition, wrapped up in the lies he told me, the thing he had done to me in Chicago when he left me alone in the room and went to the banquet without me.

Soon after that I left him. Closed up the apartment, gave the furniture away, took a series of lovers, then married the wealthy Jewish lawyer, who should have known better, and moved away.

I was burned out for a while. When I recovered it was work that saved me. The work I had abandoned when the fire that made my sons consumed me.

What will you write? my mother asked me, terrified. The truth, I answered. Stories, poems, plays.

Drunk Every Day

IT ENDED in a rape. It ended with Sally being raped behind the Jeffersons' high brick fence. It ended with Sally taking off her blue jeans at knifepoint and being raped by a sixteen-year-old kid within sight of the five-hundred-thousand-dollar addition to the Jeffersons' house that was the cause of the Jeffersons' divorce and the reason no one was there to hear Sally's cries for help. If she cried out. I don't remember if she said she did or not. She said, "He was sixteen years old and he was black as the ace of spades and I did what I was told to do, but I was not afraid. I swear to God I was not afraid."

"How did you know he was sixteen?" Jodie Myers was sitting on the bed with the stethoscope around his neck and his hands in his lap. We had both been in love with him all week. Now he was sitting on my bed being a doctor. That was not what Sally and I had in mind, but it was what we got. Have you ever noticed how things seem to build and build until finally they reach a point where something has to give? That was what happened in February of 1975. We had gone as far as we could go. We had built a pyre and something had to burn.

To begin with it was Mardi Gras and my friends and I were drunk every day. There was no reason why we should not be. We were the privileged ones. The ones who did not have to work or take care of our children or do a goddamn thing we didn't want to do. My name is Rhoda Manning, by the way, and I am older now and wiser. Still, I don't regret the life that I have lived. I don't regret a goddamn minute of it. I left no stone unturned. I will never have to sit back and say, Where did my life go?

A week before Mardi Gras I ran a twenty-six-mile marathon and finished it in four hours and five minutes. Afterward I drove to Mandeville and stayed alone all afternoon watching it rain on the porches of the summer house Eric bought me the first time I tried to leave him. I will never understand why he wanted our marriage to go on and on and on. Long after I didn't love him anymore. Long after we had stopped sleeping in the same bed. He wanted me to stay so he bribed me and I agreed to be bribed. He gave me all the money that I wanted and he let me do anything I wanted to and in return I kept on pretending to be his wife. I will never understand those years. That marriage without passion or desire. What I did to make up for the frustration was play tennis and drink. I see women now in situations like the one I was in, and I think to myself, This is bondage, as old as the hills and still going on. Young women married to old men who can't make them come. Women buying houses and cars with money old or second-rate men give them. Women with that look that says, I was bought and paid for, here I am.

So that is where I was at that time in my life and I was making up for it as best I could. I played tennis like a fiend. I ran six miles every morning in the park. I got my hair dyed. I planned vacations. I drank. The great thing about living in New Orleans in those years was that there were lots of people to get drunk with. This was before everyone started cleaning up their acts.

So it was Mardi Gras and Sally Stanfield was staying at our house and we were drunk every day. Luncheons at Galatoire's or

Commander's Palace. Breakfast in the French Quarter. Nights at parties or viewing the parades. Men we knew rode the floats in the parades. We stood on certain corners and they showered us with doubloons. We didn't even bother to bend over and pick them up. We wouldn't have bothered to pick up silver dollars if they had thrown them at us. Sally's father was the richest man in Tennessee and mine was almost as rich, and besides, I had Eric to pay for everything I could think up to charge to him. What did all this mean? I will never be able to figure it out. But I know what was missing. We didn't have anything to do. We didn't have to work. There would have been no reason to work. We had power without responsibility and we were bored to death with the hand we had been dealt. Don't start judging this. Annie Dillard said to write as if you were dying and I'm trying to.

More about Sally. She was a twenty-five-year-old swimmer who had outgrown the sport. She had come in second in the NCAA for Tennessee the year she was a junior in college. That had been the peak. It had been downhill ever since. Still, she could run as fast as I could and once she had had an affair with a sportswriter I had a crush on, and on the basis of that we had become fast friends. She liked the illusion of a home I had created with Eric and I thought she was good enough for me. We liked the way each other looked. She was tall and blond and pretty and I was extravagantly well dressed. She was my running buddy in 1975. I liked to have a good-looking slightly younger woman riding shotgun at all times in those years. For one thing it kept Eric from saying anything when I got drunk. He was much too polite to pout in front of strangers.

So it was Mardi Gras Eve and Jodie Myers's sister was having a party to introduce her long-lost doctor-brother to uptown society. Sally and I followed him around all night. A practicing psychotherapist from San Francisco, California. It was too divine, too marvelous. "Tell me about the mists on the bay," I asked him in the den. "I've never been there. But I read *The Sorcerer of Bolinas Beach* and I couldn't put it down. If I go to San Francisco will I become a different person?"

"You might," he answered. "It will depend on what you take with you when you go."

"Go with us to Mardi Gras tomorrow. We have an invitation to watch the Wild Tchoupitoulas get ready at seven. Come with us. We're going to have a ball."

"I have to stay with my sister and her kids. We'll find each other before the day is through. I'm sure of that."

"He's the cutest man I've ever seen," I told Sally later. "One of us has to have him. There has to be a way."

"He might be gay. He's never married."

"He isn't gay. I would know if he was gay. His mother told me she wanted me to have him. His mother is one of my best friends. She's been wanting me to have him for ages. She wants him to fall in love with me and come back here and live."

"But you're married, Rhoda."

"So what. My marriage is irrelevant in the larger scheme of things." I waved my wineglass in the air. I shimmered in the lights from the chandeliers. I was thirty-six years old, at the height of my wildness and my powers.

We wandered back into the party. Four drawing rooms on the ground floor of a white mansion on Saint Charles Avenue. Black waiters serving champagne and drinks. Jazz playing on a stereo. Beautiful blue sofas in the rooms. Swings on the porches. The children of the house sitting on the stairs in their best clothes watching the grown people get drunk. They were soaking it in. Learning how to be uptown New Orleanians. Let the good times roll. Roll all night long.

Which is not what we did. We went home at twelve to get some sleep. We had to be up at dawn to get ready for the parades.

At that time my three wild sons lived in my house. My husband, Eric. Fifty or sixty gerbils and hamsters. Three Old English sheepdogs. One or two parrots. A white rat that smelled like old cheese. Some turtles in a turtle pond. I guess that's all.

When we got home the children were still up. They were having a party in their rooms. A party or a fight. Sometimes it was hard to tell. The two older boys had people spending the night. The youngest boy was asleep in his room with a barricade at his door so they couldn't get in and do anything to him. The baby-sitter was in the kitchen eating ice cream with her boyfriend. There was a full moon. Every light was on.

I followed Sally into the guest room and watched while she pulled a white negligee over her head. She had a gorgeous body but I had no jealousy of her or anyone. I wanted friends with gorgeous bodies whose fathers were the richest men in Tennessee. I added their power to my power and if we were lucky we ended up with all the good men. What did we want them for? That's what I ask myself now. We didn't want to live with them. We didn't want to mate with them. We didn't want to mother them. Maybe we wanted to be admired by them. Maybe all women want is an audience.

"Did you see anyone you liked at the party except Jodie Myers?" I asked. "I didn't think anyone was there. There wasn't a man at that party I wanted to fuck."

"Me either." She sat down at a dressing table and began to remove her makeup. She lathered theatrical cold cream all over her face and carefully began to remove it with tissues. "I'm going to wear a feather mask that was made in Mexico tomorrow. It's in that box. You can look at it if you want to. What are you going to wear?"

"Eric's old tails. He gave them to me. He's crazy about you. He's so glad you're here."

"Do you ever fuck him?"

"Not much. I might tonight though, if he wants to. He's been such an angel all week. He hasn't moped or frowned or said a word about anything."

"He's a darling man. He's a perfect husband. You're lucky to have him."

"I am, aren't I? Yes, I am. Thanks for reminding me of that." I kissed her on the top of the head and went into my bedroom and took off my clothes and got into bed and held my husband in my arms. He had on Brooks Brothers pajamas. He was asleep. He felt like a large, sweet child asleep in my arms. Marriage, what a lovely, stupid, completely misunderstood idea.

We woke at dawn and all began to run around the house getting on our costumes. The children were going as hippies, which was easy since that's what the older two aspired to be. The little boy was going as a clown, only he got mad when he saw himself in the mirror and refused to wear the costume. Then Sally took over and painted his face and lent him a mask and turned him into a wild man from Borneo, complete with spear.

Eric refused to dress up. He was a Harvard lawyer and he did not forget it, even on Mardi Gras day. Sally put on some tight blue jeans and an even tighter T-shirt with no bra and the feather mask. I put on my jeans and the top of Eric's old black tails. We stuffed money in our pockets and locked the dogs in the back yard and set off down Webster Street to Tchoupitoulas. The streets were already full of maskers. We walked for many blocks, waving at everyone, admiring costumes, giving beads to people. The children ran ahead, then ran back. It was a perfect February day. Seventy degrees, a cloudy sky.

We stopped on a corner and bought doughnuts and coffee

from a vendor and sat on the curb eating breakfast. The neighborhoods were poorer and blacker in this part of town. We were lucky white people who had been invited to the warehouse where the Tchoupitoulas Indians got ready for their stomp. They were the most beautifully costumed participants in all the parades. The wildest and the best dancers. Race relations were not a problem in New Orleans in the seventies. Or if they were I was too rich and drunk to know it.

Let me put it this way. Race relations had taken a back seat to the Vietnam war. The war had redrawn the alliances, had brought the young people into an understanding that transcended race. Hell, no, we won't go. Won't go into your armies, your factories, your law firms, fuck you. For better or for worse I had sided with the young in this matter. I hardly had a friend over thirty.

We arrived at Tchoupitoulas Street, which runs along beside the Mississippi River. We crossed the street to walk beside the piers. It smelled like diesel oil and fish and the rich, brown smell of the river. I began to think maybe it was time to drink some wine but Sally had a better idea. She pulled out a bottle of pills and we each swallowed a five-milligram Dexedrine and offered one to Eric. "No, thanks, no," he said. "I haven't recovered from that last diet you put me on."

"You lost ten pounds," I said. "You were the only one who lost weight on it."

The children had run ahead. They were half a block ahead of us, playing and fighting, jumping around like hunting dogs. What did they think of the life we were leading? What do any children in New Orleans think of Carnival? They knew one thing for sure. Pretty soon they would be able to get anything they wanted out of Sally and me. They would have been crazy if they didn't know that.

We arrived at the warehouse just as the Tchoupitoulas Indians were coming one by one out a side door. Their costumes are the only thing at Mardi Gras that rival the costumes in Brazil. They are made of feathers and have wide skirts that swish around from side to side. Men in tuxedos with decorated umbrellas dance around them, protecting them from sun and rain.

A journalist I sometimes fucked for fun was with them. They loved him because he wrote flattering things about them that were printed in newspapers in New York City and Washington, D.C. "Hey, Rhoda," he called out and hurried to my side. "Aren't they magnificent. I'm so glad you came."

He was a very tall, very skinny journalist with an I.Q. of 150 and the mind of a small child. He had been born on my birthday, same day, same year. We were astral twins. We adored each other and Eric understood it and was not jealous of him.

"This is Mick McVee," I told Sally. "You can't have him. He belongs to me. He got us the invitation to come down here. Where do we go, Mick? What are the tickets for?"

"Well, it's too late now. They're going to Gertrude Geddis Funeral Home to join Zulu. Come on, we'll follow them. I think you're going to get a coconut from Zulu. One of the young Nevilles promised he'd get you one. But you can't tell what will happen. He might back out. Come on, follow me." He struck off after the Wild Tchoupitoulas and we followed him. We wound around some small streets to Jackson Avenue and went down Jackson to Simon Bolivar where the elite of black society in New Orleans was gathering for the first parade of the day. Zulu, the heart of black power and black pride.

Sometime in the next hour the first bottle of wine appeared. Before long I had one to carry with me.

We followed Zulu all the way to Lee Circle, where a law firm Eric was friendly with had a building with a fenced-in lawn from which we were going to watch the parades. There was a buffet inside the building and servants to watch the children. There were bleachers to sit on. All the powerful Jewish lawyers in town seemed to be there, buying into this Christian pageantry and mess without a qualm. Why should they have qualms? A party is a party to a New Orleanian. If you don't like it, move away.

Around eleven o'clock Sally and I left Eric with the children and wandered down to the French Quarter to look for Jodie Myers. We had some vague idea of which building the Myers family used to watch parades. "I think they use the Lang Building on Royal Street," Eric said. "You'd better call before you go wandering down there."

"We'll find it. We won't be gone long. Sally's in love with Jodie. I promised I'd help her find him."

"You can't even move in the Quarter on Mardi Gras. There's nothing there you can't see here. This is the best place in town."

"Then stay here and watch the boys. I'll be back soon." I put my arm around his waist. I flirted with him. I made him part of a wilder, bigger, braver world. He fell for it, as always. He had read too many novels as a child. He was always up for fantasy. He gloried in it, to tell the truth. He loved having wild, rich Christian women on his hands. He was even glad to nurse the children.

"I'll bring her back," Sally said. "We really just want to see the costumes the gay men wear." She gave him a kiss on the face. We surrounded him with madness and drunken charm. Then we left.

We wandered down Camp Street to Canal. Rex was passing now, with its long string of homemade truck floats carrying all the peons from the suburbs. Their fat queens, their happy children, their dogs. I should have been a pair of ragged claws scuttling across the floors of ancient seas, and so forth.

In the Quarter the streets were thronged with people, but Sally and I were not worried. We were safe in wine and Dexedrine. We caught beads and threw them back. We gave away money. We stopped at a bar and had a drink. We moved down Royal Street toward Jackson Square. Gay men were on the balconies in their elaborate and bawdy costumes. We threw beads to them. We praised them. They tossed us flowers. They praised us back.

A handsome man with a British accent stopped us on the street. "Do you know the way to the Royal Orleans?" he asked.

"Who are you?" I answered. "Why are you wearing a business suit?"

"I'm an engineer. I came on business. Lucky to get here for this, wouldn't you say?"

"Why do you want the Royal Orleans?"

"Because I'm staying there. I've lost my way."

"We'll take you home. I'm Rhoda and this is Sally. We are looking for a psychiatrist."

"You need to talk to one?"

"We are in love with one. We'll call him from the hotel. We'll get him to come and have a drink with us. Come on along. Don't lose sight of us."

Back on Lee Circle Eric had lost my two oldest sons. They had borrowed twenty dollars from him and told him they were going across the street. Two hours later they had not come back. When I called the law firm to talk to him, he was frantic. "What can I do?" I asked. "I'm at the Royal Orleans with a British engineer. I'll come back as soon as I can. You stay there. And don't lose Teddy."

"I didn't lose Malcolm and Jimmy. They ran away."

"They'll come back when they want some more money. Don't leave. I'll be there as soon as I can." I turned back from the phone. We were in the Englishman's room. Sally was sprawled on the bed, her mask in her hand. The Englishman was sitting on a chair. He was a game and very well-behaved Englishman. He didn't ask questions. He just went along. "I have to go back to the law firm," I told Sally. "Eric lost Malcolm and Jimmy. I'll take this Englishman with me. Do you want to go with us or stay here and look for Jodie?"

"I'll stay here," she said. "I like it here."

"You can use my room." The Englishman handed her the room key.

"Well, come on then." I stood up. "We may have to fight our way back to Lee Circle."

There is a strange malaise to Mardi Gras afternoon. Like the let-down of Christmas afternoon when you were a child. The presents are all unwrapped and nothing has changed. It's still your same old life. Only on Mardi Gras you are drunk or half-drunk and it's the middle of the afternoon and all the parades have passed.

The Englishman and I fought our way to Canal Street and crossed it and began to walk down Camp Street to Lee Circle. "I say, I never meant to take up your whole day," he said. "It's awfully nice of you to let me tag along."

"My oldest sons are lost. You may be in for more than you bargained for. They are very wild. American children have gone crazy the last few years. You may have heard about that."

"It isn't only American children, you know. We have our problems also. How old are they, these two oldest sons?"

"Fourteen and fifteen. They might be back when we get to the law firm. It's an historic old building. It was a library and then a radio station during the Second World War. Now it's a law firm. Well, maybe they'll be back."

"I hope your friend will be all right alone. Should we have left her there?"

"She can take care of herself. She was a swimmer. She came in second in the NCAA. That's our college competition. Well, since then she can't find anything that good to do."

"Fascinating. How much farther do we have to go?"

"A few more blocks. We can ride the streetcar home from Lee Circle to my house. It goes right to my house." We were passing the blood banks and homeless shelters now, the part of Camp Street that might not appeal too much to an Englishman. I hurried down the street. Somehow the spilled beads and plastic trinkets and straggling maskers seemed so much sadder here. One thing about being a distance runner. You can move fast when you need to. I moved, and the Englishman kept up with me.

Eric was out on Camp Street when I got back to the law firm. He was waiting for me. I introduced him to the Englishman and he was charming to him. He was always charming to everyone. I can't imagine a better husband than Eric. It wasn't his fault I was not cut out to be a wife. The gene pool is wide and deep. There are plenty of homemakers in the DNA. Plenty of angels like my mother. There are also women like Sally and me. I suppose we are there in case of war.

This wasn't war, however. This was Mardi Gras and it was winding down into a mess. "Teddy's inside with Trip Devereaux," Eric said. "No one's seen the boys. I called the house several times. I was hoping they'd gone home."

"Maybe the gypsies stole them. I bet if they did they'll bring them back."

"'The Ransom of Red Chief,'" the Englishman said.

"How did you know about that?"

"I was a student of American literature as a youth. I had an aunt who married an American. She sent me books."

"Where is Sally, by the way?" Eric asked.

"She's at the Royal Orleans. She's looking for Jodie Myers. I told you, she's in love with him."

"But Jodie's gay." Eric laughed his most boyish laugh and I went to his side and hugged him tight. He was a darling husband and a wonderful father to my terrible children. He was a jewel of the earth and I was a fool not to appreciate it. "She shouldn't be in the Quarter alone on Mardi Gras afternoon. How will she get home?"

"She could run. She has on running shoes."

"We should call her before we go home. Let's go inside and call the house and the hotel. I don't like having everyone spread out like this. I think we should go on home and wait for all of them there. Come home with us, Robert. Come see where we live."

"Please do," I added. "I'm committed to your Mardi Gras. I want you to experience the real thing."

"Good of you to want me," he answered. "Perhaps I will be of some help."

We alerted the guards at the law firm to be on the lookout for the boys. We called the hotel to look for Sally, but she was not there. We called the house and one of the boys' friends answered the phone. "They were here a little while ago," he said. "But then they went to the park."

"What are you doing, William?" I asked. "What's going on at my house?"

"We're just sitting on your steps," he said. "Jimmy gave us some Cokes."

"If they come back tell them to stay until we get there. Stay there and wait for them and tell them that, will you?"

"Sure. If you want me to. I don't have anything to do."

"What were they doing, William? Who are they with?"

"They're not doing anything. Just walking around to see what's going on."

Years later I found out where they were. They were in the park feeding marijuana to the sheepdogs. "Those dogs loved getting stoned," Jimmy told me, one rainy afternoon a million years later. He was visiting from the Virgin Islands, where he is the captain of a charter boat. "They'd curl up in our laps and go to sleep."

"Don't tell me that. I can't stand to know that."

"Everyone at our house was high on something, Momma. We all lived to tell the story, didn't we?"

"Jesus. Maybe Randolph is right. Maybe we should have pretended to believe in God."

But back to Mardi Gras in 1975.

We did not have to take the streetcar home after all. The law firm had hired limousines for the day and we rode home in one of those. We drove home down Magazine Street through the straggling crowds. We hung out the windows and threw the rest of our beads to people. Teddy sat on Eric's lap and threw nickels and dimes and quarters to other children. All our loose change. We had made it through another Carnival. I wasn't even drunk. I had walked off all the wine and Dexedrine.

When we got home my sons were sitting on the front steps with seven or eight of their friends. I got out of the limousine and introduced them to the Englishman.

"Mrs. Myers called," the oldest one said. "She called three times. She wants you to come over. She has something to give you."

"She's the mother of the psychiatrist Sally is chasing," I told the Englishman. "She lives around the corner. She's a genius."

"Is everyone you know a genius?" he asked.

"A lot of them are. Do you want to go and meet her?"

"I'll stay here and talk to the young people, if you don't mind."

"I'll take care of him," Eric said. "Go on and see what she wants."

I left the men and boys and walked around the corner to pay a call on Jodie Myers's mother. She was a true ally of mine in the years I lived in New Orleans. A fabulous woman who had done everything there was to do and now was an invalid who had to stay in bed and live vicariously through her friends. At one time or the other she had offered me everything she owned, her paintings, her ball gowns, her sons. She had three handsome sons and she was always offering them to me, even the one who was married. Her name was Rachel and I loved her and always came when she summoned me.

It was five in the afternoon when I arrived at her house. The maid let me in and I climbed the winding staircase to Rachel's exotic bedroom. Four blocks away Sally was being raped in the Jeffersons' front yard. Behind a high brick wall, within twenty feet of Saint Charles Avenue, a sixteen-year-old kid was holding a knife on her while she took off her socks and shoes and her blue jeans and her underpants and lay down upon the ground underneath a live oak tree.

The maid brought a tray of coffee and cookies to the room and set it upon a table. I sat down on the edge of the bed and began to tell Rachel about the day.

"What did you think of Jodie?" she asked, and we both began to giggle.

"I fell in love with him, of course. What did you think would happen, you white witch, you? He looks like you. He has your eyes."

"He liked you too. He told me so this morning. He's going to be here for a week. You can come over tomorrow and I'll have him here." She laughed out loud. She moved her beautiful hands across the satin bedspread. Beside the bed was the incredible Monet. Across the room was the Van Gogh drawing. There was a Calder mobile. She had lived her life. She had not been consigned to this bed until she was seventy.

I moved closer to her. I propped pillows behind my head and kicked off my shoes and stuck my legs down underneath the covers. She handed me a demitasse and a Lorna Doone. I sat back. I sighed. I began to eat the edge around the Lorna Doone. "Why do I need your sons?" I asked. "I have you. You're more fun than they are."

"You can have them and me too." She reached for a package of Camels, took one out and began to fit it into a small ivory holder. "How many do you want?"

"Jodie would do. Only my friend, Sally, is in love with him too. I sort of agreed to let her have him. I have this Englishman I picked up in the Quarter. He's over there now, with Eric and the boys. He says he's an engineer. But I keep having this paranoid idea that he might be some sort of writer."

"What do you mean?"

"Like some undercover reporter writing about Mardi Gras for some English magazine. What if he was?"

"Then he certainly found the best material. What's his name?"

"Robert something. I forgot. Anyway, I wish I could have Jodie but I think Sally really wants him."

"You can both have him. There's enough to go around, I imagine. If he's anything like his father." She started really laughing now. Holding her unlit cigarette and laughing. I got up from the bed and got another Lorna Doone and began to walk around the room nibbling it and looking at things. It was the biggest bedroom in uptown New Orleans. It had been made from three rooms on the second floor of a Victorian mansion. The room was a curve, as the rooms had curved around a central hall. There were dormer windows that looked out upon a garden and a wall. Pots of geraniums were on the wall, a cat curled up on a picnic table, beds of daisies, a hedge of cape jasmine beginning to put out blooms.

"I don't need any men right now," I said. "There's too much going on. Malcolm's so bad. He quit the football team. And he won't be nice to Eric's parents. He's so rude to them."

"Good for him. They would make him the scapegoat if they could. I know those people. Good for him for seeing through them." The phone began to ring. Rachel found the telephone beneath a pile of magazines and extricated the receiver and began to listen. "Oh, no," she said. "She's right here. I'll put her on."

There is a strange thing about being involved in a rape. You don't feel guilty like you do after a car wreck or something like that. A rape is an act of God. It's a matter of being in the wrong place at the wrong time. It's not as if I could have stopped it by being more caring or aware.

"Something's happened to Sally," Eric said, when Rachel handed me the phone. "She's been hurt. She's here with us. You better come home now."

"Hurt? How hurt? What happened?"

"She says she was raped. Just a short while ago. I called a doctor. I called Uncle Harris."

"I'll be right there." I hung up the phone and dropped the Lorna Doone on the plate. "Sally's been raped. Call Jodie, will you? Tell him to come to my house and help us." I bent over and kissed Rachel and she took a pearl ring from her finger and held it out to me. "This is what I had for you. An amulet to keep you safe. Take it. You will need it. Put it on." I looked down at the little ring she was holding. I slipped it on my finger. "Okay," I said. "I'll wear it for a while. I have to go, Rachel. I really have to go."

"I know you do. Go on. Run as fast as you can." This was a private joke between us. Once she had been teasing me about running in the park and I had said to her, *When I am worried I run as fast as I can.* She had written it down on a piece of paper and taped it to the door.

I ran now. I ran out of the room and down the stairs and out the front door and across the yard and through the gate and all the way home.

The teenagers were still sitting on my front steps, petting the dogs. There must have been twenty of them by then. They knew what had happened. They had seen Sally staggering down the street. They had helped her into the house. Had been the first to hear the story.

Sally was in my bed with Eric and the Englishman sitting beside her. I made them leave. "She needs a bath," I said. "I want to get her into the tub." I lay down beside her on the bed and petted her and crooned to her and finally convinced her to get up and go into the bathroom and take off her clothes and get into the tub. I knelt beside the tub and sponged water over her shoulders and her arms and listened to her whimper. She was bruised and trembling, but she did not seem to be bleeding anywhere.

Eric's internist uncle arrived and I put a robe on Sally and led her back to the bed. He examined her and said she wasn't hurt and gave us some pills to give her. Then Eric came back into the room and we sat on the bed on either side of her and petted her and finally she began to talk. She said the same three or four things over and over again. "He was just a kid. I should have kicked the shit out of him. I wasn't afraid. I swear I wasn't afraid."

About dark Jodie Myers arrived and took over. He sat beside her and got her to take the pills Uncle Harris had left for her. That was what he did in San Francisco. He worked in a trauma center in an emergency room at a hospital. He had seen worse things than this. "Much, much worse," he told us, after Sally fell asleep.

At eight o'clock I ran the teenagers off and made my children come into the kitchen and eat supper. The Englishman ate with them. "Very unlucky," he said several times. "Damned bad luck."

"Can I go to William Gill's house and get my algebra book?" Jimmy asked. "I left my book over there."

"No, you cannot," I answered. "Tomorrow is a school day. Everyone's going to bed as soon as they eat. You can call him and tell him to bring it for you."

I took my children to their part of the house and watched while they brushed their teeth and stood by the door while they took showers and put on their pajamas and got into their beds. I tucked them in and talked to them about Sally and promised to drive them to school so they wouldn't have to ride the school bus.

Eric drove the Englishman back to the Royal Orleans. I went into the bedroom several times and checked on Sally but she was fast asleep. I picked up her clothes and threw them in a pile in the laundry room. I put the feather mask on a shelf by a box of laundry powder.

We did not call the police. It never occurred to us to call the police and take a chance on Sally's name getting into the paper.

*   *   *

When Eric got back from the Quarter we went into the guest room to go to sleep. We curled up in each other's arms. We were married to each other. We helped each other out when things went wrong. "I'm going to quit drinking for Lent," I said. "Except for my birthday and Sundays. I might go to Ash Wednesday service tomorrow. Sally might want to go if she feels better."

"Let's go to sleep. I'm really tired."

"I know you are. Goodnight, sweetheart. Sweet dreams, my pet." I held him in my arms. I will wear my white wool suit to church, I decided, and that white-and-black Chanel scarf I got in Paris. It might be too hot, but I can't worry about that. You can't worry about being hot if you want to look good. You have to put up with some discomfort in this climate.

Joyce

IN 1976 Doctor Wheeler taught Joyce for the last time. He had sworn never to teach it again but the graduate students begged and pleaded and the dean cajoled and finally, one Sunday morning at breakfast at The Station, with the graduate students all around him and a piece of pumpkin pie topping off his scrambled eggs, he gave in and said yes.

"I will teach it," he said. "If you will read it. I won't lecture if no one reads the books. My notes are not the works of James Joyce. Don't take it unless you're going to read the books."

"We will," they swore. "You can count on us." And all around the long table of young writers and graduate students a great sigh of determination took place and moved from one to the other and rose like a cloud and joined the smoke from Doctor Wheeler's cigarette. Nothing is free. To be in the presence of so much brilliance was also to be in the presence of cigarette smoke. Doctor Wheeler chain-smoked. He smoked because he liked to smoke. He smoked until the very last minute of the clock that ticked away his life. After all, how much oxygen does a man with one leg need?

One of the students at the table was a woman named Rhoda Manning. She was a housewife from New Orleans who was trying to learn to write poetry. All morning every morning she sat at a Royal portable typewriter in a small apartment near the campus and tried to turn everything she saw or experienced into metaphor. She was forty years old and she considered this the time of her life. She had this one semester to be a student in a writing program, with other students all around her and people like Doctor Wheeler to adore. She knew about Joyce. She had tried to read Joyce. She had an old recording of Siobhan McKenna reading Joyce. Now she was going to study Joyce. She stood up. She raised her glass. "Champagne," she said. "Let's order champagne. This demands a celebration. He's going to teach the Joyce seminar. We will read *Ulysses*."

Also at the table was a tall unhappy man named Ketch Mc-Sweeney. He had been in Vietnam and had brought his wife and daughter to Fayetteville to learn how to write a book about the war. He couldn't stop thinking about the war. He couldn't stop dreaming about the war, so he thought he might as well make some money writing about the war. Not that he had much in the way of alternatives being offered to him at the moment. He was from Pennsylvania and had come to school to find a way to begin to make a stand. His wife had a job teaching second grade and his daughter was in a cheap Montessori school. He was making twelve thousand dollars a year being a graduate student in the writing program and teaching semiliterate freshmen to read and write the language that they spoke. He didn't mind. He was a good-looking man and the young girls all made eyes at him and he was sure that sooner or later he would make a killing of some kind in the writing business. Meanwhile, he was determined to make the best of it and have all the fun he could while he waited.

"I will teach it in the fall," Doctor Wheeler said. "Sign up now because I'll limit the size of the class."

*   *   *

The next afternoon Ketch McSweeney and Rhoda Manning met at the registrar's office. "You too?" she said. "Jesus, we're lucky. I can't believe he's teaching it."

"I thought you were going back to New Orleans after this semester. You decided to come back?"

"I will now. I can't miss this."

"What about your husband? He's going to let you do this?"

"I'm doing it. I'm going to be a poet if it takes the rest of my life."

"That's how I feel. Only I want to make some dough. There's got to be a way to make some money writing books."

"Well, I'll see you in class then, won't I? If not before."

They didn't see each other again until the fall. But they were thinking about it. Both of them had been on the make most of their lives. Not to feed off other people or do intentional harm. Just to sample the wares of the world, to trade at the fair, to know the mornings, evenings, afternoons and not to hesitate when something fine or plump or juicy was at stake. They both liked excitement and they both knew how to generate it.

Doctor Wheeler thought about them too. He read over the list of writers and graduate students who were signed up for the course and as he read he knew much of what would transpire. He had taught this class too many times not to know its generative power and its dangers. He had taught it the year Amanda McCamey showed up on campus. He had taught it to Barry Hannah and Frank Stanford. He had taught it the year Carolyn Forche was the poet in residence and would come and sit in on his classes and look at him with her wide, beautiful, Eastern European eyes.

He walked out into his garden and thought about it. His garden overlooked the Confederate Cemetery. In it he had planted all the flowers he remembered from his youth. Hollyhocks and morning glories, pansies, delphiniums, foxglove and four o'-clocks and bachelor's buttons.

"Virag speaks," he said out loud. "(Agueshaken, profuse yellow spawn foaming over his bony epileptic lips.) She sold lovephiltres, whitewax, orange flower, Panther, the Roman centurion, polluted her with his genitories. . . .'"

The first meeting of the class took place on a warm September night. A new moon was in the sky. A thin silver curve deep in the dark sky. Eight o'clock. The students had gathered in the hall, they milled around and talked about their summer adventures, they looked each other over, they overcame their egos and were kind. "Let's go in," Ketch said. "He'll be here in a minute." Rhoda went inside and found a seat in the middle of the room. He came and sat beside her and propped his legs on the rungs of an empty chair. She laid a notebook on the desktop and turned and smiled at him. Good, there wasn't going to be any pretense. He wasn't going to be coy.

Doctor Wheeler came into the room and sat down behind the desk and lit a cigarette. He adjusted his artificial leg so that it rested against one of the legs of the desk. He looked out across the thirty-two faces waiting to be filled. He took a drag on the Camel and began. "We will begin with *Portrait of the Artist as a Young Man.* This is Stephen's story, the young Stephen who later will be the lover in *Ulysses,* and Leopold's foil. His name is Stephen Daedalus. 'The archaic Greek mind ascribed all things cunningly wrought, whether a belt with a busy design, the rigging of a ship, or an extensive palace, to the art of the craftsman Daedalus, whose name first appears in the *Iliad.* Homer, describing the shield Hephaistos makes for Achilles, says that the dancing floor depicted on it was as elaborate as that which Daedalus designed for Ariadne in Crete. This dancing floor is perhaps what Homer understood the Labyrinth to be. Joyce did, for the ground on which he places all his figures is clearly meant to be a labyrinth.' This from Guy Davenport. The book's on the desk. You can look at it when we take a break."

"Now, you won't have to wander into that labyrinth so soon in the fall. Read the first two hundred pages of the *Portrait* for next week. How many of you have a copy already?" He waited while fifteen or twenty students held up their hands.

"Good. How many have it with you?" The same twenty or so held up their hands. Ketch and Rhoda were among these good students.

"Fine; and here are seven or eight copies I brought along from the library. The rest of you can share them." He sat back. Nodded his head. Rhoda opened her fresh new copy of the book and beside her Ketch opened his. "What are you doing after class?" he asked. "Let's go and have a glass of wine."

"Fine. I'd love it. We can go to my house. I have some wine I brought back from New Orleans. Better than anything you can get around here." She smiled and looked him in the eye. Good, better, best, no hesitation, no fooling around or wasting time. She scooted her chair an infinitesimal bit closer to his.

"Take the role of Aristotle," Doctor Wheeler was saying. "He plays in the minds of the characters. He appears over and over. Stephen Daedalus in 'Proteus' is conversant with Aristotle and ponders and tests his ideas. Bloom in 'Lestrogonians' is interested, perhaps unwittingly, in many of the same matters that interested Aristotle, and Molly knows or probably cares so little about him that she turns his name into Aristocrat. Many streams like this flow between the minds of the characters. You can get an A in here if you find one I haven't seen. . . ."

Ketch looked at Rhoda. Watched as her dress slid up her silk stockings when she crossed and uncrossed her legs. He sighed. She turned her head and acknowledged it.

*   *   *

They left the building by the wide front door and walked out onto the main street of the campus. "I wish we could walk," she said. "It's such a pretty night. It's only a few blocks to my house. Want to leave the cars and walk?"

"Sure. Why not?"

"We can walk home through the old cemetery on Spring Street. Have you ever been there?"

"No. Not that I know of."

"It's nice. The old families that built the town are buried there. I used to go up there with a photographer friend of mine and try to make art photos." She shifted her notebook and bag to her other arm and began to walk briskly down the street. "What do you think? Do you think it's going to be good? I think he's a genius. I love to watch him smoke. Sometimes he has two cigarettes going at once."

"I need the credits. I want to get out of here as soon as I can. All I want is a novel and an MFA and I'm gone. I've got to earn a living."

"I don't have to worry about that right now. We can go up there and take the path through the cemetery if you want. Are you ready?" She was walking very fast, and he quickened his pace and caught up with her. They went up a gravel road and came out at the top of a small old cemetery with huge maple trees hiding the sky and walked in darkness past the massive tombstones. "This will put it in perspective, won't it," Rhoda dropped the notebook and the bag on the ground and let him kiss her. Then she took his arm and they walked more slowly down the hill and across the street to her apartment building.

They opened wine and lit candles and then Rhoda went into her bedroom and put on a long blue silk kimono and they took the wine into the bedroom and made love with the window open and the thin moon, now brilliant in a cloudless sky, making their skin luminous and white. They made love out of curiosity and greed, without passion or tenderness or joy. They made love to prove they were mean enough to do it. When it was over he got up and put on his clothes and went home to his wife.

It became a ritual. They went to the Joyce class and listened to Doctor Wheeler explicate the material which they usually had not read, since the semester had heated up and they were busy writing and exploring the world. Rhoda would read the assignment in the car as she drove to class, get there half an hour early, take a seat and read very fast until Doctor Wheeler came in the door. When she met him on the campus she would tell him about it. "I'm behind," she would say. "But your lectures are brilliant. I want to hear them."

"Don't worry about it," he would answer. "Just read as much as you can."

And every Wednesday night after class Rhoda and Ketch would go to her apartment and make love and drink wine and talk about their work and where they were submitting it and what had been accepted where. As the semester wore on they became thinner and meaner. The anxiety of writing and not being published began to wear on them.

"I'm writing a short story," she told him one night. "I know it won't be any good. I'm just writing it to please Randolph. He said I have to write one to get an MFA."

"Oh, what's it about?" Ketch sat up. This wasn't right. She was a poet. He was a fiction writer. On this basis they fucked each other. No, it wasn't right. "I wouldn't waste my time on that if I was you," he said. "You're publishing poems. Fuck Randolph."

"Well, I just want to try. It's pretty funny really. It's set in New Orleans."

"Oh."

"Well, that's where I live. Where else would it be set?"

"I'd like to see it when it's finished."

"Sure. It would be nice if you'd read it." But Rhoda had seen the jealousy. She knew she would never show him a line she wrote after that. Fuck him, she was thinking. His stories aren't that good. They're too violent. No one's ever going to want to read them.

In the middle of November they had come to the "Sirens" in *Ulysses*. "A husky fifenote blew. Blew. Blue bloom is on the gold pinnacled hair. A jumping rose on satiny breasts of satin, rose of Castille. Trilling, trilling; Idolores. . . ." Rhoda's plans had changed. She was going to have to go home to New Orleans and finish the semester by correspondence. Her youngest son was in trouble and her husband had demanded she return. She was glad to go. She was bored with being a graduate student in a writing program and living in an apartment and doing her own laundry. She was tired of going to classes and writing papers and waiting for her poetry to be published. She was bored with fucking Ketch on Wednesday nights. It was so cold, so pointless, so rude. The week before she had been menstruating, bleeding like a stuck pig from her Lippes Loop. They had gotten drunk and made love anyway. In the morning there was blood everywhere, on the carpet, on the sofa, on the lining of her blue silk kimono. She never threw the kimono away. After being cleaned six times it still showed the bloodstains on the hem. She kept it anyway, out of some sort of abandoned rebellion, to remember how bad she had been and how free.

*   *   *

"This is a fugue," Doctor Wheeler was saying. "The sirens sit on a meadow on the bones of sailors. The music is a flight of song. The barmaids are the sirens. Twin sirens, they sing and dance and draw the sailors in. It is one of the most intense parts of the book. Joyce believed he should leave behind him a burnt-out field. . . ."

"I have to go home Friday," Rhoda was whispering. "For good. To see about my son."

"This Friday?"

"As soon as class is out. He's making bad grades, driving my husband crazy. He's sixteen. I shouldn't have left him to begin with."

"What about your classes? How can you leave?"

"I'll do them by mail. Everyone is going to let me. Well, I haven't asked him yet." She looked toward Doctor Wheeler, who was lighting one Camel from another. He was leaned over his desk, his artificial leg propped against the desk leg, papers spread out before him on the desk.

"He'll let you. He's crazy about you."

"Joyce's mother was a pianist," Doctor Wheeler was saying. "His father was a tenor. Joyce himself was both a pianist and a tenor. Everywhere in this chapter, which is a small inset in 'Scylla and Charybdis,' of course, are references to preludes, overtures, fugues. Fugue means flight, by the way. Pound disapproved of this episode, wanted it out of the manuscript, but Joyce insisted on it. As the sailors are taken in by the sirens, likewise the sirens are enchanted by the sailors' voices. It is like a prelude stuck in the middle of 'Scylla and Charybdis.' There are so many nice touches. The piano brings in Bloom, for example. In music you can play two themes at once, of course. And everywhere is blue and white, the Virgin's colors. . . ."

"My short story was accepted by *Intro*," she said. "So that's nice. I didn't tell you that, did I?"

"What?"

"Randolph sent it to *Intro* and they took it. It's going to be the lead piece."

"*Intro?*"

"What's wrong?"

"We better be quiet."

She watched him seethe. *Intro* was the epitome for a writer in a writing program in 1976. It was the springboard. New York agents read it. *Intro* could be the start of a real career. Ketch had five stories on his desk right now that had been turned down by *Intro*.

"This is a song from an opera," Doctor Wheeler was saying. "Oh, my Delores. Later they will toast the thirty-two counties of Ireland. Joyce hated Rome and thought it inhospitable. Rift in the lute. Well, it's getting late. Be sure and get up to page four hundred for next week." He stood up, began to gather his papers, laid a cigarette down on the edge of the desk where it teetered precariously, messily smoking. Rhoda went up to him and began to have a conversation about her leaving and he shook his head from side to side and up and down and agreed that she should go home and take care of her son. "I'll miss you," he said. "I was looking forward to your paper."

"Oh, I'll write it. I can't wait to write it. I can't tell you how much I've loved this. I'll always feel like something passionate and critical was interrupted in my life. Something important." She looked into his thin sweet face, his clear good face. Ketch was behind her, standing near the door. The other students were gone. There were only the three of them. I want to follow you home, she felt like saying. I want to sit up all night and talk to you.

Ulysses had himself tied to the mast not to miss their singing, Doctor Wheeler was thinking. Sound of the sirens, sound of the sea.

"Mail it to me when you write it," he said. "What episode would you like?"

"Oh, 'Penelope.'"

"Of course. You've finished the book then?"

"No. I've always known it. I had a recording of it by Siobhan McKenna when I was young. I may know it by heart."

"Then do that. I'll look forward to reading it." He waited.

"Come on," Ketch said. "We better go."

They went out the door and down the long hall and the marble stairs and out into the parking lot. "Let's walk to my house," she said. "For old times' sake and go up to the cemetery. I can walk to school tomorrow. I like to."

"Okay. If you like." They began to walk down the sidewalk in the direction of the gravel road behind the buildings. It was a cloudy night. A waning moon rode the spaces between the clouds. It was cool but not too cold. Ten o'clock on a Wednesday night. The campus was deserted. They walked without talking up to the cemetery and stopped under a maple tree by a large granite tombstone with a kneeling angel and lay down upon the grave, upon his coat, and fucked each other without mercy.

When it was over he got up and buttoned his pants and stood leaning on the tombstone waiting while she stood up and shook off his coat and gave it back to him. He put it on. She took his arm and they walked down the hill to her apartment.

"Why does this remind me of the poets versus the fiction writers baseball game?" she asked.

"I don't know. Well, I've got to be going now. Joanne's waiting for me." He left her then and she went inside and sat down at her typewriter and went back to work on a poem she had started that morning.

> *At any moment you may meet the child you were*
> *There, by the Sweet Olive tree.*
> *If you turn the corner by the faucet*
> *He will come around the other way*
> *Carrying your old sandbucket*
> *And your shovel*
>
> *You may notice the displeasure in his eyes,*
> *A sidelong glance, then he'll be gone,*
> *Leaving you holding your umbrella*
> *With a puzzled look, while the spring day*
> *Drops like a curtain between the clocks*
> *And the dialogue you rely on stops.*

Doctor Wheeler walked up the dark steps to his house. His cats were waiting beside the door. "Darlings," he cooed. "Simonedes. Dave. Well, wait a second. Let me find the key." He laid his papers on the wooden porch floor, found the key in the pocket of his jacket, turned it in the latch, and went into the darkened room. The cats followed him. He walked back out onto the porch to collect his papers. Above the house the maple trees stood guard. Doctor Wheeler knew them in every weather. Had seen them bent double by wind. Had known them in lightning, rain, snow, or when fall turned them saffron and gold, as they had been only a week ago. They were fading now. Winter was coming on.

He went back into the house and lit the fire and fed the cats and sat down in his armchair. Homer was on the table by the chair. He picked up the book and held it to his chest, patting it as though it were a child. Finally, when he had almost fallen asleep, he reached up above him and turned on a lamp and opened the book at random.

> *The old nurse went upstairs exalting,*
> *with knees toiling, and patter of slapping feet,*
> *to tell the mistress of her lord's return,*
> *and cried out by the lady's pillow;*
> > *"Wake,*
> *wake up, dear child! Penelope, come down,*
> *see with your own eyes what all these years you longed for!*
> *Odysseus is here! Oh, in the end he came!*
> *And he has killed your suitors, killed them all*
> *who made his house a bordel and ate his cattle*
> *and raised their hands against his son!"*

He closed the book and pressed it back into his chest. Then he reached into his jacket pocket and took out a crumpled package of cigarettes and turned off the lamp and lit the cigarette and sat in the dark looking into the fire and smoking.

Going to Join the Poets

RHODA LEFT THE HOUSE on Webster Street early in the morning on a November day. Teddy may have already left to go to school. Maybe the school bus had picked him up to take him to Metairie Park Country Day School and maybe it had not. She didn't mother him anymore. Eric mothered him. He was all that Eric had because she was almost never there. It was a marriage that had failed. She wouldn't have a child for Eric and he wouldn't fuck her anymore. Not that sex between them had ever made either of them happy. It had always been a tortured, patched-up affair. Because they didn't love each other. She loved his money and he loved her cousins getting them into the tennis club. He loved Faulkner. Had written his paper on Faulkner in undergraduate school. Now he was living Faulkner. He was in the middle of a Grecian Faulkner tragedy.

After Rhoda drove off in the new green car, the green Mercedes she had bought with the bonds her father gave her, Eric got Teddy up and made breakfast for him and walked with him to where he caught the bus.

"Your mother's going to be gone awhile," he said. "Let's have some fun while she's gone. Let's go out on the boat. Invite some of your friends."

"Sure." Teddy turned to his stepfather. Trying to decide how to make him feel better. Teddy felt responsible for Eric. "She'll be back, Eric. She always comes back."

"Yeah, I know. Look, there's Robert Skelton hanging out the window looking at you." Eric patted Teddy on the arm. They were the same height now. Every month Teddy grew another inch. He was fifteen years old. Had grown so tall, so sweet, such a sweet young man, such big brown eyes. Eric's heart melted when he looked into those eyes.

Teddy climbed aboard the bus and joined his friends. They waved to Eric. They all loved Eric. He was the best of the best. The best parent any of them had.

The bus drove off down Webster Street in a cloud of black exhaust. Eric walked back to the house to get the dogs and take them for a walk. Three Old English sheepdogs, an outrageous collection of dogs, an unbelievable problem on a fifty-by-one-hundred-foot lot in uptown New Orleans.

The day was cool and fresh. The dogs went crazy when they got outside the fence. They ran everywhere, jumping and turning, making their low muffled sheepdog barks. They overwhelmed Eric, licking him and jumping up beside him. They trembled, waiting to run to the park, in the cool of the morning, waiting to jump into the lagoon and swim out through the lily pads, chasing the geese and ducks.

Aboard the bus Teddy went to the back where the dealing was being done. Robert had a bottle of pills he had stolen from his physician father. David Altmont had a small amount of marijuana. Crazy Eddy had a bottle of whiskey in his lunch box. He was too crazy. He was going to get them all in trouble. Teddy had the sheet of Windowpane he had bought the day before at Benjamin Franklin. "I tried it last night. I want to save most of it for the weekend, but I'll sell ten hits. For cash. I'm not giving this stuff away and I'm not trading."

In the front of the bus the kids who weren't into dope yet looked straight ahead. They pretended not to notice what was going on behind them. "You kids sit down back there," the bus driver yelled. "Sit down and behave yourselves." Teddy took a seat next to his best friend, Robert. "We can go out on the boat this weekend if you want to," he said. "Eric's going to take me. Momma's gone."

"Where'd she go?" Robert liked Teddy's mother. She was always nice to him and talked to him about his father.

"To Arkansas. She's gone up there to find an apartment. She's going to be gone all winter."

"Where will you stay?"

"With Eric and grandmother."

"So where'd you get the Windowpane?"

"They made a batch at Benjamin Franklin last week. It's good. I had a good time last night." He pushed up the window of the bus and stuck his arm out to shoot the peace sign to some kids in a car. He was in a good mood. Nobody was going to bother him this week. The coach was letting him suit up for the game on Saturday morning. Ellie Marcus was going to let him see her Friday night. It was okay. If only he could stay away from his grandmother, he'd be all right.

Rhoda pulled out onto the Bonnet Carré Spillway and speeded up. Hammond, then Brookhaven, then Jackson, then Vicksburg, and Raine would be waiting to drive her up to Arkansas. Well, I'm not in love with him, she was thinking. I just want him to show me how to get there. Arkansas. My God! I don't even know where it is. And I won't feel guilty. It's Eric's fault, goddammit. He shouldn't have stopped fucking me. I can't have a baby. It would kill the children if I did that. It would kill me. She shuddered, thinking of it.

It didn't matter. It didn't matter. She had loved them with all her heart and they were breaking her heart. Especially the oldest, Malcolm, who was so beautiful it seemed the sun came out when he walked into a room. Now he was gone, God knows where. Walking like a god among the hippies. Her golden son, the one who was going to swim the channel for her. She tightened her mouth, speeded up, took a curve doing ninety. It didn't matter. To hell with them. She'd do it herself, would be a poet, would have her name everywhere. Fools' names and fools' faces, always seen in public places. But it wouldn't be like that. It would be like Anne Sexton. Women would weep when they read her poems, would be fused together and save themselves because of it. She slowed down. Tears were welling up in her eyes, the tears she shed every time she thought about the day she started writing. It had happened because of a poem she read. She had gone on her bike to the Tulane track to run. Then she had changed her mind and gone to the Maple Street Bookstore instead and bought a book of Anne Sexton's poems. A posthumous book. *45 Mercy Street.* She had ridden over to the track and sat down upon a bench and started reading. "I am torn in two, but I will conquer myself. I will take scissors and cut out the beggar. I will take a crowbar and pry out the broken pieces of God in me." Then she started crying.

She came around the last curve of the Bonnet Carré Spillway and out onto the long flat bridge across the marshes. Up ahead was the high span of the bridge at Pass Manchac, then the farmlands would begin, then Mississippi, her home. Then Vicksburg, and Raine would be waiting for her, her lover, her one and only love, the one who never stopped loving her no matter how long it was or what she did. Because she was as bad as he was. Because someday she would be as strong. Someday she would overpower him, but she did not know that yet. All she knew now was that he owed her favors and she was going to collect one.

She went to the motel where she had arranged to meet him and got a room and called him and sat down upon the bed to wait. Then he was there, with his exotic smell so terrible and real, so far away from the Chi Omega sorority and anything to do with modern poetry. It was a smell for Homer and the Greeks, for Odysseus, Julius Caesar, the Kha Khan. "How've you been?" she asked him.

"I've been great, baby. How about you?"

Then she took off her clothes and lay down upon the bed with him and tried to remember how to be his baby. Yes, she thought, I do not love him anymore but I will fuck him before I use him as a chauffeur.

Later she cried, because he could always make her cry. Maybe she really wanted to kill him. After they made love they went into the motel dining room and had dinner and then he left her and went back to his house and slept with his wife.

In the morning he came and got her and drove her up to Arkansas, to his state, past the small town where he had been a hero, past towns where he had fucked every other cheerleader, past plantations that belonged to men who paid to shake his hand, past Little Rock, where his sister had died in a dirty hospital, and on up to the northwest Arkansas hills, which did not belong to him or anyone, which were going to belong to Rhoda now, because that was what she wanted.

It was late in the afternoon when they found the campus of the University of Arkansas and parked outside the tall building that housed the English Department. She had been reading the poems to him. Reading some of them two or three times. They were in a blue loose-leaf notebook, more than a hundred of them. A hundred poems she had written that summer in a hundred days. "You stay here," she said, getting out of the car. "I won't be long. I just want to say hello and tell them that I'm here." She stood holding the door of the Lincoln. She was dressed in a black wool suit with a fur collar and black silk hose and high-heeled shoes. "I hate to leave you here."

"It's okay. I'll read the poems."

"Oh, good." She smiled. For a moment she stopped being scared.

She's scared to death, Raine thought. Poor baby, this is her big chance and she doesn't want to blow it. It's just a bunch of underpaid college professors but she doesn't know it. She thinks these guys can teach her something.

He smiled the smile he used for his Little League team. "Go knock 'em dead, baby. I'll be right here." She walked across the street and into the double glass doors of the building. It was growing dark. The swift dark that falls in November. Raine took a *Sporting News* out of the glove compartment and started reading it. Then he put it down and began to leaf through the poems. He liked the one about him. The one she had written years ago at Millsaps. "Pernicious sidewinder, coiled and waiting. Cold and free." She could do it. She was a winner. Well, he was pulling for her. He was on her side.

He had been a champion. He would never have to wait on jealousy, would never have to begrudge a moment's glory to another soul. He bowed his head. Raine paid obeisance to the gods of any place. He was a decent man. Most of the time he played fair and told the truth. He looked off into the west, between two buildings. What was left of the light was spreading out into the low blue clouds on the horizon. It was pretty country, no doubt about that. If she stayed up here it might be good for her.

"Raine." He looked back toward the building. She was hurrying his way with a big man beside her. "Come meet Randolph," she was saying. "He adores you. He had a fit when he found out you were with me."

Raine got out and shook the man's hand. "I'm honored," the man said. "I saw you play when I was a kid. I couldn't believe it when she told me you were sitting outside in the car."

Later, they all went over to the big man's house and the man's wife cooked dinner. Then they sat around the living room and some young people who were trying to learn to be writers came in and met them. Raine and Randolph talked about football. Rhoda and the young people talked about poetry. She acted as if she was happy. She thinks she knows what she is doing, Raine decided. She thinks this is going to save her.

The next day they drove around and found her an apartment to rent and gave a man a deposit on it and arranged for the heat and electricity to be turned on in her name the first of January. Then they went to the big man's office and told him good-bye and then they started driving home.

They stopped in Gould, Arkansas, and bought cheese and crackers and ate them in the car as they drove. It was the first thing she had eaten in days. "I'm glad to see you eat something, baby. You don't eat enough."

"Do you think they liked me? Did Randolph say anything to you?"

"They like you, baby. Hell, compared to those women that

we met, I think that skinny blonde one is a lesbian. I'd watch out for her if I was you."

"She was strange, wasn't she? They said she was a good poet but I can't believe it. She's so ugly. I don't believe in ugly poets." She scooted over closer to him and let him put his arm around her. She dropped cracker crumbs on his pants, then brushed them off. She closed her eyes and lay her head down into the crook of his shoulder. It was over. It was done. She was going to join the poets. It was okay. On the second of January she would come up here to live. Nothing else mattered. Not Eric or Teddy or Malcolm or Jimmy. Nothing mattered but the poems. The poems she would write to make women cry and break them open. To have her name in lights, to be famous, lauded and beloved. She would make it happen. It had started. Nothing could stop her now.

II

The skinny blonde girl did turn out to be a part-time lesbian. She would be whatever her ambition needed her to be. She dug her nails into poetry and held on for dear life. Poison pen, Rhoda thought of her, and it would turn out to be true.

There was also a real poet, a sweet soft girl who was married to a carpenter. The Ally, Rhoda decided. The one I can trust. The night they met they had gotten drunk on gin and laughed until two in the morning.

There was a gorgeous preppie from New England. He recognized a blanket on her bed as coming from a store in Boston. My husband went to Harvard, Rhoda told him. So they formed a bond. He's the one I'll fuck, Rhoda thought. If I can get him.

There was a dope addict and a man who ate too much and a cynical graduate student who was going to make a career of going to school. And five or six more. It was nineteen seventy-six. Writing schools were new things on the horizon. Their staffs were small and made up of people who were still writing. The students were dedicated and poor. Some of them lived on welfare and food stamps. They didn't care if they had a car. They ate and drank and slept poetry and literature.

Strangely enough, a body of poetry was arising from this heat. There was a network of poets and writing schools across the United States. Men and women were writing morning, night, and noon. Some of it was very, very good. "Like a Diamondback in the Trunk of the Witness's Buick" was a title Rhoda loved, after the poet, Francis Alter, took over her education. After he took her away from the writing program and she only listened to him.

But on this first week, this ice-cold week in January, when Rhoda drove to Fayetteville alone and moved into her freezing cold, ugly, little ground-floor apartment, the main thing she had to do was keep warm. "I don't know if you can stand the freezing winters," the director of the program had told her. "It's hard up here in winter." Now she knew what he meant. The first night she slept in the apartment she piled all her clothes on the bed and slept beneath them. It was five above zero outside. It was ten above in the apartment. The next day she went to the office of the apartment building to complain. A gas pipe was broken, she was told. We'll have it fixed sometime today.

That afternoon she went out and rented a better apartment. One in a better neighborhood, which cost twice as much. Who am I fooling? she decided. Who am I trying to fool?

Later that afternoon she walked through the snow to the English department and found Randolph, and sat around and talked to him. Another man was there, a completely beautiful man of uncertain age. "Meet Francis Alter," Randolph said. "The best poet in the state."

Their eyes met. From that moment on they would be friends. Until the day he told her good-bye and left her and went home and shot himself, not a single moment would be cruel or jealous or untrue. Many years later she knew that even the days before he did it were not untrue. He kept saying things to her that she remembered later. Look, he would say, making her look at a revision he had suggested to a poem. Look at it, Rhoda. Really listen. I won't always be here to tell you this.

Good-bye, he had said, when he embraced her, on the day before he left New Orleans and went home and shot himself. Good-bye, remember this, remember me.

She had been so lucky. All the women who made love to him, who held him in the sleepless dark nights of his soul, had never had what she had from him. She had his friendship and his help with her work. It was a gift she had longed for all her life.

So there was that first afternoon and she had met Francis in Randolph's office and they had sat around and talked, the crazy talk that writers talk, talk that transcends the food stamps and old cars and cold apartments, talk that lifts the spirit out of the realm of houses or clothes or cars. "Farewell is a sword that has worn out its scabbard," Francis had written. "Men with names like water poured from stone jugs" was the kind of line they read and talked about and marveled over.

Poetry was alive in the United States in nineteen seventy-six. I read everything that's written, Francis said. So do I, Rhoda answered. I subscribe to forty magazines.

So that was the first night and the first day. Then the classes began and Rhoda was busy from morning to night, going to classes, writing poetry, making friends. She had the new apartment with a fireplace. She had the green Mercedes. She had enough money to pay for things. She was kind and wanted to be friends with everyone. The snow fell and people had to walk uphill on dangerous icy streets to get to classes. She never complained. She never worried about the ice. She got up at dawn and wrote poetry about everything in the world, everything she could see, every person that she met. Her soul unfolded like a lotus in the freezing cold January weather, in the little mountain town, with her young brilliant broke friends.

Only the thin blonde girl was mean-spirited and angry. Rhoda tried to stay away from her, but it was hard to do. She was married to the preppie, it turned out. So Rhoda gave up on him and fucked a fiction writer instead.

In New Orleans her family was getting along quite well, so they said. "I'm fine," Teddy said, when she called him. "Stay as long as you want."

A friend of Teddy's killed himself at a party in uptown New Orleans on a Saturday night. Shot himself in the head while sitting in a car outside his girlfriend's house. We don't know why he did it, Teddy told her. It's a mystery to me.

It was not a mystery. It was LSD. The sixteen-year-old children who knew it did not tell. It never made the papers. LSD was something Rhoda could not understand. It was inconceivable to her that anyone would do something that messed with their brain. She did not know alcohol was a drug. She was dumb as a post about the brain and the things that harm it. All she knew was poetry. All she knew was fantasy and escape.

Francis had that kind of imagination. Rhoda and Francis. They had learned to throw their minds like ventriloquists. And the language they shared came from the same place, from the Mississippi Delta, from the flat black bottom lands on the Mississippi and Yazoo rivers. Francis steals from black people, his detractors said. I think I'm part black, Francis told Rhoda several times. I have the body of the black people of the Delta, the tribes from western Africa. After he said it, Rhoda began to believe it. He did have that body, those huge hip muscles, the stout intense beauty of the football players in the line at Ole Miss. I wish I had some, she answered. But I don't think I do. They made the language, Francis went on. When Africa lent its drums to English, southern speech began. Listen to the drums in Faulkner, in García Marquez, who learned from Faulkner. Can't you hear it, can't you hear the heart, the beat.

The winter wore on. Rhoda sent hundreds of poems out in envelopes to magazines she read and liked. Francis told her of other magazines, gave her things to read, the names of editors, the addresses of small presses and magazines, and, slowly at first, and then faster, Rhoda's poems began to be published. Now she didn't have as many friends as she had had at first. Now only Francis and the sweet girl poet really loved her. And Eric began to call and tell her to come home. He was lonesome for her. He was worried about Teddy. He wanted to patch up the marriage and start again.

In April, before the semester was really over, she began to leave. She took her tests, won a poetry award that made some more people hate her, began to fly home to New Orleans on the weekends. She was saying farewell to this thing she had wanted so much and now was tired of. She was tired of acting like she was poor, tired of never getting dressed up in nice clothes. She was tired of the small, poor restaurants, tired of the skinny blonde girl saying arch jealous things to her.

At that time Rhoda always kept her word. Any promise, even if she made it when she was drunk, was treated as a sacred bond. She had not learned yet how to stop people from manipulating her, had not learned how to say, I reserve the right to change my mind. I will take back promises you curry from me in moments of weakness. She was many years away from that sort of wisdom. Which is how the skinny blonde girl ended up living in her apartment, wearing all her clothes, losing half her papers, and other hardly-to-be-spoken-of invasions.

It was the last day of classes and Rhoda was preparing to go home to New Orleans. She was keeping the apartment for the summer in case she might want to come back in the fall. The clothes she wore in Fayetteville were not anything she would wear in New Orleans so she left them in the drawers and clos-ets. The worksheets of three hundred poems and five short sto-ries were in the dresser with underwear and flannel gowns and heavy socks on top of them.

Rhoda woke up early and packed the car, meaning to begin driving at three o'clock. She left the car in the parking lot and walked to school. It was a lovely spring day, the trees were covered with small new leaves so delicate and clean they took Rhoda's breath away. She had been living in New Orleans for so many years she had forgotten how the seasons come and go. How one day there are buds, then fatter buds, then tiny leaves which grow and darken. There was a hickory tree be-hind her apartment that she had been watching with great de-light. On this day, at the very first of May, the leaves were half the size of her hand and she marveled at them as she walked to school.

The preppie rode up beside her on his bicycle. When he was alone he was a lovely man. He got down off the bike and walked along beside her. "I really liked the story you put on the worksheet. The one that *Intro* took. It's really good, Rhoda. The best thing that's been written all year. I bet it made Ketch jealous."

"He's mad about it. He liked me as long as I stuck to poetry. You wouldn't believe what he did to me the other night. Well, who cares. Let him fuck his boring little wife. I'm going home."

"I wish you weren't leaving. We're having a party this afternoon. That's why I stopped. To ask you to join us. We're going to barbecue a goat. Wedge is bringing it from his mother's farm."

"You're going to sacrifice a goat?" She started laughing. The preppie laughed too.

"No, it's been in a freezer. I think it's an old goat."

"Who all is coming?"

"Randolph and his wife and Doctor Wheeler. We're going to have a symposium. Judy got some acid. Have you ever done it?"

"God, no. I couldn't do anything that changed my brain. I've only smoked marijuana once and then I got paranoid and almost went crazy. I stick to gin and vodka and I've about stopped that."

"You ought to try it. Everyone ought to try it once."

"Not me. I'm too afraid."

"Well, we're going to this afternoon. You can watch. If you decide to stay, come on out."

Understand this. Rhoda had no intention of going to the goat roast even if Randolph and Doctor Wheeler were going to be there. All she wanted to do was go to her last two classes, tell a few people good-bye, and start driving.

She went to her nine o'clock Form and Theory class. Then she wandered upstairs to see if she had any mail. She had three letters. A story had been accepted in the *Prairie Schooner.* A poem had been accepted by the *Paris Review.* Her mother had written to say she better hurry home.

She threw her mother's letter in the trash can and ran into Randolph's office to tell him about the poem and the story.

"This demands a celebration," he said. "Are you coming out to Ron and Judy's this afternoon?"

"They're going to take LSD."

"No one told me that. Where'd you hear that?"

"I just did. Well, I meant to drive on home. But I might as well stay another night. I'd be too excited to drive. I can't believe it. They want the story."

"It's a good story. You can write fiction as well as poems."

"Oh, God. I can't believe it. It's too good to be true." She held the letter up in the air. She shimmered. She levitated. She left the earth and flew around the ceiling of Randolph's room. He was elated too. Students being published made them all look good, made the program defensible to the dean and the board of directors of the university.

"You better come on out there this afternoon and celebrate," he said. "Nothing's going to happen. They're just going to barbecue a goat, for Christ's sake."

So she went to the party. She took half an Antabuse so she couldn't drink and ate part of a sandwich she had made the night before. She hadn't learned how to be happy yet. She didn't even know how to feed herself or treat herself to the simple joys of life. All she knew how to do was to run from pathology and become ecstatic when someone in Nebraska, whom she'd never met, told her that her work was good. That's all most people ever learn. To see their reflections in other faces.

She ate her paltry little chicken sandwich and took a bath and changed her clothes and put on tennis shoes and socks and drove out to Markham's Hill. She went up a gravel road to a yellow mailbox and turned onto a dirt road that led to a pasture on the top of the hill. An old lady owned most of the houses on the hill. She imagined herself to be a patron of the arts and rented the various houses and shacks to painters and potters and writers. It was a little community, with an open-air hot tub built by hippies in the sixties that was said to be the place where twenty people got hepatitis one winter. Rhoda was fascinated and repelled by Markham's Hill, as she always was by squalor.

Not that anything seemed squalid to her that afternoon. She had sold a story and a poem. She was going home in glory. She had come and seen and conquered. If Judy and Ron were taking LSD, or dropping acid as they called it, it would be all right. Randolph would protect her and maybe later she could write about it. Nothing is ever lost on a writer, she told herself. Since today she believed she was one.

The barbecue pit was dug. The goat was roasting on the coals. Ketch was standing by the pit looking glum. He barely glanced up when she said hello to him. She shrugged it off and went over to the steps where the overeater poet was holding forth about hogscalds in the Ozark Mountains.

Judy came down the stairs wearing a cotton dress that made her look like a farm wife. "I sold a story and a poem," Rhoda couldn't resist saying.

"Who to?" Judy asked.

"The *Paris Review* and the *Prairie Schooner.*"

"You ought to send them to *Ironwood*. It would be better."

"Is Randolph here yet?"

"He's in the backyard, at the horseshoe pit." She motioned around the side of the house. Rhoda walked that way and found him pitching horseshoes with two of the students.

This afternoon was going to be a wash. That much was clear. This afternoon would waste the fine happiness of the morning, not to mention a day of driving time.

"Here's Rhoda," Randolph said. "She sold a story and a

poem. Give her a drink, somebody. Come on, girl, you want to pitch horseshoes with us?"

"Not that I know of. I'll just watch. I just want a Coke, Tom. A Coke will be fine." The young man walked over to a tub of ice and reached down and retrieved a Coke and gave it to her. The preppie who was married to the skinny blonde bitch was behind him.

"I heard there was a hot tub that spread hepatitis from here to Maine," Rhoda said to the preppie. "Where is it? I'd like to see it."

"Come on. It isn't far. I'll walk you there." They set off down a path behind the house.

"Should you leave?" Rhoda asked. "What about the goat?"

"They'll take care of it. Wedge is doing it." He took her arm. They walked in silence for a hundred yards or so. When they were out of sight of the house, he pulled her to him and kissed her. "There," he said. "Sooner or later I had to do that."

"You're married to Judy," Rhoda said. "I'm swearing off married men."

"I married her when I was drunk. I'd leave today if I had anywhere to go. We live together because it's convenient. We don't fuck."

"Well, I don't want her mad at me. I'm scared to death of Judy." Rhoda stepped farther back.

"She's dropping acid. She wouldn't care if you fucked me by the barbecue pit."

"When is she going to do it?"

"She's doing it now. She did it this morning. Didn't you think she looked sweet? She gets sweet when she's high."

"Let's go back. I really want to go on back. I need to start driving. I need to get to Little Rock by midnight." Rhoda started back up the path. Judy was coming down the other way to meet them. Randolph was behind her. "I wanted to talk to you about something," Judy said, when the four of them met at a clearing in the path.

"Sure," Rhoda said.

"I was wondering. We're being evicted here in two weeks. I wonder if you'd let us sleep in your apartment for a few days while we wait to get our new apartment. I know it's an imposition, but Randolph said you were keeping it for the summer. It would be such a help. We have all this stuff and nowhere to put it."

"Sure," Rhoda said. "If it's only for a few days. But you have to take care of things. I left all my papers there. And I might come back at any time. I mean, I'm not going to be gone all summer. I have to come and get my mail."

"How could we get in?" Judy asked. She was beaming, standing in the shadow of divine Randolph, who was the most generous of men. Weighed down with Randolph's goodness and the triumph of the day and the need to escape and the shameful burden of her husband's money, Rhoda looked at the preppie, not at Judy, and said yes.

"You have to stay clear of my papers," she repeated. "I don't want anyone to even touch them."

"Of course," they said. So Rhoda took a key ring out of her pocketbook and removed a key and handed it over.

"Thanks so much," Judy exclaimed. "You don't know what this means to us."

Randolph was shaking his head from side to side. Randolph was not pleased.

By seven o'clock that night Rhoda was on the road. By ten she was in Little Rock. She stopped at a restaurant and called home and talked to her husband and Teddy. "I miss you so much," she told them and it was true. Then she called Raine and told him to come and meet her and he did. He got into a car and drove to Dumas, Arkansas, and met her there in the middle of the night and held her in his arms and made her cry. "Everything you said came true," she told him. "My work is being published everywhere. It terrifies me and I love it. I don't know what I'm doing. I have to go home and see what's wrong with Teddy. I have to mend my marriage. No one can live two lives at once. I'm schizophrenic from all this traveling. Now that bitch is going to stay in my apartment. I'm scared to death to have her in the same place as my papers. I'm paranoid and schizophrenic and I miss my sons."

"It's okay, baby," he said to her. "Go to sleep now. It will be better in the morning."

It was better. She spent the morning with Raine and took strength from him. She showed him the poems she had been writing. She sat beside him on a bed and ate breakfast on a tray and giggled and was happy. Then she dressed and drove home to New Orleans. It would be all right. The world was a goodly place. People could be trusted. There was time for everything.

In New Orleans Teddy and Eric were straightening up the house to get ready for her homecoming. They had been vacuuming for hours to get the dog hairs off the rugs and sofas. They had filled the refrigerator. Their mother was coming home.

In Fayetteville the skinny blonde poet and her husband and a lesbian friend were moving into Rhoda's apartment. They took all her clothes and papers out of the drawers and put them in boxes and lined them up against the wall. They brought in their typewriters and bicycles and the remains of the goat. They turned the air conditioning down to sixty-eight degrees. It was going to be a splendid summer. Living off the rich bitch from New Orleans. Off the fat of the land.

Rhoda walked into her house in New Orleans late that afternoon. Eric and Teddy were waiting for her. They had taken the sheepdogs to the vet to have them cleaned. They had put on clean shirts and combed their hair. They took her to the darkroom and showed her the photographs they had made of people in the park. After a while Teddy went down the street to a friend's house and Rhoda awkwardly made love to her husband. "I love you," she said, and she meant it. She did love Eric, his intelligence and goodness, his kindness and hope and gentle charm, his love for her child.

"We will start again," he said.

"Good," she answered. They both hoped it was so.

May went by and June and July. Rhoda took Teddy to a child psychiatrist. Teddy went to the psychiatrist on Monday and Wednesday and Friday. Eric and Rhoda talked to the psychiatrist on Thursdays. "You have to discipline him," the psychiatrist said. "He wants you to."

"Well, we aren't going to hit him." Rhoda laughed and looked at Eric. The psychiatrist was seventy years old. He was a friend of Eric's parents. Both of his children were doing all right. In a world of insane children, his children were married and sane. Rhoda and Eric had decided to take his advice.

"Be stronger than he is. Don't give him money."

"Is he taking dope?" They leaned toward the psychiatrist.

"I don't think so. But his friends are. Watch his friends. Keep him busy."

"He won't go to camp. He came home the first week last year. We wasted two thousand dollars on that camp."

"Get him a job."

"Okay. We'll try."

Teddy got himself a job. He got a job being a roadie for the Neville Brothers. He carried their instruments in and out of Tipitina's when they did their gigs.

Eric and Rhoda didn't know what to think about Teddy's job. They didn't know what was going on in the world enough to understand Tipitina's. Rhoda had seen the graduate students taking dope in Fayetteville but she didn't believe that applied to Teddy. Not sweet little Teddy with his sheepdogs and his camera and his bright red hair.

"I think it's a terrible idea," Eric said. "It's a bar."

"At least it's music," Rhoda answered. "At least it's art."

"We'll wait and see." Eric was in a quandary. He was so glad to have his wife back that he didn't want to queer it by being too suspicious of Teddy. He took Rhoda's arm. He smiled his Holden Caulfield smile. He was rewarded. She took him into the bedroom and made love to him.

In July Rhoda got an electric bill from Fayetteville for three hundred dollars. She got a phone bill for more than that. "I'd better go up there and see what's going on," she told Eric. "I want to get my mail. I have to kick those kids out of my apartment."

"Okay," he said. "If you have to. But don't stay too long. We need you here. Teddy needs you. I need you." He held his breath. He controlled his mind. He was a mensch.

In the morning Rhoda called her apartment and told the skinny blonde girl that she was coming to Fayetteville. "Be sure you're gone by then," she said. "I'm going to be real tired when I get there."

"Don't worry about the bills," the skinny blonde girl said. "We'll pay you back. I applied for a National Endowment grant. I'm pretty sure I'm going to get it."

"Just be sure you're out of my apartment, Judy."

"Oh, we will be. Don't worry about that. It was nice of you to let us stay."

Rhoda drove all afternoon and spent the night in Little Rock. The next morning she drove to Fayetteville and got there at noon. Judy and Ron were just getting up. The lesbian on the sofa was still asleep. They had had a party the night before.

"My God," Rhoda said. "I can't believe this. You promised me you'd be gone."

"Our place wasn't ready yet."

"Well, you have to get out of here. I mean right now." Rhoda stood in the living room trying not to look at the lesbian, who was a small, thin girl who only seemed to be along for the ride. Rhoda kept on standing there while Ron and Judy got dressed and packed some things and started taking them to the car. "I want all this stuff out of here right now," Rhoda said. "I mean it. My God, where are my things?"

"Calm down," Judy said. "You don't understand."

"I understand that this is my apartment and you said you were going to stay a few days and it's July. For Christ's sake. And you owe me six hundred dollars for the phone and electric bill."

"You can afford it," Judy said. "Get your husband to pay for it." She shifted the canvas bag to her other side. She waited.

"Get that typewriter off the dining room table. I mean it, Judy. Get all this junk out of here by the time I get back. I'm going to see Randolph."

"He knows we're staying here. We had him over one night to eat supper."

"Oh, my God." Rhoda walked through the apartment opening drawers and closets. The bedroom closets were stuffed with piles of half-clean clothes. There were milk crates marked *Do Not Remove From Premises,* filled with bric-a-brac.

Rhoda walked back into the living room and glared at Ron and the lesbian and went out to her car and drove over to Wheeler Hall.

"I wondered what you'd think," Randolph said. "I should have called you, but they said you knew. Christ, the suitors from Ulysses. We went over there one night. Shannon was appalled. She told me to call you. I should have done it."

"They'd better be gone when I get back."

"Good luck."

"I'll go get my mail."

"Why wouldn't you let us forward it?"

"I don't know. There's something about having a mailbox here. It's important to me somehow. It feels lucky." She smiled. Her work. Something of value that she alone had created. Her heart lifted, as it often did in Randolph's presence. How did he have the bounty, the largess, to go on giving and giving and giving. "I feel bad about being so mean to them. After all, they're broke."

"They're grown people, Rhoda. Her parents are physicians in Kansas City. She went to Duke. She's doing what she wants to do."

"Who's the lesbian?"

"Someone from Sassafras in Eureka Springs. They rescue housewives." He started laughing. Rhoda started laughing too. They wept with laughter at the madness and divinity of humankind. Above Randolph's desk was a poster of Botticelli's *Primavera.* Rhoda laughed into the flowers on the heavenly woman's dress.

The day got better. There were five good letters in the stacks of mail. Two were acceptances of poems. Another was an encouraging letter from the *Atlantic Monthly*. One was an apology from Ketch. He was working in Washington, D.C., at the Library of Congress. He was reading the Christian Existentialists. He said he was sorry he had treated Rhoda as a Thou.

The fifth was from the *Prairie Schooner*. They were giving her a prize. A thousand-dollar prize for the story they were publishing in October.

Rhoda clasped the letters to her bosom. She was lucky again. Fayetteville was lucky for her. She was the luckiest woman on the earth. She went back over to the apartment and helped Ron and Judy pack up their things. She let them leave some of their stuff in the coat closet in the hall. She let them leave a whole closet full of musty half-clean clothes piled from floor to ceiling in the only storage closet in the house. She forgave them their debt. She offered to buy them dinner soon. She watched them drive away. She took an envelope the lesbian had given her into the house and wrote a check for fifty dollars to the place in Eureka Springs that saved the housewives and almost mailed it. She found the vacuum sweeper. She vacuumed the rugs. She called a housecleaning service and made a date with them for the following afternoon. She wiped off the table. She got her old Royal portable typewriter out of the pantry and set it on the table. She put a new ribbon in it. She found a ream of bond paper and set it on the table. She was a writer. In the morning she would begin to write.

She put on her old shoes and left the apartment and began to walk. She walked up to the campus and watched the sun go down. What the hell, this was her life as a writer. This crazy town that she had found that had nothing to do with any other life that she had ever led. She was here. She was back where she belonged. She could stay awhile. Maybe she would come back in the fall.

*   *   *

That night Eric called. She told him about the prize from the *Prairie Schooner.* She told him about the lesbian. She told him about the piles of dirty clothes. She laughed uproariously as she told it. "Fateville," she said. "Home of the Hogs and the Poets."

"Sounds like the suitors from Ulysses," Eric answered.

"That's what Randolph said. God, Eric, I forget how smart you are. How educated. I envy you your education. Listen, I won't stay long. Just a week or so. I need to clean this place up for the fall and answer all this mail. Is Teddy okay?"

"He's fine. You're going back in the fall? You definitely have to do that?" He sighed. He looked off into a bank of ferns growing in the dormer windows of his kitchen. His wifeless kitchen.

"Oh, please. Don't be mad about it. I have to have my turn. I never had a turn, Eric. All I had were babies."

"It's all right. But come home soon if you're going back in the fall."

"I'll fly home every weekend. I'll fix it so I don't have classes on Friday. I'll stay here from Monday to Thursday and be home every weekend. I thought about that driving up here. I figured it out. I love you, Eric. The happier I am, the more I love you. Don't you know that? Be happy for me. Let me have this. I have to have this. It's so important to me." She drew in her breath. She waited.

"Of course. Whatever you want, Rhoda. Whatever you have to have. But I miss you."

"I miss you. I love you. Take care of Teddy. It won't be long. Well, I better go now. I want to do some work."

She hung up the phone. Then she took it off the hook. Then she made a pot of coffee and went to her typewriter and decided to write all night. It was her one and only life. Her one and only chance. The best year of her life. The year her dreams might all come true.

A Statue of Aphrodite

IN NINETEEN EIGHTY-SIX I was going through a drought. I was living like a nun. I was so afraid of catching AIDS I wouldn't sleep with anyone, not even the good-looking baseball scout my brothers ran in one weekend to see if they couldn't get me "back into the swing of things." My brothers love me. They couldn't stand to watch me sit out the game.

My name is Rhoda Manning, by the way. I write for magazines. I've lived in a lot of different places but mostly I live in the Ozark Mountains in a little town called Fayetteville. "I live in a small city, and I prefer to dwell there that it may not become smaller still." Plutarch.

During nineteen eighty-six and nineteen eighty-seven, however, I lived in Jackson, Mississippi, in the bosom of my family. I had gotten bored with the Ozarks and I wanted to make my peace with my old man. "The finest man I've ever known," as I wrote in the dedication to a book of poems. I don't think he ever read them. Or, if he did, he didn't read them very hard. He reads the *Kiplinger Newsletter* and *Newsweek* and *Time* and books he orders from the conservative wing of the Republican Party. He has large autographed photographs of Barbara and George Bush and Nancy and Ronald Reagan and flies an American flag in the front yard. You get the picture. Anyway, I admire him extravagantly and I was riding out the AIDS scare by being an old maid and eating dinner nearly every night with my parents.

Then this doctor in Atlanta fell in love with me and started writing me letters. He fell in love with a piece I did for *Southern Living* magazine. It was all about how we used to sit on porches at night and tell stories and the lights would go out when it stormed and we would light candles and coal-oil lamps until the power company could get the lines repaired. One of those cute, cuddly "those were the good old days" pieces that you mean while you are writing them. Later, you remember that you left out mosquitoes and flies and how worried we were that it wouldn't rain and make the cotton or that it would rain at cotton-picking time. The reason I leave that out is that I was a child at that time and thought the world was made of gold. It was made of gold and my daddy came home from the war unscathed and mostly we were able to pick the cotton and the black people on Hopedale Plantation were not miserable or unhappy and were treated with love and respect by my deeply religious family. I will never quit saying and writing that no matter how much people who were not there want to rewrite my personal history.

Anyway, this doctor was recently widowed. He was the head of obstetrics for Emory University Hospital and he fell in love with my article and the airbrushed photograph of myself I was putting into magazines at that time. I guess I was still having a hard time admitting I was pushing the envelope of the senior citizen category. Anyway, I kept putting this soft, romantic photograph into magazines and I still think it was that goddamn photograph that caused all the trouble and cost me all that money. I figured up the other day what my affair with the widowed physician cost me and it is upwards of ten thousand dollars. Do you know how many articles I have to write for magazines to make ten thousand dollars?

Back to the letters from the doctor. They were full of praise for my writing and "an intense desire to have you come and speak at our hospital enrichment program. We are very interested in keeping our staff in touch with the finer things in life and have a series of programs featuring writers and painters and musicians. We could pay you two thousand dollars and all your expenses and would take good care of you and see to it that we don't waste too much of your valuable time. Anytime in April or May would be fine with us. If you are at all interested in coming to light up our lives with a short reading or lecture please call collect or write to me at the above address. You could read the fine piece from *Southern Living*. And perhaps answer a few questions from the audience. Yours most sincerely, Carter Brevard, M.D."

Can you imagine any fifty-year-old woman turning that down? I could read between the lines. I knew he was in love with me before I even got to the second paragraph. I've fallen in love with writers through their work. And here's the strangest thing. You don't care what they turn out to be. If you fall in love with the words on the page, you are hooked. They can be older than you thought they were, or messily dressed or live in a hovel. When their eyes meet yours all you hear is the siren song that lured you in.

Of course this doesn't work for romance or mystery writers or people whose main objective is to get on the *New York Times* best-seller lists. This only works for writers when they are singing the song the muse gives them. I don't sing it all the time, like my cousin Anna did, but sometimes I do. Sometimes I trust myself enough to "know the truth and to be able to tell the truth past all the things which pass for facts," and when I do, people who read it fall in love. Re: Carter Brevard, M.D. Actually, if you subtract the two thousand dollars he paid me, I guess he only cost me eight thousand dollars. Which isn't all that much, considering the fact that I was living in an apartment and eating dinner with my parents every night. I guess I could afford eight thousand dollars to remember how nice it is to come. Have an orgasm, I suppose I should say, since this might make it into a magazine. But not *Southern Living*. They don't publish anything about what happens after people leave the porches and go to bed. It's a family magazine.

So I gave Doctor Brevard a date in April and his secretary called and made travel plans and sent me a first-class airline ticket, which is an absurd waste of money between Jackson, Mississippi, and Atlanta, Georgia, and made me a reservation for a suite of rooms at a four-star hotel and in short behaved as though I were the queen of England coming to pay a visit to the provinces. It was "Doctor Brevard wants to be sure you're comfortable," and "Doctor Brevard will meet your plane," and "Oh, no, Doctor Brevard wouldn't hear of you taking a taxi."

So now there are two people in love. Doctor Carter Brevard in love with an airbrushed photograph and a thousand-word essay on porches and yours truly in love with being treated like a queen.

My parents were very interested in this visit to Atlanta. "You ought to be thinking about getting married, Sister," my father kept saying. "It would be more respectable."

"It's against the law for me to get married," I would answer, wondering how much money someone made for being the head of obstetrics for Emory University Hospital. "I have used up my allotment of marriages."

*   *   *

February and March went by and unfortunately I had gained several pounds by the time April came. I trudged down to Maison Weiss and bought a sophisticated black three-piece evening suit to hide the pounds and an even more sophisticated beige Donna Karan to wear on the plane. I was traveling on Friday, April the sixth, leaving Jackson in the middle of the morning and scheduled to speak that night to the physicians of Emory University and their significant others. I was an envoy from the arts, come to pay my respects to applied science. I put on the beige outfit and high-heeled wedge shoes and got on the plane and read Denise Levertov as we sailed through the clouds. "The world is too much with us . . . Oh, taste and see. . . ."

He was waiting at the gate. A medium-sized white-haired man with nice eyes and a way about him of someone who never took an order and certainly almost never met planes. I could tell I was not exactly what he had ordered, but by the time we had collected my luggage and found a skycap and started to the car he was taking a second look. Letters can always win out over science. Letters can articulate itself, can charm, entice, beguile. Science is always having to apologize, is hidden in formulas, statistics, inexact results, closed systems. An obstetrician can hardly say, "I saw a lot of blood this morning. Pulled a screaming baby from its mother's stretched and tortured vagina and wondered once again if there isn't a better way."

He tried. "I did three emergency C-sections in the middle of the night. I'm going crazy with this AIDS thing. I'm trying to protect an entire operating room and I'm not even allowed to test the patient. It's the charity cases that scare me. Fourteen- and fifteen-year-old drug addicts. My sons are doctors. I was covering for one of them last night. Sorry if I don't seem up to par." He opened the door to a Lincoln town car and helped me in.

"I know what you mean," I answered. "I haven't been laid in fourteen months I'm so afraid of this thing. My friends call from all over the United States to talk about it. We're all scared to death. I don't think there's anyone in the world I would trust enough to fuck." Except maybe a physician, I was thinking. I don't suppose a doctor would lie to me. He got behind the wheel and started driving, looking straight ahead. "My wife died last year," he said.

"That's too bad. What did she die of?"

He took a deep breath. He went down a ramp and out onto an expressway. "She died of lung cancer. You don't smoke, do you?"

"I haven't smoked since the day Alton Ochsner told my mother it caused cancer. She was visiting them one summer and came home and told us of his findings. I don't do things that are bad for me. I'm too self-protective. I'm the healthiest person my age I know and I'm going to stay that way. I can't stand to be sick. If I got cancer I'd shoot myself." There, that should do it, five or six birds with one paragraph.

"I hope you enjoy the evening. It's at the University Club. The staff will be there and the resident physicians and their wives. They're all very eager to meet you."

"I hope I won't disappoint them."

"Oh, I don't see how that could happen."

He delivered me to the hotel and three hours later picked me up. He was wearing a tuxedo and looked very handsome. I began to forget he was of medium height. In the last few years I have decided such concerns limit the field too much for the pushing the senior citizen category. After all, I don't want to breed with the man.

The dinner and reading went well but there were two incidents that in retrospect seem worth noting. Two things I did not give enough weight to when they occurred. There was a woman with him when he picked me up. A thin, quasi-mousy woman about my age who introduced herself as his interior decorator. "I'm doing his country house in English antiques," she told me.

"I used to have a house full of antiques," I answered. "Then one day I hired a van and sent them all back to my mother. I couldn't face another Jackson press or bearclaw chair leg. I like simple, contemporary things."

"He likes antiques," the woman said. "In furniture, that is." She and Doctor Carter Brevard laughed and looked at each other with shy understanding and I felt left out. Later, in the ladies room at The University Club she made certain to tell me that they were not "lovers." Did he tell her to tell me that, I wondered. Or did she think it up for herself.

Later, while we were drinking wine and eating dinner I was telling the people on my right about my father. "He's a heroic figure," I was saying. "He has never told a lie. He's too stuck up to lie to anyone. And he's very funny. When he was about seventy-five he decided he was getting impotent. He told everyone about it. He told my brothers the minute that he noticed it. They said he came down to the office that morning shaking his head and laughing about it. 'I can't do it anymore,' he told them. 'Imagine that.'"

"What?" Doctor Brevard said, turning fiercely toward me. "He told your brothers that? He thought that was funny?"

"He's a great man," I answered. "He doesn't have to worry about his masculinity. It's grounded in stuff much more imperishable than whether he can get it up or not." I was laughing as I said it but Doctor Carter Brevard was not laughing. Maybe this is Atlanta society, I decided. Or what happens when people climb into society on their medical degrees.

*   *   *

So that sort of soured the evening, although I partially made up for it by making the doctors laugh by reading them a story about a woman who tries to stop drinking by going to live in the woods in a tent. It's a really funny story, a lot funnier than you'd imagine just to hear me tell about it.

Anyway, after the reading the doctor and his quasi-mousy interior decorator friend drove me back to the hotel and he walked me through the lobby to the elevator and stood a long time holding my hand and looking sort of half-discouraged and half-sweetly into my eyes. Then, suddenly, he pulled me to him and gave me a more than friendly hug. "I have a check for you in my pocket but I'm embarrassed to give it to you."

"Give it here. I'm embarrassed to take it, but what the hell, I have to work for a living like everybody else." I kept on holding his hand until he withdrew it and reached into his tuxedo pocket and took out the check and handed it to me. "You were marvelous," he said. "Everyone was so pleased. I wish we could have paid you more."

"This is fine. It was a nice night. You were nice to want me here."

"Maybe I'll come and visit you sometime. I'd like to see where you live."

"Come sit on the porch. I'll take you to meet my parents."

"Your father really said that to your brothers?"

"He did indeed. Well, I guess I better go upstairs. Linda is waiting in the car."

"She's only a friend. She's my decorator."

"So she said." I left him then and went up to my suite and turned on CNN and C-Span. Then I took a Xanax and went to sleep. What a prick-teaser, I was thinking. Is this what I've come down to now? Flying around the country letting aging doctors flirt with me and give me terrified hugs in hotel corridors? I stuck my retainer in my mouth to keep my capped teeth in place and went off to sleep in Xanax heaven. I only take sleeping potions when I'm traveling. When I'm at home I don't need anything to make me sleep.

Well, I didn't forget about it. When you haven't been laid in fourteen months and a reasonably good-looking doctor who makes at least two hundred and fifty thousand dollars a year hugs you by the elevator, you don't forget it. You mull it, fantasize it, angelize it. Was it him? Was it me? Am I still cute or not? Could you get AIDS from a doctor? Maybe and maybe not. All that blood. All those C-sections on fourteen-year-old girls. There is always nonoxynol-9 and condoms, not that anyone of my generation can take that seriously.

So I was mind-fucking along like that and five or six days went by and I was back to my usual life. Writing an article on Natchez, Mississippi, for a travel magazine, exercising all afternoon, eating dinner with my parents. Then, one afternoon, just as I was putting on my bicycle shorts, the phone rang and it was Carter calling me from his office.

"I've been thinking about you. How are you? Are you all right?"

"Sure. I'm fine."

"You were a big hit. You did the series a lot of good. Several people told me they'd attend more of the events if all the speakers were as entertaining as you were."

"That's nice to hear. That cheers me up and makes my work seem worthwhile."

"I don't suppose you'd like to come and visit me. I mean, visit in the country at my country house. It's very nice. I think you'd like it."

"The one with the antiques?"

"Oh, you really don't like them?"

"I don't care if you like them. I just don't want to have to dust them."

"Oh, I see." Was I actually having this scintillating conversation? Was I actually going to buy an airline ticket to go see this guy and have conversations like that for three days when I could pick up the phone in Jackson, Mississippi, and talk to writers, actresses, actors, television personalities, National Public Radio disc jockeys, either of my brothers, any of my nine nieces and plenty of other people who would have talked true to me and gotten down and dirty and done service to the language bequeathed to us by William Shakespeare and William Faulkner and Eudora Welty.

You bet I was and that was not the worst of it. I was going to a wedding. "I'll tell you what," he proposed. "I'm having a wedding for my daughter in June. Would you come and be the hostess? She's a lovely girl. I have four children Two are my wife's from a previous marriage. Two are my own, also from a previous marriage. It's going to be a garden wedding in my country house."

"With the antiques?"

"Very old-fashioned. The girls will all wear garden hats. The gardens will be in bloom. Some other famous people are coming. You won't be the only famous person there."

"I'm not famous."

"Yes, you are. Everyone here has heard of you."

"Well, why not. Okay, I'll come and be your hostess. I won't have to do anything, will I?"

"No, just be here. Be my date."

"Your date?" I started getting horny. Can you believe it? Talking to this man I barely knew on the phone I started wanting to fuck him?

*   *   *

Oh, yes. After the wedding, after the guests went away singing my praises, we would go upstairs and with his obstetrical skills he would make me come. Oh, life, oh, joy, oh, fecund and beautiful old world, oh, sexy, sexy world. "With everything either concave or convex, whatever we do will be something with sex."

The next morning two dozen yellow roses arrived with a note.

I tried to lose a little weight. Every time he would call and do his husky can't-wait-to-see-you thing on the phone I would not eat for hours. Remember, it was late spring and the world was blooming, blooming, blooming, "stirring dull roots with spring rain."

I had my white silk shantung suit cleaned and bought some new shoes. It is a very severe white suit with a mandarin jacket and I wear it with no jewelry except tiny pearl earrings and my hair pulled back in a bun like a dancer's.

"I want you to have gorgeous flowers," he said on the phone one afternoon. It was raining outside. I was sprawled on a satin comforter flirting with him on the phone. "What are you going to wear?"

"A severe white suit with my hair in a bun. All I could possibly wear would be a gardenia for my hair and I'm not sure I'll wear that."

"Oh, I thought you might wear a dress."

"I don't like dresses. I like sophisticated suits. I might wear a Donna Karan pantsuit. Listen, Carter, I know what looks good on me."

"I thought you might like something like a Laura Ashley. I'd like to buy you one. Let me send you some dresses. What size do you wear?"

"Those tacky little-girl clothes? No grown woman would wear anything like that. You've got to be kidding."

"I thought. That picture in that magazine."

"In that off-the-shoulder blouse? I only had that on because I was in New Orleans and it was hot as hell. Then that photographer caught up with me. It was the year I was famous, God forbid."

"I wish you'd wear a flowered dress from Laura Ashley. I'll have them send you some. I know the woman who runs the store here. She's a good friend of mine."

Wouldn't you think I would have heard that gong? Wouldn't you think that someone with my intelligence and intuition would have stopped to think? Don't you think I knew he was talking about his dead wife? A size six or eight from smoking who let him go down to Laura Ashley and buy her flowered dresses with full skirts and probably even sheets and pillowcases and dust ruffles to go on the antique beds and said, Oh, Daddy, what can I do to thank you for all this flowered cotton?

Listen, was I that lonely? Was I that horny? Right there in Jackson, Mississippi, with half the old boyfriends in my life a phone call away and plenty more where they came from if only I could conquer my fear of AIDS and quit eating dinner every night with my parents.

"All right," I said. "Send me one or two. A ten will do. I can take it up if it's too big."

So then I really had to go on a diet. Had to starve myself morning, night, and noon and add three miles a day to the miles I ran and go up to six aerobic classes a week.

By the time the dress arrived I was a ten. Almost. It was blue and pink and green and flowered. It came down to my ankles. Its full skirt covered up the only thin part of my body. Its coy little neckline made my strong shoulders and arms look absurd. Worst of all, there was a see-through garden hat trimmed in flowers.

Was I actually going to wear this out in public? I had the hots for a guy who had to have everything I take for granted explained to him. In exchange for which he had given me a dead wife, three C-sections performed in the middle of the night wearing double gloves, two dozen roses, a check for two thousand dollars, and one long slow hug by the elevator. You figure it out. Women and their desire to please wealthy, self-made men. Think about that sometime if you get stuck in traffic in the rain.

I found a Chinese seamstress and we managed to make the dress fit me by taking material out of the seams and adding it to the waist. We undid the elastic in the sleeves and lengthened them with part of the band on the hat. I found an old Merry Widow in my mother's cedar chest. Strapped into that I managed to look like a tennis player masquerading as a shepherdess.

In the end I packed two suitcases. One with the Laura Ashley special and its accoutrements. The other with my white shantung suit and some extremely high platform shoes, to make me as tall as he was.

I left Jackson with the two suitcases, two hatboxes, and a cosmetic kit. An extra carry-on contained my retainer, my Xanax, a package of rubbers and a tube of contraceptive jelly containing nonoxynol-9 and a book of poems by Anne Sexton.

He was waiting at the gate, wearing a seersucker suit and an open shirt. He was taking the weekend off. We went to his town house first and he showed me all around it, telling me about the antiques and where he and his wife had bought them. "My first wife will be at the wedding," he said at last. "Don't worry about it. She's very nice. She's the bride's mother."

"How many wives have you had?"

"Just those two. You don't mind, do you? There's a guest cottage at the country house. She and her husband are staying there."

"Oh, sure. I mean, that's fine. Why would that matter to me?"

"You won't have to see her if you don't want to. I thought we'd stay in town tonight and go out there tomorrow morning. The wedding is in the afternoon. Everything's done. The caterer is taking care of everything, and Donna is there to oversee him."

"Donna?"

"The bride's mother."

"And I'm your date."

"If you don't mind. I thought we'd go downtown and hear jazz tonight. There's a good group playing at the Meridien."

My antennae were going up, up, up. This was turning into a minefield. I had starved myself for two weeks to show off for his ex-wife and tiptoe around this minefield? I could have been in New Orleans with my cousins. I could have been in New York City seeing the American Ballet Theatre. I could have been in San Francisco visiting Lydia. I could have gone to Belize to go scuba-diving. I could have driven to the Grand Canyon.

"I can't wait to see the country house," I said. "Since you've told me so much about it." But that was a thrill postponed. We went first to his town house.

He showed me to my room. A Laura Ashley special. Enough chintz to start an empire. So many ruffles, so many little oblong mirrors and dainty painted chairs.

"You want me to sleep in here?" I asked. "Where do you sleep?"

"You can sleep wherever you like. I just thought you'd like your own room. Would you like to see the other ones? To see if there is one you might like better?"

Always play your own game, my old man had taught me. Never play someone else's game. "The room's fine. I mean, aren't you going to sleep with me? I'm a grown woman, Carter. I didn't come down here to dress up like a shepherdess and let you show me off to your friends. I thought you wanted to make love to me. What was all that talk on the phone? I mean, what are we doing here?" I sat back on the chintz bed. It was not the sort of atmosphere in which a fifty-year-old woman can feel sexy, but I tried.

"I wanted to take you to dinner first. Then to hear some jazz."

"What's wrong with now? We are alone, aren't we?"

"Now?" He stood very still. I could see the receding hairline and the bags under his eyes and there was no spark, no tinder, sulfur, or electricity.

"Never mind," I said. "Well, if you'll leave me, I'll unpack. I wouldn't want my wedding clothes to be wrinkled."

"If you really want to . . ."

"Never mind. I just wanted to know what was going on. Go on, I'll unpack and freshen up and we can go out to dinner."

"I have reservations at the club at eight."

"Fine. I'll be ready."

I patted him on the arm and he turned and left the room. I opened the suitcases and hung up the dress and suit. I took a bath and put on a black silk Donna Karan with small pearl ear-rings and went downstairs and waited in the overstuffed living room. In a while he joined me and we went out and had din-ner and he got drunk and then we heard some jazz and he got drunker and then we went home and he got into the chintz-covered bed with me and made me come with his fingers. I'll say this for him, he lived up to my expectations in that corner. He knew how to use his fingers. In maybe two minutes he made me have an incredible orgasm and he had done it with his fingers. "I can't make love," he moaned into my shoulder after it was over. "I can't desire women I admire. I can only desire young girls that I can't stand to talk to. I don't know what's wrong with me."

"It's okay," I said. "Go to sleep. Go on to sleep."

I woke up in a really good mood. An orgasm is an orgasm and it's a hell of a lot better than Xanax. By nine o'clock we were in the Lincoln headed for the country house. I had one suitcase in the trunk. The one with the white suit and extremely high platform heels.

The country house was very nice. Most of the chintz and printed cotton was green and white and there were plants everywhere and plenty going on in every room. His interior decorator was there and his first wife and her husband and all four of the children and their wives and husbands. The bride-to-be and the groom-to-be were busting around fixing flowers and watching the caterers set up the tents and the bandstand. The children were all loudly and publicly fighting over a diamond ring the bride-to-be was wearing. It had belonged to wife number two and her children claimed it and were angry that Carter had given it to his daughter. Since he had given it to wife number two Carter thought it was his to bestow and he had given it to the bride because her impecunious bridegroom couldn't afford one yet. "She'll give it back to you in time," he told the stepchildren. "Don't spoil her wedding day."

But it was being spoiled so there was no chance of my being bored that morning. The hostility rose to fever pitch now that Carter was there to suffer it and I sat at the kitchen table with wife number one, who was sipping rum and tonic, and I thought, it's true I could be somewhere where the natives speak my language, still, nothing is ever lost on a writer. Notice everything, the older stepdaughter washing dishes in a fury. The grandchildren, the first wife smoking, the pool cleaners trying to clean the pool, the striped tent being raised, the lobster salad, the uncomfortable sofas, the yard full of BMWs, the permanent waves, the eyelash liner, the way the ring has taken the heat off my being Daddy's date. "I have ten grandchildren," I told Donna and her dishwashing daughter. "Things won't always be this hectic in your family. It will settle down when you reach my age."

"How old are you?" they asked.

"I'm pushing sixty," I told them. "The older you get the better."

The day went from bad to worse. It got hot and hotter. The air conditioning couldn't deal with the doors being opened and slammed as the hour for the wedding drew near and the two-carat diamond ring belonging to the dead wife's children was still on the bride-to-be's hand.

I went upstairs and put on the white suit and heels. The guests arrived. An anorexic internist cornered me in the hall and told me about his addiction to running. Two of his colleagues joined the conversation, praising him for looking fatter. I talked to the interior decorator. I talked to the husband of the mother of the bride, who was getting drunk enough to be jolly.

The wedding party gathered. We all pressed around. A minister read the ceremony. Video cameras were everywhere. I hid behind a group of pedestals holding potted ferns. The guests went out to the tent and began to eat and drink and listen to the music. I went upstairs and lay down on a bed and read medical journals and a bestseller on the doctor's bedside table. I read his little black book, which was beside it. There was a list of women with their names checked off. Mine was at the bottom. I went back to the novel, *Russia House*.

After a long time Carter came upstairs to find me. "What's wrong?" he said drunkenly. "Aren't you having a good time?"

"Are you going to make me come again or not?" I asked. "I'm tired of waiting."

"Well, not right now," he said.

"Why not? What's wrong with now?"

"I don't know, Rhoda. I don't think this is working out, do you?"

"No. As a matter of fact I was thinking of catching an earlier plane. I mean, now that we have them married and everything. There's a plane that leaves at nine. Could someone take me there? Or perhaps you could lend me a car." I got up off the bed. "You can mail the things I left at your house. Especially that nifty dress you bought me. Someday I might want it to wear to a Halloween party."

"I don't understand," he said. "What have I done wrong?"

"It's a class thing," I answered. "Your M.D. doesn't make up for the chintz."

Well, that isn't exactly what I said. I said something more subtle than that but probably equally mean. He didn't answer for a long time. Then he handed me the keys to the Lincoln and offered to have his son drive me to the airport but I refused. The band was playing Beatles' songs. I sneaked out the kitchen door and got into the Lincoln and drove myself to the Atlanta airport and flew on home.

Where did the rest of the ten thousand dollars come in? you might well ask. Well, that's what it cost to call up my old boyfriend in Fayetteville, Arkansas, and get him to fly down to Jackson and take me to New Orleans to make love and eat oysters and beignets. That's what it cost to spend a week at the Windsor Court getting nonoxynol-9 all over the sheets and then fly back to Fayetteville, Arkansas, with him and make a down payment on a house on the mountain.

In a small city that needed me back so it wouldn't be smaller still. In a small, free city where no one I am kin to lives and where being respectable means getting your yard cut every two weeks in the summer and not smoking dope or getting your hair dyed blue.

Plus, three hundred and fifteen dollars for a reproduction of a statue of Aphrodite, which I belatedly mailed the bride and groom for a wedding present.

Mexico

JULY THE TWENTY-SECOND, nineteen hundred and eighty-eight, Agualeguas, Mexico, on the road to Elbaro, a Las Terras de Los Gatos Grandes.

It was the last day of the trip to Mexico. Another six hours and Rhoda would have been safely back in the United States of America where she belonged. Instead she was on the ground with a broken ankle. She was lying down on the hard stubble-covered pasture and all she could see from where she lay was sky and yellow grass and the terrible tall cages. The cats did not move in the cages. The Bengal tigers did not move and the lionesses did not move and the black leopard did not move. My ankle is torn to pieces, Rhoda thought. Nothing ever hurt this much in all my life. This is real pain, the worst of all pains, my God. It's karma from the bullfight, karma from the cats, lion karma, oh, God, it's worse than wasp stings, worse than the fucking dentist, worse than anything. I'm going to die. I wish I'd die.

Then Saint John was there, leaning over her with his civilized laconic face. He examined her ankle, turned it gently back into alignment, wrapped it in a strip of torn cloth. A long time seemed to go by. Rhoda began to moan. The Bengal tigers stirred in their cage. Their heads turned like huge sunflowers to look at her. They waited.

Dudley stood beside the fence. The lion was sideways. He was as big as a Harley-Davidson, as wide as a Queen Anne chair. Dudley kept on standing beside the flimsy fence. No, Dudley was walking toward her. He was walking, not standing still. My sight is going, Rhoda decided. I have been blinded by the pain.

"Now I'll never get back across the border," she moaned. She pulled on Saint John's arm.

"Yes, you will," he said. "You're a United States citizen. All you need is your driver's license."

He carried her to the porch of the stone house. The caretaker's children put down the baby jaguar and went inside and made tea and found a roll of adhesive tape. Saint John taped up Rhoda's ankle while the children watched. They peered from around the canvas yard chairs, their beautiful dark-eyed faces very solemn, the baby jaguar hanging from the oldest boy's arm. The youngest girl brought out the lukewarm tea and a plate of crackers which she passed around. Saint John took a bottle of Demerol capsules out of his bag and gave one to Rhoda to swallow with her tea. She swallowed the capsule, then took a proffered cracker and bit into it. "*Yo soy* injured," she said to the child. "*Muy triste, no es verdad?*"

"*Triste,*" the oldest boy agreed and shifted the jaguar to his left arm so he could eat with his right.

Then Dudley brought the station wagon around and Rhoda was laid out in the back seat on a pillow that she was sure contained both hookworm larvae and hepatitis virus. She pulled the towel out from under the ice chest and covered the pillow with the towel, then settled down for the ride back through the fields of maize.

"Well, Shorty, you got your adventure," Dudley said. "Old Waylon didn't raise a whisker when you started screaming. What a lion."

"I want another one of those pills, Saint John," she said. "I think I need another one."

"In a while," he said. "Wait a few minutes, honey."

"I'll never get back across the border. If I don't get back across the border, Dudley, it's your fault and you can pay the lawyer."

"You'll get across," Saint John said. "You're a United States citizen. All you need is your driver's license."

It is nineteen eighty-eight in the lives of our heroes, of our heroine. Twelve years until the end of the second millennium, A.D. There have been many changes in the world and many changes in the lives of Rhoda and Dudley and Saint John since the days when they fought over the Broad Jump Pit in the pasture beside the house on Esperanza. The river they called the bayou was still a clean navigable waterway back then, there was no television, no civil rights, no atomic or nuclear bomb, no polio vaccine. Still, nothing has really changed. Saint John still loves pussy and has become a gynecologist. Dudley still likes to kill things, kill or be killed, that's his motto. Rhoda still likes men and will do anything to get to run around with them, even be uncomfortable or in danger.

Details: Dudley Manning runs a gun factory in San Antonio, Texas, and is overseeing the construction of Phelan Manning's wildlife museum. Saint John practices medicine on Prytania Street in New Orleans, Louisiana. His second wife has just left him for another man to pay him back for his legendary infidelities. She has moved to Boston, Massachusetts, and is fucking an old hunting buddy of his. She was a waitress in Baton Rouge when Saint John aborted her and fell in love. A bartender's daughter, a first-class, world-class, hardball player. Saint John has met his match. He is licking those wounds and not in top shape in nineteen eighty-eight. Rhoda Manning is in worse shape.

She is fifty-three years old and she has run out of men. That's how the trip to Mexico began. It began because Rhoda was bored. Some people think death is the enemy of man. Rhoda believes the problem is boredom, outliving your gonads, not to mention your hopes, your dreams, your plans.

Here is how the trip to Mexico began. It was two in the afternoon on a day in June. Rhoda was in her house on a mountain overlooking a sleepy little university town. There was a drought and a heat wave and everyone she knew had gone somewhere else for the summer. There was nothing to do and no one to go riding around with or fuck or even talk to on the phone. Stuck in the very heart of summer with no husband and no boyfriend and nothing to do. Fifty-three years old and bored to death.

She decided to make up with Dudley and Saint John. She decided to write to them and tell them she was bored. Who knows, they might be bored too. Dudley was fifty-six and Saint John was fifty-eight. They might be bored to death. They might be running out of things to do.

Dear Dudley [the first letter began],

I am bored to death. How about you? Why did I go and get rid of all those nice husbands? Why did I use up all those nice boyfriends? Why am I so selfish and wasteful and vain? Yesterday I found out the IRS is going to make me pay twenty-four thousand dollars' worth of extra income tax. My accountant's computer lost part of my income and figured my tax wrong. So now I am bored and *broke*. How did this happen to me? I think I have been too good and too sober for too long. Let's get together and get drunk and have some fun. I miss you. Where is Saint John? I bet he's as bored as I am. I bet he would like to get drunk with us. I heard that beastly woman he married was up in Boston fucking one of his safari club buddies. Is that true?

I'm sorry I've been so mean to everyone for so long. It was good to see you at Anna's funeral. You looked great. Considering everything, we are lucky to be alive. Write to me or call me. Your broke and lonely and undeserving sister, Rhoda Katherine.

Dear Saint John [the second letter began],
   Let's get Dudley and go off somewhere and get drunk. I'm tired of being good. How about you? Love, Rhoda.

In five days Rhoda heard back from Dudley. "Hello, Sister," the message said on the answering machine. "It's your brother. You want to go to Mexico? Come on down to San Antonio and we'll go to Mexico."

Rhoda stood by the answering machine. She was wearing tennis clothes. Outside the windows of her comfortable house the clean comfortable little town continued its easygoing boring life. Why did I start this with Dudley? Rhoda thought. I don't want to go to Mexico with him. Why did I even write to him? My analyst will have a fit. He'll say it's my fascination with aggression and power. Well, it's all I know how to do. I wrote to Dudley because he looked so great at Anna's funeral, so powerful and strong, immortal. The immortal Eagle Scout who lived through polio and scarlet fever and shot a lion, ten lions, a thousand lions.

Now Saint John will call me too. I shouldn't do this. I have outgrown them. I have better things to do than go down to Mexico with Saint John and Dudley. What else do I have to do? Name one thing. Water the fucking lawn? I can get out the sprinklers and waste water by watering the lawn.

Rhoda slipped on her sandals and walked out the door of her house into the sweltering midmorning heat. She set up the sprinklers on the front lawn and turned them on. Then reached down and began to scratch her chigger bites. Fucking Ozarks, she decided. Why in the name of God did I come up here to live in this deserted barren cultural waste? What in the name of God possessed me to think I wanted to live in this little worn-out university town with no one to flirt with and nowhere to eat lunch?

She pulled the last sprinkler out from under the woodpile and set it on the stone wall of the patio. Scientific method, she was thinking. Germ theory. I'll go down there with them and the next thing I know I'll have amoebic dysentery for five years. Saint John will bring his convertible and I'll get skin cancer and ruin the color of my hair and then Dudley will get me to eat some weird Mexican food and I'll die or spend the rest of my life in the hospital.

Rhoda stared off into the branches of the pear tree. She was afraid that by watering the lawn she might make the roots of the trees come up to the surface. World full of danger, she decided. How did I come to believe that?

She reached down to pick up the sprinkler. Her index finger closed down upon a fat yellow and orange wasp who stuck his proboscis into her sweat glands and emitted his sweet thin poison. "Oh, my God," Rhoda screamed. "Now I have been bit by a wasp."

An hour later she lay on the sofa in the air conditioning with a pot of coffee on the table beside her. Hot coffee in a beautiful blue-and-white thermos and two cups in case anyone should come by and a small plate holding five Danish cookies and an ironed linen napkin. She was wearing a silk robe and a pair of white satin house shoes. Her head was resting on a blue satin pillow her mother had sent for her birthday. Her swollen finger was curled upon her stomach. She dialed Dudley's number and the phone in San Antonio rang six times and finally Dudley answered.

"What are you doing?" she said.

"Watching the boats on the lake. Waiting for you. Are you coming down? You want to go or not?"

"I want to go. Call Saint John."

"I already called him. He's free. Gayleen's up in Boston, as you noted. When do you want to go?"

"Right away."

"How about the fourth of July?"

"I'll be there. Where do I fly to?"

"Fly to San Antonio. We'll drive down. There's a hunting lodge down there I need to visit anyway. A hacienda. We can stay there for free."

"How hot is it?"

"No worse than where you are."

"I'm sorry I've been so mean to you the last few years."

"It's okay."

"No, it was mean as shit. I'll make it up to you."

"Let me know when you get a flight."

"A wasp bit me."

"You know what Kurt Vonnegut said about nature, don't you?"

"No, what did he say?"

"He said anybody who thinks nature is on their side doesn't need any enemies."

"I miss you, Dudley. You know that?"

"You know what a wedding ring is, don't you?"

"No. What?"

"A blow job repellent."

"Jesus," Rhoda answered.

"You know what the four most feared words in the United States are, don't you?"

"No. What?"

"I is your president."

"Jesus. Listen, I'm coming. I'll be there."

"I'll call Saint John. He'll be glad."

Rhoda hung up the phone, lay back against the satin pillow. My rubbish heap of a heart, she decided. I'm regressing. Well, they are my oldest compadres. Besides, where else will I find two men my own age who are that good-looking and that well-preserved and that brave? Where else will I find anybody to go to Mexico with in the middle of the summer? My ex-husbands are all snuggled down with their wifelets on little trips to Europe. Thank God I'm not sitting somewhere in a hotel room in London with someone I'm married to. About to make love to someone I've fucked a thousand times.

Well, I wouldn't mind having one of my old husbands here this afternoon. Yes, I must face it, I have painted myself into a corner where my sex life is concerned. I should get up and get dressed and do something with my hair and go downtown and find a new lover but I have run out of hope in that department. I don't even know what I would want to find. No, it's better to call the travel agent and go off with my brother and my cousin. Mexico it is, then. As Dudley always says, why not, or else, whatever.

Rhoda slept for a while, resigned or else content. When she woke she called Saint John at his office in New Orleans and they made their plans. Rhoda would fly to New Orleans and meet Saint John and they would go together to San Antonio and pick up Dudley and the three of them would drive down into Mexico. She would leave on July second. A week away.

*   *   *

During the week Rhoda's wasp sting got better. So did her mood. She dyed her hair a lighter blond and bought some new clothes and early on the morning of July second she boarded a plane and flew down to New Orleans. She took a taxi into town and was delivered to Saint John's office on Prytania Street. A secretary came out and took her bags and paid the taxi and Saint John embraced her and introduced her to his nurses. Then a driver brought Saint John's car around from the garage. A brand-new baby blue BMW convertible with pale leather seats and an off-white canvas top. "Let's take the top down," Saint John said. "You aren't worried about your hair, are you?"

"Of course not," Rhoda said. "This old hair. I've been bored to death, Saint John. Take that top down. Let's go and have some fun."

"We'll go to lunch," he said. "The plane doesn't leave until four."

"Great. Let's go."

They drove down Prytania to Camp Street, then over to Magazine and across Canal and down into the hot sweaty Latin air of the French Quarter. Tourists strolled along like divers walking underwater. Natives lounged in doorways. Cars moved sluggishly on the narrow cobblestone streets. Saint John's convertible came to a standstill on the corner of Royal and Dumaine, across the street from the old courthouse where one of Rhoda's lovers had written films for the Wildlife and Fisheries Commission. "Do you ever hear from Mims Waterson?" she asked.

"No," Saint John said. "I think he went back to North Carolina."

"If I hear North Carolina I think of Anna." They hung their heads, mourning their famous cousin.

"Anna," Saint John said, and moved the car a few feet farther down the street. "She was a strange one."

"Not strange, just different from us. Gifted. Talented, and besides, her father was mean to her. Her death taught me something."

"And what was that?"

"To be happy while I'm here. To love life. Tolstoy said to love life. He said it was the hardest thing to do and the most important. He said life was God and to love life was to love God."

"I don't know about all that." Saint John was a good Episcopalian. It bothered him when his cousins said things like that. He wasn't sure it was good to say that God was life. God was God, and if you started fucking around with that idea there wouldn't be any moral order or law.

"I thought we'd go to Galatoire's," he said. "Will that be all right?"

"That's perfect. Stop in the Royal Orleans and let me work on my face, will you? I can't go letting anyone in this town think I let myself go. I might have to come down here and scarf up a new husband if something doesn't happen soon with my life."

"What have you been doing?"

"Writing a travel book. Anna's agent is handling it for me. It might make me some money. At least pay my bills and get me out of debt."

"Will you write about this trip? About Mexico?"

"If there's anything I can use. Okay, there's the garage and they have space. Go on, Saint John, turn in there." He pulled into the parking lot of the Royal Orleans Hotel. The hotel was filled with memories for both of them. Secret meetings, love affairs, drunken lunches at Antoine's and Arnaud's and Brennan's. Once Rhoda had spent the night in the hotel with a British engineer she met at a Mardi Gras parade. Another time Saint John had had to come there to rescue her when she ran away from her husband at a ball. He had found her in a suite of rooms with one of her husband's partner's wives and a movie star from Jackson, Mississippi. Rhoda had decided the partner's wife should run off with the movie star.

"The wild glorious days of the Royal Orleans," Rhoda said now. "We have had some fun in this hotel."

"We have gotten in some trouble," Saint John answered.

"What trouble did you ever get in? You weren't even married."

"I was in medical school. That was worse. I was studying for my boards the night you had that movie star down here."

"I'm sorry," Rhoda said, and touched his sleeve. Then she abandoned him in the hotel lobby and disappeared into the ladies' lounge. When she reappeared she had pulled her hair back into a chignon, added rouge and lipstick, tied a long peach and blue scarf in a double knot around her neck, and replaced the small earrings she had been wearing with large circles of real gold.

"How do I look?" she asked.

"Wonderful," Saint John said. "Let's go." She took his arm and they walked down Royal Street to Bourbon and over to Galatoire's. Their cousin Bunky Biggs was standing outside the restaurant with two of his law partners. "Saint John," he called out. "Cousin Rhoda, what are you doing in town?"

"She's taking me to Mexico," Saint John said. "With Dudley."

"Oh, my Lord," Bunky said. "That will be a trip. I wish I was going."

"He's taking me," Rhoda said, very softly. It was all working beautifully, the universe was cooperating for a change. Now it would be all over New Orleans that she and Saint John were off on a glorious adventure. Bunky could be depended upon to spread the word.

"What are you going to do down there?" Bunky said. "There's no hunting this time of year."

"We're going to see some animals," Saint John said. "To have some fun." He was saved from further explanation. At that moment a delivery truck pulled up across the street and a tall black man emerged from the back of the truck carrying a huge silver fish. The man was six and a half feet tall. He hoisted the fish in his arms and carried it across the narrow crowded street. A small Japanese car squeaked to a stop. An older black man wearing a tall white hat opened a door and held it open and the fish and its bearer disappeared into the wall. We live in symbiosis with this mystery, Rhoda thought. No one understands it. Everything we think we know is wrong. Except their beauty. They are beautiful and we know it and I think they know it but I am far away from it now and get tired of trying to figure it out. Forget it.

The maître d' appeared and escorted them inside.

The restaurant was crowded with people. The Friday afternoon professional crowd was out in force. Women Rhoda had known years before were seated at tables near the door, the same tables they might have occupied on the day she left town with the poet. People waved; waiters moved between the crowded tables carrying fabulous crabmeat salads and trout meunière and trout amandine and pompano en papillete and oysters Bienville and oysters Rockefeller and turtle soup and fettucini and martinis and whiskey sours and beautiful French desserts and bread pudding and flán.

"I should never have left," Rhoda exclaimed. "God, I miss this town."

Two hours later they emerged from Galatoire's and found the blue convertible and began to drive out to the airport.

"Dudley's been looking forward to this," Saint John said. "I hope we don't miss that plane."

"If we do there'll be another one along."

"But he might be disappointed."

"What a strange thing to say."

"Why is that? Everyone gets disappointed, Rhoda. Nothing happens like we want it to. Like we think it will."

"Bullshit," Rhoda said. "You're getting soft in the head, Saint John. Drive the car. Get us there. You're as rich as Croesus. What do you have to worry about? And take off that goddamn seat belt." She reached behind her and undid her own and Saint John gunned the little car and began to drive recklessly in and out of the lanes of traffic. This satisfied some deep need in Rhoda and she sat back in the seat and watched in the rearview mirror for the cops.

The plane ride was less exciting. They settled into their seats and promptly fell asleep until the flight got to Houston. They changed planes and fell back asleep.

Rhoda woke up just before the plane began its descent into San Antonio. She was leaning against the sleeve of Saint John's summer jacket. My grandmother's oldest grandson, she thought. How alike we are, how our bodies are shaped the same, our arms and legs and hands and the bones of our faces and the shape of our heads. Apples from the same tree, how strange that one little grandmother put such a mark on us. I was dreaming of her, after she was widowed, after our grandfather was dead and her hair would stray out from underneath its net and she gave up corsets. Her corsets slipped to the floor of her closet and were replaced by shapeless summer dresses, so soft, she was so soft she seemed to have no bones. Her lovely little legs. "Tell me again the definition of tragedy, I always forget." In my dream she was standing on the porch at Esperanza watching us play in the rain. We were running all over the front lawn and under the rainspouts, barefooted, in our underpants, with the rain pelting down, straight cold gray rain of Delta summers, wonderful rain.

How burning we were in the cold rain, burning and hot, how like a force, powerful and wild, and Dan-Dan standing on the porch watching us, worrying, so we were free to burn with purpose in the rain. In the dream she is calling Dudley to come inside. Saint John and Floyd and I may run in the rain and Pop and Ted and Al but Dudley must come in. She holds out a towel to wrap him in. He was the sickly one, the one who had barely escaped with his life, three times, whooping cough and malaria and polio. And yet, he was stronger than we were. He was stronger than Saint John, stronger than Bunky Biggs, stronger than Phelan even. How could being sick and almost dying make you strong? Gunther told me once but I have forgotten. It was about being eaten and fighting, thinking you are being eaten and becoming impenetrable. Anna seemed impenetrable too but she turned out not to be. Rhoda shook off the thought. She got up very gingerly so as not to wake Saint John, and wandered down the aisle to the tiny bathroom to repair her makeup. She went inside and closed and locked the door. She peered into the mirror, took out her lipstick brush and began to apply a light peach-colored lipstick to her lips. A sign was flashing telling her to return to her seat but she ignored it. She added another layer of lipstick to her bottom lip and began on her upper one. How did being sick when he was little make Dudley so powerful? What had Gunther said? It was some complicated psychological train of thought. Because a small child can imagine himself being consumed, eaten, burned up by fever, overwhelmed by germs, taken, as children were taken all the time before the invention of penicillin and streptomycin and corticosteroids. Before we had those medicines children died all the time. So Dudley must have lain in bed all those terrible winters and summers with Momma and Doctor Finley holding his hand and waged battle because they begged him to live, because they sat with him unfailingly and held his hand and gave him cool cloths

Rhoda finished her makeup and returned to her seat just as the stewardess was coming to look for her. "I'm sorry," she said, and slipped into the seat beside her cousin. He was shaking the sleep from his head. "We slept too long," he said. "We must have drunk too much at lunch. Don't know what's wrong with me." He squinched his eyes together, squirmed around. "It's okay," Rhoda said.

"Where have you been?"

"I was in the restroom. I figured out Dudley. Want to hear?"

"Sure. Put on your seat belt."

"He has to kill or be killed."

"What does that mean?"

"He hunts to keep from dying because he was sick when he was a child."

"Rhoda." He gave her his bedside look. Indulgent, skeptical, maddeningly patronizing.

"Never mind," she said. "I know you don't like psychiatry."

"Well, I'm not sure it applies to Dudley." Rhoda gave up, began to leaf through an airplane magazine. Outside the window the beautiful neighborhoods of San Antonio came into view, swimming pools and garages and streets and trees and trucks, an electric station, a lake. The modern world, Rhoda decided, and I'm still here.

Dudley was waiting for them, standing against a wall, wearing a white shirt and light-colored slacks, beaming at them, happy they were there. They linked arms and began to walk out through the airport, glad to be together, excited to be together, feeling powerful and alive.

They stopped at several bars to meet people Dudley knew and danced at one place for an hour and then drove in the gathering dark out to the lake where Dudley's house sat on its lawns, filled with furniture and trophies and mementos of his hunts and marriages. Photographs of his children and his wives covered the walls, mixed with photographs of hunts in India and France and Canada and the Bighorn Mountains of Wyoming and Africa and Canada and Tennessee. Rugs made from bears were everywhere. Four rhinoceros heads were on one wall. Jaguar, tigers, lions, cougars, mountain sheep. He should have been a biologist, Rhoda thought. He wouldn't have needed so much room to hang the trophies on.

They cooked steaks on a patio beside the lake and ate dinner and drank wine and played old fifties music on the stereo and went to bed at twelve. Rhoda had an air-conditioned room on the second floor with a huge bearskin rug on the floor and a leopard on the wall. She cleaned her face and brushed her teeth and put on a gown and fell asleep. At three in the morning she woke. Most of the lights in the house were still on. She wandered out onto the sleeping porch and there were Dudley and Saint John, stretched out on small white enamel beds with a ceiling fan turning lazily above them, their long legs extended from the beds. If I had one chromosome more, she decided. One Y chromosome and I'd be out here on this hot sleeping porch in my underpants instead of in an air-conditioned room in a blue silk dressing gown. I'm glad I am a girl. I really am. They are not as civilized as I am, not as orderly or perfect. She turned off the lights they had left on and went back into her room and brushed her teeth some more and returned to bed. She fell into a dreamless sleep, orderly, perfect, civilized.

When she woke Dudley was in the kitchen making breakfast. "You ready to go to Mexico?" he asked. He handed her a tortilla filled with scrambled eggs and peppers. "Did you bring your passport?"

"No, I didn't think I needed it."

"You don't. It's all right. Well, we'll get off by noon I hope. I have to make some phone calls."

"Where exactly are we going, Dudley?"

"To see a man about a dog." They looked at each other and giggled. It was the thing their father said when their mother asked him where he was going.

"Okay," Rhoda said. "When do we leave?"

It was afternoon before they got away. They were taking a blue Mercedes station wagon. Rhoda kept going out and adding another bottle of water to the supplies.

"How much water are you going to need?" Saint John asked. "We'll only be there a few days."

"We can throw away any we don't want," she answered. "But I'm not coming home with amoebic dysentery."

"Take all you want," Dudley answered. "Just leave room for a suitcase and the guns."

"Guns?"

"Presents for Don Jorge. You will like him, Shorty. Well, Saint John, are we ready?" They were standing beside the station wagon. Saint John handed him the small suitcase that contained their clothes. In a strange little moment of companionship they had decided to pack in one suitcase for the trip. Dudley had pulled a dark leather case from a closet and each of them had chosen a small stack of clothes and put them in. They stuck the suitcase in the space between the bottles of water. Dudley put the gun cases on top of the suitcase. They looked at one another. "Let's go," they said.

"You got the magical-gagical compound?" Saint John asked, as they pulled out of the driveway.

"In the glove compartment," Dudley answered. Saint John

reached down into the box and brought out a little leather-covered bottle that had come from Spain the first time the two men went there to shoot doves, when Saint John was twenty-nine and Dudley was twenty-seven. Saint John held the bottle up for Rhoda to see. "The sacred tequila bottle," he said. Dudley smiled his twelve-year-old fort-building smile, his face as solemn as an ancient Egyptian priest. That's what the Egyptians did, Rhoda thought. Had strange bottles of elixir, went on mysterious expeditions and ritual hunts. The Egyptians must have been about twelve years old in the head, about Dudley and Saint John's age. Remember Gunther told me I was arrested at about fourteen. I don't think Saint John and Dudley even made it into puberty.

Saint John raised the little vial-shaped leather-covered bottle. He removed the top. Inside the leather was a very thin bottle of fragile Venetian glass. He took a sip, then passed the sacred bottle to Dudley.

"Exactly where are we going?" Rhoda asked. "I want to see a map." Saint John replaced the top on the sacred tequila bottle and restored it to its secret resting place in the glove compartment. Then he took out a map of Mexico and leaned into the back seat to show it to her. "Here," he said. "About a hundred and twenty miles below Laredo."

Then there was the all-night drive into Mexico. The black starless night, the flat fields stretching out to nowhere from the narrow asphalt road, the journey south, the songs they sang, the fathomless richness of the memories they did not speak of, all the summers of their lives together, their matching pairs of chromosomes, the bolts of blue-and-white-striped seersucker that had become their summer playsuits, the ancient washing machine that had washed their clothes on the back porch at Esperanza, the hands that had bathed them, the wars and battles they had fought, the night the fathers beat the boys for stealing the horses to go into town to meet the girls from Deer Park Plantation, the weddings they were in, the funeral of their grandmother when they had all become so terribly shamefully disgustingly drunk, the people they had married and introduced into each other's lives, the dogs they had raised, the day Saint John came over to Rhoda's house to help her husband teach the Irish setters how to fuck, the first hippie love-in ever held in New Orleans, how they had gone to it together and climbed up a live oak tree and taught the hippies how to hippie. Their adventures and miraculous escapes and all the years they had managed to ignore most of the rest of the world. The way they feared and adored and dreamed each other. The fathomless idiosyncrasies of the human heart. All of which perhaps explains why it took all night to go one hundred and eighty miles south of the place they left at three o'clock in the afternoon.

First they goofed around in Laredo. Then they stopped at the border to get temporary visas, then searched for diesel for the Mercedes, then crossed the border, then parked the car, then went to the Cadillac Bar for margaritas, then had dinner, then found the car.

It was black night when they left the border town of Laredo and began to drive down into Mexico. "Why don't we spend the night here and go on in the morning?" Rhoda asked a dozen times. "Why drive into Mexico at night?"

"Nowhere to stop," Saint John and Dudley said, and kept on going, taking sips out of the sacred bottle, which seemed to hold an inexhaustible supply of tequila. Rhoda was curled up on the back seat using her raincoat for a pillow, trying to think Zen thoughts and live the moment and seize the day and so forth. I could be getting laid, she kept thinking. If I had expended this much time and energy on finding a new boyfriend I could be somewhere right now getting laid. I could have called an old boyfriend. I could have called that good-looking pro scout I gave up because of the AIDS scare.

"We were the lucky ones," she said out loud. "We got to live our lives in between the invention of the birth control pill and the onslaught of sexually transmitted diseases. We lived in the best of times."

"Still do," Dudley said.

"There was syphilis," Saint John added.

"But we had penicillin for that," Rhoda answered. "I mean, there was nothing to fear for about twenty years. If someone wanted to sleep with me and I didn't want to, I apologized, for God's sake."

"That's changed?" Dudley asked.

"It changed for me," Rhoda said. "I'm scared to death to fuck anyone. I mean it. It just doesn't seem to be worth the effort. I guess if I fell in love I'd change my mind, but how can you fall in love if you never fuck anyone? I can't fall in love with someone who has never made me come."

"Her mouth hasn't changed," Saint John said. "Rhoda, do you talk like that in public?"

"In the big world? Is that what you're saying? You're such a prick, Saint John. I don't know why we let you run around with us. Why do we run around with him, Dudley?"

"I like him. He's my buddy." The men laughed and looked at each other and Saint John handed Dudley the tequila bottle and Dudley handed Saint John the salt. They poured the salt on their folded thumbs and licked it off. They shared a lime. They replaced the top and put the sacred tequila bottle away. Nothing had changed. Dudley and Saint John understood each other perfectly and Rhoda sort of understood them, but not quite.

"Unless you are both just as dumb as fucking posts and there is nothing to understand."

"What's she saying now?"

"I said I want to drive if you are going to get drunk and I want you to stop the car and roll up the windows and let's sleep until it's light. I don't like driving down through this desolate country in the middle of the night. I thought we were going to some hacienda. No one told me I was going to have to spend the night in a car."

"We're going," Dudley said. "We'll be there in an hour."

"It's two o'clock in the morning and you've already been lost twice and I don't think you have the slightest idea where you're going."

"You want some tequila, Sister?"

"No, I want to get some sleep."

"You stopped drinking too? You don't get laid and you don't get drunk, that's what you're telling me?"

"That's what I'm saying."

"Then why do you want to be alive?" Dudley shook his head. "Have some tequila, honey. We'll be where we want to be when we wake up tomorrow. You'll be glad, you'll see."

"Why baby her?" Saint John said. "If you give in to her, she'll bitch all week."

"Fuck you," Rhoda said. She sat up and straightened her skirt and blouse and arranged her legs very properly in front of her. He was right, what was she living for? "Hand me that tequila," she said. "Is there anything to mix it with?"

"Wasting away again in Margaritaville," Rhoda started singing. Dudley and Saint John joined in. They worked on country and western songs for a while, which are hard songs to sing, then moved into hymns and lyrics from the fifties and back into hymns and finally, because it was the fourth of July even if they were in Mexico, into God Bless America and oh, say can you see and oh, beautiful for spacious skies, for amber waves of grain.

"Wait till you see the maize fields in the daytime," Dudley said. "That's how they bait the paloma blanca. Maize fields on one side and irrigation ditches on the other. The whitewings are moving this way, and Don Jorge Aquillar and Mariana have been buying up all the leases for miles around. We're going to have some hunting this fall. Right, Saint John?"

"Who are Don Jorge Aquillar and Mariana?" Rhoda asked.

"The people we're going to see," Saint John said. "Right, Dudley," he went on. "If enough birds come. I can't bring my friends down here if the birds are scanty."

"Jesus, you've gotten cynical," Rhoda said. "Why are you so negative about everything?"

"Why are you picking on me?"

"I don't know, because I'm sick of riding in this car."

"Have another drink," Dudley said. "We'll be there in a little while. It isn't far now." He was right. They went another fifteen miles and began to approach the outskirts of a town. "Agualeguas, 1000 Habitantes," the sign said. They drove past small adobe buildings, then around a curving dirt road, then past a two-story building and a store and through a darkened neighborhood and went down a paved road and drove another three miles and came to a long brick wall covered with bougainvillea. A tall wrought-iron gate was in the middle of the wall with painted white wooden doves on either side of the lock. Attached to the dove on the right and fluttering in the breeze was an extra wing. Dudley stopped the car and got out and pulled the wing from the dove. It was a billet-doux. "Dearest Dudley," he read out loud. "I am waiting for you with a worried heart. Ring the bell and we will let you in. Love, Mariana."

So this is why we couldn't stay at a hotel at Laredo, Rhoda thought. So this is why we had to drive all night in the goddamn car. Because his new girlfriend is waiting. I should have known. Well, who cares, I signed on for this trip and this is what is happening. Who knows, maybe she has a brother.

Dudley rang the bell and a girl in a white skirt came running out of a building and began to fumble with the lock. Then the gates were open and servants appeared and took Rhoda's bag and led her to a room with beautiful red stone floors and windows that opened onto a patio. They set her bag on one of two small beds and brought her water and turned down the other bed. Rhoda took off her clothes and lay down upon the small wooden bed and went immediately to sleep. Outside the window she could hear Dudley and Saint John and Mariana laughing and talking and pouring drinks. They never stop, Rhoda thought. Fifty-six years old and still spreading seed. "This is Mariana," Dudley had said when he introduced the girl. "Isn't she beautiful, Sister? Wouldn't she make great babies with me?"

When Rhoda woke she was in a hacienda in Agualeguas, Mexico. Bougainvillea, red tile roofs, a parrot in a cage, rusty red stone floors, a patio with a thatched roof and an oven the size of a cave, ancient walls, soft moist air, beside the oven a bar with wicker stools. Above the bar, cages of doves, paloma blanca and paloma triste, whitewings and mourning doves, very hot and still. I am still, Rhoda thought, this is stillness, this is Zen. A dove mourned, then another and another. The doves woke me, Rhoda decided, or I might have slept all day. It seems I was supposed to come here. It is the still point of the turning earth, like the center, the way I felt one time when Malcolm and I sailed into an atoll in the Grenadines below Bequia and I said, This is the center of the earth, we must stay here forever.

Well, we can anchor overnight, he answered, but in the morning we have to push on. No wonder I divorced him. Who could live with someone as work-drugged and insensitive as that. Mother-ridden and work-drugged. My last millionaire. Well, now I'm broke. But at least I'm happy this moment, this morning in this lovely still place with red tiles and thatch and the doves in cages and Saint John and Dudley asleep next door in case I need protection.

The stillness was broken by the sound of a Mexican man putting chlorine in the pool outside Rhoda's window. She dressed and went out onto the patio to watch. The pool was a beautiful bright blue. The man had put so much chlorine into it that the vapors rose like a cloud above the water. The birch trees beside the pool had turned yellow from the chlorine fumes. They were like yellow aspens, beautiful against the green shrubbery and the red flowers of the bougainvillea. Death is beautiful, Rhoda thought, as long as it isn't yours. She remembered something. A bullfight poster they had seen in Laredo advertising a bullfight in Monterrey. Let's go, she had said. I'm in the mood for a bullfight. Of course, the men had answered. They were amazed. When last they messed with Rhoda she had lectured them for hours about going to football games and eating meat.

Mariana came out from the thatched kitchen carrying a tray with coffee and two cups. Brown sugar and cream.

"Will you have coffee?" she asked.

"Con leche, por favor," Rhoda answered.

"What will you do today? Have they said?"

"We are to go see the fields. And maybe to a bullfight. There's some famous matador fighting in Monterrey."

"What's his name?"

"Guillarmo Perdigo."

"Oh, yes, with the Portuguese. They fight the bull from horseback. It's very exciting."

"*Muy difícil?*"

"Oh, yes."

"Your English is so good."

"I am from Acapulco. I just came here to help my uncle."

"Dudley said it would be a famous place soon. That everyone will be coming here."

"We hope it will come true. If the doves come. We have bought up all the leases. We will have a monopoly."

"And some fun?"

"Oh, yes. That too." Mariana smiled, poured the coffee, looked away.

"Maybe the shopping clubs will come," Rhoda said. She watched Mariana, hoping to make her smile. Dudley had told Rhoda that groups of women came down to meet the hunters in Brownsville and Laredo and McAllen. Busloads of women from Shreveport and Baton Rouge came to meet the hunters at the Cadillac Bar and the bars of the Hilton Hotel and the Holiday Inn. It had begun by chance. First the men started coming down to hunt the doves. Then a group of women happened to be shopping in the border towns the same week. There were the bars full of good-looking hunters from all over the United States. So the women went home and told their friends and soon busloads of bored housewives from all over the South were down in the border towns buying up all the Mexican wedding dresses and piñatas in the world and getting laid at night by the hunters.

"That would be nice," Mariana said. "Do you think I should wake your brother?"

"No. Let sleeping men lie, that's what I always say."

"He told me to wake him at ten so he'd have time to see the fields. Carlos is here to drive you."

"Then wake him up. As long as you don't make me do it."

"Excuse me then." Mariana got up and moved in the direction of the men's rooms. I can't tell if she's shacking up with him or not, Rhoda thought. How Spanish not to flaunt it one way or the other. Spanish women are so mysterious, soft, and beautiful. They make me feel like a barbarian. Well, I am a barbarian, but not today. Today I feel as sexy as a bougainvillea. Rhoda sat back. The sun shone down between the thatched roof and the pool. The servants moved around the kitchen fixing breakfast, the yellow leaves fell into the bright blue pool, the carved tray holding the white coffeepot sat upon the wrought-iron table. Rhoda drank the coffee and ate one of the hard rolls and in a while Mariana returned with melons and berries, and the chlorine in the pool rose to the trees and the breeze stirred in the bougainvillea. The still point of the turning world, Rhoda thought. And what of the bullfight? Of the carnage to come? Death in the afternoon. What would it be? Would she be able to watch? It was getting hotter. Rhoda was wearing a long white skirt and a green and white striped shirt tied around her waist. White sandals. She was feeling very sexy, enchanting and soft and sexy. She looked around. There was no one to appreciate it. I'll just think about it, she decided. It's beautiful here, very Zen and sexy. This is a thousand times better than being at home in the summer, a lot better than being bored.

The servants brought more coffee. Mariana returned. Then Dudley appeared, buttoning his khaki safari shirt. Saint John was behind him, dressed in white duck pants and wearing a cap with a visor.

"Why the cap, Saint John?" Rhoda asked. "Not that I don't like it. I do, a lot."

"It's from the Recess Club's last outing." He took off the cap, handed it to her so she could see the design. It was a man and woman locked in an embrace. "A Rorschach test," he added.

"Fabulous," Rhoda said. "How amusing."

"Give me back my cap." He retrieved it and planted it firmly back on his head. He had decided to be adamant about his cap. Rhoda moved nearer to him and put her arm around his waist. Poor Saint John, she decided. He could never wear that cap in New Orleans. All the trouble he's had all his life over pussy, he ought to get to make a joke out of it when he's in Mexico. "I think you're the sexiest man your age I've ever seen in my life," she said out loud. "I bet the ladies you treat fantasize about you all day long."

"I hope not," he said, but he was pleased and looked to Dudley to save him from himself.

"I thought Saint John got in the business to do it in the examining room," Dudley said. "Saint John, do you do it in the examining room?"

"Only with the nurses," he said, and they laughed and were relieved.

A driver appeared and they all piled into a four-wheel-drive vehicle and headed out of town toward the maize fields where the whitewing doves were already arriving in small numbers. From July to October more and more would come. Flying from the orange-red tops of the maize plants across the road to the irrigation ditches and then into the bush. It was all there, everything they needed, water and food and cover. All I need, Rhoda was thinking. All any creature needs.

"It will be a great fall," Dudley said, and opened a bottle of wine and began to pour it into paper cups. "Paloma blanca bastante, right, Mariana? Right, Pablo?"

"We have a monopoly all along the river and the ditches," Mariana said. "And twenty-three rooms and three vehicles. Now if Dudley brings us hunters we are happy." She reached across the seat and touched his knee. I can learn from these women, Rhoda thought.

"A great fall," Dudley said again. "A great year." He leaned out the window, admiring the maize and the doves flying back and forth across the road as the vehicle approached the trees.

"I think I'll come twice," Saint John said. "Once in August and once in September. Look at that maize, Dudley. This place is going to be spectacular. I've counted twenty whitewings since we passed the dam."

"This place is going to be dynamite," Dudley agreed.

"I hope we make some money," Mariana said. "Uncle Jorge has invested very much."

"I'm coming back too," Rhoda said. "I know how to shoot. Don't I, Dudley?"

"Tell us which ones are the palomas blancas," he answered. "Start practicing."

On the way back to the hacienda they stopped at a native market and bought fruit and packages of orange tortillas. The tortillas were such a beautiful shade of orange that Rhoda forgot her vow not to eat native food and began to gobble them up.

"They are also good with avocado on them," Mariana suggested. "I will find you some when we get home."

"I like them like this," Rhoda said, and brushed orange crumbs from her skirt.

"If you get lost we can find you by the crumbs," Saint John suggested. "Like Hansel and Gretel."

"If I get lost I'll be with some good-looking bullfighter who fell for my blond hair."

"Dyed blond," Saint John said.

"Sunbleached. Don't you remember, Saint John, my hair always turns blond in the summer."

"Rhoda, you never had blond hair in your life. Your hair was as red as Bess's mane, that's why we said you were adopted."

"Is she adopted?" Mariana asked.

"No," Dudley answered. "She is definitely not adopted."

It was after one o'clock when they got back to the hacienda. Time to get ready to leave for the bullfight.

"It starts at four-thirty," Rhoda said.

"They are always late," Mariana answered. "If we leave here by three we'll be there in time."

"Time for a siesta," Dudley said.

"Siesta time," Saint John echoed.

There was an hour to sleep. A dove mourned, then another, a breeze stirred an acacia tree outside the window, its delicate shadows fell across the bed and danced and moved. Dance of time, Rhoda thought, light so golden and clear, and Zeus came to her in a shower of gold, clear, dazzling, and clear. Rhoda curled up into a ball and slept on the small white bed. She had not felt so cared for since she was a child. No matter how much I hated them, she thought, they protected me. They would throw themselves between me and danger. Why, I do not know. Taught or inherent, they would do it. How spoiled I am, how spoiled such men have made me.

The bullfight was in Monterrey, a hundred and twenty kilometers to the south and west. Mariana sat up front with Dudley. Rhoda and Saint John rode in back. They drove along through the afternoon heat. Dudley had the air conditioner going full blast. Mariana had a flower in her hair. They talked of the countryside and what it grew and Rhoda asked Mariana to tell them who she was.

"My father is Portuguese," she began. "This is not unusual in the towns of the coast. The Portuguese are seafarers. There were seven children in our family. I am the second oldest."

"I'm the second oldest," Rhoda said. "We're the oldest of all our cousins. We used to rule the rest of them. The rest of them were like our slaves."

"Why does she say things like that?" Saint John asked.

"Because that's how she thinks." Dudley handed Saint John the leather-covered tequila bottle. "Whatever she does, that's the best. If she was the youngest, she'd believe the youngest child had the highest I.Q. She's the queen, aren't you, Shorty?"

"We did rule them. You used to boss Bunky and his brothers all around and I used to boss Pop and Ted and Al. We used to stay all summer at our grandmother's house, Mariana. We had a wild time. I guess those summers were the best times of my life. There were all these children there. Because of that I always thought a big family must be a wonderful thing."

"Give Mariana some of our Dudley-Juice," Dudley said. "Give her some magical-gagical compound, cuz. She needs a drink."

"It was nice to have the others," Mariana said. "But we ran short of money."

"What did your father do?" Rhoda went on.

"He is a builder," Mariana answered. "A contractor. He helped build the Viceroy Hotel in Acapulco. He will come for the hunts. If you come back you will meet him."

"How old is he?"

"He is sixty. But he looks much younger. He is a young man."

"Let's sing," Dudley said. "How about this?" He reached for

Mariana's hand, began to sing. "When Irish eyes are smiling, sure it's like a morn in spring." I wonder if that stuff works on young girls, Rhoda thought. I wonder if that old stuff gets him anywhere anymore. I mean, it's clear the child likes him, but it may be for his money. They used to like him for his basketball prowess. No, maybe it was always for money. Why did boys like me? Maybe that was only Daddy's money. Well, now I'm broke. No wonder I don't have any boyfriends and have to run around with my brother and my cousin. Rhoda, stop mindfucking. Love people that love you.

"I can't wait to see this bullfight," she said out loud. "I saw one on my second honeymoon but I was so drunk I can't remember anything about it except that my feet hurt from walking halfway across Mexico City in high heels."

"It's how she thinks," Saint John said. He took a drink from the tequila bottle and passed it to Dudley.

"How do you think?" Rhoda said. "What are your brilliant thought processes? Hand me that tequila bottle. Where is all the tequila coming from? When are you filling it up?"

"Doesn't have to be filled," Dudley said. "It's magical-gagical compound. Up, down, runaround, rebound."

They arrived in Monterrey at four-fifteen, parked the car and found a taxi and told the driver to take them to the Plaza de Toros.

"Lienzo Charros," Mariana told the driver. "Pronto."

"I do not think it is open," he answered. "I don't think they are there today."

"It said on the poster they would be there. Guillarmo Perdigo is fighting."

"We'll see." The driver shifted his cigar to the other side of his mouth and drove through a neighborhood filled with people. He went down a hill and turned sharply by a stone wall and came to a stop. They could hear the crowd and see the flags atop the walls of the compound.

"I can't believe we're here," Rhoda said. She got out of the taxi and stood waiting by a tree while Dudley paid the driver. Her sandals settled into the soft brown dirt beneath the tree. The dirt moved up onto her toes and covered the soles of the new white sandals. She was being taken, the earth of Mexico was making her its own. The taxi driver waved and stuck his arm out the window and the little party weaved its way down the incline toward a wooden ticket booth beside a gate. Rhoda was very excited, drawn into the ancient mystery and the ancient sacrifice, the bull dancers of Crete and Mycenae, the ancient hunters of France, the mystery of the hunt and ancient sacrifice, and something else, the mystery of Dudley and Saint John. What allowed Dudley to hunt a jaguar in the jungles of Brazil? What allowed Saint John to don his robe and gloves and walk into an operating room and open a woman's womb and take out a baby and then sew it all back up? What was the thing that these men shared that Rhoda did not share, could not share, had never shared? I could never cut the grasshoppers open, she remembered, but Saint John could. I could pour chloroform on them. Poison, a woman's weapon since the dawn of time. But not the knife. The knife is not a woman's tool. She shuddered. Women give life. Men take it. And the species lives, the species goes on, the species covers the planet.

She took a twenty-dollar bill out of her pocket and tried to buy the tickets but Dudley pushed her hand away and gave the ticket seller a handful of thousand-peso notes. Then they walked across a dirt enclosure to the entrance to the stands. Small boys played beneath the stands, chasing each other with toy pics, charging each other's outstretched arms. A blindfolded horse

was led by, wearing padding and a double rein, a tall white Andalusian horse that looked quite mad. The excitement was very
sexy, very intense. Four students wearing shirts that said Stanford University were in front of them on the stairs. They were
drinking beer and laughing.

"These guys are just hairdressers," one student said. He was
carrying a minicam video recorder.

"A high school football game," his companion added. Rhoda
felt the urge to kill them. Rich spoiled brats, she decided. If they
start filming this on that goddamn minicam, I'm going to throw
up. How dare they come and bring that goddamn California
bullshit to this place of mystery, this remnant of ancient sacrifice
and mystery, this gentle culture and these lithe sexy Spanish
men, how dare these California rich boys spoil this for me. She
looked at Saint John and Dudley and was very proud suddenly
of their intelligence and quietness. Dudley held the arm of the
young Spanish girl. Both Dudley and Saint John spoke intelli-
gible Spanish to anyone they met. We are civilized, Rhoda decided. We are polite enough to be here, to visit another world.
But those goddamn muscle-bound California pricks. Who
would bring a minicam to a bullfight? Fuck them. Don't let
them ruin this. Well, they're ruining it.

They found seats and arranged themselves. Mariana on the
outside, then Dudley, then Rhoda, then Saint John. The music
began, terrible, wonderful music. Music that was about death,
about sex and excitement and heat and passion and drama and
blood and death. The music was about danger, sex was about
danger, sex was the death of the self, the way men and women
tried themselves against death. Ancient, ancient, Rhoda
thought. Oh, God, I'm so glad to be here. So glad to be somewhere that isn't ironed out. "Without death there is no carnival." A long boring life with no carnival. That's what I've come

down to, that's what I've been settling for. And will settle for, will go right back to. Well, fuck safety and security and fuck the fucking boring life I've been leading. She put her hand on Saint John's arm. Reached over and patted her brother on the knee. "Thank you for bringing me here," she said. "Thank you for this."

"You want a Coke?" Dudley said. "Do you want a beer or anything? You want a hat?" He motioned to a vendor and the man came over and Dudley bought a black felt matador's hat with tassels for Mariana and tried to buy one for Rhoda but she refused his offer. "I don't wear funny hats," she said, then looked at Mariana. "You have to have black hair to wear that hat. On black hair it looks great." Mariana pushed the hat back from her head so that it hung down her back on its black plaited cord. Her gold earrings dangled about her shoulders. It was true. She did look nice in the hat.

A vendor passed before them carrying a huge basket full of candy and cigarettes and packages of M&M's and sunflower seeds. His wares were spread out like a flower opening. It was a beautiful and heavy load and he displayed it as an artist would. Over his shoulder Rhoda could see the Stanford students standing side by side in their muscle shirts rolling film on the mini-cam and she hated them with a terrible and renewed passion.

"This is a small corrida," Mariana said. "Three bulls, but the matadors are good. Especially Guillarmo. I have seen him fight. He fought last year in Mexico City. And the last matador is Portuguese. Yes, you are lucky to get to see this. This is unusual for Monterrey."

"*Como se dice in Español,* lucky?" Rhoda asked. "*No recuerdo.*"

"*Fortunata,*" Dudley answered. "*Bendecire* and *fortunata.*"

The music stopped for a moment and the vendor passed by again, this time carrying Cokes and beer in aluminum buckets.

He was assisted by two small boys who looked like twins. "*Gemelos?*" Rhoda asked, and added, "Are they yours?" The vendor laughed and shook his head. He opened a Coke for Rhoda and one for Mariana and beer for the men. The mini-cam crew from Stanford had turned the camera Rhoda's way. She held up her hand before her face and waved them away. They kept on filming. "Tell them not to do that to me," she said to Saint John. "I mean it." Saint John waved politely to the young men and they turned the camera back toward the arena. Rhoda drank her Coke. The vendor and the twins moved on. The band picked up their instruments. They were wearing red wool jackets with gold buttons and gold trim. "They must be burning up in those uniforms," Rhoda said. She shook her head. They raised their tarnished brass instruments and the wild dangerous music began again.

"Look," Saint John said. "At the toriles, the bull pens, you can see the bulls." Rhoda looked to where he was pointing. She could see the top of a bull beyond a wooden wall, then the horns, then a second bull. They were very agitated. Very large, larger and more powerful and more agitated than she had imagined they would be. The blindfolded horse was led into an arena beside the toriles, a picador in an embroidered suit was sitting on the horse, another leading it. A bull charged a wooden wall, then disappeared out of sight. The door to the arena containing the blindfolded Andalusian horse was open now. The bailiff came in. He was wearing a tarnished gold uniform, riding a tall black horse with a plaited mane. Other men on horseback joined him. The paseo de cuadrillas was forming. Three small boys chased each other with paper pics across the barrera. "We could sit down there," Mariana said, "if you don't mind getting blood on your clothes."

Dudley and Saint John didn't answer. They were getting serious now, the homage athletes pay each other. "The seats near the arena are barrera," Mariana added, addressing her remarks to Rhoda. "The torero's women sit there." The women exchanged a look. In the bull pen a bull broke away from its keepers. There was a rush to corner it. Rhoda thought of Ferdinand, the old story of the bull that wouldn't fight. My sweet little mother, she thought, trying to deny all mystery and death for me. Except for the soft passing of Jesus into heaven, she would shield me from all older worlds.

But there are no Ferdinands, put out to pasture if they will not fight. The ones that won't fight go to the slaughterhouse. My sweet mother, smelling of talcum powder and perfume, reading to me of Ferdinand smelling the flowers. Then she would get up and go into the kitchen and cut the skin from a lamb, as happy as Saint John in the operating room. Contradictions, half-truths. But this is true. Death in the afternoon is real danger, real death.

One of the toreros came up the stairs toward where they were sitting. He stopped in the barrera and spoke to a group of men. Two men stood up and embraced him. They are his father and his brother, Rhoda decided. The torero was tall, and lithe, like a dancer. Beneath his white shirt his skin seemed soft and white. Rhoda wanted to reach out and touch him, to wish him luck.

He sat down between the men he had embraced. The one who appeared to be his brother put an arm around his shoulder. They talked for a while. Then the torero got up as swiftly as he had arrived and left and went back down the stairs. The music grew louder, rose to a crescendo, descended, then rose again. The gates to the arena opened. The alguacil rode out in his tarnished suit, leading the paseo de cuadrillas. Then the matadors, the banderilleros, the picadors. The mayor threw down the key to the toril. The matador who had come into the stand was wearing a short black jacket now, a montera, a dress cape.

The procession filed back through the gate. The gate to the toril was opened and the bull ran out. The matador, Guillarmo Perdigo, walked out into the arena and the ceremony began. This was no hairdresser, no high school football game, this was the most exquisite and ancient ceremony Rhoda had ever seen. The matador spread his cape upon the ground, squared his shoulders, planted his feet. The bull charged across the arena. The matador executed a pass, then another, then turned and walked away, dragging his cape. The bull pawed the ground, was confused, walked away. The matador turned to face the bull again, spread out his cloak, called to the bull. The bull charged again, and then again. The matador passed the bull's horns so close to his body, to his balls, to his dick. Rhoda held her breath. It's amazing, Rhoda thought. Where have I been while this was going on?

Dudley and Saint John had not moved. Mariana was still. A second matador appeared. Then the third. The matadors each did a series of passes, then the picadors came out on horseback and stuck the pics into the shoulder muscles of the bull. Rhoda was sickened by the sight. Fascinated and repelled, afraid for the matador and trying to hate the bull, but there was no way to hate him now since he was outnumbered. She turned her eyes from the bull's wounds, turned back to the matador who was alone with the bull again. This is so sexy, so seductive, she was thinking, the hips on that man, the softness of his face, of the skin beneath his white shirt. How many years has he worked to learn this strange art or skill? To allow that bull to move its horns so close to his hips, to his dick, then to turn his back and walk away. Still, to torture the bull. Rhoda, don't fall for this mean-ness. It is mean. Still, it doesn't matter, not really, not in the scheme of things. It is how things are, how things have always been. Men learned these skills to protect themselves from ani-mals, to protect their children and their women. And it's so sexy, so fucking wonderful and sexy. I would fuck that bullfighter in a second, AIDS scare or not. I bet they think everyone from the United States has it. I bet no one in a foreign country would fuck an American now. They probably wouldn't fuck an American for all the money in the world. Rhoda leaned into the arena. The matador spread out his cape and made four beautiful and perfect passes, then drew the cape behind him and turned his back to the bull and walked away. He walked over to the barrio and was handed an older, redder cape and a sword. He came back out into the arena and displayed the sword against the cape and then prepared the cape for the kill. The bull looked confused, hesitant, worried. Perhaps he smelled his death. He walked away. "Toro," the matador called, "toro, toro, toro." The bull pawed the ground, made a fake pass, then moved back. The matador prepared again, spread out the red cape upon the ground, displayed the sword upon it, then moved the sword behind the cape, moved his feet very close together, then waited. The bull charged, the matador stuck the sword between the spinal column, planted it all the way to the hilt, and the hull's lungs filled with blood and it fell to its knees.

"The sword goes in and severs the spinal column," Saint John said. It was the first time he had spoken in thirty minutes. "It punctures the lungs and the lungs fill with blood. An easy death."

"Compared to what?" Rhoda said.

"Anything you can think of."

"What would be the easiest one?"

"Anna's wasn't bad. The shock of the freezing water would cushion the shock of the cyanide."

"What would be the easiest thing of all?"

"Fifty Demerols. I have a jar at home in case I have a stroke. I don't want to recover from a stroke."

"Nor I," Dudley said.

"Well, you probably won't have to," Rhoda said. "You'll just ruin your liver getting hepatitis down here in Mexico and call me up and ask me to give you one. God, I hope I don't have to give you a liver."

"I hope so too."

"Kidney," Saint John put in. "They don't transplant livers."

The picador ran out onto the dirt floor, took out a silver dagger, delivered the coup de grâce. The matador stared at the bull, then turned his face to the sky and walked back across the dirt arena. Rhoda rose to her feet with the crowd. This is what theater was trying to do, she decided. This is what plays aspire to but this is real death, real catharsis, real combat and real battle, and the thing I cannot understand and my shrink cannot understand. This is not subject to Freudian analysis because this is older than Freud and besides I am not a German Jew. I am from a culture more deadly and cold than even these Spanish people descended from Moors. She looked at the face of her brother and the face of her cousin. They were completely satisfied. She was satisfied. The young men from California were still sitting. They had put their camera away. Even they knew that something had happened. Later, Rhoda thought, they will get drunk and blow it off. Whatever the matador represents they will not allow it in. They are future people, remaking the genes. No second-rate Mexican bullfighter can impress them. Perhaps nothing can impress them. They will just get on a talk show and explain it all away. They are the future, but I am not. Rhoda stood up, extracted some dollar bills from her purse, excused herself, and walked down through the still cheering crowd toward the barrio. She wanted to be near the matador, to breathe the air he breathed, to experience the terrible sexiness of his skin, to look at him. She walked down the steps toward the concession stand underneath the stadium. He was standing with his back to her, his back was sweating underneath the soft white cotton of his shirt, his hair reminded her of a painting she had seen once of a Spanish child, so black it was no color, his neck was soft and tanned and the skin on his shoulders beneath his shirt seemed to her to be the sexiest thing she had ever seen in her life. He turned and handed something to a woman in a yellow blouse. Rhoda withdrew her eyes and walked on down the stairs and stood by a long concrete tub which held beer and Cokes. Two men were selling the drinks. "*Un Coke,*" she said. "*Por favor.*" The vendor extracted one from the depths of the icy water and removed the top with a church key. He handed it to her and took her dollar. The blindfolded horse stood against a fence. A few tourists walked toward the stand, two small boys chased each other with make-believe swords, the heat was all around her. She drank the cold sweet drink, felt her body melt into the heat. She stood there a long time. Finally the matador came out of a gate and walked toward two men in black suits who were awaiting him. The men embraced. The matador held one of the men for a long time. They were the same height and their arms slid around each other's shoulders. The black-suited man patted the matador's wet shoulder. The matador looked past his friend and saw Rhoda watching him. He met her eyes and received her tribute. I could fuck him, Rhoda thought. If I were still young enough to have hope, I would walk across this twenty feet of earth and hand him a paper with my name on it and tell him where to find me. He would find me. He is young and still has hope. She set the cold sweet Coca-Cola down on the waist-high concrete tub and walked toward the matador. He excused himself from the men and came to meet her.

"*Esta noche,*" she said. "*Donde?* Where will I find you?"

"At the Inn of the Sun." His lips were as soft and full as the skin on his shoulders. His hips were so close to her. The smell of him was all around her.

"I will come there," she said. "When? At which hour?"

"*A los siete.* At seven." He reached out and took her arm. "I was watching you. I knew you wished to speak with me."

"I am called Rhoda. *Se nombre Rhoda Katerina.*"

His fingers held her arm. "At seven," he said. "I will wait for you." He moved closer. "Will you sit with me now?"

"No, I am with my brother. I will come at seven." She turned to walk back to the stairs. He walked with her to the first landing. The tourists were watching them. The men at the concession stand were watching them. The children were watching them.

She walked back upstairs and rejoined Dudley and Mariana and Saint John. The afternoon grew hotter. Two more bulls were killed, including one from horseback. Then the corrida was finished. The band put up their tarnished instruments and recorded music began to play from the speakers. Rhoda and Dudley and Mariana and Saint John went out on the street to find a taxi but there was none so they began to walk toward the hotel where they had left the car. I have to ask Mariana how to get to the inn, Rhoda thought. I have to get her alone and get her to help me.

"There is too much violence in the world," Saint John said. They were walking along the uphill dirt street, following the crowd in the direction of the town.

"Too much violence," Rhoda answered him. "What do you mean? You're as bad as those goddamn Stanford boys."

"You're all fascinated by your father's violence," Saint John said. "Look what it's done to Dudley."

"What are you talking about, Saint John? Make yourself clear. Jesus, it's hot as noon." They had walked out from the shade of the hill. It was as hot as noon, hotter, for the earth had had all day to soak up heat. Rhoda shuddered, thinking of the earth soaking up the blood of the bulls, blood soaking down into the earth and turning black. The matador's soft hands, the silver sword, the red cape and blood soaking down into the earth, the heat. I'm too old for him, Rhoda thought. But then, what difference would my age make? Remember when Malcolm gave that speech at the medical college and we went to the party with all the surgeons. The oldest man in the room was the most powerful. God knows how old he was, but he came across the room and took me. Just took me because he wanted me. And I allowed it. I left everyone else that I was talking to and followed him out onto the patio and he said, I want to take you somewhere tomorrow. Where was it he wanted me to go? To see a cadaver or something terrible or grim and Malcolm came and found me and brought me back inside because even Malcolm knew what was going on. So it has nothing to do with age or even violence although violence is one of its manifestations. It's power that matters, and in this Mexican town on this hot day power is killing bulls and Saint John knows it and is pissed off at the matador and pissed off at me.

"Goddamn, I wish we'd find a taxi," Saint John said. "I'm not sure this is the way to town."

"We can catch a bus," Mariana said. "If we go this way we will come to the main street and a bus will come by." They trudged up the dusty street and arrived at a main thoroughfare, and in a few minutes a dilapidated city bus picked them up and took them into town. She told them on the bus. First she told Saint John. "I'm going to meet the bullfighter," she said. "I'm going to his hotel."

"Of course you aren't," Dudley said. He turned around from the seat in front of her. "No, that's final."

"You don't tell me what to do. I don't take orders from you."

"He's right," Saint John said. "You can't go off with those people."

"Why not? Why can't I? What do I have to live for that's so important I'm supposed to be careful? My children are grown. I'm going to his hotel at seven o'clock tonight."

"You aren't going off with a Mexican bullfighter," Dudley said. "That is that. You aren't going to do that to us, Shorty."

"Is not a good idea," Mariana put in. "He would not really expect you to come even if you said you would. Not if he saw you were with men. He would think they would not let you." She lowered her eyes. "Even American men."

The bus had stopped at the downtown square. They filed off with the other passengers and found themselves in the middle of a parade which was forming to circle the square. A young girl in a red dancing dress was seated on a throne on a car. Her attendants were around her. A band was getting out its instruments.

"Be a good sport," Saint John said. "Don't start something with a matador. Not tonight, please, Rhoda." He took her arm. They began to walk toward the hotel where they had left the station wagon. "It was such a nice day. Why spoil it?"

"It's about death," Rhoda said. "I can't stand to do nothing constantly but displacement activities, amusements, ways to pass the time, until we get into the ground to stay. What's happening to us, Saint John? We are getting so old. We haven't got enough sense to be alive and it's almost over. We'll be crippling around with a pacemaker soon. We'll be completely dried out and ruined and I've never slept with a bullfighter in my life and I've always wanted to."

"Stop and get her a margarita," Dudley said. "Let's go in there." They had come to a restaurant on the square and went in and ordered a round of margaritas. They drank to the bullring and the brave matadors and Dudley began to give toasts.

"I'm going," Rhoda said. "I'm going over there at seven o'clock."

"Here's to the girl from the Delta, who never would say you are right, who never gives in, please give in, Rhoda, your brother and cousin are begging and begging you tonight." Dudley raised his margarita and signaled the bartender to bring them another round.

"Here's to the girls growing old," Rhoda raised her glass. She was into it now. "Who think they didn't get laid enough. Lost their youth and their puberty and their childbearing years being good for Daddy and big brother and fucking Jesus."

"Rhoda, you've had all kinds of husbands and boyfriends. What did you miss out on?"

"Normal relationships. Having one husband and loving him forever. Getting laid on a regular basis. Remember, Saint John, I missed from the time I was thirteen to nineteen. I never got laid during the great primitive fertile years, thanks to no birth control and our Victorian upbringing."

"So you want to go fuck some Mexican bullfighter in a cheap hotel to make up for not having a normal life?"

"Don't lawyer-talk me." Rhoda put down her margarita. She had decided to take it easy and not get drunk. "And you're not getting me drunk," she added. "So don't try that. It will just make me go over there more."

"He won't expect you to be there." Mariana reached out a hand and touched Rhoda's arm. This woman was so different from her brother. This woman was not careful. It would not be good to hunt with her.

"I want to go and fuck this guy. I'm fifty-three years old. It's none of anybody's business. I don't mess around with your sex lives."

"Hey, look," Dudley said. "Here come the musicians." Three guitarists had come in the door and were gathering around a table. The music began, beautiful, sexy, exciting music. A song

Rhoda had heard once coming over a wall at a resort in Acapulco. "I heard that music in Alcapulco at Las Brisas once," she
said. "I was having a terrible honeymoon with a man I didn't
love. See, think of the terrible life I have been forced to live because I only liked power."

The music rose. Dudley motioned to the musicians to come
their way. "I was on a honeymoon," Rhoda went on. "But all I
did was get drunk and swim in this pool where you swam over
to the bar. It was New Year's Eve and the musicians on the boats
in the harbor played that wonderful music but it was all feet of
clay, feet of clay." Rhoda finished the first margarita and started
in on the second. The musicians came nearer. Dudley gave them
money. "Let's dance, Shorty," he said. "I want to dance with my
baby sister." Then the two of them went out onto the dance
floor and began to dance together. My closest closest relative,
Rhoda was thinking. My own big brother. My own hands and
legs and arms and face. The gene pool, Jesus, what a fantastic
mess.

"*Que paso, mi hermano,*" she said. "We shall dance a little
while and then go and see the bullfighter."

Dudley was a wonderful dancer and Rhoda loved to dance. He
had Rhoda where he wanted her now and he knew it. They
drank many margaritas and some wine and danced until the sun
was far down below the horizon and seven o'clock had come
and gone. "I have to go over to the Inn of the Sun," Rhoda kept
saying. "What time is it?"

"Let me dance with her," Saint John said. "I never get to
dance with Rhoda."

Sometime later they found a restaurant and ordered tortillas
and frijoles and chili with mole verde sauce. They drank sangria
and ate the wonderful gentle spicy food. "The food of a thou-

sand colors," Rhoda said. "The food of orange tortillas and green avocado mashed and red peppers the color of the bull. I have to get over to the hotel, Dudley. I want to change clothes and go and see the matador."

"Let him wait," Saint John said. "The longer he waits the more he'll want you."

"You're just saying that," Rhoda said. But she was in a wonderful suggestive drunken state and so she began to picture herself as she had been at fifteen, sitting in her room for fifteen minutes while her date cooled his heels waiting for her to come down the stairs. Fifteen minutes, LeLe had always insisted. You have to make them wait at least fifteen minutes. Don't ever be on time. Don't ever be waiting for them.

When they had eaten all they could eat of the exotic dangerous food, they wandered back out onto the street where the parade had ended and the carnival had begun. There were street vendors selling food and musicians playing, children everywhere, young men and women walking in groups and couples, drinking beer and sangria and calling out greetings. Dudley and Saint John and Rhoda and Mariana walked back to the hotel where they had left the station wagon and took possession of the rooms Mariana's friends at the hotel had saved for them. There were two large adjoining rooms with big tiled bathrooms and a common sitting room. They carried their small amount of luggage up the stairs and went into the rooms and all fell down on one enormous walnut bed. Dudley was still making up limericks.

"There was a young girl from Brownsville, who always wanted to swill wine, and when they said no, she said, 'You know where to go,' and now she is there waiting for them."

"That's terrible," Saint John said.

"There was a young doctor from New Orleans, who always said, 'I am going to warn you, you'll get into trouble if you go out with me, for I won't marry you but I'll charm you."

"Worse."

"There was a young girl from the womb," Rhoda began. "Who barely got laid from there to the tomb. She said, 'Well, goddamn, so that's where I am, who did this to me. I must find a way to blame whom.' Sinking spell," she added. "I am having a sinking spell." She rolled up on the bed, cuddling into Saint John's shirt.

"Don't worry," he said. "It will pass."

A short while later Rhoda made a recovery. "Wait a minute," she said. "Where's my cosmetic kit? I have to do something about my face." She got up and found the small leather kit and carried it into the bathroom. She put the kit on the counter and examined herself in the dark mirror. I'll have to start all over, she decided. She took out a jar of Charles of the Ritz face cleanser and began to apply it to her face. Then she decided it was going to get all over her hair so she dug around in the bag until she found a shower cap and she put that on. She went back into the room and opened the suitcase and took out a clean blouse and disappeared back into the bathroom. Dudley had gone downstairs to procure a bottle of wine and some glasses. Saint John and Mariana were propped up on the bed having a conversation about whitewing dove hunting and how to get the birds to come to Laredo instead of Brownsville.

Now Rhoda decided to take a bath in the stone bathtub. She took off all her clothes and wrapped herself in a towel and took her clothes back out to the room and hung them over the back of a chair. "Don't mess these up," she said. "They're all I have to wear."

"He won't expect you to come," Mariana said, in a voice so low only Saint John could hear her.

"Don't talk about it," Saint John said. "Don't say anything. So tell me, how much land has your uncle leased? Has he got it all, all along the irrigation ditches?"

"Yes," she said. "*Para ustedes solamente.* All of it. All the land."

Rhoda ran water in the tub and washed the tub out. Then she filled the tub with hot water and got in. What was I going to do? she was thinking. Oh, yes, I'm going over there and see the matador. LeLe will have a fit. She'll die of jealousy. If Anna was alive what would Anna say? Anna would say, Rhoda, you are drunk. Rhoda giggled, the thought was very heavy, the thought would sink the hotel. That's why you got cancer, Anna, she decided. From always thinking shit like that just when I was about to have a good time. Rhoda examined her legs as they floated in the water. They didn't look very good anymore. There was something wrong with the quality of the flesh, with the color of the skin. I hate my fucking body, Rhoda decided. I just fucking hate growing old. There isn't one single thing about it that I like. She got out of the tub and wrapped the towel around her and went out into the room.

"We should give all our money to young people," she said. "It is wasted on people as old as we are."

"What's wrong now?" Saint John asked.

"The skin on my legs looks like shit. I mean, the flesh. The flesh looks terrible. There's something wrong with it. It's mottled looking. I hate myself. I hate getting old, Saint John, it sucks to hell and back."

Dudley came in the door with a tray. A Mexican boy was behind him with the glasses. There was fruit and cheese and champagne and Dudley opened the champagne while the young boy tried not to notice that Rhoda was wearing a towel. She picked up her clothes from the chair and took them into the bathroom. Dudley brought her a glass of champagne and she drank it. Then she sat down at the bathroom stool and began to put on makeup.

Saint John turned on the radio beside the bed. Wild music began to play. United States music. It was a broadcast from Tom and Jerry's in Laredo. They were interviewing people who had come there to party all night. The music rose and fell and the people who were being interviewed told where they were from and what they had come to find in the border towns. It was funny. It was hilarious. The people were drunk and the broadcast was from Nuevo Laredo on the Mexican side so the interviewees were saying anything they wanted to say. It was amazing to hear people telling the truth on the radio. "I came down to get laid." "I came down to get drunk and let it all hang out." "I came down to find chicks." "I came down to find some guys to party with." "I came down to get away from it all." "It's cheap here." "You can find a party, you can have a good time." And so on.

Rhoda was getting back into a wonderful mood. The champagne had erased time. Her face was starting to look mysterious and beautiful. The bathroom was beautiful and mysterious. There were baskets of beautiful colored towels. There was a tile wall of fine blue and white figured tiles, each one different, each one made by hand. Everything in the room had been made by hand. The wicker stool was high and comfortable. The lights were soft. Rhoda applied more rouge, added some blue eye shadow, then a small single line of silver. She was beautiful, perhaps the most beautiful woman in the world. She thought of the matador pacing around the lobby of the hotel waiting for her. Waiting and waiting, thinking she wasn't going to come. Then she would appear. Fresh and lovely, his dream come true.

Dudley came into the bathroom and filled her champagne glass. He kissed her on the cheek. "I'm about ready to go," Rhoda said. "As soon as I finish my face."

"You're sure you want to go there?"

"I am sure. I have to have experiences, Dudley. I can't live my whole life in a straitjacket." She peered into the mirror. A deep line furrowed her brow. She was not quite as beautiful as she had been a moment before. "Don't back out on taking me. You said you'd take me. You promised me."

"I'll take you. We're going to see the matador. El matador." He was serious. He was playing the game. He wasn't making fun of her. One thing about Dudley, Rhoda decided. He never makes fun of me. Their eyes met. Yes, they were going to take the world seriously. Otherwise it wouldn't be worth ruling in case they were ruling it.

"What's going on in there?" Saint John called out. "I thought we were going to the Inn of the Sun God to see a matador. You better hurry up before I go to sleep instead."

"Let's go," Dudley said. "Come on if we're going."

It was eleven o'clock when they left the hotel and walked back to the square to look for the matador's inn. The fiesta was in full swing. The cafés were full. Mariachi music was playing. Music was coming out of the doors of the cafés. Drunks were falling off of benches on the square. People had been drinking all day. The car with the throne perched on top was parked sideways on a curb.

"Where is the Inn of the Sun?" Rhoda kept asking people.

"Keep going," someone said, "you will come to it."

"I'm just going over there," Rhoda kept saying. "I may not stay."

It was a square brick hotel on the corner of a street two

blocks off the square. There was a lamp over a desk in the lobby. The light was dim and no one was behind the desk. They went into the lobby and waited. "Anybody here?" Rhoda called out. Dudley and Saint John didn't say a word. Mariana cuddled into Dudley's arm. A sleepy-looking man came out a door and asked what they wanted.

"I am looking for the torero, Guillarmo Perdigo," Rhoda said. "Is he staying here?"

"He was here," the proprietor said. "With his family. But he is gone now. He has been gone for a while."

"Will he be back?"

"I do not know. Perhaps in the morning. Perhaps not."

"Thank you," Rhoda said, and turned and led the way out of the inn and back out onto the street. They walked back to the hotel and went up to their rooms and told each other good night. Saint John was sleeping on a pull-out bed in the sitting room. After a while Rhoda got up and went into the room and got into the bed with him. "I'm lonely as shit," she said. "I want to be near you."

"Get in," he said. "It's okay. I love you. You're our little girl. Are you okay?" He reached over and pulled the cover up over her shoulder. He patted her shoulder. He patted her tired worn-out head. Her used-to-be-red, now sunbleached, hair which was not standing up very well under the trip to Mexico.

"No," she said. "I drank too much and besides I wanted to go and meet that bullfighter. I wasn't really going to sleep with him, Saint John, I just wanted to get to know him."

"But you might catch something, Rhoda. Kissing is worse than intercourse for some of the viruses. You should see what I see every day. It's really depressing."

"I never think of you getting depressed."

"Well, I do."

"I really wanted to go over there and meet him."

"We went there."

"No, you got me drunk to keep me from going."

"I was afraid for you, Rhoda. I love you." He patted her shoulder. He felt old suddenly, very old and far away from the world where he and Rhoda and Dudley had been alive and hot and terrible.

"I miss my children," Rhoda said. "I am lonesome for them."

"I know you are," Saint John said, and kept on patting until Rhoda settled down and was still.

"Thank God," he said out loud and moved his hand and went to sleep beside her.

In the morning they drove back to the hacienda. No one mentioned the matador or having gone to the inn to look for him. Rhoda folded her arms around herself and thought about the softness of his shoulders and his black eyes seeking out hers across the concrete concession stand. Win some, lose some, she was thinking. Outside the windows of the station wagon the hills were purple in the early light. I love this country, Rhoda decided. Any place that can produce a man like that is okay with me. Oh, God, I wish Anna were here. I could call up Anna and tell it to her and she would say, What a wonderful story. What a lovely encounter. Remember when she fell in love with that tennis player that summer in New Orleans and he fell in love with her? Some enchanted evening, only it was afternoon at the New Orleans Lawn Tennis Club right after they moved to the new club and the next day she showed up at my house at about eight in the morning so excited and horny and borrowed my makeup because she had been up all night making love to him in his apartment on Philip Street. God, what a summer. What a hot exciting world. It's true, we got to live in the best of times. Now they have to have rubbers and spermicides and be scared to death of catching things.

We weren't afraid of anything. Oh, God, Guillarmo's back and arms are the most beautiful things I've ever seen in my life. I would like to see him fight bulls from now till the dawn of time.

"Rhoda?"

"Yes."

"Are you all right back there?" It was Dudley speaking. Saint John was asleep beside him in the front seat. Mariana was asleep beside Rhoda.

"Let's stop and get something to eat," Rhoda said. "I didn't have any breakfast."

"We'll be at the hacienda soon. Can you wait till then? I don't think there's anywhere to stop between here and there, except maybe a native market."

"No, it's all right. I forgot. I forgot where I am."

"I want to take you to a special place this afternoon. To meet some friends of mine."

"Sure."

"They're Americans who live down here. The man's from Austin and his wife is from Ireland. You'll like them. They have a really interesting place. An animal farm. You've never seen anything like it."

"Where do they get the bulls?"

"For the fights?"

"Yes."

"They raise them. It's quite an art, to keep the bloodlines pure and keep from overbreeding them. I'll take you sometime to one of the ranches where they are raised."

"I want to go back to Monterrey and see another bullfight."

"I bet you do."

"Okay, Dudley. Well, I'm going back to sleep." She closed her eyes. Went into a fantasy of meeting Guillarmo on an island off the coast of Spain. Having babies with him. Raising bulls.

*   *   *

They got back to the hacienda in Agualeguas at noon and had lunch and packed up and said their farewells to Mariana. Mariana was wearing a new gold bracelet with the teeth of a saber-toothed tiger embedded in the gold. Does he carry that stuff around with him in the glove compartment? Rhoda wondered. I mean, does he just have it ready in case he gets laid or does he go out at night and buy it? Maybe the fairies deliver it. God, what a man.

"I wish you could stay another night," Mariana said. "The rooms are free."

"We have to get back," Rhoda said. "Saint John and I have to catch a plane tomorrow. Look, Mariana, could you get me a poster of that bullfight we saw yesterday? I mean if you see one or if you get a chance." Rhoda held out a twenty-dollar bill. "Keep this in case you see one and buy it and send it to me."

Mariana refused the money. "I'll send you one if I am able to find it." The women's eyes met. "Well, come back," Mariana added. She took Rhoda's hand. I love Mexico, Rhoda decided. I adore these people. I wish they'd all cross the border. This lovely tropic heat, the bougainvillea, Guillarmo's shoulders, blood on the arena floor.

"I'll come back," she said. "When the doves are here." Then Dudley embraced Mariana and Saint John embraced her and Rhoda embraced her and they got into the station wagon and drove off.

"One more thing we need to see," Dudley said, as he turned onto the asphalt road. "One more thing to show Shorty."

"What is that?" Rhoda asked.

"The cats," Saint John said. "Dudley wants you to see the cats."

It was two o'clock in the afternoon when they left the hacienda. They turned onto an asphalt road leading northwest to Hidalgo and Candela. A few miles outside of Candela they left the main road and followed the course of a stream until they came to a fence and a gate. Dudley stopped the car and got out and spoke into a microphone attached to the gate. In a few minutes a boy came on a bicycle and opened the gate with a combination and held it while they drove in.

A well-kept road made of crushed stone led uphill between acacia and scrub birch trees. Dudley drove the station wagon carefully up the road. The road grew steeper and he shifted into second gear. Rhoda was leaning up into the front seat now, trying not to ask questions. They had all slipped once again into their childhood roles. Dudley, the general and pathfinder. Saint John, the faithful quiet lieutenant. Rhoda, lucky to be there, lucky to get to go, interloper.

"You may see a lion along here," Dudley said. "Don't be surprised if you do. They get loose. Dave Hilleen and I had to shoot one last month. Hated to have to do it."

"A lion," Rhoda said. Very softly, very quietly. "He's kidding, isn't he, Saint John?"

"No, he's not," Saint John said. "You'll see."

The road wound down a small hill, then across a wooden bridge. The bridge covered a creek that crossed and recrossed the road.

"There's a springbok," Saint John said. "Oh, there's the herd." Rhoda looked and there beneath the trees was a herd of twenty or thirty African springbok. Their tall sculpted horns rose like lilies into the low hanging limbs of the scrub brush. They quivered, then disappeared like a school of fish.

"My God," Rhoda said. "How lovely. How divine."

"There are kudu and sheep and deer," Dudley said. "We're hoping to get some rhino in the fall."

"You're kidding."

"No, he's not," Saint John put in.

"They'll love it here," Dudley said. "It's exactly like parts of central Africa. Only safer and there is hay. It's conservation, Shorty. Someday, this may be the only place these creatures live. The African countries are destroying their herds. They're being hunted out and their preserves raped. They're beautiful, aren't they?"

"Do you hunt them?"

"Very little. We sell them to zoos. Sometimes we trade them for cats."

"All right. I'll bite. What cats?"

"You'll see," Saint John said. "Wait till you see."

"Cats the circuses can't train. Ones that go bad. The one Dave and I shot was an old lion that went bad. Ringling Brothers paid us to take him."

"Who does this belong to?" Rhoda asked. "Who pays for all of this?"

"It pays for itself. Dave paid five thousand to shoot the lion. He was scared to death. I didn't think he was going to pull the trigger when it charged. Jesus, I never saw a man get so white. Afterwards he said to me, I was scared to death, Dudley. How do you do that in the wild? Just like you did it here, I told him. It's him or you. It took him two shots." Dudley was talking to Saint John now. "One glanced off the ear and one went in an eye, ruined the head. I shot for the heart and lung when I saw his first shot miss. Old Dave. I never saw a man go so white."

"Who started all this?" Rhoda asked. "Who does this belong to?"

"These are nice folks here," Dudley said, suddenly stern. "They're friends of mine. Be nice to them and try not to talk too much."

"Of course," she said. "I'm always nice to everyone." Saint John sniggered, and Rhoda started to tell him to go fuck himself but for some reason she didn't feel like making Saint John or Dudley mad at her right that minute.

They had come to the top of a rise. A Caterpillar tractor with a grader blade was parked beside the road. Two Mexican boys sat underneath an umbrella drinking from a stone jar.

A house was at the end of the road. An old stone house like something out of a nineteenth-century English novel. It was three stories high with turrets and a tower. In the field behind the house were structures that looked like huge greenhouses. They were tall cages, sixty feet wide by eighty feet long. There were three of them, at intervals of forty feet, constructed of steel bars three inches thick. Swings were suspended from the ceiling beams and some of the cats were sitting on the swings. A leopard, Rhoda thought. That's a leopard. And that's another one. She was struck dumb. Now she did not have to try to be quiet. Nothing could prepare you for this, she decided, no words could prepare anyone for this.

Dudley drove the car up to the house and parked it. Children appeared on the back porch. The caretaker's children. A tall girl, maybe twelve or thirteen, a boy a little older, a smaller girl, an even smaller boy. They were dark-skinned and dark-haired but did not look like Mexicans. "Are they Mexican?" Rhoda asked.

"Of course."

"They don't look it."

"Their mother is Italian. Where's your momma?" Dudley called out. He opened the door and got out. "Hand me that sack of rolls," he added. They had stopped at a bakery in Anahuac and bought sweet bread and raisin loaves for the children. Dudley handed the sack to the oldest girl. The boy smiled and held out an animal he was wearing on his arm. "Baby jaguar," the boy said. "They are all gone for the day, gone hunting with Redman."

"We just came by to see the cats," Dudley said. He patted the jaguar. He got back into the car. "We'll be back to the house. I want to show my sister the cats." Rhoda was half in and half out of the car. Now she got back in and shut the door.

"The momma killed the other one," the boy said. "We are raising this one on a bottle."

"We'll be back," Dudley said. He put the car in gear and backed out of the parking place. The children arranged themselves on the porch stairs, the boy held up the baby jaguar, flies buzzed around the porch and the car, the ground was dry and yellow. Rhoda sat on the edge of her seat. Behind them was a fourth cage. It was full of very large cheetahs, at least three cheetahs. "That cage isn't big enough for the cheetahs," Dudley said. "We have to do something about it. We didn't know we were going to have so many. The cougar need better cages, too. There are fourteen cougar now. Too many, but everyone keeps sending them and no one wants to hunt them."

"Embarrassment of riches," Saint John muttered. Dudley ignored him and drove the car from the driveway and out into the field where the cages rose like monuments in the hazy blue sky. We will get bogged down in the field, Rhoda thought. The car will stop and we'll have to get out. Why do the men in this family always have to drive cars into fields? Why do I always end up driving on a field or in a ditch? Why can't we stay on the road like other people? Don't talk. Don't say a goddamn word. If you object it will just make him do it more. You can't stop Dudley by telling him not to do something. Just be quiet and it will soon be over.

"How do you like it?" Dudley said, and laughed. He began to circumnavigate the cages. Tigers were in the first one. At least five tigers, four gold-and-white-striped tigers and one black tiger lounging on top of a concrete shelter. As they passed the cage Rhoda saw that a sixth tiger was inside the shelter, a huge black tiger twice as large as the others, taking up the coolest, most protected spot in the concrete shelter. She shuddered, tried to take it in. Dudley drove on. In the second cage were Bengal tigers, with faces as big as car windows. Three Bengal tigers sitting together on swings looking at her with their huge heads. In the third cage were lions. A lioness and three young cubs. Dudley drove down to a fourth cage, which could not be seen from the house. Jaguars were in that one. There were more cages in front of the house, protected by shrubbery and trees.

"What are in those?" she asked quietly.

"Leopards and cougar and some more lions," Dudley said. "We have three lionesses with cubs now and the ones in the pasture."

"What pasture?" But then she knew. Dudley had stopped the station wagon beside a flimsy-looking thirty-foot-high fence. Inside the fence was a huge lion. Behind him in the tall grass were two lionesses with their cubs. The lion turned his head their way. Dudley rolled down the automatic windows and opened the sun roof. "Aren't they gorgeous, Shorty?" he said. "Aren't they something?"

"My God," she said. Dudley got out and walked over to the fence. "Hello, Waylon," he said. "Long time no see." The lion roared, a long deep rattling in the throat. Dudley turned his back to the lion and walked away.

"Don't worry, Shorty," he said. "He wants me but not badly enough to do anything about it today." Rhoda could hear him but she was only looking from the deepest part of the back seat. She had tried looking at the lion out the window but it was like staring over a precipice. Still, she could hear every word Dudley said, every sound of the world, suddenly she could hear every nuance, every blade of grass.

"Don't talk to him," she said. "Don't do anything else. Get back in the car." Dudley turned back to the lion.

"Get in the car," Rhoda called out. In a very soft voice. "Roll up those windows. Get in the car and get me out of here. Saint John, roll these windows up."

"The windows wouldn't stop him," Saint John said. "If he wanted to get in the car he could do it."

"Well, drive it then," Rhoda said. She called out the window in the loudest voice she could muster: "Dudley, get in the car. Get in this car and get me out of here. I don't like it. I don't like that lion. Or those cats. Get me out of here."

"I thought you were into violence now," Saint John said. "Bullfighters and blood and all that."

"Not when I'm part of the ring. Roll the windows up, Saint John, this is madness. That fence isn't big enough to stop a dog, much less a lion. Get Dudley back in the car. Let's get out of here. I don't like it here."

Dudley spoke to the lion again. "You want me, don't you, Waylon. Show Rhoda what you need." He turned his back to the lion again and began to walk away from the fence. The lion moved toward the fence.

"Oh, shit," Rhoda said. "I'm driving off, Dudley. I'm leaving you here. Roll those windows up, Saint John. Roll them up this minute, do you hear me?"

"It's okay," Saint John said. "You're okay."

"I am not okay. I am scared to death." Rhoda pulled herself into a ball in the very middle of the back seat. She considered climbing into the trunk, but there was no trunk, it was a station wagon.

Dudley turned back to the lion. "Old Waylon," he said. "He hates me but he doesn't know why. You don't know why, do you, Waylon? Except you know I'm not afraid of you."

"Get in the car," Rhoda yelled. "Get in the car this very minute. Roll those windows up. Oh, God, why did I come down here to fucking Mexico in the middle of July. Have they closed the window yet? Please close the window, Saint John. Dudley, close the goddamn sunroof and get back in the car and get me out of here. I have had all I can take of these goddamn terrifying unbelievable cats. I don't want to see them anymore. Take me to that house." He was still standing by the lion. "It's bad karma," Rhoda continued. "It's terrible karma to have these animals here. They should not be here. They should be dead or else back where they came from, where the Indians or Chinese or Africans or whatever can kill them themselves. If they lived where I lived I'd kill them all tonight. Get back in the car. Leave that lion alone." The lion bounded for the fence. Dudley laughed. Saint John got back in the car.

"Start the car," Rhoda said. "Saint John, start the car."

"Not yet. Go on up to the house if you're scared."

"Hell no."

"They can't get out, Rhoda. Oh, I guess the lion could get over the fence, but he doesn't really want to."

"Okay, I'm going. I can't take any more of this." Rhoda opened the car door. She looked toward the house. The children were standing on the stone steps holding the baby jaguar. "I'm going to the house," she said. "Fuck being out here with these goddamn lions." She stepped down on the grass, shut the car door, and began to run. "Don't get so excited," Dudley yelled. *Don't get them excited,* she thought he said.

"Watch out," Saint John called. "Watch your step." Rhoda sprinted toward the house, which seemed a mile away. She ran faster and stepped into a gopher hole and turned her ankle and went sprawling down across the dry yellow grass. Pain shot up her leg, then something was on top of her. It was Saint John. He knelt beside her and began to feel the bones in her foot. "Get me into the house," Rhoda was yelling. "Carry me into that house and lock the door."

Rhoda lay on a filthy horsehair sofa in the parlor of the stone house. One-half of the sofa was covered with the skin of a mountain sheep. Her broken foot lay propped on the sheepskin. By her side was a marble table with a statue of Mercury, wings on his feet. Saint John had gone into the kitchen to call the hospital in Laredo. Dudley was outside the window helping the young girls feed the jaguar. I am lying on this sofa catching ringworm, Rhoda decided. The worms are going into my ankle through my wound and into the soles of my feet from where that dreadful little abandoned jaguar shit upon the floor. The children will have ringworm too. They will be bald and dead from the bad karma in the place. Live by the sword, die by the sword. There's no telling what will happen now. I don't even know if Saint John is a good doctor. Being my cousin doesn't make him good enough to set my foot, even if we do think our genes are superior to everyone else's in the whole fucking world. "It hurts," she called out. Then yelled louder. "My goddamn foot is killing me, Saint John. Please come give me something for my foot."

Dudley stuck his head in the open window. "What's wrong, Shorty? What's wrong now?"

"My foot is broken. And I want to go to the hospital. I don't want to wait another minute. It's your fault for not taking me to the house when I asked to go. I didn't know we were going to see these lions. Who said I wanted to go see a bunch of real lions? That fence wouldn't hold a lion for a minute if it wanted to get out. It could get out and kill everyone in the place."

"We're going in just a minute," Dudley said. "As soon as Saint John gets off the phone."

"Then hurry up," she said. "It's killing me. It's about to kill me, Dudley."

Saint John entered the room carrying a glass of water and a bottle of Demerol pills and stood by while she swallowed one. The water will give me amoebic dysentery, she decided. But I can't help that for now. "Where did the water come from?" she asked. "What kind of pills are these?"

Then the pain was better and finally stopped, or, at least, Rhoda didn't have to suffer it any longer. They carried her out to the station wagon and laid her out in the back seat beside a box of frozen palomas blancas and two cases of German wine and the guns. Saint John borrowed an embroidered pillow from the children and arranged it underneath her head and propped her injured foot on a duffel bag and then Dudley made long elaborate farewells and they drove off down the line of caged animals. The panthers scurried around their cages. The lionesses flicked their tails. The lion cubs played with their paws. The Bengal tigers turned their stately faces toward the car like huge Indian sunflowers. The kudu pricked up their ears, they moved like leaves before the wind. The peacocks flew up to the fence posts. The Mexican guards waved and opened the gate. Dudley returned their wave and drove on through. Then he reached down into the glove box and took out the secret leather-covered tequila bottle and passed it to his cousin.

"When was the first time you two ever went hunting together?" Rhoda asked drowsily.

"When Saint John was ten and I was eight," Dudley answered. "Remember, Saint John, Uncle Jodie lent us his four ten and that little rifle, that twenty-two, and we went bird hunting, across the bayou behind the store."

"We were quail hunting," Saint John added. "We scared up a covey but we missed and then you shot a rabbit. Back where Man's cabin used to be."

"We skinned it and Babbie cooked it for us that night for dinner." They leaned toward each other in the front seat of the car, remembering.

"I took my old harpoon out of my dirty red bandanna," Saint John began singing. "And was blowing sweet while Bobby sang the blues."

"Blowing soft while Bobby sang the blues," Rhoda corrected sleepily from the back seat. "Not blowing sweet." She sank back down into the Demerol. The hunters looked at each other and shook their heads. A hawk high above them in the air spotted the car and was blinded by the reflection of the sunlight in his eyes.

"From the coal mines of Kentucky," Saint John started again. "To the California hills, Bobby shared the secrets of my soul."

A few days later Rhoda was back in her own house, safe from spotted fever and hookworm and amoebic dysentery and adventure. Her ankle was in a cast. She had a pair of rented crutches and a rented wheelchair. She had a young girl from the nursing school who was coming by in the mornings to fix her breakfast. She had an old boyfriend who taught history who was coming over in the afternoons to cheer her up. She had accepted an offer to teach Latin during the fall semester, replacing a young man who had gone crazy in the summer and run off to California without telling his department chairman. He had sent a note. "I can't bear their wretched little faces," the note said. "What do they need with Latin?"

The department chairman had called Rhoda and asked her if she could fill in. He had gotten her on the phone the day after

Dudley had delivered her to her house. "Yes," she had said. "I will teach your class. I need some order in my life."

Now she sat in the wheelchair on the patio and watched the robins picking up seeds on the freshly mowed lawn. Her hands lay on her legs. She thought about her boring boyfriend. She thought about the sweet little nursing student who was fixing her such boring sweet little meals. She thought about lying in the back of the station wagon all the way home from Mexico and Saint John's hopeful, grating, off-tune voice singing the collected works of Kris Kristofferson and the collected works of Willie Nelson.

She thought of Dudley and how long they had all managed to live and how strange that they still loved each other. We know each other, she decided. Nothing has to be explained. No questions asked. *I wish them well.* Even if they do think it is all right to fuck around with a bunch of lions and tigers and risk their lives and keep on hunting when it is the twentieth century and for a long time men have dreamed they could evolve into something less dangerous and messy and bloody. Still, there was that bullfight.

The sun came out from behind a cloud and flooded the patio. Rhoda sank deep into herself. Moved by the light.

She considered her boyfriend, who did good dependable useful work in the world and how boring and pointless it was to make love to him. With or without her foot in a cast she had no passion for the man. Her chin fell to her chest. We are not making progress, she decided. This is not progress.

I will go back with them in September. To kill the beautiful and awkward palomas blancas and pluck them and cook them and eat them. Anything is better than being passionless and bored. There's no telling who might be down there this fall. No telling what kind of gorgeous hunters might shut me up for a few hours or days and make me want to buy soft Mexican dresses with flounces and rickrack and skirts that sweep around my ankles. Bullfighters are waiting and blood on the arena floor. Blood of the bull and fast hot music and Mexico. "I should have left a long time ago," she began humming. Progress is possible, she decided. But it's very, very slow.

Several weeks later, when her ankle had healed enough that she could walk, she drove downtown to the travel agency to buy her ticket back to San Antonio. At the corner of Spring Street and Stoner she changed her mind and went to her old psychiatrist's office instead. She parked the car and went in and asked the receptionist to make her an appointment. Then she went home and began to write letters. It was a cool day. The first cool day in months. The light was very clear. The trees were just beginning to turn their brilliant colors. Fall was coming to the mountains. Life was good after all. Peace was possible. Ideals were better than nothing, even if they were naïve. Here I go again, Rhoda thought, one hundred and eighty degrees a minute. She stuck some paper in the typewriter and began to write letters.

Dearest Dudley [the first letter began],
We have been the victims of Daddy's aggression all our lives. The pitiful little victims of his terrible desire for money and power. All he understands is power. He doesn't have the vaguest idea how to love anyone and neither do you and I. We must save ourselves, Dudley. Don't go back to Mexico and drink tequila and run around with lions. Come up here and visit me and we will sit on the porch and drink coffee and try to think of things to do that are substitutes for always being in danger. We could play cards. I will play cards with you for

money, how about that? *I don't know anything now. I don't know where to begin.*

We need to talk and talk and talk. Please come.

Love, Rhoda

Dear Saint John,

Don't go back to Mexico and catch amoebic dysentery. Come up here instead. We don't need to kill things in order to eat. All we need to do is stay alive and work and try to appreciate life and have a good time.

Come on up. Dudley and I are going to revive card games. We are going to play poker and drink a lot of coffee and I'll make biscuits for breakfast.

We'll have new times instead of old times.

Love, Rhoda

P.S. I'm sorry about that bullfighter. I really am.

P.P.S. I had this vision of the three of us huddled together on the floor at Esperanza sucking on each other for sustenance and love. Trying to get from each other what we couldn't get from the grown people. All those terrible years — our fathers at the war and our mothers scared to death and the Japs coming to stick bamboo splinters up our fingernails and you and me and Dudley trying to mother and father each other. Life is not easy for anyone. That's for sure. I don't think we really understand much yet and may be losing the little that we used to know. We don't need Mexico, old partner. We need something to hold on to in the dark and someone to remind us of where we really are. We are spinning in space on this tenuous planet. I won't let you forget that if you won't let me.

Love and love again, me.

Rhoda sealed the letters into envelopes and addressed them. Then she got into the car and drove down the hill and deposited them in the box at the post office. She was in a good mood. She even remembered to think it was miraculous that man had learned to write, not to mention invented a system to get letters from one place to another. Not to mention taming horses and fighting bulls and living to grow up. Every now and then someone grows up, she decided. I've heard about it. Why not, or else, whatever.

Paris

A YOUNG MAN is dead and maybe we could have stopped it. That's what I wake up with every morning. Until a month ago I was a completely happy person. Who knows, maybe I'll be happy again.

Reality expands exponentially. It meets itself coming and going. It is a net, a web; touch one strand and the whole thing quivers. Get caught and you cannot get away. Sticky stuff, reality. Spiders understand this metaphor. It had nothing to do with me. I say this over and over again, like a mantra.

There was no reason why I shouldn't go to Paris. My young friend, Tannin, was writing a book about me. He needed me to inspire him and give him material. I don't think he knew he was writing about me. He thought he was writing a book about three girls in Paris living in an apartment and talking all the time about their lovers. Only all three sounded like me, my hysteria, how I make every utterance an oath or a promise. I can't help it. I was poisoned in the womb. If you don't buy first causes, don't read on.

I'm a journalist and a writer of novels. My name is Rhoda Manning and I'm fifty-eight years old and you'd never believe that either. People who believe in fairies don't age.

So on the fifth of May I climbed into the belly of the whale and crossed the Atlantic Ocean and arrived at Orly about seven in the morning. Tannin met me at the plane. His fifty-eight-year-old muse in a wrinkled white linen suit and two-inch spectator pumps getting bravely off a plane with her hair cut short for the mission. I used to have lovers his age. Now I only want the good part, the youthful energy, the sheer delight. Coming out to Orly at seven in the morning to squire me through customs. The ones I had for lovers might have done that. But none of them spoke flawless Parisian French.

There are many love affairs in the world, more ways to love, Horatio, than you dream of. I had been practicing all my life for this. Having brothers, raising sons, loving young men. And now, in my Senior Citizenship, Tannin had been delivered to me. To love, to understand, to nourish, to adore. He had written me a letter to say he liked a book I wrote. It was a book about a friend who died an early death. I will write about you, I had told the friend. I will not let you die. Do it, he had answered. If you write it from the heart, it will be good. I had and it was and I was as proud of it as anything I had ever written.

Also, it gave Tannin to me. The book had come to him from the Book-of-the-Month Club and he forgot to send it back. So he read it and then he wrote to me and told me he wanted to be a writer. I throw such letters away every day. This one was different. It had a lilt, a ring, it made me laugh. He asked my advice about writing schools and I told him to come up here. That Randolph was a genius and would not harm him. Randolph is the director of the writing program.

So Tannin came to Fayetteville and became my friend and the next thing I knew I was flying to Paris to "hang out with him" while he wrote his book.

He called me frantically two days before I left to say he had a visitor, a young man who had gone to Sewanee with him. "He's driving me crazy," he said. "He's in a terrible mood. He hates everything in Paris. I took him to hear Ravel at the Sorbonne. He hated Ravel. I hope he'll be gone by the time you get here, but he might not be. I'm really sorry. He just showed up. I invited him a year ago. I never dreamed he'd come."

"Maybe he's disoriented. That happened to me once, in Heidelberg. I just got completely disoriented. I had to go home."

"I don't know what's wrong with him. He quit his job a month ago. Maybe that's it. He was working for his dad in Nashville."

"Don't worry about it. Nothing will stop us from having fun in Paris. Did you get tickets to the ballet?"

"Yes. They're supposed to be good seats. They'd better be."

"My cousin plays in the orchestra. We'll meet her after the performance. I haven't seen her since she was in high school."

"Good. That's fine. We'll do anything you want to do. I'm so glad you're coming."

As soon as we collected my bags we went to my hotel and sat in the café drinking coffee and talking. We hadn't seen each other in four weeks but it seemed a year. Our sagas engage us. His are as real to me as mine. "So what's the friend's name?" I asked. "And is he better?"

"His name is William and he's worse. Now he has a cold. He's asleep in my room. He's going to the ballet with us tomorrow night."

"That's fine. I want to meet him. Don't worry, Tannin. Nothing is wrong. I'm elated to be here. Look at this weather. This is paradise. My plan is to stay awake all afternoon and take a sleeping pill and crash about six and sleep till dawn. How does that sound to you?"

"Fantastic. Should you be drinking coffee?"

"It won't matter. I have a Xanax. It will knock me out." We giggled. We laughed as if that were the funniest thing in the world, as if it were deeply, wildly, madly, hysterically funny.

We left the hotel and walked up the rue de Montalembert to the boulevard St.-Germain and followed it to the Seine. We stood on the bridge and watched people and talked about the swimming pool that had sunk in the river the night before.

"A floating swimming pool that's been here since the forties. Think what would have happened if it had been in the daytime. If people had been there. I wish I could have seen it sink."

"So do I. What a phenomenon. A huge floating swimming pool sinking into the Seine. *Mon dieu!*" We laughed again. It was incredibly, divinely, hilariously funny. No one ever gets that tickled when they are alone. Only two people can know something is that funny.

"In sight of Notre Dame Cathedral. This may be a sign. Listen, I told William I'd meet him for lunch. I never thought you'd want to stay awake. We don't have to go. I could go by there and tell him I'm not coming."

"I want to. Come on. I want to go. I really do. Why are you so worried about my meeting William?"

"Because it's your vacation. You shouldn't have to baby-sit my friends."

"I want to meet him." I took his arm and we walked along the river to the Jardin des Tuileries and across the gardens to the Café du Palais Royale, a bright café with pots of orange flowers and brilliant paintings on the walls. We found a table and sat down and began to read the menu. A young man came hurrying toward us through the tables. He had curly blond hair and blue eyes and looked enough like Tannin to be his twin.

"William Watkins Weckter," Tannin said. "The fourth or fifth. My old roommate at Sewanee. He's dying to meet you."

"I read your books," he said. "I used to talk about them all the time."

"Oh, my. Sit down. Are you feeling better? Tannin said you had been sick."

"It's nothing. A summer cold. Well, I quit my job last month. I'm out on the street. That should give you a cold, don't you think?" He laughed and took a handkerchief out of his pocket and stood up and went outside and blew his nose. When he came back in he picked up the conversation and went right on. He didn't seem depressed to me. Just at loose ends, like half the young people I meet. No children, no responsibilities they can't leave. They are free, in the deepest and most terrible sense of the word. Cut loose, dismounted, disengaged. Not Tannin though, he's in love with the muse, the sight of his words upon the page. Artists are the same in any age, always lost and always found.

So here was William with a degree in history and a minor in biology and nothing to do. He had worked for his father in an office supply store in Nashville for a while, now he was wandering around the world. "I better see it while I can," he said. "When I go back to work I won't have a vacation for a year."

"The age of commerce may be over," I said. "I've been thinking of this. It's time for live theater, beautiful buildings, parks. There must be things for young people to do that will engage them in their brightest minds. It's this transition that is painful. Find out what you want to do and do it. What do you want to do, William? Do you have any idea?"

"Something worth keeping. Something I could talk about. When I was young I liked to keep records. I wrote down what I did each day." He looked off into the gardens outside the café.

We finished our coffee. William insisted on paying for our lunch. Nothing would dissuade him. Then he left us, and Tannin and I walked back to my hotel. There were young people dressed in costumes from the seventeenth century wandering around the Tuileries looking beautiful and mysterious. They weren't selling anything. We couldn't figure out why they were there.

"Gratuitous beauty," Tannin declared. "France. I am happiest when I am here. It's my mother's fault. She did this to me."

"I'm fading," I answered. "Take me to my bed. I'll see you in the morning."

Tannin delivered me to my hotel and I went upstairs and unpacked and ordered some Evian and drank half a bottle of it with a Xanax and went to sleep with the windows open. I was on the seventh floor of the Hôtel Montalembert, where Buckminster Fuller used to stay with his entourage. Outside my window I could see the Eiffel Tower and the streets leading to the river and les Champs Elysées. I slept. Like a lamb in a meadow I slept away the hours until dawn.

I woke in Paris. I stretched out my muscles in the bed. Pulled the beautiful pillows into my arms. Goose down, from some lovely flock of geese somewhere in the land of France. This elegant old culture. I lay in bed and looked around the room. It was black and white. White walls, black painted furniture, a soft design on the chairs. Another bolder print on the bedcover. White linen drapes pulled back from dormer windows. I won't do a thing I don't want to do, I decided. I will not hurry. I curled back into a ball and daydreamed for a while, imagining the ballet we would see that evening. The Paris Opéra House with its ceiling painted by Chagall. Ballets by Balanchine and Robbins. I had not seen ballet in fourteen months. I was badly overdue for a ballet.

*   *   *

I rose from the bed and walked over to the window and stood leaning out the casement in my white silk nightgown. When I'm at home I sleep in flannel. See what this city does for me. I drank the rest of the Evian and dressed in a black pantsuit and went down to the café for petit déjeuner. A waiter brought me the *Herald Tribune* and I read Russell Baker's column and drank the best coffee in the world and ate a brioche and raspberries from the Dordogne. I was getting more civilized every minute. I was almost urbane. The city and the day stretched out before me. I thought of Tannin, not ten blocks away in his room overlooking the Luxembourg Gardens. I thought of William, with his upper-respiratory infection and his pretty face. I thought of my young cousin playing her violin at the Paris Opéra. I thought of Chagall and the light coming in the glass windows onto my table and the perfect weather and how lucky I was to live in such a world.

I went upstairs and changed into street shoes and left the hotel and walked for an hour, exploring side streets, stopping at a salon to make an appointment for my hair, windowshopping.

When I got back to the hotel there were messages. Tannin was coming to take me to lunch. My cousin was home and would I call her. It made me giddy, to be in a city this beautiful, in cool weather, with young people to talk to, and nothing, not a single thing going wrong, and no longer in boyfriend jail. I was not in love with anyone and I did not want to be. BOND NO MORE, it said on notes I had scattered around my house. I had written it and I meant it. I was free to let the whole world be my lover.

Free at last from the obsessive weight of love affairs. Free from waiting around a hotel room for a husband or a lover to decide what I could or could not do. Free from men turning on television sets.

I combed my hair, put on my two-inch heels, went down to

the lobby and Tannin was there, smiling and embracing me, as excited as I was. We left the hotel and walked until we found a sidewalk café that we liked and sat in the shade of a plane tree giggling and talking and telling stories and watching everything. There is nothing on earth like friendship. It is God's love, God's ambrosia, the one thing we never have to pay for or regret.

"That man is looking at you." Tannin laughed. "Men have been checking you out all morning."

"It's the damnedest thing. I mean, *mon dieu,* the minute you stop being available, men start wanting you. They can smell it a mile away. It has nothing to do with age or beauty."

"It's true. If we think we can't have it, it becomes interesting to us."

"You can't manufacture it. You have to really be out of the game. I am. You can't imagine how much I do not want to have another affair of any kind."

"Look at that, Rhoda. Over in the corner." I glanced at the couple kissing in the corner. A middle-aged man and a woman in a low-cut blouse. They looked like some inferior breed of human, the expression on their faces was completely infantile.

"Do you think they just did it or are they just about to go somewhere and do it?"

"Probably both." A waiter approached the couple and set a huge glass of ice cream with whipped cream and cherries and chocolate sauce down in front of the woman. The man picked up a spoon and began to feed her. Tannin touched my arm. We shook with laughter. We almost fell off our chairs. We could not contain ourselves. We paid the bill and walked off down the street and found a building to lean against and laughed until we cried.

I slept in the late afternoon and dressed and met Tannin and William in the lobby and we set out for the opera house.

"I've never seen a ballet," William said. "Is it okay to admit that?"

"I was older than you before I saw one that was good," I answered. "This is the World Series you're going to see. Except for Maurice Béjart and the Ballet of the Twentieth Century. That's the best to me, the nonpareil."

Later, after the first ballet, which was the Balanchine, he said, "Don't the ones in the chorus mind? They never get to be the star?"

"Prima ballerinas," I told him. "Listen, these are great athletes. They don't mind someone being the prima ballerina any more than a football team minds having a great running back. They have a wonderful life. They live to dance, to be up there on that stage, with that music, doing this for us. Dancers never grow old. I wish I could have been one."

"Well," I grudgingly admitted, later, in the lobby, at intermission, with a glass of wine. "They ruin their feet. They tear up their toes. What they're doing is unnatural, but that's why it's so hard and why the excitement of it never dies."

We went back to our seats, which were in a box to the left of the stage. Above our heads, the divine ceiling by Chagall. The curtains opened. Two dancers came on stage. Behind them were the flats which had also been painted by Chagall. *Entrée et pas-de-deux.* Magic. *Danse des garçons* with tables covered by umbrellas. More magic. Then the *danse des filles,* with small umbrellas everywhere. It was the dance of the day we had just spent in Paris, with the burden of weight dissolved in color. The human spirit turned loose to fly, transcend itself. This ballet alone would have been worth the trip across the ocean.

I had arranged for us to meet my cousin after the performance. May Chatevin Debardeleben. Her name was almost whispered in my family. She's in Paris, they would say. She plays the violin for the Paris ballet.

She was just as I remembered her, a blithe young girl with long dusty blond hair and violet eyes. Even as a child she had carried herself with dignity and grace. It had not surprised me when I heard she had flown the coop, escaped the massive tentacles of our family.

We found her in the orchestra pit, holding her violin against her black taffeta dress. I introduced everyone, embraced her, and begged her to come to dinner with us. "All right," she said. "Let me put this violin away. I won't bother to change to street clothes, if you don't mind." She was so absolutely Southern, the same young girl from Abbeville, Louisiana, where her mother played the organ at the Episcopal Church.

While she put the violin in the case I squeezed Tannin's hand. I was so proud of my lovely young cousin. All this time William had not spoken. Now, when May Chatevin snapped the clasps on the case, he reached out a hand and took it from her. "I played a violin when I was a kid," he said. "But I had to stop."

"Oh, why was that?" She was wearing large hornrimmed glasses. She reached up and took them off as she waited for his answer.

"Because it interfered with baseball practice. Then I broke a finger and it was in a cast for a year."

"That's terrible." She moved near him. "That's the worst thing I ever heard."

"I used to love the way it fit into the case."

"You could start again. It's not too late."

"You think so?"

"Sure. There are wonderful teachers here. Do you speak French?"

"I won't be here long."

"Let's start walking," Tannin said. "You can't solve this on an empty stomach."

We had dinner at a brasserie along the Seine. The lights from the barges going along the river climbed the trunks of the trees, then filled the crowns, then climbed back down. Afterward, an afterglow. A heavy metaphor for love, if anyone needed one in Paris.

May Chatevin and William were in love before we even got to the brasserie. They had paired up as soon as we left the opera house. They walked behind us, their heads bent toward one another. I had forgotten how fast it happens, had forgotten young men's bodies, the cold shaking power of desire, had been glad to forget it, as I now had other things to do, being in the universe on this clearer, older plane.

"My guardian angel must have finally made it across the ocean," William was saying across the table. "Everyone who goes to Sewanee gets a guardian angel. When we go onto the campus we check him at the gates. When we leave we pick him up again. We don't need him at Sewanee, you see, as it's the closest place to heaven." William laughed out loud. He was laughing at everything. And his cold had disappeared. It was the truth, what I told his parents later. He was the happiest young man I'd ever seen. In contrast to Tannin, who is as hysterical as I am. Searching, searching, dreaming, playing out the string. Philip Larkin has a metaphor for this. People sitting on the cliffs waiting for a white-sailed armada of hopes to come in. They arrive, Larkin says, but they never anchor. "Only one ship is seeking us," the poem ends. "A black-sailed unfamiliar, towing at its back a huge and breathless silence. In its wake, no waters breed or break."

*   *   *

The four of us became inseparable. We went to the Sorbonne to hear a string quartet play Brahms. We walked in the Tuileries and had lunch at Les Deux Magots. We strolled the boulevard St-Germain and went to Sulka to look at the ties. We walked along the Seine and saw the small blue asters in the flower shops and I told the story of V. K. Ratcliff's trip to New York City to the wedding of Eula Varner Snopes to the Jewish Communist and how V.K. bought a tie the color of asters and how the Russian woman kissed him on the mouth as she tied it around his neck.

We talked of writing and painting and music. We harvested the beauty of the city and fed it to each other. One day we rented a car and drove to Dieppe to see the coast. On the way home the skies were full of clouds and over a field of young corn we watched three parachuters playing with the wind. We talked of books we had read and artists we admired. We went to the Rodin museum and stood in line for fifty minutes. "Rilke came here every afternoon," Tannin said. "He adored Rodin. '*Rodin, c'est lui qui a inspiré le poete,*' Ran Rilke."

"I want to buy the tickets," I said. "Tell me what to say?"

"*Quatre. S'il vous plaît.*"

"*Quatre. S'il vous plaît,*" I told the lady in the cage and counted out the money as if I were six years old.

The *billets* were beautiful, reproductions of the statue called *Le Bourgeois de Calais,* 1895. Musée Rodin, 77 rue de Vareene, Paris.

We had an audience with the brilliant translator, Barbara Bray, and took her to a concert with us at a cathedral. May Chatevin and I had our hair done at Julien et Claude, Haute Coiffure, St-Germain-des-Prés. We stood outside the Louvre and watched the tourists going in. We bought a disposable camera and took photographs of each other by the statues of the continents. We went to Chanel and saw Catherine Deneuve shopping for costumes for a movie. We pretended not to know who she was and looked the other way.

Often, in the afternoons, May Chatevin and William would disappear until suppertime. Tannin had sworn off women until his book was finished. And I had found out a wonderful thing. You do not have to be getting laid to be ecstatic in this city which worships love.

Often while they were gone we went somewhere and wrote in our notebooks. He needed a château for a love scene in his book and we found one in the country and went there several times to draw it in our minds.

"William's sister is calling him twice a day," Tannin told me. "His family's furious. They want him to come home."

"His sister?"

"She's visiting Rome with her husband. She wants him to come there and go home with them."

"What does he tell them?"

"He tells them no. He says he's in love with a girl from the States."

"What's going on?" I asked my cousin, when I had her alone one afternoon.

"I'm in love with him. I want him to stay here with me."

"How could he work? An American can't get work in Paris."

"It's a problem." She looked right at me. That old fierceness, selfishness, call it what you will. In the last two generations our family has a divorce rate about twice the national average. The reason is that look. This arrogance we breed or foster, here it was again, in Paris, in this twenty-nine-year-old girl with her perfect ear and talented hands. "I'm writing a symphony. The Saint

Louis Symphony is going to perform it when it's done. I can't leave now. This city is my muse. I have to stay another year or two."

"Then what will happen?"

"I don't know. I want him to stay. He can live with me. He knows that. He can get a visa."

"What would he do for money?"

"I don't know. Maybe we have to live today and not think about it." I had been wrong. She had stopped being Southern. She stood beside the window in my room, looking out onto the roofs of Paris. She was where she had meant to go, she was where she meant to be.

I changed my plane reservation. I decided to stay another week. One morning Tannin met me in the hotel café for breakfast.

"He's leaving at noon," Tannin said. "He's run out of money and his sister won't leave him alone. He's going to Rome and fly home with them in his brother-in-law's plane. His family has lots of money, but they won't give it to him."

"They shouldn't. That's good. That's right."

"He's in love with your cousin. That's our fault, Rhoda. We did that, you and I. He's really broken up about leaving. Do you think she loves him?"

"She loves her work. She's writing a symphony. She wrote one last year that was played by the New Orleans Symphony Orchestra. She has an agreement to write one for Saint Louis. She's going to be a star. Yes, I think she loves him. She wants to keep him here for a pet."

"He came home early last night. I guess they had a fight."

"It's not our fault, Tannin. That's nuts to think that."

We left the café. We walked to the Champs Elysées and window-shopped. We went to the Luxembourg Gardens and rode the carousel. We bought beignets with powdered sugar and sat upon a bench and ate them with our fingers.

"I'd better call May Chatevin when I get home," I said. "She has to play tonight. Maybe we can meet her later and get some supper."

"It's not our fault, Rhoda, remember that."

"I know. It isn't. By God, it has nothing to do with us. We didn't do it."

Neither was it our fault that the Italian Mafia chose that day to load up a car with plastic explosives and drive it into the train station in Firenze just as William got off the train. For what? To turn around and come back to Paris? To buy a package of cigarettes? To call May Chatevin?

I don't buy group guilt. Or any of that politically correct bullshit. Most of the people in the world are doing the best they can with whatever knowledge they have managed to attain or been fed by whatever myths they were raised under. So, somewhere in the darkness of the underside of existence, in the ancient land of Italy, someone, or two or three benighted souls, stuffed a Fiat full of explosives smuggled in from God knows where and with or without a driver ran it into the side of the old section of the Firenze train station where maybe William had just disembarked long enough to buy a sandwich or a drink or a newspaper. He was trying to learn Italian, he had said, one night when we were sitting beside the Seine using all our pidgin languages. Tannin is the only one of us who has mastered anything other than English, although May Chatevin's French is charming and she gets by.

Tannin and May Chatevin and I were together that night. We left my hotel about six and walked to the Jardin des Plantes to see the menagerie. It was cool that evening and May Chatevin was wearing pale yellow silk pants and a green silk jacket. Her hair was pulled back into a chignon. I thought she looked like her mother that night, as she was sad and trying to hide the sadness. "I couldn't leave now," she said a dozen times. "I couldn't just leave all this and go back home. I think he understood that. Did he say anything to you, Tannin? What did he say?"

"That he is in love with you, of course. He doesn't know what he's going to do. Maybe go to work for his brother-in-law. Make some money and come back for you."

"You could go and visit him," I put in. "Surely you don't have to work incessantly."

"Until I finish the symphony I can't take a day away from it. I've wasted two weeks as it is, but not entirely. I've been working in the mornings." We were walking along the rue Claude Bernard, trying to find our way to the boulevard de Vaugirard, where there was a Brazilian restaurant Tannin knew about.

After dinner we decided to see the late showing of *Much Ado About Nothing* in English with French subtitles. It was over about eleven-fifteen and the two young people left me at my hotel and Tannin walked May Chatevin home. He is struggling with his novel and takes every opportunity to put off going home to write it, which he does in the middle of the night no matter how much I lecture him on the efficacy of the morning hours.

I went up to my room and turned on the television set for the first time since I'd been in Paris. I turned on CNN and settled back into the pillows with a glass of Evian. It was the first event on the news. The train station in flames, people running with their hands up in the air, firemen spraying the flames with chemicals, demolished automobiles parked outside the station.

*   *   *

I watched the full report. Then I called Tannin. He returned to my hotel and came up to my room and we began to call crazily around three countries trying to find something out.

"Let's go down there," I said. "Rent a car."

"We have to stay here. He might have my address with him if he was hurt. He might call."

"What about May Chatevin?"

"Wait until morning. If she knew she would have called. What could she do this time of night?"

"It wouldn't be him. He wouldn't die. He's not the type."

"Anyone can die, Rhoda. Anytime. Anywhere."

"Thinking he was a failure?"

"He didn't think that. He just couldn't decide what to do."

"We're overreacting. I shouldn't have called you. You should be at home doing your work."

"Do you think he was in it?"

"I don't know."

"Neither do I."

Tannin slept on the sofa in my room. We woke up early and dressed and went to May Chatevin's apartment. She had read it in the paper. "If he wasn't hurt, he would have called us," she kept saying. "He said he'd call when he got there."

"We can't be sure."

"Then why hasn't he called?"

"What's his sister's name?

"I don't know."

"Should we call his parents in the States?"

"No. Oh, God, no. What if he's all right?"

In the end Tannin and May Chatevin had a car delivered and started driving. I stayed by the phone. They stopped and called every two hours. In between the second and third call the American embassy called to say his name was on the list of the dead.

THE LIST OF THE DEAD. In June, in a peaceful Europe, the summer he was twenty-five. Random, inexplicable.

I told her when she called at three that afternoon. They went on to Firenze to see if they could claim the body. I asked the embassy to get me his parents' phone number. I sat in zazen on the floor of my room and waited for the courage to make the call. I could have looked out the window and seen the Eiffel Tower if I wanted to.

I got his father on the phone. I told him his son had been completely happy when he left for Rome. I told him his son had been the happiest man I had ever known. I asked if I could meet the daughter in Firenze. If I could do anything at all for them. I gave them my phone number in the United States. I said they could come to visit me and I would tell them about every minute of the weeks gone by. "He was the happiest young man I've ever known," I told them. "What fine parents you must have been. What a delightful son you had." Had. Here in the maya of space and time. On the planet Earth, in nineteen hundred and ninety-three A.D., in the only world there is.

Two days later Tannin and May Chatevin got back to Paris. They had met the sister. Tannin had helped identify the body. May Chatevin had lost ten pounds. I put her to bed in her apartment with one of my three remaining Xanax tablets. I sat in her living room while she slept and tried to read *Le Monde*. Tannin had gone home to rest.

"Get up tomorrow morning and write," I told him. "Now will you believe? Now will you go on and write your hero's death?"

"No," he answered. "I'm going to skip over to the part that takes place in the United States. After the child is born."

"Requiem. Yes, go on."

"We got a dog the last year we were at Sewanee. This brown dog we found at the pound. We had to hide it from the landlord."

"What happened to it?"

"He took it to Nashville and gave it to his mother. I guess she's still got it. He used to let it ride in the car with him everywhere he went. That dog loved to ride in automobiles. He'd put his paws up on the window and stick his head out. Everyone knew our dog. We called it Vain for a girlfriend he once had."

"I told his father he was the happiest man I had ever known."

"He might have been. Now he is. Now he doesn't care." We had been whispering. Now we embraced. He left me there. I opened French *Vogue* and began to read an article about how to dye the hair on my legs. We don't really need hair on our bodies anymore. But nature keeps it there in case things change.

A Wedding in Jackson

THEY WERE NOT getting married in a fever. Although they were young and full of hope and at least the bride seemed bright with passion. The boy was scared to death. His parents were there from Minnesota and his sisters stuffed into their ridiculous pink bridesmaid's dresses. Well, there's no point in getting judgmental. The point is, I was there. I hadn't been to a family wedding in five years. I'd been too busy getting yet another anal-retentive Momma's boy to like me to have time for my family. From the age of fifty-four to fifty-eight I spent all my time and money getting this slightly younger man to squire me around and show the world I was still physically attractive. What a bore I must have been. Mooning around and getting dressed up to go to movies just so people would think I was getting laid. Not that what we were doing could be called getting laid. Still, it got the job done and I'm not complaining about him. It was my idea to begin with, then, suddenly, that spring I had let it go and I was free to go back to the bosom of my family.

My name is Rhoda, by the way. Rhoda Katherine Manning. You might have heard of me. I'm a famous scandal in some circles in the South. Our crazy cousin Rhoda, my respectable cousins call me, in Birmingham and Nashville and Memphis

and New Orleans. Even some of the ones who are making it in
New York City run me down.

Who cares, you might ask. Well, I cared enough to spend
four years on this quasi-respectable man just to keep them at bay.

Then I was free again and the first thing I did was call my
mother and tell her I would come to Jackson for the wedding of
my great-niece, Annie Laurie. She's the first of her generation in
our family to be married and I had made up my mind to be
there. Was it my fault the plane couldn't take off from our goddamn fog-ridden mountain town?

I had gotten up at five-thirty in the morning to be out at the
airport for a flight at seven. I had spent two days packing a dress
and hat and shoes and pearls and even bought new earrings. I
had called my ex-daughter-in-law and begged her for an hour
to bring her new boyfriend and my grandchildren and meet me
there. I had acted with enthusiasm and good faith. No, it was
not my fault that I was late.

If I were writing this as a play I would begin in my mother's
house on Woodwind Lane in Jackson, Mississippi, where she is
waiting for me to come and take her to the wedding. She won't
ride in the car with my father and besides, he always rides with
my brothers. The men against the world and so forth.

My plane was supposed to get in around noon, which would
have given us plenty of time to make the wedding at four. Only
the plane was not taking off. The plane was sitting on the runway with a light flashing in the cockpit saying the right engine
needed oil. It didn't need oil. The switch to the light was broken
and they didn't have one in Fayetteville, Arkansas. So, fifteen
minutes went by and it was hot as Hades in the plane and I was
wearing my allergy mask and reading Rilke. "All this was mission, but could you accomplish it? Weren't you always distracted
by expectation, as if every moment announced a beloved?"

I'm a published author by the way, in case you want some credentials. I'm an ex-alcoholic. My face is wrinkled but my legs are good and I'm in perfect health except for the allergies. Pollen, house dust, grasses, and seven kinds of mold. What else? I'm a lot of fun. People like to be with me. I'm likable and aware. Sometimes I'm smart. Lots of times I'm smart.

But back to the light in the cockpit. By the time they got it fixed the fog had rolled in and by the time it cleared I'd missed my connection in Memphis. The stewardess finally opened the door and told us to go back into the terminal and we did. I ran for it and reached the desk first and began to demand satisfaction.

There was none to be had. The best I could do by flying around half of Arkansas and Louisiana was to get to Jackson at two-forty. Give me back my money, I demanded. I'm driving. I had just spent seven hundred dollars putting Pirelli racing tires on my BMW and I was in the mood to drive. I collected my suitcase and ran for the car.

It was ten to eight. I have a friend who once made the trip from Fayetteville to Jackson in seven and a half hours and I thought I could do it. If I failed I would still make it to the reception. Seven and a half hours to drive, five minutes to dress, ten minutes to make it to the church. If I didn't stop to eat or drink I could make it. It was Holy Saturday, the day before Easter. I could make it if I tried.

I started up the curving mountain road leading from Fayetteville to Alma. I once killed a character in a novel on that road. Later, I brought him back to life in a short story.

Meanwhile, at Momma's house in Jackson, she is waiting for me. "I knew something was going on," she said, when I called to tell her where I was. She's an intuitive. Nothing gets past her.

She is eighty-five years old and she has been there for every minute of her life. She is beloved in the world, worshiped really. She has never put down her pack for a moment or stopped to complain, except once when Daddy was going through his midlife crisis and "acting like a horse's ass." There are three profane things my mother has been heard to say. Hell's bells, tacky, and "he was acting like a horse's ass." She was a classics major. She believes in the Graces, in service and gentleness. I love her, that's the long and short of that, and I have given her plenty of heartbreak and disappointment. Also, I have acted out for her the life she never got to lead, have been selfish, spoiled, hot-tempered, all the things she married my father for. Is it my fault that's how the genes fell out? Is it my fault I have red hair?

So she is in Jackson waiting for me. Putting the bedspread I sent her from London on the bed in my room, making the pound cake, putting out the towels and the pink Vitabath, picking roses for the dresser. Here I am, up in the Ozark Mountains, dying of allergies and she is out in her backyard spraying poison on the roses without a sneeze. She could have given me her immune system in the gene exchange. I wouldn't have minded that.

The Pirelli tires were great. I drove up the mountain taking the curves at twice the speed on the posted signs and the car was sweet. The sun was bright, the mountains were beautiful, I had Mozart on the CD player, and I was going to make it. I stopped once to buy gasoline and a bottle of drinking water and kept on driving. At nine I drove into Alma and took the ramp to Highway 40, bound for Little Rock. Not a policeman on the road. Hardly any traffic. Holy Saturday. Everyone who was going anywhere was already there.

Wildflowers were growing in profusion along the highway.

Blue cornflowers and the vibrant red triflora Lady Bird Johnson caused to be planted when she was First Lady. They bloom beside the highways all over the American South.

I drove eighty for a while, then eighty-five. The radar detector I paid five hundred dollars for in a fit of thinking the movies were going to make me rich scans five miles to the front and five miles to the back. Not a sound, not a beep.

Back at Momma's house she has decided what to do. Wait for me even if she's late to her great-grandchild's wedding. She wants to enter the church with her daughter on her arm. Her other choices are driving with Daddy or one of my brother Dudley's wives. The first one, the grandmother of the bride, the second one, who is still everyone's friend, or the fourth one, a twenty-eight-year-old student in graduate school. The third wife had not been able to come.

Maybe Mother is not waiting on me because she doesn't want to pick and choose among my brother's wives. Maybe she is waiting on me because she loves me. There's a thought. The squeaky wheel gets the grease and so forth. The squeaky middle child, that's me. Whoever is in need. Isn't that the deepest truth of the maternal instinct? Once a physician and I were sitting in a bar in New Orleans on a rainy day in August discussing that. One of those hot muggy New Orleans days that has finally turned into rain. We were in the Napoleon House on Royal Street looking out into the rain and talking about women. This was years ago, before I believed in Germaine Greer, when I only read her in a sort of dazzled haze. "There is an act of volition in every pregnancy," he was saying. "And something else. If I threw a baby down on the floor every woman in sight would rush to pick it up. And some men too." I looked around me. It was true. Even the woman wearing black and pretending to be gay. Even the girl in the lace hat and patterned stockings, even the two charmers at the bar.

"Then how will we ever control the world's population?" I asked.

"We won't. How about another drink?"

I passed the turnoff to Subaico, the Benedictine Academy where the poet Francis Alter is buried. He was my first true writer friend. The first blessed, gifted, cursed poet that I knew. Also, the most beautiful human being I have ever seen. To be in his presence was to understand why men became the disciples of Christ. Existence changed when he was around, became finer, clearer, more alive. He dedicated his life to beauty, art, poetry, freedom. Then he killed himself. He showed me how to make my first book, chose the poems, put them into order. He taught me how to find a cover, how to demand perfection. But that's another story. I didn't have time to take the turnoff and visit his grave. Francis's bones are laid to rest. He has been in the grave for fourteen years, has turned to dust. Dust also the roses we laid upon his coffin, the tears the poets of Arkansas shed upon that hill on that cloudy day that later turned to rain.

The highway from Russellville to Little Rock was deserted. Not a beep on the radar detector as I cruised along at ninety miles an hour. I was getting cocky now. If I got a ticket I could get it fixed. So I was driving along like that, confident and cocky, and I made it to Little Rock in three and a half hours. I cruised through the town and on down to Pine Bluff, the ugliest town in the world. Then I was into the hardest part of the trip. The two-lane road from Pine Bluff to the Greenville, Mississippi, bridge.

The hardest and most sentimental. My most perfect lover was raised in a small town I was passing through. He had led his schoolmates to state victories in three sports. I could have stopped on any corner and said, I used to be Raine's girlfriend, and men would have bowed to me.

Instead I kept on driving. I passed the state penitentiary at Cummins. I passed catfish ponds. I passed rice fields. I passed the place where I had been stopped once by a good-looking black patrolman who was immune to my scrawny white charms. Once I was going into a courthouse in New Orleans to pay a parking ticket and a black prisoner hanging out of a window in a neighboring jail had yelled down to me. "Where you going, you little ole dried-up white pussy?" I cherish that memory. It was such a beautiful piece of language, so funny and so bitter and so true. The sun had been so hot that day, beating down on the parking lot, and I had thought I looked so great in my new green dress.

At one o'clock I crossed the old suspension bridge that spans the Mississippi River at Greenville. I turned right onto Highway 454 and the vast fields of the Delta were all around me. The place that I call home. I passed the house built on top of an Indian mound. To my left were plowed fields, flat and verdant, waiting for seed. On my right were the dense woods of Leroy Percy Park, where I was taken for picnics as a child. I turned onto the River Road, Highway 1, famed in literature and legends. At the entrance to the park I turned left and headed east to Yazoo City. Nothing could stop me now. I was in the Delta and could drive a hundred miles an hour if I liked. No traffic, no policemen, roads as flat and straight as a line drawn with a T-square. Nothing to run into and nowhere to go but into a cotton field.

In Yazoo City I was stopped by a train crossing the main street of town. Forty minutes from my mother's house. One hour and ten minutes until the wedding and there I was, on the main street of Yazoo City with the streets full of Easter shoppers and a slow-moving train barring every street going east. I turned off the ignition and ran around to the back of the car and started getting out my things. I hung the suit up in the car. I got out high heels and hose. I put on a string of pearls and the earrings. I took the hat out of the hatbox and put it on my head.

"I'm late to a wedding," I called out. All around me the black and white citizens of Yazoo had stopped to watch.

"Hope you make it," a man called back. "Good luck to you." The caboose came into sight behind the broken skyline of the town. Everyone waved and pointed. I turned on the motor, clutched the wheel, got ready to drive, my wide straw-colored hat at a rakish angle on my head.

At twenty minutes to four I pulled into my mother's driveway and honked the horn. She came out the door to the kitchen and shook her head. I loved her. She loved me. We had lived so long since I was formed inside her womb. She had held my head when I threw up. Had taught me to believe in fairies. Did I get out of the car and throw my arms around her and say, I love you, love you, love you, never die?

I did not. "Get that suit out of the backseat," I yelled. "I'll be dressed in five minutes."

She helped me carry the things into the house and stood leaning on the bedpost while I put them on.

"Where's the wedding?" I asked.

"Out in Madison County. Don't wear that silly hat, honey. This is only a little country wedding."

"I don't care. I want to wear it. I'm going to be me no matter where I go."

"Well, it looks ridiculous."

"I told my granddaughters to wear theirs. I have to match them."

"All right. Do as you please, as always."

"Let's go in your car. But I'm driving. I won't drive fast, I promise."

"The key's in the kitchen, on the rack." She led me out

through the den. Every flat surface of the den is covered with photographs of her children and her sisters and her nieces and nephews and their children and husbands and wives and step-children and dogs and prizes and awards and sports events. Every person who comes into that room goes from wall to wall look-ing at photographs of themselves, checking to make sure they are well represented. One of the great moments of my life was one day when I walked into that den and noticed she had re-moved a photograph of Dudley standing over a dead lion and replaced it with one of me that had been in *Mississippi Magazine*.

We passed through this gallery and out into the hall and into the garage and got into her car and she opened the garage door with her genie.

We arrived at the church just as my youngest niece and her husband were going in the door. We followed them and found ourselves in a wide hall full of costumed people. The main sanc-tuary was in the midst of a dress rehearsal for the Passion Play.

There was a sign saying "Wedding" with an arrow pointing down a narrow hall and we followed it and made it to the cere-mony just as the bride and groom were approaching the minis-ter for the rites. I slid into a seat by my grandchildren and Momma sat with my brothers. The Baptist minister said a lot of things that burden the ear of an Episcopalian. Then the bride-groom kissed the bride and the recessional began. Everyone marched back down the aisle and the family rose and started kissing each other. I kissed my brother and his three wives and all their children and grandchildren. I kissed the people from Minnesota. I kissed my grandchildren, my ex-daughter-in-law, and her new boyfriend. He was a handsome man, as handsome as my son, who is the father of these children. She can pick them, I was thinking. She only wants the best. She doesn't care how long it takes. She waits for what she wants.

The boyfriend kept her close to him, his hand around her waist. He seemed kind, a kind man, the children seemed okay, at least the little girls did, they swirled around him, dancing with this idea of a daddy, even a borrowed one. I tried to get objective, really watch. In these days of reported child abuse everyone is suspect. The idea of a strange man in a house with their small precious bodies bothers me, even the kindest, most civilized-seeming man.

I pulled my grandson to me. He had gained weight, grown taller, was almost as tall as me. He looked at me as from a distance, resisted me somehow. That has never happened before between us.

"Let's go to the reception," Momma said. "They want us to get started."

"I'll take the children with me," I told my daughter-in-law. "Let Mother and me take them in the car." I pulled my grandson to my side. I held him there. I wanted to overpower him, surround him, make him safe, but maybe this time he wasn't going to let me tell him who to be.

Mother took the little girls by the hand. I followed with my arm around my grandson. As we moved down the hall we passed some of the costumed players. A sixty-year-old Mary Magdelene and a pair of Roman soldiers. "What's all that?" my grandson asked.

"A reenactment of the passion of Jesus," I answered. "A religious rite still practiced in many parts of the South."

"I don't believe any of that crap," he said. "It's just myth and superstition."

"Be quiet," Momma whispered, and swept us out the door. "This is someone's place of worship."

The reception was held at a lodge in the woods. An open building surrounded by pine trees and dogwoods in full bloom. There was a lake and a pier, which soon was filled with little girls in white dresses. Small boys fanned out along the lake's edge looking for snakes and frogs.

There were many delicate small trees just bursting into leaf. There were azalea bushes, pink and white and red with fresh May flowers. Inside were two huge cakes and a marvelous feast spread out upon a table. The bride and groom were shaking everyone's hands. "I want to talk to the bride," my six-year-old granddaughter whispered to me.

"It's just your cousin Annie Laurie. You've talked to her lots of times."

"I want to talk to her. Take me over there." She took my hand and we went over and talked to the bride.

I have mellowed. I went around to each of my sisters-in-law and embraced them with real tenderness. I danced with my brother. I danced with my oldest grandson and taught him the two-step. I danced with my youngest granddaughter and one of her friends. I danced with every little girl at the party who looked like she needed someone to dance with. By then I had abandoned the hat. Mother had been right about the hat. Live and learn and mellow. Drive as fast as you can and try not to get a ticket.

At fifty-eight I have finally left my adolescence behind me. Lucky old fecund world. Whatever we lay down, there is always someone behind us to pick it up.

My grandson was sitting glumly in a chair. He had never had to put up with his mother having a boyfriend and he wasn't going to put up with it now. "What's wrong?" I asked him.

"Him. Edward. He kicked me going into the hotel."

"You must be mistaken. He wouldn't kick anyone. He's a sweet man."

"He kicked me. I don't like him."

"Oh, my. You want to ride around in the car for a while? Come on, get some cake and let's get out of here."

"I don't know."

"Please. I want to talk to you. I want to be alone with you. Get some cake and meet me at the door. Get me a piece of the chocolate one." He went off to get the cake and I found my mother and asked her for the car keys.

"What for?"

"I have to talk to Malcolm. He's having a fit."

"About the boyfriend?"

"Yes."

"It won't do, Rhoda. He's too young."

"No, he's not. You don't care how young Dudley's wives are. Ingersol's girlfriends. Why shouldn't she have some happiness? She's a wonderful mother. The best mother I've ever seen in my life. She's the light of my life. I want her to be happy."

"Don't talk so loud. This is Annie Laurie's wedding. Well, here they are." She found her keys in her pocketbook and gave them to me. "Don't be gone long. I don't want to stay forever. I don't want to drive home with your father." She looked in his direction. He has grown old this year, lost his power. All he cares for now is living, he wants to live forever, to go on breathing at any cost and she has begun to despise him for it. Her power, which was never physical, is still keen, and she still tries to use it.

I collected Malcolm and we walked out on the porch to go to the car. His mother and the boyfriend were sitting at a glass-topped table, laughing and drinking wine, talking to my nieces and their husbands. "We're going riding," I told her. "We want to be alone."

We went out to the parking lot and got into the car and my daughter-in-law followed us and got in the backseat.

"He's mad at Edward," I said. "He says Edward kicked him."

"They were just horsing around." She leaned up into the front seat and touched my hand. "He's the gentlest man on the earth. He wouldn't harm a child."

"You have to let your mother have a boyfriend," I began. "There's nothing wrong with that. She loves you. So do I. We love you more than anything in the world. We would never let anyone harm you in any way. We would kill or die for you. But you ought to let her have a boyfriend. She lets you have friends. Edward's a nice man. He's the nicest man I've met in years."

"No, he's not. He's mean to me." He scrunched down into the seat, looked at the floor. Heart of my heart, the dearest thing on earth to me. I touched his mother's hand. My son had destroyed every relationship I'd ever had after I divorced his father. That was with us in the car. And the pain my son had caused this woman. And the pain she had caused my son. And these children, our inheritance and legacy, our treasure.

"Okay," I said. "You need to have a meeting. You and your mother and Edward sit down and talk this over. Your mother says he was horsing around. Maybe you took it wrong."

"He did it to be mean."

"Okay. I'm going to send you some books about what to do when your mother has a boyfriend. Hell, maybe I'll send you Sophocles." My daughter-in-law laughed. For a moment the tension wavered. Like a thermocline, the water of laughter invaded the heat. Then the heat returned.

"If he's going to be around, I'll come and live with you," he said. "If you like me so much let me live with you."

Above us the beautiful light green leaves swayed in the breeze. Above them stretched the sky with its immensity and wonder. I looked into my ex-daughter-in-law's wide brown eyes. We had fought this child's father together. I had fought his father and grandfather and great-grandfather. We knew what we were up against. This will that grew stronger from generation to generation. That finally, in this child, had been mixed with her German, Dutch, and American Indian genes. Hybrid vigor. My Celtic craziness dissolved in more rational, cooler genes. Will and imagination and a sense of order remained of my genetic contribution. And the strongest of these was will.

There he sat, in the passenger seat of his great-grandmother's car, the end product of all this random *genius,* ready to defend his territory at any cost.

"I'm going to send you a book about a man named Oedipus," I said. "It will explain the psychological ramifications of this problem. Call me up when you've read it and we'll talk about it."

"I don't know what any of that means." He raised his head and looked at me. Gave me the full force of his gaze. He's an intuitive too. Nothing gets past him. There is no barrier between him and the world. Not a membrane to separate him from all that burgeoning wonder, all the glorious and inglorious knowledge of our being.

"I will love you till I die," I said. "I love you more than anyone. You are the dearest thing on earth to me."

"Let's go back to the party."

"We better," his mother added. "I have to see about the little girls."

The day wore on into evening. The little girls went off to spend the night with cousins. My ex-daughter-in-law and her boyfriend went off to party with my nieces.

I took my grandson to the mall. We bought some baseball shirts and a pair of striped shorts. We ate some junk food. We held hands and walked around and looked at things. He is five foot five inches tall now. As tall as I am. Soon it will be over, this part of it. The part when he was a child and I was his guardian angel. He will leave me and go off to the world. He will leave me here with memories of many days in many malls, of buying transformers and Lego sets and books and basketball shoes and posters of Jose Canseco. Baseball hats and tacos and pizza and frozen yogurt. Goofy golf and batting cages and long walks and bike rides and swimming pools. We have heard the chimes at bedtime, oh, the malls that we have seen.

"I love you," I kept telling him. "It's okay if your mother has a boyfriend. It will make her stronger. Anything that makes her stronger, makes you stronger. We are a family. We stick together."

"I wish you lived where I do. I wish you lived next door."

"I wish I did too. I hate to miss a day of seeing you."

After a while the mall began to close and we walked out into the parking lot and watched the black teenagers forming into groups. I held his hand and let him find the car for me.

We went over to my momma's house and slept in my old bed. We snuggled down into the sheets from London. I pulled his fine strong eleven-and-a-half-year-old body into my arms and held him there. "You are my angel," I said. "No one will ever take your place with me. Your mother and I love you more than you will ever know. No one will ever take her or me away from you."

"I don't think so," he said. I found his hand and held it. It is still the same size as mine. Delicate, with long thin fingers like his mother's. He is the catcher on his baseball team, the goalie at soccer. Always the dirtiest, hardest job in any sport. Because he can be depended upon.

"Go to sleep," I said. "Tomorrow's Easter. Grandmother dyed eggs for us to hide."

*   *   *

In the morning everyone reconvened in my mother's yard to hide Easter eggs and take photographs of each other. It was about evenly divided, between children who had been to Sunday School and the children of apostates.

The boyfriend moved among the children being charming. "My father is taller than you are," I heard the six-year-old girl tell him.

"No, he's not," I said. "Edward is taller than your father." He raised his eyebrows just an almost imperceptible amount and sighed, and seemed to thank me.

"Why did you introduce him to the children?" I asked my ex-daughter-in-law. "Why did you even let him meet them?"

"He asked to. I put it off as long as I could. Well, it's done now. Let's get this Easter egg hunt over and I'll take him home."

"This was a stupid idea. I shouldn't have talked you into coming. It was nuts. Coming up here into your ex-husband's family. Mother acting like the high priestess of a cult. The shrine of the double standard. My family in Jackson, Mississippi."

"It's okay. I know what I want. I won't let this stop me."

"Good. I'm glad to hear it." I hugged her to my side. This woman six inches taller than me who is the only daughter I have ever had, who has never let me down or disappointed me. This giver of grandchildren, whom I worship.

An hour later they drove away. The boyfriend driving. My ex-daughter-in-law riding shotgun with the six-year-old beside her. The older children on the back seat with their Walkmans plugged into their ears. "Thank goodness that is over," my mother said.

"What a mean thing to say," I said. "I'm pulling for her. I want her to be happy."

"He's too young," my mother said. "It's embarrassing."

*   *   *

RHODA 408

Five days later I was in the kitchen of my house, leaning on a counter, hearing the fallout on the phone. "The boyfriend's gone," my ex-daughter-in-law is saying. "They scared him off."

"I'm sorry. It's my fault. I shouldn't have asked you to come."

"It had to happen. I'm a group of people. I'm four of us."

"Do you really believe that?"

"No."

"Is there something I can do?"

"I don't think so. I guess I have to ride it out."

"Fuck love. Fuck having lovers."

"Come on, Rhoda. It's not that bad. I had a good time for a while."

"Next time keep him to yourself. Don't even tell him you have kids. Don't tell me."

"I've had enough to last me for a while."

We hung up and I went out into my garden and started to water the hostas and the lilies. I pulled the garden hose around the hickory tree and started to turn it on. Then I changed my mind. To hell with nature. Let it take care of itself. I spotted a wasps' nest under the eaves by the garage. I went into the house and got a can of flying insect spray and sprayed it good. I doused it and then I sprayed some on a spider's web.

If I had been one of my grandfathers I would have gone out to the stables and saddled a horse and put a bit in its mouth and gone riding with my dogs at my heels. Instead, I went into the house and put on my running shoes and started out around the mountain. I don't have any German-Jewish or American Indian or Dutch genes. I'm a Celt. I pile up stones and keep a loaded pistol in my underwear drawer. My ancestors painted themselves blue and impaled each other on oak staves. I can't stand tyranny. From the world outside or the tyranny of the heart. How can I help anyone? I can't even help myself. I was GLAD HE HAD WON. GLAD NO ONE COULD TAKE HIS MOTHER FROM HIM. GLAD HE KNEW HOW TO KEEP HER.

Even as I suffered for her I was glad no man would be in the house with those little girls, not any man, not the sweetest man in the world, in this chaotic world, vale of sorrows, vale of tears.

The Uninsured

August 1, 1993

Dear Blue Cross, Blue Shield,

I got your letter advising me that you are redoing our health insurance plans. I guess this means you are going to be raising our rates again. I know you *want* to raise my rates since for the past ten years it has cost you more to pay my psychiatrist than you have collected from me. We may be getting tired of each other. It may be time to sever our relationship especially since I am about to cut down on the number of times I see him each week and aside from that am in perfect health.

> Yours most sincerely,
> Rhoda K. Manning

September 3, 1993

Dear Blue Cross, Blue Shield,

While I wait to see if you have figured out a way to make money from me instead of me making money from you I have done the following at your expense. Had a mammogram and Pap smear. Had a bone density evaluation and scan. Had an

AIDS test. Had a blood profile and blood pressure check. Had ten small skin lesions removed from my hands and arm and lower legs. Had all my prescription drugs filled.

I have also driven up to Jackson, Mississippi, to visit my eighty-six-year-old parents and found them both in perfect health. From all these tests and the evidence of my genes it is clear that, barring accidents, I will live to be about ninety years old with no bone, heart, liver, lung, or brain disease. My blood pressure is ninety over sixty. My bone density is that of a thirty-year-old woman. It is obvious that if you raise my rates I will have to consider bailing out of your Flex-Plan.

Yours most sincerely,
Rhoda K. Manning

October 10, 1993

Dear Blue Cross, Blue Shield,

I have applied to the John Alden Insurance Company of Springfield, Illinois, for inclusion in their Jali-Care Program. I am going to let the two of you bid for my healthy body. A healthy body, I might add, that has been shored up by twenty years of psychotherapy which has taught me to love, care for, and value myself.

The John Alden representative in our area has come to visit me. He is a very nice man about my age who once was a forest ranger in Oregon. We chatted and drank bottled water and he took my medical history. He said that, with the exception of my twenty years of psychotherapy, he was certain my record would be well received at the John Alden Jali-Care Evaluation Center. "I am not mentally disturbed," I told him. "I am a writer. The reason I have never been blocked is because I have been in psychotherapy and therefore am able to withstand the pressures of society upon my artistic nature. It is also the reason I have never been depressed or had accidents."

You people at Blue Cross may think the four hundred dollars a month it has cost you to pay my psychiatrist is a lot of money but think of what it might have cost you if I had harmed myself with food or drink or drugs or unhappy love affairs. You are coming out ahead, I assure you.

Well, this is just to keep you updated while I wait for my letter telling me about the restructuring of Farm Policy Group Seven's Comprehensive Major Medical Coverage for the Future.

Yours most truly,
Rhoda K. Manning

November 7, 1993

Dear Blue Cross, Blue Shield,

I just got my flu shot. I didn't charge it to you since I just ran by the Mediquik and it only cost five dollars so I thought it wasn't worth the paperwork. I have been racking my brain trying to think of something else I can have done to myself before I bail out of the health insurance business and devote myself to staying in perfect health until I am sixty-five and can get some of my tax dollars back in Medicare.

The John Alden Insurance Company sent a sweet young woman out to do a medical check on me. She called one afternoon at four and asked if she could come the next day at noon. I guess that was to make sure I wasn't forewarned in case I secretly smoke or drink. I told her to come on and she said I had to fast from eight that night until noon. That was the hard part. I never go eight hours without food as I believe in controlling the blood sugar levels at all times.

She arrived promptly at noon. It turns out she lives in my part of town. She said when she was ready to buy a house she asked a policeman where the safest place in town was and he said these old neighborhoods on the mountain. The houses were built in the sixties and look like there would be nothing here to steal.

She came in and weighed me on a pair of scales she carries with her in a carpet bag. Then she drew blood and separated it in various little cylinders and sealed them up and put them in a pack to be taken by Federal Express to a lab in Kansas City. I had to sign a paper saying they could do an AIDS test. That's two in two months' time. I was glad to do it. As I told Sharon Cane, that's her name, if you aren't part of the solution, you are part of the problem. A gay friend of mine tells that to anyone who won't be tested for HIV.

Next I gave Sharon a urine specimen. She explained to me that they could tell from it if I had smoked a cigarette in the last ten days or had a drink. I have not had a drink in twenty years. A hypnotist in New Orleans talked me out of that years ago.

The way I feel now is that if the John Alden Jali-Care people don't have enough sense to want my $157.69 a month after all of this they can go to hell.

You may think from the tone of this letter that I am getting mad at you, but you would be wrong. I have appreciated all those checks for fifty percent of my psychotherapy. I don't blame you for trying to figure out a way to get your money back but I don't think there's any reason for me to give it to you.

Yours sincerely,
Rhoda K. Manning

December 4, 1993

Dear Blue Cross, Blue Shield,

John Alden Jali-Care is considering my application. I passed all my physical tests with flying colors but they are worried about the years of psychotherapy and have requested a letter from my psychotherapist, which he is drafting now.

I assume that the reason I haven't heard from you about my policy is that you have been busy with the lawsuit the Arkansas Senate is bringing against you for raising all the rates of people with preexisting conditions to such exorbitant amounts that they (we) are all going to have to quit. In the meantime I am pursuing other options as I have told you in our correspondence.

It said in the paper today that you had begun all this in order to get ready for the great Health Care Debate of 1994. Well, all I can say is I am losing interest in the whole thing. I have always paid for the things that made a real difference to my health, like eyeglasses, running shoes, good books, good music, movies, food. I know how to go to Mediquik and get shots. Not to mention the dentist, which you do not cover either.

Good luck with your lawsuit.

> Yours sincerely,
> Rhoda Manning

December 5, 1993

Dear John Alden Jali-Care,

Here is the letter from my psychiatrist which you requested. From it you will see that the only reason I have been going to him all these years is because I am a writer. It has nothing whatsoever to do with health problems. It is preventive medicine, and besides, I'm cutting down on my sessions and you won't be responsible for them anyway as they are a preexisting condition. Hope everything is clear now.

> Yours most sincerely,
> Rhoda K. Manning

December 15, 1993

Dear Blue Cross, Blue Shield,

I received your offer to continue to provide me with health insurance for $567.69 a month with a three-thousand-dollar deductible and a fifty-thousand-dollar stop-loss. I have decided to decline this offer. It's been nice doing business with you but I think I'll quit while I'm ahead.

Stay well,
Rhoda Manning

January 1, 1994

Dear Blue Cross, Blue Shield,

This is my first day of being uninsured. It feels great. I have had the snow shoveled from my sidewalk, am wearing my seat belt at all times, and have invested two thousand, three hundred dollars in a new Exercycle from the StairMaster people.

If I subtract the one thousand, six hundred and seventy dollars quarterly payment I would have sent you that is only about seven hundred dollars for the Exercycle.

Looking ahead to the second quarterly payment I have bought a new fur jacket to keep me from catching cold. With the two hundred dollars I saved by having all my prescriptions filled in 1993 I bought a matching hat and muff.

Yours for a happy and
healthy new year,
Rhoda Manning

February 1, 1994

Dear Blue Cross, Blue Shield,

Now that a month has passed and all is well I have decided to look ahead to the money I would be paying you the next few years and put in a lap pool. The pool people don't have much to do this time of year and have given me a twenty percent discount.

February 27, 1994   Sorry I didn't get this off sooner but they came and started digging the hole for the pool and it's been chaos around here. All is well now. The pool is nine feet wide and sixty-nine feet long. It has an electric cover that can be opened or closed from a switch in the kitchen. Talk about high technology.

Do you remember Sharon Cane, who came to draw blood for the John Alden Jali-Care Evaluation? Well, she is swimming with me three days a week. She starts at one end and I start at the other to make waves for each other to swim against. We usually bet five dollars on who can swim the most laps in an hour. A lot of times we lose count because we are having so much fun. I am down to seeing my analyst three times a month now that I have to pay for it. No ill effects so far, only I can tell I am not working as hard as I was when I had him to drive me to it. Why should I work seven days a week? It's almost spring. The long winter is over and I didn't catch the flu. That five-dollar flu shot may be the best money I spent all year.

Yours for a healthy America,
Rhoda Manning

March 19, 1994

Dear Blue Cross, Blue Shield,

I had a long talk with my ninety-year-old neighbor, Kassie Martin, yesterday. She praised me for letting my insurance run out. She said that if I have a stroke or a heart attack it is best to arrive at the hospital uninsured as that might lower the chances of them putting you on a life support machine. She has seen many unpleasant things happen to older people who arrive at the hospital fully insured. Greed is nothing new in the world but why should we be victims of it?

On another note I have only had one prescription filled since I left you. I drove around town doing some comparison shopping. That pharmacy that used to fill my prescriptions is twice as high as the one at Wal-Mart. You should look into this.

Yours in spring,
Rhoda Manning

March 21, 1994

Dear Blue Cross, Blue Shield,

Well, it looks like John Alden Jali-Care is going to come through with a cheap policy for me. Their representative called this morning to say all they needed now were some copies of my books with pages marked showing them where I used the information I got in psychotherapy to help my writing.

It's difficult to believe that health care professionals could be that unlettered and that dumb, isn't it? Now that I have gotten accustomed to being uninsured and dependent on myself it is going to be hard for me to pay anyone anything for health insurance. I'll let you know what I decide.

Stay well,
Rhoda Manning

March 26, 1994

Dear Blue Cross, Blue Shield,

I can't bring myself to take John Alden up on their offer. Why would I want to do business with people who are dumber than I am?

Instead, I have decided to go to Italy. A hotel near the Ponte Vecchio. I don't know where that is yet, but I will soon. A young man of my acquaintance who speaks perfect French and Italian is going with me. We are going to stay at a hotel in Rome where Sartre and Buckminster Fuller and Isamu Naguchi and lots of other artists stayed. If I get sick in Italy, who cares? What could I have that Italian pasta and Italian men couldn't cure? We are going to Rome for twelve days and then to Florence for seven.

Arrivederci,
Rhoda Manning

April 10, 1994

Dear Blue Cross, Blue Shield,

Well, here we are in Florence after a heavenly time in Rome. The sun is shining and the world seems "to lie before us like a field of dreams, so various, so beautiful, so new." We arrived yesterday morning and walked around for a while. Then we slept awhile and ate dinner in a piazza. Tomorrow we will go to see the Uffizi Gallery. There are paintings there by Botticelli, Titian, and Raphael, to name a few. I'll probably faint, but don't worry, it won't cost you any money.

It's pretty amazing to step off an airplane and be in Italy. Thanks so much for making this possible by raising my rates so much that I couldn't keep my insurance.

I picked up a paper as I was leaving Fayetteville and noticed that you had made a deal with State Farm to keep everyone's group policies in effect another year with only a twenty percent increase. I started to call my insurance agent and see if I could get in on that, but then I decided to hell with it. Why should I pay you three thousand dollars a year? That's ten more nights in first-class hotels in Tuscany. Well, stay well. This is the last letter

I am going to write to you. I'm going to see paintings, eat Italian food, then rent a sports car and drive up to the mountains to go skiing. My young lover and I have a motto. We'll take today. I know we aren't the first to think of that but it still works.

Arrivederci,
Rhoda